RED HOT PEPPER

LOVE ON THE MENU
BOOK TWO

MELLANIE SZERETO

amatoria press

Red Hot Pepper
Copyright © 2016 Mellanie Szereto
Published by Amatoria Press
Cover art by Dragonfly Press Design

ISBN-13: 978-1-942522-05-8
ISBN-10: 1942522053

This story is a work of fiction, and any resemblance to real persons and/or events is coincidental.

BOOKS BY MELLANIE SZERETO

Romancing the Phone series ~

Call Me…Maybe

Smooth Operator

Hang-Ups (2024)

Telephone Lines (2024)

Dialed Up (2024)

Mixed Messages (2024)

The Homegrown Café Book Club series ~

Makin' Bacon

The Farmer Takes a Husband

The Butcher and the Baker

When Harry Met Wally

And Baby Makes 2½

The Homegrown Café Book Club Boxed Set

Love on the Menu series ~

Love Served Hot

Red Hot Pepper

Hot Tamale Nights (2024)

Love on the Menu...Extra Hot standalones ~

Just Desserts

Iced Latté

A Little Appetizer

The Main Dish

Dressing on the Side

Flavor of the Day

Love on the Menu…Steamed trilogy ~

Egging Her On

Sweetening Her Up

Reeling Her In

Love on the Menu: Steamed Boxed Set

Short Stories ~

Death Benefits ~ paranormal romance

Mad About You ~ romantic suspense

Behind the Mask ~ contemporary romance

Frostbite ~ contemporary holiday romcom

Snowballed ~ contemporary holiday romcom

You Had Me at Goodbye ~ contemporary romcom

Kiss My Sass ~ contemporary romcom

Divorce Actually ~ contemporary romcom

Not Quite Cupid ~ contemporary romcom

Diner 49er ~ contemporary romcom

Nerds & Babies series ~

The Nerd Next Door

The Nerd Upstairs (Foxy Professor anthology 1/17 - 4/15/24)

The Nerd Downstairs (2024)

The Sextet Anthologies ~

Volume 1: Sharing

Volume 2: Dirty Dancing

Volume 3: Occupational Hazards

Volume 4: Entanglements

Volume 5: Mistletoe & Ménage

The Sextet Presents standalones ~

Playing in the Raine: A Toy Story

Bound by Voodoo: Legends

Bewitching Desires series ~

Two if by Sea

Two Knights of Passion

Two Fated for One

Two Pirates to Treasure

Two Times the Trouble

Two Roped and Ready

Two from the Triangle

Beyond Bewitching

CHAPTER ONE

STUFFING ANOTHER PAIR OF JEANS INTO HIS DUFFLE BAG, DREW Fulton swallowed the impulse to mutter every swear word he'd ever learned. He'd give his boss an earful at the breakfast meeting tomorrow morning when his daughters weren't within listening range.

Who the hell plans a company conference the week between Christmas and New Year's?

"Daddy, when's Aunt Colleen picking us up? Shouldn't she be here already?" Kristin clucked her tongue as she hurried to the bed. She pulled out the pants and everything beneath them. "Your shirts will get all wrinkled. Don't you want to look nice?"

Drew coughed to cover a snort. Considering he was supposed to have the week off to spend with his girls, he didn't give a damn if he impressed his workaholic boss. "Thanks, squirt. I don't know what I'd do without you. Did Hannah remember to pack pajamas and her toothbrush?"

"I remembered!" His younger daughter skipped into his bedroom, the locket he'd given her for Christmas swinging and bouncing at her neck. She hugged him around the waist. "Did *you* remember to pack pajamas and your toothbrush, Daddy?"

"Yep." He sat and lifted Hannah onto his lap.

When he patted the bed next to him, Kristen sat, her lanky frame and wavy reddish-brown hair reminding him of Kate for about the four-hundredth time. "Your mom would be proud of you for being so grown up, even though you're still my baby girls. I promise to call you every night while I'm gone."

Hannah shook her head and scrunched up her face. "I'm not a baby. I'll be seven in one month and four days."

"I know, but I still remember when you were born. It was one of best days of my life." The knot is his stomach wound tighter.

How would he survive three nights of not tucking in his children? He hadn't spent more than a day away from them since Kate's death, and the day before yesterday had been harder than he'd expected. The second Christmas without her had been almost as tough as the first.

No matter how much he'd loved her, he couldn't keep his promise to Kate yet. Taking a leap of faith required the will to jump, and he didn't have it. She wouldn't want him to rush back into reality when he was still learning his way through single parenthood and being a widower.

God, I hate that word.

Kristin knelt and wrapped her arms around his neck. "We'll be okay, Daddy."

But will I?

The ring of the doorbell sent Hannah scrambling off his lap and running out of the room. "Aunt Colleen is here!"

After a quick kiss on his cheek, Kristin followed her sister. "Come say good-bye."

"I'll be right there."

As he zipped his bag closed, the thought of composing a resignation letter crossed his mind, effective immediately. He'd have to dip into his retirement savings while he looked for a new job, but he wouldn't have to abandon what was left of his family. Unfortunately— or fortunately—his current employer allowed him to work from home more than half the time. He wasn't likely to find another local marketing firm with that flexibility. He had no choice unless he went out on his own or took his chances, and likely a pay cut, with an online company.

A slow inhale and exhale did little to calm his jangled nerves. He'd have to hold his tongue during the conference and look at his options in more detail over the next few months. Then he would put together a well-thought-out plan, one that didn't put his financial resources in jeopardy.

Shouldering the suitcase strap, he snagged his laptop case from the desk. *Clothes, computer, keys. Wallet, phone, charger.* If he forgot anything, he'd have an excuse to cut out early.

As he neared the top of the steps, his sister-in-law's voice carried up from the foyer. "Go load your stuff while I talk to your dad, munchkins. We'll be out in a minute."

The front door clunked shut a few seconds before he reached the bottom of the stairs. "Hey, Colleen. You sure you're up for this?"

Her smirk warned him she wasn't falling for his desperate attempt to get out of the trip. "I'm pregnant, not sick with the flu. You're thinking of canceling, aren't you? They'll be fine, Drew, and so will you. Enjoy some adult interaction for a change. Have a beer and relax. Try to have a good time."

The tension spread to the back of his neck as he handed her the envelope he'd stowed in the outside pocket of his computer bag. "It's business. I should be here with Kristin and Hannah instead of working this week. Here's the power of attorney and my insurance card in case one of them gets sick or hurt. Your parents have a copy of my will—"

"Stop that. Nothing's going to happen." She stared at him with the same stubbornness Kate had aimed his way countless times. "Now lock up and get on the road so I don't have to drive you there myself. The forecast is calling for some nasty weather this afternoon."

Her tone advised him not to argue, not that he had the opportunity when she headed out the door. The females of the Hastings clan had a streak of Irish tenacity ten miles wide, and he'd learned early on to pick his battles wisely. No way would he win this skirmish.

He surrendered to the inevitable, mostly because Colleen was right. Kristin and Hannah would be happy and safe while he was gone, and he'd live through being away from them for a few days. If anything happened to him, Kate's family knew his wishes.

Shifting the computer case to his right hand, he locked the front door and then headed to the kitchen entrance to the garage. He finished loading his gear in the car as the garage door rose.

I can do this.

Colleen waited in the drive, probably so she could follow him to the highway. She'd been the first one to offer babysitting services when he'd mentioned the badly timed trip, practically threatening to kidnap his kids if he refused to go. He should've kept his damn mouth shut.

Maybe I can convince Morton to wrap things up a day early.

Giving in to necessity, Drew trudged outside to say good-bye while he pulled on his coat. Life had taught him he couldn't change what was meant to be and, aside from exercising some caution, he had little control over his fate or that of those close to him.

"Hey, girls, I need some hugs that'll last me until Wednesday afternoon." Opening his arms, he dropped to one knee and braced himself for a double attack.

Hannah sprang at him half a step ahead of her sister. "I love you, Daddy!"

With slightly more dignity, Kristin pounced on him next. "Love you, Daddy."

Closing them both in a hug, he focused on the flowery scent of their shampoo and the sweet sound of their giggles. "I love you too. I'll miss you a bunch. Be good for Aunt Colleen and Uncle Brett. And no picking on your cousins."

His older daughter pressed her cool cheek to his. "We'll be good. Promise."

He swallowed past the lump in his throat and gave them another squeeze. "I should get going. I'll call you when I get there."

A second later, they were out of his reach, leaving him empty and alone.

"Bye, Daddy!" The farewell came in stereo as the girls scrambled into their aunt's car.

Too choked up to speak, he waved and turned to get in his own vehicle.

"Be careful, Drew. I'll take care of the kids. You take care of you." Colleen slid in behind the steering wheel, shutting the door before he could thank her. She sat idling in the driveway when he backed out of the garage and closed the door.

With the GPS ready to guide him, he waved again and set off on the three-hour drive. If he was lucky, he'd reach Logan by three o'clock and his cabin by three thirty. Then he'd have a little downtime before he ordered and picked up carryout for supper. A loaded pizza paired with a beer and a quiet evening of studying the specifics of his next contract wouldn't be so bad. He wouldn't have to rush to unpack groceries and cook, and cleanup couldn't get any easier than a paper plate.

When was the last time he'd gotten the toppings he wanted or had a beer?

Before Kate got sick.

His life had been one giant holding pattern for a year and a half, every decision he'd made based on his wife's and children's needs. He wouldn't trade a second of it for all the freedom in the world, but he still had no idea why the love of his life had been taken from him.

What had he done to deserve that kind of punishment?

Kate certainly hadn't deserved the pain and agony she'd suffered. Neither had their girls.

He would've exchanged places with her in a heartbeat. She sure as hell would've dealt with the stress a lot better than he had—and being strong while he watched her die for six months had almost destroyed him. Kristin and Hannah had saved him from losing his sanity, although sometimes they did a pretty good job of making him crazy.

Pushing the dark thoughts from his mind, he focused on the road. The gray southwestern sky ahead matched his mood. A few flurries skittered across the windshield as he followed the entrance ramp of the highway leading west.

Two hours later, the flakes had grown in size and number, covering the edges of the road and the median strip. Cooking supper when he wanted to eat made more sense than having to come back out in a winter storm.

The light traffic slowed near the last town before the park, crawling past the shopping center and south toward Hocking Hills. Several inches of snow already coated the landscape. A few hundred yards past the reservoir, headlights shone upward from the opposite ditch through the steady back-and-forth motion of his wiper blades.

With less than fifteen miles to go, Drew vowed to be patient. He'd get there when he got there, preferably with him and his car healthy and undamaged, which could be a challenge on the hilly, winding roads on a good day.

Forty-five minutes later, the sign for the park office finally signaled his arrival. He eased into the left turn, glad for a break for his tense neck and shoulders. If not for fresh tire tracks, he wouldn't have had any idea where the road leading toward the check-in building was. At least six inches of snow lay on the ground at his destination and, from the looks of the mostly undisturbed surface, no plows had come through.

Stopping in the parking lot, he finally breathed a sigh of relief. Kyle Morton was getting worse than an earful for not canceling the stupid conference because of the weather. With his luck, Drew was probably the only responsible fool nuts enough to make the drive, if he actually managed the last couple miles to the cabins without incident.

Cell phone in hand, he jogged from his car to the building. The CLOSED sign in the window registered as the door refused to open when he twisted the handle.

What now?

Wait a minute. Didn't the reservation confirmation say something about the cottage being unlocked if the park office was closed?

He returned to his car and sorted through the file on the passenger seat. At the bottom of the reservation page, the e-mail confirmed his hope. He only had to drive to Cabin 12. Check-in could wait until tomorrow morning.

As he buckled his seatbelt, he checked for cell signal. It was weak, the winter storm and hilly terrain likely playing havoc with reception.

He opened his text messages and clicked on Colleen's contact.

Made it. Storm here already. Almost no signal. Probably won't be able to call tonight. Tell the girls I love and miss them.

A long minute yielded a sent message, but the signal vanished almost immediately afterward. At least they'd know he was okay.

Another twenty-minute drive got him to the road lined with cottages, each one an indistinct shadowy blob in the blowing snow. If not for the open area around the community fire-ring area next to his destination and a detailed map, he wouldn't have been able to identify his cabin. They probably all looked the same on a clear day. With near-zero visibility, he never would've found the right one.

The first vehicle he'd seen in over an hour was parked in the pull-off between numbers 12 and 13. Only about an inch or two of snow had accumulated on the roof of the car, meaning its owner had to have arrived not long before him. The wind had already obliterated any tracks leading away from the car.

At least I'm not the only one crazy enough to be out in this mess.

He would grab as much gear as he could carry, but he'd still have to make a second trip. Winter had struck with a vengeance, and he was in no mood to traipse through it any more than necessary. Whether Morton had canceled the damn conference or not, Drew had no intention of driving or hiking down to the building that housed the restaurant and meeting rooms to meet up with his boss tomorrow. If Kyle wanted a damn conference, he could make the trek to Cabin 12.

Lights glowed in the faint outlines of the closest windows. The cleaning crew had evidently left them on when they'd finished preparing the cabin for his stay.

He winced at the sharp wind and icy pellets biting at his cheeks while he grabbed his duffle bag and laptop from the trunk. Then he hefted a bag of groceries, leaving a free hand to open the door. A careful jog along the barely discernible path brought him to the front porch. Kicking the snow from his hiking boots, he twisted the knob. It didn't turn.

No. No fucking way.

Closing his eyes, he rolled his head back.

What else could go wrong?

Forget I asked that.

Something else could always add to an awful day. Experience had taught him that the hard way.

He exhaled and opened his eyes, focusing on the porch ceiling above the door. A flash of silver caught his attention. Hanging from the exterior light was a key attached to a large plastic key ring.

Hallelujah.

Warmth hit him in the face as he entered, beckoning him inside, but he set down his load and went back for the rest rather than bask in the heat. He'd have the rest of the afternoon to thaw and relax.

He finally slogged through the deepening drifts with the cooler, balancing the second bag of groceries on top. Even if he got stranded for a few days, he wouldn't starve.

After shedding his coat and boots inside the door, he rolled the cooler to the refrigerator to unpack. As he removed the lid, he opened the fridge, only to discover shelves laden with enough supplies to last a family of three at least four or five days.

Had he let himself into the wrong cabin?

No, the key has a number twelve on it.

Had somebody else moved into his accommodations by mistake?

Strange clanking noises and the clomping of boots on the porch made him turn toward the entrance. The door swung inward, and a pair of snowy tennis rackets preceded their owner.

Tennis rackets?

In stepped a smaller-than-average person, maybe a young teenager, bundled in matching ski pants and a jacket, a scarf and gloves, and a facemask.

Snowshoes.

A pair of narrowed eyes—angry, feminine eyes—met his gaze from inside the holes of the mask. "What the hell are you doing in my cabin?"

CHAPTER TWO

W<small>EIGHING HER OPTIONS</small>—<small>ATTACK</small>, <small>RETREAT</small>, <small>OR WAIT FOR THE MAN IN</small> her kitchen to come after her, Pepper McCann locked stares with the intruder. Self-defense moves probably wouldn't be terribly effective against someone close to a foot taller than she was and almost twice her weight, especially when she had the mobility of a pregnant elephant in her snow gear.

She eased backward, keeping her hand on the open door for a hasty escape. "I asked what you're doing in my cabin."

A deep furrow in his forehead accompanied his frown. "This is *my* cabin. Number 12. I have a copy of my reservation confirmation in the file right there."

"Like I'm going to fall for that. *I* have the key to this cabin, given to me by the cashier at the park office, plus an e-mail confirmation on my cell phone. *And* I was here first." *So there!*

He took a step toward the table, triggering a small shot of adrenaline in her veins. Flight or fight tried to kick in, but she held her ground.

His gentle push sent a folder sliding across the smooth surface. It stopped at the edge of the table.

Holding up his hands, the man stepped back again. "I'm guessing somebody screwed up. The park office is closed and neither of us should be out driving in this mess. The cabin has two bedrooms. I'm willing to share if you are."

She rolled her eyes and laughed. "You expect me to stay the night with a stranger out in the middle of nowhere? Sounds like a bad slasher film."

A muscle popped in his not quite clean-shaven jaw. "Do you have a better solution? I'm sure as hell not risking my life out there to soothe your paranoia."

He made a good point. The roads were treacherous. However, paranoia was a bit over the top to describe her right to be careful.

Reaching for the file, she kept both eyes trained on her would-be roomie. A glance at the first paper confirmed his assertion, and the name on the reservation made her blood boil. "Damn it, Mort, you manipulative ass. I should've known you'd pull something like this."

"Mort?" The squatter shoved his fingers through his perfectly mussed hair. Intermittent silver strands fell into place between wavy brown ones, almost disappearing. "Not Kyle Morton?"

"None other than. Let me guess. You're Drew Fulton and your next project is an advertising package for the Red Hot Pepper deli, right?"

He rubbed the fingers of both hands along the bridge of his nose. "Yeah. Would you mind closing the door?"

Fairly certain her cousin wouldn't endanger her life by forcing her to share quarters with a sociopathic creep, she shut out the cold and snowy day. "What line of bull did Mort feed you about this…arrangement?"

Fulton withdrew a bottle of beer from the cooler at his feet. "Company conference to discuss all the new contracts starting in January and some upcoming changes in procedure. He was supposed to give me an information packet about your business, sort of an outline of your expectations of the marketing campaign."

"Sneaky twerp." She tugged off her gloves. "Pepper McCann, owner of the Red Hot Pepper. He wanted me to prepare all the meals for his little get-together and have a one-on-one conversation with you so you'd have an idea about what kind of food I serve at the deli. He claimed you'd do a better job with the project. Like I said, he's manipulative."

A tinny clink sounded as she bent to loosen her bootlaces, the familiar noise easy to place. Her ad man had tossed his bottle cap into the trashcan.

"Want a beer? Or I brought coffee." His attempt to be nice caught her off guard.

She yanked off the ski mask as she toed off her boots. Static snapped in her ears, and her hair likely stood on end more than usual. "Not a coffee or beer drinker. I'll make a pot of tea when I'm done undressing."

Drew's lips twitched. Maybe he had a sense of humor after all. That would be an improvement over their first contact.

"Um, removing my snow gear." She unzipped her coat. "I should get supper started, too, since we'll probably lose power at some point. I'd rather not have to resort to propane-stove cooking already."

"You brought a camp stove?"

Hanging her coat on the kitchen chair, she gave him another annoyed look. "Can't cook on an electric stove if there's no power. I also brought a few candles, two flashlights, and extra-long matches for the gas fireplace's pilot light. We'll still have a little bit of heat if the electric goes off. That happens sometimes with a really heavy snow."

By the dip of his eyebrows, he clearly hadn't considered that possibility. "Okay. Good. I brought a radio and a flashlight. And we should have plenty of food."

He took a long swallow from his beer and then set to work unpacking his cooler. Every few seconds, he seemed to look her way as if he didn't quite believe she knew what to do in a power outage.

Did he have any clue how to survive being stranded in a snowstorm?

She pushed her ski pants to her feet and stepped out of the legs. "Have you ever been camping? Like in a tent. Not in your parents' backyard?"

His low laugh held no humor. "My parents wouldn't have tolerated having a tent set up in the backyard unless they were hosting an event. I went on a few geology field trips when I was an undergrad."

Drew Fulton's childhood sounded too much like her own— unachievable expectations and more time spent in the company of nannies and housekeepers than with the man and woman who'd conceived her. The memories weren't worth remembering.

She scooped up her damp clothes and walked to her bedroom to hang them up. "Would you mind setting out the leeks and carrots? I need to finish making supper before the power—"

Silence fell with a noiseless crash. The furnace no longer blew as hard as the wind outside to maintain the temperature in the cabin. The fridge had decided on a nap too.

"Damn." Abandoning her task, Pepper returned to the kitchen. "Put your cooler on the screened porch. The fruits and vegetables will be fine in the refrigerator for now, but we'll have to move the milk, eggs, and cheese out there."

He hesitated a moment. "No generator?"

The urge to roll her eyes was strong, but she resisted. "No."

Tipping up his beer, he drained it. "You've done this before, haven't you?"

"Yeah."

He set down the empty bottle, the worry lines around his mouth suggesting that tidbit of knowledge didn't help.

With a shrug, she picked up the lid to his cooler and handed it to him. "It's not so bad. In fact, we could be a lot worse off. We have plenty of food and a roof over our heads. If you take care of moving this stuff and closing all the curtains, I'll carry all the blankets out here and close off the bedrooms to conserve heat."

"Okay. You can sleep on the couch. I'll take the floor."

His chivalry surprised her. "The couch folds out."

Turning away, he reached into the fridge. "I'd rather sleep on the floor."

Instead of relief, another reaction hit her square in the gut. It wasn't exactly disappointment, more like what she'd experience if someone insulted her. Most men she met tried to get her into bed, not refuse to share accommodations in favor of dirty, unpadded carpet.

Did he find her repulsive? Or maybe he wasn't into women. She was hardly an expert when it came to reading the opposite sex.

Then again, with her luck, he could be a married man, an escaped convict, or a psychopath. Her cousin wouldn't have booked a single cottage for her and Drew if he was any of those things, would the obnoxious little twit?

"Excuse me." Drew's stilted voice brought Pepper back to reality. He stood less than two feet from her, the cooler handle in one hand and a gallon of milk in the other.

"Sorry." Butterflies stirred up a squall in her stomach—and it wasn't from concern for her safety.

Ready to retreat to the bedroom, she spun on her heel and slipped on the linoleum flooring, her wool socks giving her no traction. Her tight leg muscles were no help, either, and she grabbed for the chair for balance. It slid with her, sending her sprawling and ruining her dignified departure. She winced at the loud bang and the pain in her hip.

"Are you hurt?" The poor guy paled, his voice sounding panicked. He hovered over her for second before lifting her into his arms. A few seconds later, he laid her on the couch as he knelt beside her. "Damn, I shouldn't have moved you. What if something's broken?"

Pushing up on her elbows, she let out a disgusted sigh. "Nothing's broken. I'm just a klutz."

And a fool for a hot hunk.

He frowned. "It's my fault for leaving a puddle on the floor. If you're sure you're okay, I'll put the food outside and get the bedding. You should rest."

"I'm fine." More embarrassed than in pain, she scooted past him to stand. The last thing she needed in her life was a complication. Physically attractive or not, Drew Fulton wasn't going to lure her into acting like a hormone-crazed idiot. *Been there. Done that. Have the kid to prove it.* "Let's get to work."

NOTHING HAD CHANGED IN THE YEAR AND TWO MONTHS SINCE KATE had died. Females still confounded Drew.

He'd learned to recognize some signs that he'd said or done something wrong with his wife, but Pepper McCann gave off more mixed signals than a short-circuited traffic light. She'd suggested they share the sofa bed, taken off layer after layer to reveal a body most women would kill for, and offered to cook for him. Then she'd run away the minute he'd gotten within two feet of her.

He'd touched her, but he'd only been worried that she'd hurt herself when she fell. He hadn't groped her or tried to kiss her, even if kissing her had crossed his mind when she'd pulled off the ski mask. Intelligent eyes and full pink lips had sucker-punched him in the chest. He'd wanted to tame her wild copper hair, the short strands begging for some finger combing while he explored the rest of her body with his mouth.

Making love with Kate had been beautiful and full of love. Sex with Pepper McCann would be uninhibited and—

What the hell am I thinking? She's a client.

Well, not officially. Yet. But I still can't sleep with her.

One-night stands and short-term affairs weren't his style. They never had been. When he decided to take the step of getting physical with a woman, a serious relationship would be part of it.

I've gone too long without sex and a woman to hold. That's all.

Banishing his cabinmate from his thoughts, he returned to moving his cooler to the porch. He had more important issues to ponder, like surviving until the roads were cleared and the power restored.

Pepper reappeared as he closed the sliding door to their giant walk-in refrigerator, a baggy hooded sweatshirt now covering her breast-hugging sweater. She'd also traded her socks for a pair of fuzzy slippers. Setting a pile of pillows and blankets on the coffee table, she steadied the stack and then moved the camp stove to the kitchen table.

"Turn on the fireplace. If the pilot's out, I'll relight it before I start cooking." Her gruff tone warned him to do exactly as she'd told him to, without argument, question, or comment.

The next few days promised lots of misunderstandings and too many temptations to quit his job.

He flipped the switch for the gas log. Flames sputtered for a couple seconds before licking higher. "It's working."

"Good." She stomped to the kitchen, turning her back to him after she opened the stove.

A string of unintelligible words carried across the room, but he ignored them. The rhythmic *thunk, thunk, thunk* of vegetables hitting the counter didn't bode well for the day, let alone the rest of the week. More than likely, Pepper lived up to her name—a hot temper and enough bite to make him keep his mouth shut and his hands away from the salsa jar. Maybe if he got to work on logo sketches for the promotional package, he wouldn't fall victim to her venom. He might even finish the preliminary designs and wouldn't have to meet with her more than once or twice after their four-day adventure.

Digging in his duffle bag, he found shirts, jeans, and socks but no glasses. He'd remembered to pack them, hadn't he? Or had Kristin taken them out and forgotten to put them back in his suitcase?

He ran his fingers along the inside pocket on the off chance he'd accidentally put them with his shaving kit. The travel bag was right where he'd packed it. A search of the contents yielded nothing out of the ordinary except the gold wedding band he'd taken off after his conversation with Kate's brother almost two months ago. Flynn had seemed surprised when Drew announced he planned to start dating.

That milestone had yet to occur.

Glancing sideways at Pepper, he slid the ring on his finger. Would it ward off the strange compulsion to run his hands through her fiery hair and kiss the anger from her pouty lips?

Somehow, after twelve years of wearing it, he'd gotten used to having a bare ring finger already. The first week had been hell, the emptiness nearly unbearable. He'd rubbed at the naked spot almost constantly, as if the action would grant him the ultimate wish. Kate wasn't coming back to him, though. She'd wanted him to find love and happiness with someone else, to go on with his life.

The band tightened around his finger, threatening to cut off the circulation.

He slipped the ring off again. The past was done.

Zipping the bag closed, he hoped his good judgment was stronger than the need to get laid, especially since his supply list didn't include condoms. He wasn't so far out of the dating loop to risk STDs and unplanned pregnancy.

That settles it. I'm sleeping on the floor.

He'd suffer through an aching back to avoid doing something stupid. The consequences probably wouldn't last the rest of his life.

Desperate for a distraction, he checked the outside pockets. The last one had a lump about the length of his glasses case.

Finally.

He opened the zipper and grasped the contents. As he withdrew the case, the edges poked his hand rather than being smooth, and it bent like it was broken in multiple places. The crinkly texture reminded him of something that wouldn't bolster his willpower.

Damn. This better not be what I think it is.

A short inspection of the perforated foil packets triggered a twinge below his belt. He was in a shitload of trouble. Temptation, he could probably handle, but being prepared put a new spin on the problem.

Fuck.

No. No fucking.

He dropped the strip of Trojans into the pocket and zipped it closed. Out of sight might not mean out of mind, but throwing condoms out the door would be a bit conspicuous. Why hadn't he unpacked them after the last trip?

Gotta find my glasses.

The computer bag was next. Going through each compartment, he failed in his search. His patience wore thinner by the minute. He had to have brought his damn glasses. He'd packed for a work conference, not a vacation.

Pulling out a sketchpad, he blew out a frustrated sigh. His favorite mechanical pencil wasn't in its usual slot, either. He reached inside his sweater to check his shirt pocket. The round metal end of the pencil rested against the glasses case.

I'm losing what's left of my mind.

He settled in the chair near the window, putting on his reading glasses and adjusting the pencil lead. With a dozen calming strokes, he drew a bunch of short, curved peppers hanging from the bottom hook of an "R."

"Do you have any food allergies?"

Pepper's brusque question made him look toward the kitchen.

She stood at the counter, her attention seemingly on a large knife poised above a tomato on a cutting board. As she turned to meet his gaze over her shoulder, her wind-chapped cheeks lost every bit of color and the knife clattered into the sink. "I think I'm gonna be sick."

CHAPTER THREE

THE ROILING IN PEPPER'S STOMACH THREATENED TO SEND HER LUNCH on an unpleasant trip to the kitchen floor. She swallowed hard and closed her eyes. A deep breath calmed her insides a little bit, but her pulse continued to thump in her ears.

Zack's grown up. Nobody can try to take him away anymore.

An arm closed around her shoulders, and the irritating scrape of a chair being pulled across the linoleum brought her out of the daze.

"Sit down and put your head between your knees." Drew pressed her forward as she plopped into the seat. He sounded more panicked than she'd been seeing him with those damn glasses on. "You're not going to pass out, are you?"

She smacked at his legs, embarrassment once again getting the best of her. "Let me up! I'm fine."

"No, you're not. Now stay put while I get some water." His feet moved out of her peripheral vision for a several moments. "Do *not* sit up."

"Geez, okay. Bossy much?" She turned her head to find where he'd gone.

He snorted, the sound almost as annoying as the squeaky plastic as he freed a water bottle from its shrink-wrap packaging. "And you aren't?"

"You're an expert at first aid as well as making do when the power goes out, Mr. Generator Man? For your information, head between the knees isn't for nausea." Antagonizing him seemed wiser than admitting she had control issues. That flaw had helped her survive on her own for a good long time, but he didn't need to know that. "You reminded me of somebody. The glasses caught me off guard."

The cap snapped free with a quick twist, and he handed her the water bottle. "Caught you off guard? You looked like you saw a ghost. Is somebody stalking you? Sit up and drink this."

"Don't sit up. Sit up. And I'm supposed to drink and talk at the same time?" Sarcasm was her most effective tool. It had chased off numerous guys who'd thought to play her for a fool.

"Sit up. Drink first." Crossing his arms in front of his chest, he frowned. Faint lines fanned out from the corners of his mouth.

Was he genuinely concerned about her well-being?

To pacify the overgrown worrywart, she drank several swallows. "Happy now?"

"No." His expression softened, but his jaw stayed tense. "Who is he?"

Her personal life was off-limits. Ready to drop the subject, she gave the only answer she could. "Someone I knew a long time ago."

"Did he hurt you?"

No one had ever asked that, including her parents. "No. I made a bad choice. It's over and done."

He shook his head. "It isn't done if a man in glasses can scare the shit out of you."

Why couldn't Drew let it go? She had—nineteen years ago.

Setting aside the water, she stood to finish chopping the tomato. "I wasn't scared. You're reading way more into this than there is."

He stomped to the living room. "Women! Done trying to figure you out. Done trying to be helpful. Where's the information packet you put together for Morton? The sooner I get done with this contract, the better."

His implied insult stung. She should be happy that she'd managed to piss him off so easily. Most men were persistent to the point of aggravation, but Drew Fulton hadn't tried to pick her up at the grocery store or the gym. He'd picked her up off the floor and rescued her from her imagination.

I'm officially a bitch.

She owed him an apology. If life hadn't taught her that everyone had an ulterior motive, she might've accepted the friendly gestures with gratitude. Trust wasn't her strong suit, even when she had no reason to doubt.

The steady *tap, tap, tap* of the knife on the cutting board nagged at her. She scraped the last ingredient into the pot, wracking her brain for the right words. Rinsing her hands under the tiny stream of water left in the faucet didn't bring inspiration, either.

She stirred the soup as she checked the flame and then forced her legs to carry her across the room.

Drew didn't look up from the sketchpad on his lap. His pencil skimmed over the paper, forming what appeared to be strings of jalapeños, serranos, and cayennes. Wavy lines rose above them, as if to signify their spicy heat. He'd drawn the name of her deli in block letters on the page in several places, one even peeking out from under his forearm.

"I'm sorry." The simple statement didn't taste as bad in her mouth as she expected it would. "I'm used to depending on myself, and I don't like to dredge up the past."

He offered her the tablet. "What do you think?"

Disappointment made her chest tighten. He must've decided to keep their conversations all business after her appalling behavior.

So much for smoothing out the rough spots.

She tipped the notepad toward the window, studying his creations in the fading light. His artistic skill was outstanding, especially given the short time he'd been working. The pepper strings could've been modeled from the ones hanging from the wall menu in the deli. Each name had a different style. Along the right edge, bold lettering caught her attention—the logo that had been half hidden beneath his arm as she'd watched him. The design matched one of the fonts on her short list for the new sign.

Red Hotheaded Pepper. Long red and green peppers hung in a decorative garland beneath the name.

While it fit her to a T, did he mean it as a joke? Or was he poking fun at her?

Peeking past the notepad, she tried to decipher his mood.

His lips twitched, but he didn't meet her gaze.

She pointed to the could-be insult as she set the pad on his lap. "This one is the best. The info packet is on the end table."

He grinned up at her. "Apology accepted."

An uncomfortable twinge in her lower belly stole any relief at his willingness to forgive and forget. He was too handsome, too charming, and too nice to be real. Her only hope of enduring their forced cohabitation was to tell him the truth, to let him know in no uncertain terms that experience had taught her all she needed to know about men.

She stepped backward out of his reach and braced herself for his assumptions. "You reminded me of a guy I met in college. He denied that he was the father when I got pregnant."

Drew's mouth froze in an awkward grimace, and the paper crinkled in between his fingers. "The bad choice. You demanded a paternity test, didn't you? For child support?"

Shaking her head, she revealed the rest. "He and his friends told my parents I slept with all of the guys in the fraternity. How could I possibly know who the father was?"

The long silence was confirmation enough that Drew doubted she had any idea who'd actually fathered her son. He'd obviously made the same assumption her parents had—that she'd been stupid drunk and had sex with every guy at the party. The only person she'd ever shared the whole truth with was Zack.

Mission accomplished, she headed to the camp stove. She wasn't compelled to glance toward the man still staring at her—and he was. The skin-crawling tingle along her spine was all the evidence she needed. He sat there judging her, like everybody had nineteen years ago.

Except Mort.

Her pain-in-the-ass cousin hadn't stopped trying to help her since he'd found her walking on the road a mile from home. He'd tossed her suitcase in the backseat, offered her a ride, and given her a place to stay.

You crossed the line this time, though, Mortie.

He always meant well, but she wasn't interested in a fix-up. Nothing in her life was broken. She'd remained single by choice, and she planned to stay that way.

Lifting the iron skillet from her crate of cooking gear, she sifted through the recipe file in her brain. Somewhere in the organized mess was her favorite biscuit recipe. The challenge of remembering the details would de-stress her faster than reading the measurements from an index card.

She wouldn't get the third degree from her roommate for throwing things, either.

NO MATTER HOW HARD HE TRIED, DREW COULDN'T CONCENTRATE ON the paperwork for Pepper McCann's vegetarian deli. Something about her revelation left him wondering what the hell she hadn't told him. He had no doubt she'd abbreviated the story to the absolute bare bones.

She might exude wariness and sarcasm, but her color-changing eyes held naïveté.

No, not naïveté. Innocence?

Yeah. And a boatload of distrust.

Her eyes had gone from forest green to muddy brown as she'd told him about the guy with the glasses. She could pretend aloofness all she wanted, but he wasn't buying it.

Two scenarios came to mind. Either the guy and his friends had raped her or the friends had lied. She hadn't chosen to screw a bunch of frat boys.

A bad choice.

What choice had she made?

It's none of my business. Why do I even give a damn?

The rattle of dishes brought his attention to Pepper standing at the kitchen table. She set bowls next to the propane stove, her stiff posture warning him her mood hadn't improved. Metal clanked against metal as she ladled soup from the pot into the dishes, and the aroma of freshly baked bread made his mouth water.

Helping her carry their meals to the coffee table would be the polite thing to do, but she didn't seem receptive to a friendly gesture. He'd evidently gotten himself into a no-win situation. He sent up a silent thank-you that Kristin and Hannah hadn't reached the age of unpredictability yet. They were still his sweet and lovable girls.

Pepper donned an oven mitt and transferred a skillet from the camp stove to the cabin's electric stove. The movement sent a stronger waft of warm bread carrying to him. Using tongs, she removed some sort of biscuits or rolls from the pan.

Huh. Stovetop baking.

Her solemn eyes finally met his for a brief second. "Supper's ready."

Though the invitation wasn't enthusiastic, he rose to get a bottle of water to go with his food. "Thanks."

Looking away, she set a teakettle on the empty burner. "You're welcome."

Her stilted yet polite answer added to his frustration. He couldn't spend three more days and nights tiptoeing around her, hoping he didn't say or do the wrong thing. She was a fuse and he evidently held the burning match. Too bad he couldn't tell whether—or how many times—he would spark the flame to it or not. She was destined to blow up at him again. And again.

He tucked the bottle under his arm to carry his soup to the living room. As he straightened to go back for a biscuit, she set one down beside his bowl. Loath to repeat their pathetic three-word conversation, he simply nodded.

Instead of joining him, she pulled out a chair at the kitchen table and sat with her back to the living room. The action irritated him more than her silence.

Had she lumped him in with the creeps who'd treated her like a piece of garbage?

What if she thinks I don't want to eat with her?

He hadn't had woman trouble this bad since Kate had given him a lesson on her moods and how to stay out of the doghouse. They'd been married all of a year and had already started arguing over petty nonsense. He'd wondered if they possessed the strength to avoid becoming another statistic. Love wasn't always enough to keep a relationship together, but he'd vowed to make theirs last.

It had, but only because they'd learned to compromise.

Making two trips to the kitchen table, he didn't say a word. He sat adjacent to Pepper and took a bite of soup, her lack of acknowledgment too complete to be anything but deliberate. The tasty mix of broth and vegetables warmed his body, if not the chill she projected. He was a victim of guilt by gender association.

Wisps of steam escaped from the perfectly browned biscuit as he split it open. "Would you pass the butter please?"

She set the paper-wrapped stick and a butter knife by his bowl. "We should listen to the radio for a weather update. Last I heard, Hocking County was under a blizzard warning until tomorrow morning, with up to eighteen inches of snow expected."

Banal as the topic is, at least she's speaking to me. "We aren't going anywhere for a while, are we?" He slathered butter on his biscuit. Pushing back his chair, he bit off a mouthful.

Where had he packed the radio? Had he carried it in from his car?

Did I put it in with the groceries?

The black handle stuck out the top of the bag on the armchair closest to the door, bringing a lonely moment of relief. He was still stuck.

Setting down her spoon, Pepper pursed her lips. "One of the rangers might come in on a snowmobile to check on the cabin campers after the snow stops, but we won't be able leave until everything's plowed. Maybe Wednesday or Thursday. Possibly Friday. Depends on if the park has a full staff. Not likely with the holidays and the weather."

With another bite of biscuit in his mouth, he stalked to the bag. The extra package of batteries lay next to the radio. He grabbed both, placing them in front of her as he returned to his seat. "Want to find a station? You seem to know a lot about the area."

"Okay, but I'm guessing we won't be able to pick up much. The few local stations probably lost power too, and the Columbus signals are iffy on a good day."

He finished his soup and buttered another biscuit while she fiddled with the radio dials. Static and dead air filled the silence. "Supper was really good. Thanks for making it."

Her wary look warned him she might be about to serve up another helping of sarcasm. "Just doing my job, but I suppose you're welcome."

Seizing the opportunity to get to know more about her, he focused on her work. "My brother-in-law Flynn's a chef. Where'd you go for training?"

Her laugh was anything but humorous. "The kitchen."

She obviously meant to maintain a healthy distance between them, given that she ignored his prompt to talk about herself. Unfortunately, the harder she pushed him away, the more he wanted to sneak past the defensive walls she'd built around herself. That fortress wasn't impenetrable, and he was determined to stand at the door until she opened it.

Exactly what I don't need—another stubborn female in my life.

Or maybe he did.

He'd tried to imagine the kind of woman he would choose to fill the empty spot Kate had left in his heart and his family, and a hotheaded, obstinate sort like Pepper had never entered his mind. He'd pictured a soft-spoken, feminine type with long dark hair. His girls needed someone to talk to about girlie stuff and to take them shopping. He needed a companion willing to help him raise his daughters and grow old with him. Not once had he thought about finding an abrasive, self-reliant nymph with wild red hair.

I shouldn't be thinking about it now. Even if I'm ready, she's a client. Business before pleasure.

Under normal circumstances, he could make the decision to keep his personal and professional lives separate, but he was trapped. He had no escape hatch if the attraction got out of hand. Lack of electricity was the least of his worries.

Gathering his dishes, he stood. "I'll clean up since you cooked."

She switched off the radio. "You realize you'll have to heat water to wash dishes, don't you?"

Her reminder didn't deter him. "No big deal. We have a stove."

"We also have no running water."

That, on the other hand, could pose a problem. She didn't seem bothered by the prospect, so they had to have another source.

He set his bowl and spoon in the sink as wind and icy pellets rattled and pelted the window. Snow obscured his view of the cars, although they were probably too buried to see anyway. Eighteen inches sounded like a gross underestimation.

"Snow." A jolt of satisfaction almost sparked a snide comment about her lack of confidence in his survival skills. "Do you have any big pots or plastic containers? I'll bring in enough snow to wash dishes and flush the toilet a few times."

"Well done, Mr. Fulton. You aren't completely helpless after all." She obviously hadn't expected him to think of what she'd planned on from the start. "I put four buckets on the screened porch. You can put the leftover soup out there when you get them. Use the canning pan under the sink to heat the dishwater."

She obviously had no qualms about him earning his keep until the power was restored.

Toting the soup pot past the table, his sense of justice got the better of him. "Gotta give a bossy woman credit. She knows what she wants and how to get it done, without actually doing it herself."

Now they were even.

By the time he'd retrieved the buckets from their giant walk-in fridge, she had scooted the coffee table into the tiny hall by the bedrooms. She grabbed a couch cushion and marched to the armchair as he slipped on his boots. It tumbled to the floor when she set it on the seat. She growled, and he bit the inside of his cheek to hold in a snicker. He'd truly nailed her temper with his "Red Hotheaded Pepper" spoof.

With his coat and gloves on, he headed out the door with the buckets. Had he laughed, she probably would've locked him outside.

Then again, she still might.

He stepped back in to grab the oversized key off the end table before he closed the door behind him.

"Damn it." Her curse came with the click of the bolt.

She wouldn't have really left him to freeze in a blizzard, would she?

CHAPTER FOUR

Drew set his toothbrush in the glass on the sink and picked up the flashlight. Getting ready for bed in a dark bathroom with no running water was a serious step down from the shower house he'd had access to the last time he'd been camping.

It's an adventure. That's what Kristin and Hannah would tell him.

Colleen had likely put them to bed more than an hour ago, and he'd been too wrapped up in bringing in snow and washing dishes to even notice. For the first time in almost two years, he hadn't tucked them in for the night.

Guilt nibbled at his conscience, but he shook it off. He'd done what he had to do.

Sleep well and sweet dreams, my girls. I miss you.

Gusty wind threw flurries against the window as another round of whistling and howling started. The storm hadn't let up since his arrival, only worsening from time to time. According to the static-filled weather report he'd finally picked up, it would go on through the night and end sometime tomorrow morning.

Pepper had continued arranging sheets and blankets on the folded-out couch after the announcement. He hadn't argued with her when she created two cocoons on the lumpy mattress. Sleep was foremost in his plans, sleeping with her a far distant second. Besides, the floor sounded about as inviting as another verbal battle.

He exited the bathroom and walked to the closest side of the bed to climb in. The flickering firelight cast shadows on the walls and across the woman already snuggled in the covers. Her eyes were closed and her face relaxed, as if she didn't have a care in the world—nothing like when she was awake. Her untamed hair and delicate features brought to mind the fairies from one of Hannah's favorite books. She was breathtakingly beautiful.

What had happened to her to cause such wariness and cynicism?

Having some jackass deny being her kid's father and calling her a slut couldn't have done that by itself. Had she ended the accidental pregnancy by choice? Or because she had no other choice?

What if she'd been unable to care for her baby? Did she live every day wondering about the child she'd given up? Or maybe raising a child on her own was a lot more challenging than his experience.

He hoped to hell his initial thought was wrong. Drunk or not, no woman asked to be raped.

Laying his head on the pillow, he pulled the chilly blankets higher. Goosebumps spread over his bare arms and legs, boxer shorts and a T-shirt not quite the kind of pajamas the temperature warranted. Unfortunately, he'd have to live with the cold until the layers warmed him.

He would've been in a lot worse position if not for Kyle Morton's self-serving meddling. Without Pepper's knowledge and extra supplies, Drew would've been hard-pressed to figure out heat and water sources, and homemade vegetable soup beat the hell out of cold canned stew. Pepper deserved better than the retaliatory teasing he'd given her earlier.

An apology might improve their chances of getting along, but he'd wait until morning. Slow, even breaths came from her side of the bed, a pretty good indication that she was asleep. If she wasn't, she was putting forth a real effort to look like it. Bothering or waking her now wouldn't gain him any points.

Shadows danced on the ceiling, drawing him closer to sleep. Mostly, they distracted him from Pepper's tempting presence.

I finally share a bed with a woman again, and I can't touch her. I can't even talk to her.

He missed sex, but he wouldn't complain about having someone to hold while he fell asleep. Soft skin and feminine scents were as comforting as they were arousing. A little anticipation wouldn't kill him, either. Getting laid didn't begin to compare to making love, the physical connection less satisfying without the emotional bond. His years of marriage had taught him the value of truly loving another person.

A yawn escaped, and he rolled to face his temporary roommate. Her outline blurred in his watery eyes.

Goodnight, Pepper. I'm glad neither one of us has to be alone tonight.

LETTING OUT A FRUSTRATED GROWL, DREW SHIFTED TO REMOVE A lumpy spring from his back. Another poked him in the thigh as he rolled to his stomach. He turned over again, only to discover the support bar with his hip. If he lived through the night without the steel coils skewering him, he'd convince Pepper they needed more padding and less covers. That, or he was sleeping on the floor. It couldn't be any less comfortable than a cheap mattress with little stuffing.

He punched his pillow and sat up to frown at his bedmate. How the hell did she sleep on the lump-filled torture device?

The cocoon next to him was misshapen, half the blankets under her instead of on top. She'd evidently fixed her problems with the sprung springs. Being half his size undoubtedly made a difference too.

Following her example, he repositioned the layers to fold over top of him, braving the cold for a minute in favor of a more comfortable bed. As he settled into his makeshift sleeping bag, Pepper's bedding shook. A noise like chattering teeth came from the pile.

Although flames still fluttered in the fireplace, the wind and frigid weather prevented their only heat source from maintaining the room's temperature. They wouldn't freeze to death, but the cold required a secondary method of creating warmth.

With no alternative, he stripped the bedspread from his padding and flung its length over Pepper. Moving closer to her, he tugged part of the cover over him and put his arm around her. They'd have to depend on each other for body heat, whether she liked it or not. He could almost guarantee she wouldn't.

She continued to shiver for what seemed like an hour, but the chattering finally stopped, and he found a position that didn't make him a human pincushion. Now he only had to contend with the temptation to press his half-hard dick against the sexy curve of her butt.

The physical attraction, he understood. Wanting to get to know her confused him. As sharp-tongued and stubborn as she was, he shouldn't have the urge to pound the shit out of the guy who'd gotten her pregnant. She didn't need a protector or someone to console her. If he asked her to confide the details of her past, she'd tell him to take a flying leap and give him directions to the nearest cliff. Hell, she'd probably lead him there and give him a push.

Kate had been unbelievably strong, facing death with more courage and grace than he'd thought one person could possess. A different kind of strength emanated from Pepper. She was independent, possibly to a fault, and she held her head high, no matter her past. The armor she wore kept him—and probably everyone else—at a distance. Her loner attitude would put off most people, but it sparked his curiosity.

Did a vulnerable woman reside behind the brusque façade she presented to the world?

She wasn't weak. That much was clear. He'd have at least a couple days to figure out the enigma lying beside him, or try to.

Easing almost close enough to rest his chest against her back, he closed his eyes and inhaled. The scent of peaches urged him to take a deeper breath.

Peach pie. What I wouldn't give for a taste of her.

Maybe he was ready to move on, after all.

His brother-in-law was a perfect example of fate deciding the right time and place. Flynn hadn't expected to meet his match at a job interview, especially at a retirement community. Fighting the attraction hadn't changed a thing, either. He'd fallen for Lilith, despite his best intentions to maintain a professional relationship.

Logic had no place in love or lust.

Is it lust? If I sleep with Pepper, will the novelty wear off?

Drew wasn't a playboy. He'd never had sex with a girl until they'd been dating for months. He'd even asked permission to hold her hand and kiss her. At thirty-eight years old, engaging in a short, hot fling with someone he barely knew was irresponsible and reprehensible. The woman was someone's daughter, for God's sake. He wouldn't tolerate that treatment of his own girls sitting down.

My girls. I never should've left them.

If he'd stayed home, he wouldn't be torn between some unexplainable force pushing him toward Pepper and common sense telling him to keep their relationship platonic.

Dating sucks, and I haven't even started.

Struggling with the blankets again, he rolled so his back faced her and tried to turn off his contradictory thoughts.

The time wasn't right.

The place was wrong.

Whether or not Pepper McCann had a place in his life remained to be seen, but he damn well wanted to know already.

ISN'T HE EVER GOING TO GO TO SLEEP?

Biting her lower lip, Pepper counted to five as she exhaled. Then she waited another full five seconds before sucking in a slow breath.

Drew finally stilled, and she savored his heat against her back, her half of the blankets alone not enough to keep her warm. Without a working blower fan on the fireplace, most of the heat went up the chimney instead of into the cabin. She also hadn't expected the temperature to drop so drastically. They'd have to resort to sharing the same covers tomorrow night if the power wasn't restored.

Why did the prospect excite her as much as worry her?

Exhibiting atypical male behavior, Drew hadn't used the situation to his advantage. Not once in his rearranging and shifting had he worked his hands under the blankets or her clothes. She should be thrilled with that small favor, but a disconcerting mix of emotions churned in her stomach.

He was too nice. He had to have a self-serving motive. All men did.

"Pepper?" His whisper made her pulse jump. "Are you awake?"

Answer? Or pretend I'm asleep? "Who can sleep with you rolling all over the place?" The smartass question came as easily as her heart beating.

"Sorry, I'm having a hard time getting comfortable." He let out a frustrated-sounding sigh. "And I miss my kids."

She nearly choked. "Kids?"

Was he married? Divorced with shared custody?

"My girls, Kristin and Hannah. They're ten and a half and almost seven." The bed shifted again, but he didn't continue.

Curiosity got the better of her, even though she half dreaded his response. "Are they home with their mom?"

"No, they're at my sister-in-law's house. Their mom—my wife—died last year." His quiet words kicked her in the gut.

He's a grieving widower. Could she have been any more tactless? "Shit, I'm sorry. I—"

"It's okay. You didn't know." He seemed to hesitate for a moment. "Will you tell me about what happened with, you know, the college thing? I'll tell you about Kate."

No one had ever had the balls to ask her about her past except Mort. He'd demanded to know what happened the minute they'd entered his apartment almost nineteen years ago. She'd refused, knowing he'd want retribution for her.

Drew tugged the blankets a little higher. "You don't have to if you don't want to."

The usual rush of anger and hurt faded with his recognition of her reluctance. He hadn't tried to coerce her. "I don't know if I can."

"I shouldn't have asked. And I doubt you want to hear about a

thirty-six-year-old woman dying from cancer. I'll just shut up now."
His voice held no pain, only surrender. He sounded tired and lonely.

Defeated.

How many times had she wished for someone who would do
nothing more than listen?

She hadn't wanted anyone's sympathy. An ear had been all she'd
needed—no hand to hold, no shoulder to cry on, no fist to punch
Zack's father in the mouth for lying. None of it would've changed
anything.

"I was a college freshman. I'd seen this guy in my dorm a few
times, and one day he invited me to an off-campus party. Naïve fool
that I was, I decided to go. He fed me a line about finding the perfect
girl and how we were meant to be. I fell for it, had sex with him, and
ended up pregnant. When I told him, he claimed I'd been drunk and I
had him confused with somebody else. His friends backed him by
saying...well, you know. My dark-haired, blue-eyed son looks just like
the loser. Want to know the kicker? I'm allergic to alcohol. Zack is
too."

Drew was silent so long, she almost shined the flashlight at him to
see if he'd fallen asleep. "You couldn't have been drunk. Why didn't
you—"

"I made a bad choice. I saw no reason to compound it by insisting
on a lifelong connection to a low-life scum."

"How old is your son—Zack?"

Running her fingertips along the finished edge of the sheet, she
searched for a loose thread to keep her fingers busy. "He turned eighteen in July."

"You raised him on your own?" Drew shifted for the umpteenth
time since he'd come to bed.

"Yeah."

"You're a survivor."

The reverence and respect in his voice brought a tiny burst of pride
and empathy. "I did what I had to do. It couldn't have been any harder
than losing your wife to cancer and raising your children by yourself
now."

"She was a lot stronger than I am. Try knowing you have six months to live without falling apart in front of your kids. Not once did she complain about how unfair life had treated her. In fact, she told us every day how lucky she was to have us." He paused, his swallow audible over the blustering wind. "I lived day to day for a long time. Going on without Kate was the most difficult thing I've ever done."

Tears stung Pepper's eyes in the near darkness. She didn't want Drew to see her cry any more than she wanted to witness that weakness in him. "Some people say it's harder to be the one who doesn't die. I guess that makes you a survivor too."

"It changed everything. Now I don't get in the car without wondering if I'm going to be in an accident and who'll take care of the girls. Before I left today, I reminded Kate's sister that her mom and dad have a copy of my will. Is that surviving?" His voice didn't break over the admission, but it had grown softer.

He hadn't exaggerated about living day to day. She'd lived through constant worry for eighteen years. Would Zack grow up happy and healthy without a father? Would he blame her for being fatherless? What if his father suddenly decided to fight for custody?

Thankfully, she didn't have to think about a possible legal battle anymore, and Zack had turned out far above average. The answer to the middle question still nagged at her occasionally, even though he'd assured her that he didn't blame her for any of her choices.

"You're doing what you have to do. It's your way of coping." She rolled to her back to stare at the ceiling. The cool sheet triggered a fresh batch of goose bumps over her skin. "I'm gonna grab another layer of clothes. Even the wool socks aren't helping. You need anything while I'm up?"

"Mind if I make a suggestion?"

Pushing up on her elbows, she tried to keep her tone less caustic than normal. "Depends on what it is."

He frowned. "I know how this is going to sound, but... If you put your head on my chest and cuddle up close to me, we can share body heat and blankets. I swear I'll keep my hands to myself. No groping or accidentally on purpose brushing against you. Just sleeping and staying warm."

His idea had genuine merit. It also triggered an intense impulse to run like hell.

Where was her usual dose of sarcasm with the side of contempt? Why couldn't she tell him what to do with his suggestion?

Tossing back the covers, he climbed out of bed. "I'll get your stuff. I need to straighten the covers anyway."

She hadn't meant to imply a refusal with her indecision. Trust didn't come naturally to her, and she'd needed a few seconds to weigh her options. He should've given her more time instead of choosing for her.

As he bent to pick up her suitcase, she braved the cold to slide his layers to the middle of the mattress. Then she spread her bedding over top, including the bedspread he'd shared with her.

Sweats in hand, he turned toward her with his arm outstretched as she snuggled back into the nest. "Here's— What're you doing?"

She swallowed her fears. "Waiting for you to climb in and get me warm."

"Are you sure?" He lowered the clothes to his side. "I understand why you're not comfortable—"

"I'm fine. Now stop talking and come back to bed."

His nod was less than decisive, but he dropped the handful of garments on the chair and shuffled to his side of the mattress. "I promise."

The vow was solemn and utterly convincing. The man was a master of deception if he'd lied. His gaze hadn't wavered when he'd looked at her, sincerity showing in what she could see of his eyes in the low light.

Taking his promise at face value was only fair. "Okay."

Slipping in beside her, he settled on his back and held out his arm. She rested her head on his chest, scooting close enough that her legs pressed against his longer ones. His hand guided her knee over his thigh, the icy toes of her left foot settling into the warmer valley between his calves.

Enclosed in his embrace, she willed her muscles to relax. His heart beat in her ear and his warmth seeped into her body. The freshly laundered scent of his T-shirt was soothing, reminding her of home, her safe place.

Slow, even breaths lulled her toward sleep, the gentle rhythm keeping time with his pulse. She closed her eyes and exhaled. "Thank you, Drew. Good night."

"You're welcome." He leaned his cheek against her hair, his warm breath caressing her forehead. "Good night, Pepper."

CHAPTER FIVE

CAREFUL NOT TO BANG THE PANS, PEPPER SET A SECOND IRON SKILLET on the camp stove to preheat. The baked French toast she'd had to cook on the stovetop was almost ready, giving her about ten minutes to sauté the apple topping.

Drew had slept through her not-so-quiet breakfast prep. He hadn't even budged when she'd crawled out of bed at seven fifteen. Of course, neither of them had gotten much rest prior to his suggestion that they share the bed, the covers, and their body heat. Then they'd both zonked out.

And he kept his promise.

At least she was pretty sure he hadn't copped a feel while she lay nestled against him. He didn't snore, either—a definite plus. She might actually endure another night or two of the arrangement without having to boot him onto the floor.

The butter sizzled as it hit the hot pan, and she swirled it round and round to coat the bottom of the skillet. Tipping up the cutting board, she added the sliced apples, followed by a light sprinkling of sugar and a good-sized dose of cinnamon. She popped on the lid and inhaled the freshly baked pie scent wafting up in the steam. Lack of electricity didn't have to interfere with her ability to cook.

"Damn, that smells good." Drew sat on the near side of the mattress, his bare feet sticking out from the layers of sheets and blankets. As he stood, they fell away, revealing long, lean legs below the hem of his boxers.

She jerked her gaze upward when she got to the bulge in his shorts. His upper body wasn't muscle bound like a bulked-up jock, but he worked out if his broad shoulders and sizable biceps were any indication. He didn't have an extra ounce of fat anywhere. The dark stubble on his jaw and his sleep-mussed hair did nothing to detract from his underwear-model physique.

Since when did she care about men's builds and Jockey advertisements?

Forcing her attention back to the stove, she stirred the apples more vigorously than necessary. "Thanks. There's coffee in the thermal carafe and hot water in the teakettle. If you want juice, it's on the porch. I brought orange and cranberry."

"Maybe being stranded isn't so bad. Back in five for coffee." The smile in his voice was too appealing.

A promise kept doesn't make him worth the risk. The past had taught her too damn well that attraction and desire weren't to be trusted.

He moved out of her peripheral vision, and a door clunked closed a few seconds later. Hopefully, he'd put on some clothes while he was in the bathroom. Living without a man in her life hadn't been a hardship, but one night in Drew's arms had set off an unrealistic fantasy—a little girl's dream of a handsome prince sweeping her off her feet and a woman's dream of her prince taking care of her sexual frustration.

"Ouch!" She jerked her hand up to her lips, sucking on her scorched knuckle.

I'm a delusional fool.

All she had to do was *think* about falling in love and she got burned. Tripping head over snowshoes for a man still mourning his dead wife wasn't in her best interest. Remembering the consequences of making bad choices was. Independence suited her better anyway.

Steeling herself against her cabinmate's magnetic pull, she

switched off the flames under the skillets and poured hot water over her tea bag. The empty sofa bed caught her eye as she carried the mug to the far end of the table. She shook her head and walked to the cabinet for plates. Her job was to feed her ad man, not play housekeeper.

Footsteps sounded behind her, but she added two forks to the dishes in her hand before turning around. This time she got an eyeful of jeans-clad butt and a sweatshirt stretched across those broad shoulders instead of a close-up of biceps and boxers.

"Please tell me this isn't decaf." Drew gestured at the carafe next to the cup she'd set out for him.

"Full strength. Do you take sweetener or milk?" Ready to plate the meal, she removed the lids from the pans.

"Nope. Strong and black." Pouring the steaming liquid, he pulled in a slow inhale. He took a noisy sip, obviously not caring if he scalded his tongue. "Perfect. I'll make the bed while you serve up breakfast. Any suggestions on what to do with the blankets?"

He was volunteering to put the couch back together?

She tried unsuccessfully to hold in a surprised smile. "The middle shelf in the hall closet's empty. Would you like syrup or cooked apples on your French toast?"

With an overflowing armful, he looked over his shoulder at her. The hunger in his eyes sparked a twinge of unexpected jealousy. "French toast and cooked apples. Skip the socks tonight. I'll let you put your cold bare toes on my legs. Hell, I'll rub your feet to get them warm."

Her belly somersaulted. From anticipation or panic, she wasn't sure. The lust in his chocolate-colored eyes didn't help matters, either. "You haven't tasted my French toast yet. How do I know you won't change your mind about the foot rub?"

He stuffed the pile into the closet. "After a year and a half of cold cereal and frozen waffles, your cooking would have to really suck for me to renege on that promise."

"You don't know how to fry an egg or make oatmeal?" Topping the first helping with apples, she shuddered. Waffles from a box were for people with broken taste buds.

"My girls informed me that my scrambled eggs are slimy and my oatmeal tastes like paste." A loud squeak from the bed frame nearly drowned out his words. He shoved the cushions into place. "I've learned to pick my battles carefully."

She prepared the second plateful. "Such is the life of a parent. Breakfast is served."

Joining her in the kitchen, he sat across the corner from her like he had last night for supper. "It looks fantastic. If you don't mind my asking, how did you ever manage to raise your son by yourself? I can't imagine eighteen years of single parenting."

Giving a shrug, she squeezed the moisture from her tea bag. "Like I said before, I did what I had to do. It helped that Zack was always a good kid. He still is."

"I'm guessing you're a good mother too. I have no idea how I'll get two girls through the teenage years. Makeup, dating, driver's licenses. Why can't they stay little?"

"Everybody has to grow up sometime, and you hope your best does the job." She picked up her fork and willed him to let the subject drop. Talking about their personal demons and challenges was fine in the dark, but the light of day dragged too much reality out of the shadows. "You should eat before it gets cold."

He nodded and cut into the French toast, seemingly content to eat in silence. If not for an occasional glance at her, she would've thought he was completely absorbed in his breakfast.

Did he realize she'd prefer a lighter topic?

His low groan incited cold sweat over more than her neck and forehead. "Damn, this is really good. Do you offer breakfast delivery?"

Breakfast in bed? For you, maybe.

Going solo had distinct advantages, but some things couldn't be replaced.

She sipped her tea, hoping to wrestle her hormones into submission. "Sorry, no. The deli's only open for lunch and supper. No breakfast or delivery then, either."

"Think I can talk Kyle into letting you pay me for the promotional package with meals? Unlimited use of my designs for a month of breakfast sounds fair, don't you think?" Drew lifted another bite to his lips, the forkful not hiding his grin.

Glancing away, she ignored the flutter in her chest. Prince Charming belonged in the pages of a fairy tale. "Depends on my cost versus your normal charge."

The cost to her sanity wasn't worth any amount of marketing gimmicks. She'd have to spend far too much time in his company and expend too much effort avoiding temptation.

"I'm pretty sure I'd get the better end of the deal. Of course, when the month was up, I'd have to go back to cereal and frozen waffles." A swallow of coffee followed his next bite.

"I haven't seen anything but a few doodles, so I can hardly make an educated decision." She stuffed a slice of apple in her mouth before she suggested some other mutually agreeable exchange.

"I'd better get busy on those designs then. Do you mind if I have another helping of French toast first?"

"My motto is 'no leftovers.'"

When she started to get up, he nudged her back down in her seat with a hand on her shoulder. "Go ahead and eat. I can get it."

Warmth spread down her arm, and she struggled to form a coherent thought. "Maybe I should teach you how to cook instead of making all your meals while we're stuck here. No more cardboard waffles and soggy corn flakes when you get home."

Too late, the realization donned on her that she'd suggested they work together in the tiny kitchen, doing one of the most intimate activities a couple could engage in besides sex. Working in a restaurant kitchen with other professionals didn't fall into the same category as a woman and a man preparing food they intended to share in a private setting.

"I might take you up on that. There's only one piece left. Do you want half?" His fork was poised over the slice of bread.

When will I learn to keep my mouth shut?

She shook her head and forced her gaze to her plate. "No, thanks. I have plenty."

The world was filled with selfish, arrogant, obnoxious men, and she was stuck in a blizzard with the only one who had any decency and manners. If she'd been searching for the perfect man, she would've found him, except for a single flaw that matched hers.

He was damaged.

She might not have been smart about Zack's father, but falling for a man still madly in love with his dead wife was beyond stupid. Life had given her lemons again.

I'm tired of lemonade.

LOOKING BACK AT THE THREE PAGES OF SKETCHES, DREW STIFLED THE urge to throw the whole pad against the wall. Drawing had never failed to distract him from real life, but it wasn't working today. His room-mate confounded him with her mood swings more than Kate and her sisters—combined—ever had.

He and Pepper had finally achieved an amiable state in their forced companionship, and she'd turned quiet and pensive again out of nowhere. He'd replayed their conversation over and over in his head to no avail. He hadn't said anything that could've offended her or given her the impression he was mad at her. His offer to share the last of her amazing breakfast had seemed to trigger her sudden silence, but he had no clue as to why.

Hadn't he done the polite thing? Did she regret the suggestion that she teach him how to cook some of her specialties? Why the hell had she said anything about instructing him if she didn't want to play teacher?

The steady *chop, chop, chop* of the knife on the cutting board was getting on his nerves too. She'd been at it for at least fifteen minutes with barely a pause.

Was she planning to feed him rabbit food for lunch?

At least she wasn't vegan. The French toast proved she ate eggs and milk, unless she'd used some sort of egg substitute and soy milk. He'd starve if she gave him a plate of chopped vegetables.

Damn, I could go for a steak or a bucket of wings. Or a turkey and Swiss on rye would hit the spot.

Since he'd evidently already done something to get on her bad side, building a sandwich for his lunch probably couldn't make things any worse. He had all the necessary ingredients in the cooler.

The repetitive chopping sounds finally ended, and a few seconds later, sizzling started. A faint whiff of what smelled like frying onions carried to his nose, reminding him of county fair cuisine—grilled kielbasa with peppers and onions.

He caught himself before he laughed out loud. *Yeah, like the owner of a vegetarian deli is going to serve Polish sausage for lunch.*

His stomach growled all the same. Pepper McCann was a damn good cook, but man couldn't live without the occasional dose of cholesterol.

He almost set aside his sketchpad in favor of making his own lunch, but the sight of the foldout couch across from him brought second thoughts. Provoking his short-tempered client was probably less than wise. They had to share tight quarters for at least two more days, and she sure as hell wouldn't let him use her camp stove to cook a T-bone if she was pissed off at him.

Too keyed up to sit still, he tossed his pad on the coffee table and slipped on his boots. Though the wind hadn't died down, the snow had slacked off to a few flurries over the course of the morning. Now was as good a time as any to refill the buckets. It would also get him away from the palpable tension inside the cabin.

Donning a hooded sweatshirt, his coat, and gloves, he kept his back to Pepper. He was an adult, and he didn't owe her an explanation of where he was going or what he was doing. If she wanted to know, she could ask. He might even have the balls to tell her it was none of her business if she did.

Ha! I bet that'd go over well.

He retrieved the buckets from the porch and then shoved the cabin key in his pocket on the way out the door. He'd be able to throw Pepper a damn sight farther than he trusted her not to lock him out.

Icy wind blasted him in the face, stealing his breath for a few seconds, and filtered sunlight nearly blinded him from its reflection off the pure white snow. High-pitched whining grew louder as he descended the steps, but he had no delusions about escaping any time soon. A park ranger on a snowmobile wouldn't drive him home.

He scooped a bucketful of snow, determined to enjoy the brief respite from his claustrophobic lodgings. The chill outside wasn't significantly worse than the atmosphere inside, and he didn't have to pussyfoot around himself.

The engine noise lowered to a dull idle behind him. "Morning! You doing okay up here?"

Pivoting toward the road, Drew waved. "So far."

The ranger gave a barely perceptible nod. "Got plenty of food and water?"

"Yeah, we're good. Any idea how soon the plows will come through?"

"Wednesday at the earliest. More likely Thursday. Power and water should be restored by then too. Maybe sooner. Depends on how quick they can get the lift station going again." Trudging through a knee-deep drift, the man made a path to Drew, folding his ski mask to his forehead as he walked. He withdrew a notepad and ID badge from inside his ski gear. "Ranger Jay Vanderhogen. Can I get your name and cabin number? Gotta verify who's here."

"No problem. Drew Fulton and Pepper McCann in Cabin 12. Do you have any way to get a message to my family?"

"Fulton and McCann. Thanks." Jay frowned. "Sorry, phones are out too at the moment. If you need anything, I'll be back around tomorrow morning."

"Okay, thanks."

The park ranger slogged to his snowmobile and revved the engine once before taking off.

Returning to his job, Drew filled the other buckets and carried them up the steps. As he reached for the doorknob, the door swung inward, revealing his personal chef.

She took the first two buckets from him. "What's the prognosis?"

Hefting the second set, he stomped the snow off his boots and stepped onto the rug. "Electricity and water on Wednesday, maybe. Roads probably clear enough to get out on Thursday."

Her grunt summed up his opinion of the situation quite well. She set down her load near the kitchen sink. "Lunch is ready."

"Go ahead and eat. I'm going to have to put on dry clothes and hang up the wet stuff." He dropped his gloves next to his feet. His coat was next so he could bend over to untie his snow-caked shoelaces.

"Fine." She removed the lid from one of the skillets, setting it down on the real stove with a clank.

What the hell had he done to deserve the F-word? Did she expect him to sit down to lunch in his snowy clothes?

Figuring he was best off ignoring the further deterioration of her mood, he clamped down on his tongue and pried off his boots. No way would he come out of the conversation alive if he asked what was wrong. Her answer—*nothing*—was as predictable as the fact that she'd be lying. He might not have grown up with sisters, but Kate, Meredith, and Colleen Hastings had taught him a few important lessons about women.

When a woman says "fine," she really means you're in deep shit.

"Nothing" means you've done or said something wrong.

Banging and throwing things means you better duck and run. But, most of all, keep your mouth shut!

He peeled off his damp socks, tossing them one at a time onto the growing pile. As he stepped toward the armchair holding his duffle bag, another metallic bang sounded from the kitchen. Muttering carried to his ears, and the few words he caught warned him she wouldn't be pleased if he didn't sit his ass at the table pretty damn quick.

Snagging a dry pair of jeans, he chanced a look at her. She was busy spooning some kind of colorful mixture into whatever those hollow bread things were called for making gyros.

With a step backward toward the cabin door, he lowered his zipper and then gave his wet pants a shove. The dining chair and the package of water bottles would block her view if she happened to glance at him —which she probably wouldn't, considering her current temper tantrum.

The damp denim slid as far as the middle of his thighs and stopped. Fabric bunched and yanked on his leg hairs when he gave his pants another push. "Ouch!" *Son of a hairy-assed monkey.*

Footsteps alerted him too late.

"What are you do—" A squeak in the middle of the cut-off word was the perfect accompaniment to Pepper's wide eyes—and they weren't on his face.

He prayed to every god ever known for bodily control. A twitch of his dick warned him no amount praying would help.

She's gonna think I'm a pervert.

Her cheeks colored, and she opened and closed her mouth several times. Unfortunately, that action put a rather inappropriate idea in his head.

Then she doubled over laughing.

CHAPTER SIX

GIVING THE PINEAPPLE FRIED RICE A FINAL STIR, PEPPER STOLE A peek at the stoic man in the living room chair. He hadn't spoken since she'd been unable to hold in her laughter at his goofy boxer shorts. Not only had he jerked his damp jeans up, he'd put his socks and snowy boots back on to eat lunch out of his cooler on the porch.

Then, after two hours outside using a bucket to shovel snow, he'd finally come in and parked himself in the armchair with his sketchpad —after he'd changed clothes in the bathroom. His pencils had scratched across the paper until dusk had fallen.

Now he sat with his laptop open, its light illuminating his stern silhouette. Harsh lines accented the corners of his eyes and mouth, and his jaw jutted forward. He was obviously mad at her for the giggling fit, but she couldn't begin to guess why.

Unless...

He didn't think she'd been laughing at the barely distinguishable bulge in his boxers, did he? She hadn't been able to see anything. Besides, a guy with hands and feet as big as his had to be well endowed. Then again, most men were touchy about their penis size.

Males and their delicate egos.

Dishing up their supper, she swallowed the tough pill of having to apologize again. He should be happy she hadn't screamed and called him a pervert for dropping his drawers in front of her. She might not have even noticed if he'd remained quiet while he switched to dry pants.

Had he caught his skin in the zipper? Or he could've caught his leg hairs when he was trying to take off his jeans. He was a little on the hairy side, after all—not that he was ape-like. His well-muscled thighs and calves were covered in the perfect amount of nutmeg-colored hair.

If she'd been inclined to date, she'd search for a man a lot like Drew Fulton, in looks and in personality. He was nice enough and seemed to care a great deal about his daughters. He'd probably even been a decent husband.

Why does that matter? It's not like I'm interested in him.

Said the Queen of Denial.

Balancing a fork on the loaded plate, she carried his supper to the end table next to his seat. When he didn't look up from his work, she cleared her throat. "Supper's ready. And I'm sorry for laughing at you, if that's what you're mad about."

His expression didn't change as he glanced up at her. "Feeding a guy doesn't make up for laughing at him when his pants are halfway down his legs. Just a tip for future reference."

"You think I'm bribing you?" For the most part, she'd learned to control her temper, but Drew brought out the worst in her. "For the record, I was laughing at the ridiculous baby hippos on your boxers, not your—your...stupid salami. And I'm feeding you because it's a paying gig."

His lips twitched and he raised his eyebrows at her. "*Salami?*"

Dozens of possible comebacks he could've used pushed and shoved their way into a single-file line in her mind, starting with *Would you like a taste of my salami, Pepper?*

Her scalp tingled at the rush of heat up her neck to her cheeks. She wasn't cut out to interact with men.

She retreated to the kitchen, willing him to let the subject drop. "Eat your food before it gets cold."

How would she survive another two or possibly three days alone with him?

She certainly wasn't thrilled with the idea of sleeping with him for a second and third night. Big salami or not, freezing her ass off was better than depending on another person for anything. She'd managed all by herself for almost nineteen of her thirty-seven years, and she wasn't about to make the mistake of relying on Drew Fulton.

With a helping of fried rice on her plate, she sat at the end of the table, her back to the living room. Her stomach roiled at the aggravation yet another man had put her through. Mort owed her much more than the cost of the supplies she'd brought. If he had the balls to bill her for the advertising package, she'd make damn sure he paid her back for every free lunch she'd given him for the past decade and a half.

Five lunches a week times fifty-two weeks times fifteen years at eight dollars apiece.

Two sixty. Thirty-nine hundred. Carry the seven. Thirty-one thousand two hundred dollars. Divided by two since he isn't there every day.

A new car, and I might call it even.

She poked a snow pea, using it to plow a pile of rice, pineapple, and cashews. Too bad snow removal wasn't that simple. She'd kick out her roommate and enjoy a short vacation.

Footsteps made her pulse jump. Drew had to be on the move. Was he dumping her dinner and making his own?

He dropped into the chair adjacent to hers and set his plate on the table. "Truce?"

Giving a shrug, she met his gaze. "Okay."

"That was easier than I expected." He adjusted the hold on his fork. "I didn't have time to finish laundry before the trip. Hannah picked out the boxers when we went to the zoo last summer. She said they were silly and that I needed more fun." His voice and the lines on his face softened when he said his daughter's name. A slight smile turned up the corners of his mouth. "Kristin's much more practical. She got me a mechanical pencil with a parade of animals on it."

Pepper recognized the kind of love she had for Zack. Drew adored his girls, and he was obviously a good father. Life should've been that kind to her son, even if his parents didn't end up together.

Adding a pineapple chunk to her fork, she tried for a smile. "You miss them. I bet you'd rather be trapped here with them than me."

"I'm not touching that with a ten-foot snow drift. Remember the truce?" He rested his elbows on the edge of the table and pursed his lips. "Just because we're both a little set in our ways doesn't mean we can't get along. I promise not to get bent out of shape from you laughing at my clothes if you promise to tell me when something's bugging you instead of giving me the silent treatment. Or worse yet, saying 'fine.' Call me a prick or punch me in the arm, but please don't sulk."

His grimace assured her that sulking bothered him more than anything else.

"I punch pretty hard for a girl. Are you sure you don't prefer quiet to a bruise?"

"You wouldn't hurt me unless I hurt you. Like it or not, you're a nice person. And I might hurt your feelings by saying something without thinking, but I'd never do it on purpose."

She couldn't help but chuckle. "You think I'm nice? We've had at least four spats in the last twenty-four hours."

Shaking his head, he scooped a forkful of rice and vegetables. "If you were mean, neither one of us would've apologized and we wouldn't have slept worth a damn last night. Personally, I'd rather not spend tonight cold and uncomfortable."

He was right. She'd slept like a log once they'd rearranged the blankets to accommodate them both. Their shared body heat had warmed her until she'd crawled out of bed in the morning. Normally, she sprawled all over the mattress, but he'd held her.

And I liked it.

Crossing his heart with his finger, he took on a solemn tone. "Same promise applies. No pawing or groping. And I'll do my best to keep my salami under control."

She barked a laugh at his surprising sense of humor. "I can't believe you said that!"

"Yeah, well, neither can I." He grinned, a slight blush coloring his neck and ears as he looked toward his plate. "Thanks for supper, even if it's a paying gig. You're a good cook."

The compliment sounded sincere, and a twinge of guilt made her wish she hadn't been so defensive. "Thanks. I can teach you to make a few things tomorrow, if you want."

"Sure. See? We can get along okay. In fact, I kinda like you."

If he hadn't immediately tucked a bite into his mouth, she might've demanded to know more.

What kind of like? Like like? Or just friends?

Oh brother, what am I, twelve?

Burying the surge of panic rising in her chest, she offered simple honesty—whether she understood it or not. "I kinda like you too."

LIGHT SEEPED IN PAST THE LIVING ROOM CURTAINS, BUT DREW CLOSED his eyes tighter and savored the connection to his red hotheaded Pepper. Not only did he like her, he liked the way she fit in his arms lying next to him all night. She didn't seem inclined to want or need more than friendship, and he was fine with that, at least until she wasn't a client anymore. They'd have an opportunity to get to know each other before they decided if they should pursue a romantic relationship.

Slow. Gradual. No jumping in with both feet without testing the waters.

In the meantime, he would enjoy talking to an adult female who wasn't a sister-in-law offering to babysit his kids. Merie and Colleen had loved Kate, but they'd been pushing him to go out, if not on a date, then with friends. The problem was most of his friends had also been his wife's, and no one knew what the hell to say to him. Drifting away had been easier than the awkward conversations.

He'd been waffling over the dating issue for several months. The timing hadn't felt right, and he still sometimes had to rub his bare ring finger to get rid of the empty sensation. With Pepper, he could imagine crawling out of the hole he'd been stuck in since facing the stark reality of being a widower with two young girls.

She sighed, her warm breath tickling his neck. Her hand loosened its hold on his waist and came to rest directly below his belly button. A thin layer of fabric separated her palm from his skin. His morning erection hardened another notch not too far south of her fingers, his sudden awareness adding to the discomfort of knowing he was in big trouble if she noticed.

Inching out from under her, he eased to the side of the mattress. The cold floor made him wince as he stood to go to the bathroom, and goose bumps rose on his skin. He snagged his jeans and sweatshirt from the chair, wishing he could hop in a hot shower and have some privacy to take the edge off his lack of a sex life.

Right. Like I'm gonna jack off with a woman in the next room.

He growled under his breath on his way to the bathroom. He'd resorted to self-gratification a handful of times since Kate died, but he'd always been alone. No particular woman had made think about burying himself inside her and staying there until he couldn't move. His new fantasy starred an outspoken redhead, and he'd declared her off-limits for now.

Why didn't fate, karma, or whatever was screwing with his life go find somebody else to harass?

His best course of action was to get dressed and cool off outside. They needed more water anyway. He'd have a few minutes to chill, and with any luck, his salami would go into hiding.

Salami.

Why was he still calling it that?

Sure, he'd gotten a good laugh out of Pepper's embarrassed retort, but a dick was a dick, not a stick of deli meat. He always used anatomically correct terminology when talking to his daughters about male and female body parts. With Colleen's announcement a couple months ago that she and Brett were having another child, the discussion centering on conception had involved the insertion of part P into slot V. No salami, wiener, or sausage had been mentioned in the conversation.

Would Pepper have a special name for his cock if they reached the point of making love?

Geez, I have to stop thinking about sex.

He tugged on his sweatshirt as he returned to the living room, hoping he could make his escape before she woke. The light of day seemed to change their interaction with each other. Although they hadn't shared private stories last night like they had the night before, the cover of darkness made being close more comfortable, less demanding. Daylight revealed weaknesses and complications, reasons to maintain a safe distance.

A peek at the bed didn't help rein in his libido. She was lying on her back, with the wild cap of fiery hair framing her relaxed face. Her left arm was flung over her head, and the covers had slipped below the full curve of her breasts. She was a wet dream come true.

Forcing his gaze away, he dug for a clean pair of socks. Within two minutes, he'd layered on enough clothes to venture outside and she still hadn't moved.

Today's only Tuesday. Damn.

A hot shower and sexual relief weren't happening, but he could haul in plenty of snow for a sponge bath. He'd heat some water for his tempting roommate to shampoo her hair and wash up if she wanted to while he dunked his dick in a bucket of ice water.

"You're up." Her husky voice caressed his libido as he turned the doorknob. She stretched and yawned, making flight even more imperative. "Are you getting snow?"

He nodded, unsure if he could speak without sounding like he'd reverted to puberty.

"Thanks." She lowered the covers. "I'll start breakfast after I get dressed."

Another curt nod was all he could manage before he made a quick exit to the stoop. The blowing snow had calmed compared to Sunday and yesterday, giving him a break from the breath-stealing wind. Clear skies had allowed the temperature to dip overnight, and the icy cold nearly froze his nostrils shut when he pulled in a lungful of fresh air.

The faint buzz of a snowmobile cut through the quiet morning, sending a flock of birds scattering from the lower branches to the tree-tops. As the noise grew louder, they took flight again, this time dancing like a dark cloud past the tree line.

Shaking off the urge to meet the ranger at the road and beg for a ride anywhere, Drew descended the stairs to restock the water supply. He hefted the last bucket to the top step as the snowmobile stopped next to his car.

"Morning, Fulton! Cold enough for you?" The park ranger kept his ski mask in place instead folding it up as he tromped through the snow. "Looks like the plows'll be coming through ahead of schedule. Probably by noon tomorrow. Can't say whether we'll have power back by then. You and Ms. McCann doing all right?"

Tomorrow? "Yeah. Thanks for the update." Drew didn't even try to analyze the mix of relief and disappointment at the prospect of leaving in little more than twenty-four hours. "Anybody else stranded in the cabins?"

"Nope. We warned everybody about the incoming weather and gave them the choice of rescheduling the rest of their stays or riding out the storm. The office sent out a notice to all the incoming reservations with the same options. I'm kinda surprised you decided not to reschedule."

"I didn't get a notice. Pepper didn't, either."

"Hm. That's strange. The office should've had contact information for whichever of you made the reservation. You might want to mention it when you check out."

The reservation.

Morton had made all the arrangements for the "conference," and his name had been on the confirmation page. He'd put his employee and his cousin in danger. For what purpose? Because Drew had asked for the Red Hot Pepper account to be reassigned?

After three months of rushed projects, he'd hoped for some down-time of mundane updates and marketing plan assessments so he could spend some quality time with his kids. Instead, Kyle had dumped another new account on him.

Vanderhogen headed back along the makeshift path to his ride.

"Have a good one!"

With a wave, Drew climbed the stairs. He had some serious thinking to do concerning his job. While he didn't like leaving Pepper in the lurch by quitting, Kyle Morton deserved some major payback for manipulating the situation. As a senior project manager, Drew should've had at least some say in picking up a start-from-scratch campaign. His boss might consider the assignment a compliment, but being the most in demand shouldn't have to mean overworked. Burnout was becoming a real possibility.

"Bad news?" Pepper's question came at him as soon as he closed the door.

"No, not really." He stripped off his gloves. "The road should be clear tomorrow afternoon. Oh, and your cousin's an asshole."

Her laugh hit him smack dab in the chest. "Yeah, he can be. I already knew that. What'd he do this time?"

"You mean besides taking me away from my kids over Christmas break and endangering both of us with this trip?" His zipper stuck halfway down the front of his coat. "Damn it."

She sobered. "Endangering us how?"

"The park notified everybody with reservations about the forecast, and good ol' Mortie didn't bother to tell us we could reschedule instead of getting trapped here with no water, no heat, and no electricity." He gave the zipper a second tug. "For God's sake, will you help me out of this damn thing?"

Frowning, she marched over to him. "He'll be lucky if he can father children when I'm done with him. Hold still." After a few upward zips and an awkward reach inside his coat, she freed him. Her maniacal smirk made him glad he wasn't on her bad side anymore. "There. Now we can plan my cousin's demise."

Her full lips coaxed him to lean down and kiss them. He was also hard again, and a cold dunk in the bucket wasn't the most pleasant solution that came to mind.

Eyeing the unmade bed, he shrugged off his coat. While he wouldn't mind a bit of freelance work, chances were damn good she wasn't going to be his client anymore.

CHAPTER SEVEN

"READY TO HELP MAKE BREAKFAST? I ALMOST FORGOT I WAS GOING TO give you a cooking lesson." Pepper stepped out of Drew's reach a moment before he could raise his hand to cradle the back of her head.

Maybe it was for the best, but logic didn't cure his disappointment. Waiting until their business dealings were finished wasn't going to work, if she even felt the same attraction to him.

Mid-thirties, never been married, has no reason to trust men who want to date her. This is stupid. And hopeless.

Shedding his boots, he gave a frustrated sigh. He shouldn't be thinking about kissing or making love to her. Two days stuck in cabin wasn't anywhere near enough time to develop anything more than a sexual itch, and scratching it should be the last thing on his mind.

"Do you like omelets?" His case of poison ivy hurried into the kitchen, her hips swaying back and forth, drawing his attention to a delectable butt in snug jeans.

He'd gladly let her rub anti-itch cream on every inch of him. "Hm? Oh, um, yeah."

"Have you ever made one?"

One what?

Concentrate.

She'd asked about omelets, hadn't she?

"I don't cook eggs."

"Come on. I'll teach you how to make the perfect omelet." She removed a glass measuring cup from the cupboard. "What would you like in it? Onions, mushrooms, green peppers?"

"Can't eat peppers. They give me indigestion." With his coat and gloves in hand, he headed for the bedroom to hang them up to dry.

"We could use fruit instead. Do you like pears?"

His imagination dove into the deep end as he shoved the hanger into one sleeve. The best kind of pair would be her and him sharing an orgasm or two.

He struggled to shake off the strange sex-starved obsession that had taken over his brain. "Um, yeah. Pears. I didn't know you could put fruit in an omelet."

"Sure. Apples are good too."

Clipping his damp gloves on a pants hanger, he tried to train his focus on food. "Let's go with pears. The girls pick applesauce to go with supper at least three times a week and we had apples with the French toast yesterday."

A muffled reply came from beyond the open refrigerator door as he entered the kitchen. Only Pepper's backside was visible from his vantage point, sending his rampaging hormones into a tailspin.

He busied himself rearranging the supplies on the table. "Sorry, I didn't catch that."

"I said you should meal plan with them for the week so you have some variety." She set three pears next to the camp stove and straightened as she closed the door. "Have them make a list of their favorite fruits, vegetables, and main dishes, then mix and match."

"We're sort of limited by what I can cook. Kristin helps on the weekends, but her repertoire consists of macaroni and cheese from a box, toasted cheese sandwiches, and Rice-a-roni. If not for my mother-in-law and Kate's sisters, we'd probably be eating prepackaged foods and take-out every day."

She was quiet long enough that he finally turned to look at her.

Dark eyes stared back at him, the usual mix of green and brown gone. "You spend a lot of time with your wife's family, don't you?"

Pepper's question and the word "wife" brought a twinge of guilt. He hadn't thought about sleeping with anyone but Kate for almost fifteen years—until now. Yes, he was single again. It didn't make the sudden feeling of cheating on her any less real, even it was an irrational reaction.

He nodded, his wayward musings buried by self-reprimand. He wasn't ready to dive into a relationship, horny or not. Liking Pepper didn't change the fact that, in some manner or another, he'd be using her if they had sex. He couldn't add to her already deep distrust of his gender.

His appetite replaced by distaste, he retreated to the living room to put away the bedding. No matter how many times he replayed his and Kate's conversation days before she died, her admonition was too surreal to get past his conscience.

"I love you, Drew, and I know you love me. But I'm going soon, and I want you to be happy again. Promise me you'll find someone new to love. You're too good a man to be alone for the next fifty years. I don't want to be mourned that long. There's a woman out there who'll love you as much as I do, maybe more. And she needs you, just like you'll need her."

Stuffing the blankets in the closet, he swallowed the lump in his throat. He'd let go, but only because he'd had no choice. Moving on would mean risking his heart to a woman who could break it, walk away from him, or leave him by dying. How would he live through a second loss?

He folded the creaky metal frame into the couch, careful to avoid catching his fingers. The sudden *thwack, thwack, thwack* on the cutting board almost made him drop the cushions as he carried them from the armchair.

Pepper had evidently decided his silence meant he didn't plan to help with breakfast. If he ended up in the doghouse again, he'd have to seriously consider moving into one of the bedrooms until the roads were passable.

Actually, that tack seemed the wisest route in any case. He doubted he could uphold his end of the deal for a third night.

"Thanks for making the bed. Are you ready to learn how to make an omelet?" Surprisingly, nothing in her voice suggested she was upset, angry, or annoyed with him. "I cored and sliced the pears since you probably know how to do that. We'll sauté those in a tiny bit of butter first and add a dash of cinnamon. The number one rule of making omelets is to have everything ready before you start cooking the eggs."

Her chatter ended, but she continued to flit back and forth from the fridge to the table, not even glancing his direction.

Could he keep his hands to himself in the confined space?

Finally, she stopped at the sink, facing the window rather than him. "I'm sorry. What you feed your kids and how often you see your wife's family are none of my business. And I shouldn't have mentioned her."

Was he destined to spend the whole damn day suffering from remorse?

The battle going on inside him had its first casualty, and it wasn't him. "I brought up what I feed the girls, and I mentioned Kate before you did. You have nothing to be sorry for except being stuck here with me."

She shook her head as she pivoted to face him. "Believe me, I can think of a few guys who'd give you a run for your money for the worst-person-to-be-snowed-in-with award. Come on, let's make our damn omelets and then go for a hike. I'm sick of being cooped up in here. Besides, the cabin'll feel warm after being outside for a while."

"I guess that's a compliment, huh?" Four steps brought him within a couple feet of her. More than anything, he wanted to hug her—not so much from physical desire as thanks for listening and understanding. "Okay, teach me how to cook eggs without them turning out runny or rubbery."

"Yeah, a compliment." She pointed to the camp stove. "Do you know how to light the burner?"

"I'm thinking you better do it. I'd probably singe my eyebrows or ruin your stove."

"It isn't hard, but I'll do it if you want me to. While I get the fire started, you can cut about a teaspoon of butter off the stick. We'll put the butter in the skillet after it preheats." A few seconds later, blue flame danced in a circle beneath the grate. After an adjustment to the height of the fire, she set a pan over it. "Wait about a minute or so and then add the butter. As soon as it finishes melting, you can put in the sliced pears."

He followed her instructions, watching the second hand on his watch for a full revolution. The butter sizzled and spread into a puddle when he dropped it in the hot pan. "Now the pears?"

"Mm-hm. And sprinkle on two or three shakes of cinnamon. Just enough to give the pears a little color and flavor. Stir it gently, and while those are cooking, we'll prepare the egg mixture."

Instead of watching over his shoulder, she made a quick trip to the screened porch.

He stirred the contents, hoping he hadn't screwed up the filling for their breakfast.

"Looks good." She set the egg carton and a jug of milk on the table. "You're going to break four eggs into the big measuring cup. We'll add a dash of black pepper and a little bit of salt. I like parsley or chives in my eggs, but it's up to you. Either or neither, whatever you like."

Eyeing his choices, he grabbed the parsley. Flakes looked like they'd taste better with fruit than tiny green rings. "How much? Damn, I got shell in the eggs."

"No big deal. Use a fork to get it out. You're going to mix every-thing, so it doesn't matter if you break the yolks." She poured hot water into her tea mug. "A few shakes of parsley. Next, you're going to whisk the eggs until they're evenly colored and sort of frothy. Lots of bubbles."

He had no idea how she guessed he didn't know what frothy meant. Maybe she was simply a good teacher.

"Perfect. Now you're going to mix in about two tablespoons of milk. The omelet pan needs to preheat while you check on the pears. They should be soft but not mushy." Playing with the gas control on her side of the stove, she lit the other burner. "We're going to use a nonstick pan and just a dab of butter. Pour in enough egg mixture to cover the bottom. About half. Once the egg is set and you've put fruit on one half, you'll tip up the pan like this to let it slide out onto the plate. When the filled half is out, you guide the pan half over top to form the fold."

She made it sound much easier than it was. The first attempt had holes in the egg and the top folded in at least three places. The second more closely resembled an omelet he'd get at a restaurant.

"Great job." Pepper grinned at him, tripping his rumbling stomach into a somersault. "You take the pretty one. They'll taste the same, and you earned it."

They ate in silence, but it didn't hold the awkward is-she-mad-again tension of their previous meals. His worry about accidental touches during his lesson had been unfounded. He'd been too busy concentrating on her instructions to think about his attraction to her, and she hadn't seemed bothered by the tight space. If anything, she'd been more relaxed than usual, probably because preparing food was her job.

He leaned back in his chair, cradling his coffee mug between his hands. "Thanks for the cooking lesson. That was the best omelet I've ever had."

Her cheeks flushed a bright pink, and she poked a slice of pear without looking up at him. "You're a good student."

She was such a contradiction—strong and confident, yet shy and wary. Her hotheadedness was tempered by a forgiving nature.

He liked her. A lot.

§&

THE HEAVY SCRAPE OF METAL AGAINST PAVEMENT CARRIED OVER THE snow-covered terrain to Pepper's ears as she led Drew along the path they'd forged when they left the cabin. The plow crews couldn't have made much progress on the winding road that connected the dining lodge and cottages to the main road, but they were plowing.

Her bout of claustrophobia had faded as soon as she and her roomie had trekked into the woods. They hadn't talked much, but the silence was companionable. He wasn't mad at her and she wasn't frustrated with him. They were almost friends.

Kicking the snow from her boots, she dug the key from the pocket of her ski pants. "Ready for some hot cocoa? I figured we could reheat the soup and make sandwiches for lunch."

"Sounds good." He followed her inside and closed the door behind them. "I'm starving after that workout."

They'd hiked for almost two hours, the calm winds and slightly warmer temperatures making tromping through waist-high drifts more comfortable, but challenging nonetheless. She was fairly certain he'd enjoyed their outing.

The pile of damp, snowy outerwear grew as they shed their coats, gloves, and boots. Sorting through the jumble, she grabbed her wet things. "I'll get lunch started while you change—" A click, a rattle, and the low hum of a motor made her words stick in her throat. "Is that—"

Drew lifted her off her feet, wrapping her in a bear hug. "The refrigerator!"

The furnace fan joined it in the background noise.

"And the furnace!" He swung her around in a circle. "We have electricity!"

Clinging to his neck, she squealed and tucked her legs around his waist to keep from kicking the furniture on both sides of them. The motion put a firm ridge down the center seam of her jeans. She closed her eyes and tightened her abs to hide a sudden spasm in her lower belly. Wet heat flooded her inner muscles.

Then warm breath tickled her ear. "Sorry about that. I got a little carried away."

She released her hold and tried not melt into a puddle on the floor as he set her down. "Um, no problem. I'm excited too."

Having power wasn't the only reason, either. Vibrations still echoed through her body from the intimate contact.

Holy moly, am I in trouble.

He stepped away, turning to dig in his duffle bag, presumably for dry pants. "Do you need the bathroom before I change clothes?"

Too tongue-tied to answer, she shook her head as she aimed for the bedroom to hang her damp gear. A cold shower probably wouldn't do her any good. The outline of his erection was permanently imprinted on more than her brain—and he'd been hard as the proverbial rock.

Did he want her, or would any woman do?

For all she knew, he'd slept with a dozen women since his wife died. He didn't seem the type to screw around with every girl he met, but what did she know?

A door clicked closed, and she plunked down on the edge of the double bed. In nineteen years, one man had talked her into his bed. The consequences of that mistake had affected and still influenced her life. She'd appreciated a few fine specimens over the years, but she'd never been brave enough to take another risk.

Drew was different. He hadn't made any attempt to seduce her, even when they were sharing a bed and blankets. Losing his wife and raising his daughters alone put him in a class apart from other men. He'd admitted to struggling through some of the day-to-day tasks he had to handle on his own, showing her his weaknesses instead downplaying his difficulties like a macho do-it-all-with-one-arm-tied-behind-his-back superhero.

He was human and not afraid to admit it.

At the very least, she could imagine becoming friends with him—calling him to talk about her crappy day or giving him advice on how to deal with a little girl who wasn't so little anymore.

A thump came from the other side of the wall. "Damn it."

Had he hit his elbow on the bathroom wall as he was undressing?

"Son of a..." This time a low growl carried through the thin barrier. "Pepper!"

She frowned.

Had he hurt himself?

Hurrying to the bathroom door, she smothered the rising worried-mother concerns. She tapped on the door. "Drew? Are you okay?"

"No! Would you mind coming in here? The door's unlocked."

She rushed inside, only to stop next to the shower to stare at him. A giggle bubbled up her throat, and she immediately choked it back. Laughing at a man wedged in a corner with his legs tangled up in his pants was a bad move.

"What happened?" She edged closer.

"My jeans are wet and I'm stuck." Resting his chin on his hairy knee, he sighed. "You're allowed to laugh. We both know you want to."

His dejected grimace was pathetic enough that she didn't have the heart to snicker, let alone laugh. "How can I help?"

"Get me the hell out of my pants. Please." The wording of his request obviously registered in his brain at the same time it did in hers, because he winced even as a hoot of laughter escaped her. "Undress me, and I'll make it worth your while."

CHAPTER EIGHT

PEPPER PERCHED HER FISTS ON HER HIPS, HOPING SHE DIDN'T LOOK TOO anxious to accept Drew's deal. She never, in a million years, would've expected he'd blatantly suggest sex as payment for helping him with his problem.

He winked at her. "I forgot the girls made brownies for me to bring on the trip. I'm willing to give you half in exchange for the ability to move my legs."

I have to stop thinking the worst about him.

"Brownies, huh? Deal." She knelt at his outstretched foot to work the denim past his left knee. "How exactly did you end up like this?"

"I tried pushing them off, but they bunched up around my knees. So I figured I'd pull my foot up through. You know, turn them inside out? This is as far as I got before I lost my balance."

He was right. His pants wouldn't budge past his knee.

Changing strategies, she reached into the half inside-out pant leg to find his foot. Since it wasn't caught on a seam or the hem, she forced the waistband and thigh portion back up his calf. "Let me try tugging them off from the bottom."

She grasped the soaked hem and wiggled the fabric until his left leg slipped free. Within a minute, she'd freed his other leg as well. Reddish streaks crisscrossed both his thighs. *Ouch.*

Tossing the torture device over the shower door, she clamped her lips together to stop an offer to rub lotion on his abused skin. He could do it as easily as she could.

When she turned to face him again, a pair of rubber ducky-covered boxers stared back at her. He'd evidently stood up while she'd been hanging up his pants. They really had to stop meeting this way, especially since he filled out his boxers as perfectly as his jeans.

Heat creeping up her neck and settling between her thighs, she jerked her gaze upward. "Ducks. I'll just, um, wait in the kitchen for you to, uh, get dressed."

"Brownies are in the bag next my computer case. Help yourself." His smile touched his eyes, sending her pulse skipping.

He was handsome and too damn nice, and she had to get out of the bathroom before she did something incredibly foolish.

I should've brought one of my battery-powered boyfriends. They were safe—and disposable if they didn't meet her needs. Chocolate would have to satisfy her for now.

She twisted the lock mechanism and gave the door an extra-hard tug to be sure she couldn't go back in even if she wanted to. Brownies and lunch needed her attention.

Once she'd put the leftover soup on the stove to heat, she sorted through the mishmash of her and Drew's belongings that had taken over the armchairs and half the living room. With the power restored, they could finally settle into their respective bedrooms.

Just in time to leave tomorrow.

Their campout had been interesting, to say the least. She wouldn't have expected she could sleep with a man without him insisting they do more than sleep. Tonight, they'd go to separate rooms and separate beds. She wouldn't need him to keep her warm, and he'd be able to stretch out his long legs. Why did the prospect of going to bed alone sound so depressing?

Moving yet another bag, she found his computer. A plastic container poked out of the tote beside it. Chocolate filled every square inch, from corner to corner and top to bottom. If the brownies stuck together when she tried to take one out, she'd resort to a fork or a spoon.

She loosened the lid. Gooey fudge aroma teased her nose, and she held the container close to her nose for a deep inhale. "Dear chocolate, how I love you."

A snicker from behind her warned her that Drew had seen her sniff his brownies and heard her declaration of undying devotion. "Half of those are mine, so no drooling."

Snapping off the cover, she gave up trying to hold in a smile. "I wouldn't dream of it. Want one?"

"Dessert before lunch. You won't tell, will you?" He stepped around her to sit in the chair closest to the fireplace.

She almost choked at the sight of his sexy knees and muscular calves. She'd wanted to caress them as she removed his jeans, but the best she'd gotten was a few accidental brushes against his furry legs. "Afraid of pants?"

For two nights, he'd held her while wearing those sleep shorts. He'd climbed into bed and walked to the bathroom with them on. Why were they affecting her now?

"I only have one pair of dry jeans. If we can leave tomorrow, I'll need something to wear on the drive home. Besides, we have heat now." He bent forward, prying a brownie from the container. "Don't you like my legs?"

She scrambled for a way to divert attention from his loaded question. "Do you mean when they aren't stuck in wet jeans? Oh, here! Take these. I need to go stir the soup."

Lucky for her, she had a legitimate excuse to leave the conversation hanging.

He juggled her handoff. "Want some help getting lunch ready?"

Springing to her feet, she waved him off. "Nah. Do you want cold sandwiches or grilled cheese?"

"Ah, come on. I make great grilled cheese. You're not gonna pass up Guggisberg baby Swiss on rye, are you?"

A whimper snuck out. "You brought baby Swiss? What kind of rye?"

"Yeah, quarter of a five-pound wheel. Seedless Amish rye bread, plus a ring of Trail bologna and steaks from a meatpacking place I found out in the middle of nowhere." He scrunched up his mouth. "I guess you wouldn't want those. Sorry. I didn't think about you being a vegetarian."

Grabbing his arm, she pulled him up from the chair. "I'm not. Get busy on the sandwiches, and you're cooking steak for supper."

His chuckle didn't bother her. A man in his position deserved a few brushes with happiness, and he wasn't exactly laughing at her. Besides, the sound brightened her mood and made her insides flutter.

"If you get the cheese from my cooler, I'll butter the bread and find a pan." He set down the container, still holding his uneaten brownie. As he retrieved the loaf of rye from a grocery bag near his bare feet, he took a bite.

"Deal."

"Want some?" He raised the fudgy treat to her lips. "Can't beat Betty Crocker."

She opened her mouth, accepting his offer. Rich chocolate flavor spread over her tongue, and the intimacy of his action registered a moment too late. Not only was he feeding her, he'd taken a bite from the same misshapen square.

Popping the last piece in his mouth, he ambled to the kitchen, leaving her glued to the floor.

Thrill and panic collided. They'd forged a friendship of sorts, the unexpected attraction something she'd planned to ignore, at least for now. The food sharing, however, had caught her off guard. It had been as profound as a lover's kiss. He'd swapped spit with her, after all.

He wasn't trying to seduce her, was he?

How laughable is that?

They'd slept together—in the same bed, cuddled against each other —two nights, and he hadn't copped a feel or tried to talk her into anything remotely resembling sex.

I have one option if I want to know.

❧

DREW HID BEHIND THE OPEN REFRIGERATOR DOOR UNTIL HIS ROOMMATE stepped onto the screened porch.

What just happened?

He hadn't planned to share his brownie with Pepper, but he had. Suggestive didn't begin to describe what he'd done, and he couldn't change it. His instincts—or more likely, his hormones—had taken over. Hopefully, she'd thought he was being generous and nothing more.

At the counter, he pulled half a dozen slices of bread from the package and picked up the butter knife.

The sliding door whooshed closed behind him and then light foot-steps padded closer.

"Why'd you do that, Drew?"

Nothing more? Right.

He considered feigning ignorance for less than a second. Pretending he didn't know what she was talking about was almost as bad as lying. Given her past, the truth was his only option.

Setting down the knife, he turned to face her. "I'm not sure. I guess it seemed like the thing to do at the time."

She studied him, like some ulterior motive was written all over his face.

Uncomfortable with her silence, he forged on. "I like you, Pepper. After I finish your ad campaign, I'm hoping you might go out to dinner with me. Or something. You know, like a date."

Her cheeks flushed from pink to red in an instant, but she still didn't speak.

He should've kept his mouth shut and his brownies to himself. "If you want to. It's okay if you don't. Just friends would be okay too."

Friendship might challenge his willpower, but he'd give it a shot. Then again, she didn't seem too receptive to that at the moment, either.

"Look, forget I said anything." He pivoted around to finish buttering the bread, regret and embarrassment making him wish he could erase the whole conversation.

"I'll think about it." She reached around him to set the cheese on the counter and then moved to the stove. Setting aside the lid, she stirred the soup. "I haven't dated in forever. Not since Zack was two. The idiot made the mistake of telling my son his plans for after bedtime. Luckily, Zack thought 'getting dirty with your mommy' meant playing in the sandbox when he repeated it. I didn't want adult male companionship bad enough to put up with that kind of behavior."

"He told your two-year-old he wanted to get dirty with you?" Drew shook his head. Men tended to think with their appendages instead of their brains, but he never would've talked like that to anyone about a woman, much less to a baby. "Geesh. Apologies from all the decent guys of the world."

Disappointment poked at his gut. He didn't stand a chance with her. Even if he wasn't guilty by gender association, she had every right to distrust him. Life had taught her some cruel lessons.

Since she remained silent, he could only assume she didn't want to discuss it anymore. Letting the subject drop, he sliced through the wedge of cheese. "We should have hot water after lunch. Do you want to shower first?"

She gave him a wide berth as he set the skillet on the burner. "Sure."

Although she sounded agreeable, her one-word answer set the tone for their meal. Her mood seemed darker and she made no effort to converse. By the time he cleared the table, she'd already vanished into the bathroom.

Too frustrated to work, he spent ten minutes stabbing the steaks with a fork. The meat would probably fall apart when he cooked it, but the stress release had cleared his head enough to think. He'd take advantage of the two full weeks until the deadline for the Red Hot Pepper project. If all the time he'd have with her was job-related, he'd damn well use every last second.

Why had the thought of rejection pushed him headlong into wanting a relationship with her?

He was usually cautious and rarely made a decision without weighing every option. Putting himself out there for a woman he'd known for a few days was possibly the most ridiculous thing he'd ever done. He had little doubt she'd leave him nursing more than wounded pride when he submitted his work. He hadn't been exaggerating when he'd told her he liked her.

If he was dealing with a simple matter of physical and sexual attraction, his stomach wouldn't be sporting knots. She didn't need—or want—his protection. Her independence was part of the draw. Loneliness wasn't the cause, either.

Whether she felt it or not, they'd connected on a basic level. She didn't pussyfoot around him by avoiding Kate's name and the fact that his wife had died. Pepper had let him talk, and she'd listened. Other than his in-laws, no one had encouraged him to speak freely about that terrible time in his life. Their late-night exchange had soothed the scars of losing his wife to cancer.

Pepper McCann understood pain. She'd lived through it too, and he admired her strength.

Engine noise and scraping added to his depressing contemplation. He leaned over the sink to peer out the window toward the main road. The plow wasn't visible yet, but it would be soon. By morning, they'd be able to check out like their original reservation stated.

He was anxious to get home to his daughters. Unfortunately, heading north almost guaranteed an end to his private time with Pepper.

"Snow plow?" The hope in her tone sank any dreams of her wanting to spend any more time with him.

"Probably. I can't see it yet." He sprinkled tenderizer on the steaks, followed by garlic salt and Tabasco.

"You're gonna want to wait to shower. The water was cold when I got done."

Cold would serve him better than hot, but he'd do what she suggested. "Okay."

Tired of trying to anticipate her seesaw moods, he stowed the marinating steaks in the fridge and gathered his laptop and sketchpads. With power restored, the bedrooms had heat, meaning he could work in relative solitude until suppertime.

He had no illusions that she'd miss him, and she barely glanced up from her seat on the couch when he walked past her with his over-stuffed computer bag. A few hours by himself might set his hopes straight.

At four thirty, he left everything scattered across one of the twin beds and headed to the kitchen. Reality had begun to sink in, making him wish he hadn't promised to look for another someone to love. Fifty years of loneliness couldn't be much worse than traipsing through the land mines of meeting women and dating, could it?

With the potatoes scrubbed and wrapped in foil, he put them in the oven to bake. He chanced a nonchalant peek into the living room as he walked to the fridge to pull out a bag of salad and a package of toma-toes. Not a peep had come from the adjoining room, and now he knew why. His cabinmate lay sound asleep on the couch.

Tempted as he was to move close enough to memorize every curve and plane of her beautiful face, he prepared two salads and garlic bread to go with the steak and baked potatoes. Torturing himself wouldn't change anything. Her assertion that she'd think about going out with him had been her way of letting him down easy. She had no intention of going out with him even once.

Her actions, or rather her lack of conversation, during supper made it crystal clear. Other than the perfunctory "please" and "thank you," she was quiet. When she ran dishwater in the sink, he didn't argue about cleanup. He had no desire to spend his last hours alone with her fighting over trivial garbage.

As he headed for the shower, the snowplow noises that had faded with the afternoon grew louder. The real world had invaded his short-lived fantasy. Headlights reflected off the drifts in the dusk, announcing the arrival of an escape route.

He retreated to the bathroom before Pepper could jump up and down for joy. For all he knew, she planned to pack up and leave as soon as the road had a single lane. He'd prefer finding her gone to watching her go.

Never again.

The hot water lasted all of about ten minutes, and he resorted to shaving in the sink to put off going out to the living room. After sneaking in a nap, she probably wouldn't go to bed for hours—and he wouldn't sleep at all.

Too aggravated to even check to see if she'd left, he followed the short hall straight across to his bedroom, bypassing the issue altogether. The bed he hadn't covered in work-related paraphernalia was made up with blankets, a comforter, and pillows they'd used on the foldout couch. She hadn't seized the opportunity to sneak away, but her preference of sleeping alone was obvious with the neatly turned-down covers.

A door clicked closed, and he could only assume she'd gone in the bathroom to get ready for bed.

How had they gone from sharing a bed and their most painful experiences to avoiding each other?

Climbing into bed, he switched off the lamp. The snowplow sounds had stopped and only the blowing from the furnace kept him company in the near darkness. He should be used to the lack of another person's voice and breathing at night. Chances were he'd have to tolerate it for years to come. Thankfully, he was bushed enough to lose himself in sleep.

He closed his eyes and relaxed into the hard mattress. At least springs weren't poking him. His thoughts drifted to his big, comfortable bed at home, dragging him toward sleep.

Squeakkk. Thunk.

Bolting out of covers, he half expected the roof to cave in around him. A limb had to have fallen on the cabin to cause that racket. He tried to shake off the rush of adrenaline, but something niggled at him.

Pepper!

What if the limb had landed over her bedroom?

His heart leapt to his throat.

Three quick steps took him to the door. He swung it open, ready to dig through debris to get to her if he had to. Nothing seemed out of place, and the other bedroom door stood ajar. Light came from the living room, flickering, as if she'd forgotten to turn off the fireplace.

In the shadows near the bathroom, movement caught his attention. "Pepper? Are you okay? What happened?"

She stepped into the wavering light, an oversized T-shirt having replaced the sweats she'd worn the last two nights. Toned calves and shapely thighs drew his gaze and sparked a tightening in his groin. Her mix of innocence and pure sexuality was too enticing to ignore. "I couldn't sleep."

"We can turn up the thermostat if you're cold."

Shaking her head, she edged closer, until she stood inches from him. She rose to her tiptoes as she looped her arms around his neck and rested her cheek over his heart. "I missed you."

She rocked her hips forward, pressing against his already half-hard cock.

A growl rumbled up from his chest.

Was she testing him to see if he had the power to resist her?

I don't. Cradling her face in his hands, he leaned his forehead on hers. "I missed you too."

Then she pressed her soft lips to his.

CHAPTER NINE

PEPPER SWEPT HER TONGUE PAST HIS LIPS, AND DREW WANTED TO CRY out in relief. Unless he was dreaming, she was really kissing him, with all the passion of a woman who truly wanted him. His hopes were more than wishful thinking after all.

He glided along the welcome invader, letting the minty flavor of toothpaste cool his mouth. It didn't do a thing for the rest of his body. Warmth spread through his palms and to his cock, everywhere else they touched.

Tilting his head to the right, he sought a better angle to take the kiss even deeper. He explored her mouth, savoring the aggressive way she wrestled him for control. Her needy moans convinced him she was as desperate for more as he was. Desire wasn't his alone.

His instincts short-circuited, giving way to something far more basic. Grasping her ass, he lifted her, and she circled her legs around his waist. She fit against his erection like they'd been made for mating. Every nerve ending buzzed, and anticipation raced from his fingertips to his bare toes.

He needed to become part of her.

A moment of sanity struck as he carried her toward her bedroom, and he detoured to his duffle bag on the armchair in the living room.

The strip of Trojans wasn't near as easy to locate this time, with his mouth still enjoying heaven and his libido getting impatient. After another search of the outside pocket, he finally pulled the condoms free.

Turning toward the bedrooms, he banged his shin against metal.

Son of a—

The bed.

Did she think of it as theirs?

The sharp zing of pain vanished at the realization that he had only to lie down with her on the nearest flat surface. As soon as they hit the soft layers of blankets, he released her long enough to set the protection on the pillow and strip off her T-shirt. He almost choked at the sight of her full, rounded breasts dappled in firelight and shadows.

Invitation beckoned to him in her eyes. She reached for him.

He dragged his own shirt over his head and then leaned down meet her kiss-swollen lips again. Soft palms brushed along his ribs, sending a welcome shiver up his spine. Her taut nipples grazed his chest, and he groaned with the pleasurable pain of aching testicles and a hard-on ready to thrust inside her.

Patience. He had no intention of rushing to the end, no matter how much he wanted her. They both deserved better.

Trailing his lips over her cheek, he inhaled her faint fruity scent. It grew stronger as he got closer to her neck. He buried his nose in her hair and breathed in the intoxicating aroma. He'd always loved the finer elements of making love—the tastes, the textures, the smells.

He nibbled the outer shell of her ear, hoping to inspire more of those sexy mewling sounds. Her gasp was reward enough for now. "Tell me what you like. Where do you want me to touch you?"

She grasped his head and guided him lower, lining up his mouth with her breast. Her fingers closed around his forearm, moving his hand even farther down, past her flat stomach to a damp spot on her underwear.

Wiggling against him, she let out a throaty moan. "Play with my clit and suck my nipples."

Unaccustomed to hearing more than "touch me here" or "yes,

there," the words seemed naughty. They also jacked his craving up to a new level.

He slipped her panties past her hips as he licked circles around her areolas, trying to calm his pulse and keep his desire under control. A slow glide up the silky skin of her inner leg didn't help, but she cooed and arched into his touch. The first orgasm would be hers, not his, and he'd give to it to her the way she wanted it.

Following the curve of thigh, he found a thatch of springy curls and the slit down the middle. With a light touch, he traced her labia to the source of her heat. A slow trip through the wetness yielded a distinctive nub, and her slick fluids provided the perfect lubrication for massaging her clitoris. He matched the rhythm of his circuits, teasing the puckered tip of her breast and the swelling bundle of nerves.

She grabbed his shoulder with one hand and threaded her fingers through her hair with the other, pulling hard enough to make it sting and remind him he could feel. "Suck my nipple. Now, oh please, now. Yes, just like that. Make me come. Don't stop."

Her whole body arched against him as she cried out, the sound sweeter than he'd ever imagined it could be. Spasm after spasm set her shuddering against him, and he didn't stop until she lay limp and relaxed beneath him.

He was reluctant to let go of her for even a second, but his shorts had to go. The condom package crinkled under his palm on the pillow, and somehow he managed to tear it open without dropping it. After a moment's hesitation, he flipped over the latex round and rolled it on. He was out of practice, not stupid. He wouldn't risk putting the thing on wrong, subjecting her to a man's carelessness again.

He rose over her, bracing himself on his elbows close enough to kiss her. "I want to be inside you. Will you let me make love to you?"

She pulled him down for another tangling of tongues and guided him to her entrance. With one upward motion, she swallowed him whole, her inner muscles pulsing around his cock and sucking him deeper as she hooked her feet at his lower back.

Rocking forward, he sank in another inch. Her body surrounded him, enveloping him in a second skin. A groan rumbled up from his chest at the pure physical pleasure of joining with her. They fit perfectly, and he couldn't imagine ever wanting any other woman after her.

Dragging himself away for a breath, he nuzzled her neck. "Can you come again? This time with me?"

She nodded. "Mm-hm. Hard and fast? Or slow and gentle?"

For her bad experiences with men, she was far less inhibited than he was. He was hardly a novice, but her candor surprised him and stirred his baser needs.

"Would you mind hard and fast?" He withdrew partway and then thrust back into her. "You feel so damn good."

Her muffled cry vibrated through his jaw. "Fuck me, Drew."

Her blunt language stole the last of his restraint, and he vowed to set a pace sure to get them both off sooner rather than later. Adjusting his position, he lifted her legs to his shoulders. The rise of her hips pulled him deeper.

She opened her mouth, but a strangled squeak came out instead of words. Then she tightened around him. "I have a G-spot."

Thrilled to be the first to find it, he plunged into her. He held nothing back as he moved in and out of her. Every smooth glide brought the sensitive skin directly below the head of his cock in contact with her contracting muscles. Her wetness created a silky path. The light friction threatened to send him over the edge, especially when she dug her fingernails into his ass.

She trembled under him, and her panting quickly changed to high-pitched screams as she tightened and pulsed around him. Her body milked him until he couldn't hold out for one more second.

The pressure in his cock and balls let loose, a hot stream of semen blasting from him. A shout tore at his throat, and he drove into her a final time. His hammering heartbeat echoed in his head as his muscles tried to give out. He braced his arms to keep from collapsing on her as he released her legs.

Sex had always been good, but this time was different. Pepper had freed him from his inhibitions, her lack of reticence allowing him to truly let go. She'd invited him to a place he'd never gone before.

Leaning down, he pressed his lips to hers. They were soft and inviting, and he smiled against them. "I should make a trip to the bathroom. Need to go first?"

She sighed, warming his cheek. "Uh-uh. Not sure I could walk anyway. My legs are probably too rubbery to hold me up."

"I'd carry you if you needed to go." He hated to withdraw from her, but he'd never put her at risk for an unplanned pregnancy after what she'd gone through. "Be right back."

SURRENDERING TO A YAWN, PEPPER FOLLOWED DREW'S PROGRESS TO the bathroom until she couldn't see him anymore. His long, lean frame was breathtaking in the firelight, and not only because he was naked. He'd joined that exquisite body with hers, and she had no regrets. *None.*

The knowledge that they'd go their separate ways tomorrow had finally nudged her into action. Sure, they would meet to discuss the promotional package he was building for her, but they might never have the complete privacy of being stranded in a remote cabin again. She couldn't let him leave without acting on her attraction. He'd earned her trust, and she couldn't take it lightly.

No man had ever treated her with the reverence and care Drew had shown her.

With the little energy she possessed, she managed to tuck the remaining condoms under the pillow and wriggle under the covers. Her eyelids were heavy and drooping, but she blinked away the exhaustion. She wanted his arms around her and his heart beating in her ear when she fell asleep.

The bathroom door creaked open and then footsteps padded closer. He turned down the blankets enough to slip in beside her before assuming the position he'd taken the past two nights. As he lifted her leg over his thigh, his hand lingered, rubbing gentle circles over her hip. "Warm enough?"

Cuddled skin to skin with him, their shared body heat made her toasty enough to doze off, but she wasn't ready yet. "Mm-hm. Perfect."

He kissed her forehead. "Me too. Perfect."

The steady *ka-thump, ka-thump* of his heartbeat and his slow, even inhales and exhales lulled her toward dreamland, the place in her mind where she'd find a man worthy of a chance. If she slept, she might wake to discover she'd imagined the whole thing.

"Pepper?" He rolled toward her, pressing his chest to her breasts.

"Hm?"

"Will you go out to dinner with me on Saturday?"

He was asking her for a date?

She'd promised to consider going out with him. "Just us? Or will Kristin and Hannah be there?"

Meeting his daughters would be a huge step for a first date. It would suggest he was at least as interested in finding a stepmom for his kids as choosing a woman he could honestly love. That, or he hated single life and wanted an easy replacement.

Stop thinking. Just let it happen.

"The girls are going to their cousin's birthday party. Seems like rushing things to have you meet my kids so soon. I'd rather focus on us for a while."

The red flags that had popped up in her mind about his children fluttered to the ground, only to be replaced by a horde of butterflies in her stomach. "I guess I can't accuse you of wanting a one-night stand, can I?"

A moment too late, she wished she'd censored her thoughts before they came out her mouth.

He tightened his hold on her. "Nope. Unless you're nothing like the woman I've gotten to know while we've been snowbound, I think there's a pretty good chance I could fall in love with you."

Biting her lower lip, she blinked to stop the stinging tears. His admission had hit where it could either cause the most pain or inspire the most joy. She wasn't certain she could take his statement at face value. Experience had taught to err on the side of caution.

He trailed his palm up her spine and then cradled her head to his chest. "I'm guessing that's more than you want to hear right now, huh? I'll shut up and go to sleep."

Although he sounded more amused than upset or disappointed, she couldn't let him think she wasn't interested. "Dinner on Saturday. We'll go from there."

"Works for me. Goodnight, Pepper. Sleep well."

She kissed his bicep. "For a few hours. Then I think I'll be ready for more."

His low chuckle vibrated through her jaw. "I better get my rest."

A grin tickled her lips. "Mm-hm. Goodnight, Drew."

TOO COMFORTABLE TO LIFT HER HEAD YET, PEPPER SLID HER HAND under the pillow, hunting for the stash of condoms. If the hard length nestled in her butt cheeks was any indication, Drew's magic salami was raring to go, even if he didn't seem awake. Half the fun would be waking him up with some exploration.

Aha! Her blind search finally yielded the partial strip of foil packets. She'd need one after she enjoyed some playtime with an erection that wasn't made of silicone. Her past had made her wary of dating, but plastic playmates weren't going to cut it now that she'd seen a man could give her as much her pleasure as her toys.

A man who cares about me.

Not a single doubt remained.

She tore off a package and then stowed the rest under the pillow again. Clasping the condom in her hand, she rolled over to face him and shimmied a little farther under the covers.

He shifted to his back, pulling her along as if she was part of him. His body heat wrapped her in a cloud, and she pressed a kiss to his chest, grateful for every minute they shared. Nibbling her way lower, she traced the curve of his ribs and followed the slope of his firm abs. The light dusting of hair leading downward tickled her nose, but she didn't care. He was hers to enjoy.

Trailing her hand along his muscular thigh, she moved higher and higher, barely brushing the backs of her fingers on his scrotum. A kiss to his hipbone earned her soft groan.

She eased inward until the silky head of his cock swept over her cheek. The earthy scent drew her closer, until she found the firm ridge that ran from base to tip. She licked along the raised path to his slit. Droplets of creamy fluid spread over her tongue, bathing her taste buds in his flavor. He tasted better than any dessert she'd ever wanted to devour.

After another sample, she took him in her mouth, swallowing as much of his length as she could without triggering her gag reflex. With practice, she might be able to deep throat him someday.

Doubts about a future with him tried to creep in, but she pushed them back. She'd take one day at a time and see where it led her. He was too good a man to lump in with the losers from her past. She had to give him a real chance.

She lapped up another dribble of his tasty liqueur, getting drunk on the contrast of sweet and salty. He was her poison of choice. She'd never understood what people found so appealing about oral sex, but his addictive flavor and steely hardness wrapped in silky skin was all the explanation she needed. Giving him a blow job would put her in complete control.

I can make him feel as good as he made me feel.

Cupping his sac, she nibbled a path down his length and back up, tracing the thick ridge. She stopped short of the cap to play with a loose bit of skin. It wasn't pulled tight like the rest.

Could it be the male equivalent of a clitoris?

She sucked the tiny flap between her teeth and fluttered her tongue over it.

A muffled groan from outside the blankets boosted her confidence, and Drew arched into her as he threaded his fingers through her hair. "Mm. I love what you're doing. Want me to do it to you?"

The thought of his mouth pleasuring her as she sucked him off triggered a tiny spasm in her lower belly. "Mm-hm."

"Swing your legs around."

After struggling with the layers of blankets for a few seconds, she managed to free her legs and aim her feet toward his head. Not sure exactly how they'd be able pull off a sixty-nine, she let him guide her knee over his torso. His warm lips on her inner thigh made her breath catch, and she closed her eyes to concentrate on her part of their sexual adventure.

He rubbed his palm over her hip, making her almost jump out of her skin. "It's okay. If you don't like what I'm doing, I'll stop."

"Don't stop. I just... I've never done this before." The admission was easier in the dark, but it was still embarrassing. She was thirty-seven years old and a virgin at almost everything regarding sex except the act itself.

"I won't hurt you." His fingertips skimmed along her calf, the gentle touch soothing and sensual at the same time. "You have the most amazing skin. And I love the way you smell—ready for me to make you come with my mouth while you go down on me."

His words heated her blood, and she spread her knees farther apart to lower herself closer to his face. "I'll come for you if you come for me."

He laughed, sounding more pained than amused. "I'm sure that won't be a problem."

Returning to her task, she ran her tongue over his smooth cap in search of more nectar. As she licked him clean, she squirmed from the nibbling kisses he trailed along her panty line. His lips were inches from her clit, and his breath warmed then cooled her, making her wish he'd dive in.

"Are you wet?" His husky tone would've done it if she hadn't been drenched already.

She wiggled lower, hoping to show him how wet and ready she was. "Melting."

The slow drag of his tongue through her folds lit fireworks in her nerve endings, and she almost collapsed on top of him from the trembling in her leg muscles. He spread her labia with his thumbs as his tongue fluttered over her clit. His fingers had been wonderfully talented, but his mouth was spectacular. Now, she was truly melting.

Distracted by the sensations building between her thighs, she almost forgot about the treat he had for her. A little more oral exploration yielded his soft sac. She eased one malleable ball past her lips, rolling the testicle back and forth as she sucked.

His groan vibrated through her center, a sign that he must like what she was doing. She switched to the other side, offering it equal attention before cupping the handful and moving up to his cock again. A slow glide down his length earned her another husky rumble, the sound barely audible over her own moan as his rough breathing added a new level of pleasure.

He jerked upward and stiffened, driving his rigid length deeper into her throat. His hoarse growl caught her by surprise. Thick cream spurted onto her tongue, and the knowledge that she'd made him come sparked a sudden release of tension, sending her over the edge. Spasms rocked through her lower belly, dragging her on and on with each gentle tug on her clit.

Too drained to maintain the position, she let him slip from her mouth and dropped on top of him. She swallowed his essence and licked her lips, not wanting to waste a single drop.

He smoothed his palm over his hip, bringing it to rest on her ass. "If I ever tell you you're mouthy, remind me that's a good thing. Really good."

CHAPTER TEN

STOMPING THE SNOW FROM HIS BOOTS, DREW CLOSED THE DOOR behind him. All his gear was loaded in the car and he was ready to head home—except he wasn't. As much as he missed Kristin and Hannah, the thought of sleeping without Pepper in his bed made him wish he didn't have to go back to the real world.

Why had they wasted two whole days sniping at each other?

"Towels are bagged and trash is ready." With her back to him as she stood at the sink, she didn't sound any happier than he was about leaving. She'd been quiet and subdued since they'd climbed out of bed after making love yet again in the early-morning light. "Everything packed?"

"Yeah." Not caring if he tracked snow through the kitchen, he joined her, wrapping his arms around her from behind. "God, I'm going to miss you."

"You mean you're going to miss getting laid three times in one night." Her laugh was probably meant to make him think she was simply teasing, but it was too weak to be genuine. She was more than likely putting on a sarcastic front to keep him from seeing how much she disliked returning to reality too.

He tightened his hold on her. "I'll miss arguing with you and watching you cook. Tonight, I'll miss listening to you to breathe while I'm going to sleep, if I can sleep at all. I wish we had more time."

Turning in his arms, she buried her face in his chest. "Stop it. If you make me cry, I'm canceling our date on Saturday."

He doubted she'd actually follow through on the threat, but he didn't want her to remember their first days together with tears. "If you try to cancel, I'll hunt you down and kidnap you."

She nipped at his neck, the slight sting making his body react again. "That might be fun."

"Are you sure about that? Because if I have to kidnap you, I'm not sure I'll ever let you go." Leaning down to kiss her, he hoped his desperation didn't show in his eyes.

At the last second, she turned away and his lips met her cheek. "We should get going. We're supposed to be out by ten."

She was trying to distance herself from him already. Did she think he'd forget her once they got back to civilization?

No chance of that happening.

He nodded, unwilling to end their time together on a bad note. "Whenever you're ready." At her car, she ducked inside before he could give her a proper kiss, but he stopped her from closing the door without a good-bye. "Be careful, okay? And call me when you get home."

"Okay. You be careful too."

She seemed anxious to leave, so he stepped back to watch her pull away. A little piece of him went with her. He'd never expected to fall for a woman like her—fiercely independent, untrusting, and completely unaware of her beauty and passion.

Or so fast. How did that happen?

After a frustrated wave, he slid in behind the steering wheel of his own car and drove to the park office. He turned in the cabin keys, spending several minutes picking out souvenirs from the gift shop. His girls deserved a little something for cooperating with his "business trip," and he wasn't sure he could stand driving north with Pepper still in his sights. He'd be too damned tempted to wave her to the side of the road for more than a simple good-bye kiss.

The roads were slick but passable on the drive. The closer to home he got, the less snow covered the landscape. He hadn't seen her car—ahead of him, pulled over, or in a ditch—and he'd been watching, but that didn't stop the worry.

As soon as he parked in the garage, he checked his cell phone to be sure it was charged and that he hadn't accidently switched off the ringer. She lived less than twenty minutes from him.

Why hadn't she called?

Calling her would only make him seem overprotective and possessive. Determined not to chase her off by smothering her, he set to unpacking.

Half an hour later, he'd sorted his dirty clothes and put a load of laundry in the washing machine, emptied the cooler, and made a sandwich for a late lunch. His nerves had frayed out of control, his imagination coming up with a dozen possible scenarios of her demise. She still hadn't let him know she'd gotten home okay, and he was seriously considering a drive to her apartment above the deli.

He searched his contacts instead. As he lifted his finger to tap the icon to connect, the phone vibrated in his hand and sang out the ringtone Kristin had chosen for him. His pulse jumped into a double-time beat. "Hello?"

"Hey, Drew. The girls are wanting to know if you're home yet."

His heart sank to his knees at the sound of Colleen's voice. "Just finished unpacking."

"How was the trip? The weather report said that area got almost two feet of snow."

Not in the mood to share details of his snowed-in experience, he stuck to vague facts. "Yeah, lots of snow. Got some work done. Birthday party's still on for Saturday evening, right?"

"Yep. Merie reserved enough lanes at the bowling alley for the adults too. Are you planning to stick around?"

"Uh-uh. I have to…meet a client for dinner. Do you mind if I pick up the girls at your house about nine thirty?" His little white lie wasn't really a lie. Pepper was his client and they were having dinner.

"No problem, but it'd be better if you had a hot date." Colleen paused, as if waiting for a response. "You know, if you're having a hard time meeting women, you could always join a singles group or something."

"I don't need help." He snapped his mouth shut before he accidentally revealed more than he wanted her to know to right now.

She *tsked* in his ear. "Okay. Fine. Do you want me to run the munchkins home?"

"Yeah, if you don't mind." Hopefully, he'd be able to reach Pepper by then.

"See you in a few."

He ended the call and then went back to his previous task. For three rings, his stomach churned and somersaulted. He paced to the refrigerator, but didn't open it.

"Hello, Red Hot Pepper. Can you hold please?" Pepper's voice sounded strained. "Oh, sorry. Wrong phone. Hello?"

His insides went from roiling to relaxed at the normalcy in her greeting, and he smiled at her usual lack of pretense. "Hi, it's Drew. Is everything all right?"

"Crap! I forgot to call. Sorry. I've got a minor emergency on my hands with the deli at the moment. I can't talk now."

Relieved to know she was okay, he cut her some slack for forgetting about him. "Will you call me later when you have a few minutes?"

Her tone softened. "Yeah. Gotta go."

The line went dead, but he didn't care that she'd hung up on him. She'd gotten home safely and promised to talk to him later. He could live with that. He didn't have to like being apart from her, but a little separation might slow down his emotions enough to be sure he wasn't suffering from lust and infatuation. A little caution was a good idea.

How had he gone from thinking he wasn't ready to start dating to counting the minutes until he spoke to Pepper again?

He didn't dive headfirst into any situation. Sleeping with her was the most spontaneous thing he'd ever done. Even telling his father to stuff his snobbery and political aspirations had been months in the making. He'd waited for the right moment to announce his engagement to Kate, knowing his family would never approve of a middle-class girl joining their ranks. Then he'd cut his ties to the high and mighty Fultons. He had no regrets.

"Knock, knock! Anybody home?" Colleen's yell was nearly lost in the wake of running feet in the entry.

"Daddy! Daddy! Where are you?"

He grinned at the instant lightening of his mood. Gone was the concern about his relationship with Pepper, replaced by contentedness brought on by his daughters' presence. No matter how down he got, they always cheered him up.

"In the kitchen!" He rushed to the doorway, anxious for the boisterous hugs he was due.

Kristin reached him first. She flung her arms around his waist and squeezed. "We have a surprise for you, Daddy!"

Pushing past her sister, Hannah hopped up and down until he bent over far enough for her hook her arms around his neck. "We missed you, Daddy!"

"I missed you too." He lifted her off the floor. "What's the big surprise?"

"It's in Kristin's suitcase. We have to get it." She loosened her hold as he lowered her and then grabbed her big sister's hand. "Come on! We'll be right back."

Colleen flattened against the wall until the stampede ran past her. Then she joined him in the kitchen, rubbing her hand over the barely discernible bump of her belly. "This time I'm smart enough to appreciate how easy kids are to take care before they're born, not that the girls gave me any trouble."

He snorted. "No, they just never run out of energy. Want something to drink?"

Scrunching up her face, she shook her head. "No thanks. Morning sickness turned into afternoon sickness yesterday. So, you stayed in a cabin, didn't you?"

"Yeah." Something about her expression put him on guard. "One of the state park cabins by Old Man's Cave."

"Anybody else brave the weather?"

Unable to outright lie, he shrugged. "One of my clients showed up. We got some work done on a new campaign."

At her smirk, he replayed his answer in his mind. He hadn't mentioned his client being female or sharing the cabin with him.

"Must be some campaign." She nudged his chin to the right with her thumb. Her smirk became a full-fledged laugh. "Does it involve hickeys?"

Smacking at her hand, he willed away the heat creeping up his neck. Surely Pepper hadn't left her mark on him.

The nip when I threatened to kidnap her.

He fingered the spot, the slight sting fresh in his memory. He'd have a hell of a time sleeping alone tonight.

"That's why you said you didn't need help meeting women. Is it serious? Does she live close enough to see her again?"

Too trapped to deny Colleen's suspicions, he had nothing to lose by leveling with her. "We have a date on Saturday."

"You're kidding." Her eyes widened. "That's awesome! Congratulations!"

"Geez. I didn't say we're getting married. It's just a date." Another wave of embarrassment carried warmth to his cheeks.

"*Just* a date? I don't think so. You don't do anything halfway, Drew. When are you gonna introduce her to the munchkins?"

With a sigh, he gave up any pretense of a casual relationship. "I like her a lot, but I want to see how things go before I talk to the kids about her."

"Good plan." She enveloped him in a hug. "I hope it works out. You deserve to be happy again."

"Thanks." Pattering footsteps made him turn toward the kitchen doorway as his daughters returned.

Hands behind their backs, they stopped in front of him.

Kristin nodded as she glanced in her sister's direction, sending her ponytail flopping over her shoulder. "Go first."

Hannah's dimples deepened with the widening of her contagious smile. She held out her open palm, a plastic container from a quarter-prize vending machine balanced in the center. "It's a fancy ring."

Holding out a folded slip of paper, Kristin stepped forward. Her seriousness sent a warning shiver up his spine. "And here's the name of the lady we want you to give it to. We think you'll really like her. And she'll make a great mom."

Speechless for the moment, he took the surprises from his previously predictable daughters. They'd chosen a wife for him and a new mother for them. As much as he wanted to appreciate their gifts, he had no intention of dumping Pepper for a fix-up with a woman chosen by his daughters. Their well-meaning motives had too much Disney-princess influence, and marriage was more complicated than rescuing a damsel in distress—not that Pepper was a damsel by any stretch of the imagination.

He glanced at Colleen, hoping for a little help, but she simply shrugged and rubbed her belly. "I better get going. I have a checkup in twenty minutes."

"I'll walk you out." Clutching the paper and the ring in his fist, he gestured for her to lead the way to the front door.

"See you at the bowling alley on Saturday, kiddoes." She blew kisses in Hannah's and Kristin's direction as she turned toward the hall.

Not wanting the girls to hear, he saved his question until they reached the front door. "You didn't put them up to the arranged wedding, did you?"

She snorted a laugh. "Don't you think you're being a little melo-dramatic? Besides, I didn't know a thing about their surprise. They must've dreamed that up on their own."

"Okay. How do I talk them into letting me pick my own wife?"

Her devious grin didn't bode well. "You could tell them about the hickey lady. Just keep it rated G."

She evidently suspected the mark on his neck was only a hint at what had gone on during his business trip.

He shooed her out the door. "You're as bad as a real sister."

"I'll take that as the compliment I know you meant it to be." Pulling her coat tighter around her, she looked back at him over her shoulder. This time, her expression was sincere. "Fingers crossed for you, brother dear."

"Thanks. Let us know how the little guy's doing, okay?"

"The 'little guy' is gonna be a girl, and I'll text you the stats later." She hurried down the steps to her car.

He and all the men in the family had put money on another boy, while the women all insisted Colleen was having a baby girl. They probably knew better than he did, and he only cared that the newest addition was happy and healthy.

"Daddy, when you marry the lady we picked for you, can we have a little brother?" Hannah popped her head out the door and waved to her aunt.

Her question prompted an unexpected thought—one that he hadn't considered.

Did Pepper want more children?

Hell, do I want to do the baby thing again?

He and Kate had agreed to stop at two, neither of them having the pressing urge to try for a son. Their beautiful girls had been enough for both of them, but his sweet angels were growing up.

Scooping up Hannah, he shoved the door closed with his foot. "Let's talk about it over a snack."

"Aw, Daddy, that means no." She wrinkled up her nose at him.

"Not necessarily." The situation wasn't that simple, and the short walk to the kitchen didn't help him come up with an easy explanation. As he sat at the table, he perched her on his lap. "Family discussion time, Kristin. Have a seat."

His older daughter didn't look any happier than her sister when she plopped into the chair adjacent to his. "We don't want you to be lonely anymore. Can't you at least meet her?"

He hated denying her anything, but the truth was more important. "Here's the thing. I met a terrific lady a few days ago, and I really like her. We're going out on a date on Saturday, so meeting somebody else would feel like I'm not playing fair."

Kristin crossed her arms in front of her and lowered her chin. "You have a *date*? But we don't even know who she is."

The urge to grin at her motherly behavior was strong, but he smothered it. She was only trying to protect him.

"Now, come on. Don't you think I can decide if she's good enough for me? And you? I'd never go out with someone I thought would be less than a great mom to you two. And I know her well enough to want to spend some time with her and get to know her better."

Hannah's pout was likely more about not getting her way than being truly upset with him. "How are we supposed to meet her if we're at Cody's birthday party?"

He should've expected them to give him the third degree. "This our first date. I don't want to make her think the only reason I like her is because my girls want a mother."

"When do we get to meet her then?"

The Hastings streak of stubbornness was wide in Hannah, but he wasn't about to let his kids rush his relationship with Pepper. "Tell you what. If I still like her and she still likes me in a couple weeks, I'll talk to her about meeting you."

Pushing back her chair, Kristin stood, her spine rigid and arms crossed tighter than before. "She doesn't even know about us, does she?"

Appalled by her insinuation, he silently counted to ten to calm his rising impatience. "Yeah, actually she does. She also knows that your mom got cancer and died. Maybe you should consider how hard it'd be for her to take the place of someone we loved with all our hearts. How do you think she'd feel about becoming my *second* wife and the *stepmother*?"

Kristin glared at him for a full three seconds before spinning on her heel and running from the room. Rapid footsteps on the stairs and the slamming of a door followed.

A lump formed in his throat and his chest constricted. His words had been too harsh, too blunt. He hadn't meant to cause her pain, but he couldn't change reality.

Wiggling off his lap, Hannah glanced after her sister and back again. "Daddy, will she make us clean the ashes out of the fireplace and scrub the floors with a brush?"

CHAPTER ELEVEN

"LAST ORDER'S GONE AND THE DOORS ARE LOCKED."

Pepper wanted to hug her son for his announcement. Unfortunately, she was elbow deep in cherry tomatoes and black olives. "Thank goodness. Any word on Ona's condition?"

Shaking his head, Zack shoveled a handful of halved tomatoes into the tub of marinade. "Nothing since her mom called from the emergency room. If it's appendicitis, we'll probably have to get somebody to cover her shifts for a week or two."

"Know of anybody with counter and register experience?" Even as she asked the question, a solution formed in her mind. "Hm. Oh, yeah. That would be the perfect payback."

He grinned, clearly following her train of thought. "Uncle Mort? Yep, he deserves to be taken down a notch after sending you into a freaking blizzard. I'm thinking restroom and mop duty."

"That's my boy." She bumped her shoulder against his bicep. "Why don't you invite him for supper while I finish here? Tell him to pick up Mexican on the way. Enchiladas Verdes for me."

With a nod, he moved to the sink. "He called about four, wanting to know if you were home yet."

"Yeah?"

Zack dried his hands and then slid his cell phone out of his back pocket. "He seemed kinda anxious to know how the trip went."

Of course he did, the devious twerp. "Really? I wonder why he didn't call *me*?" Slicing the last tomato in half, she let loose her best witch cackle. "You don't suppose he's worried that I'm ticked off at him, do you?"

"Only if he knows what's good for him." He lifted the cell to his ear. "Hey, Uncle Mort. Mom wants you to come over for supper. Well, yeah. No. The usual. Okay, see you in about a half hour."

Pocketing his phone, Zack seemed to hesitate, triggering her radar.

"What did he say?"

He rubbed the back of his neck, setting off another warning signal. "He just wanted to know if you said how things went, whether you made much progress."

"Made much progress on what?" She could spot his guilty conscience a mile away. As close as they were, she was surprised he tried to cover whatever Mortie had put him up to.

Shuffling toward her, he shrugged. "Don't be mad, okay? I called Uncle Mort right after you left for the cabin. I was worried about you getting stuck there by yourself in the snowstorm, and he told me about the ad guy. He asked me not to rat him out, that you needed a vacation."

"So you knew Drew Fulton was going to be sharing the cabin with me, but you didn't tell me when I called to say I made it okay." Simply saying Drew's name caused a tickle in her tummy. She should've made calling him top priority instead of punishing her cousin.

Zack rubbed at a spot on the counter. "Mort promised me Mr. Fulton wasn't a creep. He thought you might like each other, and, to be honest, I think it's time you started dating. I'm not crazy about you living alone."

With her suspicions about Mort's interference confirmed, she focused on Zack's admission. "You're not the parent. You shouldn't be worrying about me. And my apartment is right next to yours."

"What about when I'm at class or out with friends? This isn't a bad neighborhood or anything, but stuff can still happen."

"And having a man in my life will protect me?" She wiped her messy hands on her apron and then gathered him in a hug to counter her cynical retort. "I know you mean well, and I love you for it."

"But?"

"No buts." Mustering her courage, she leaned back to him in the eye. "I have a date with Drew on Saturday. He's a nice man, and I like him. However, you have to promise me you won't say anything about it to Mortie. He already sticks his nose in my business too much."

Zack's mouth opened and closed twice before any words came out. "You're going out on a *date*? Like a real one?"

"Yeah. Pretty bizarre, isn't it?"

"Bizarre doesn't even come close." He reached behind him, and seconds later he unfolded his wallet. Holding out a square blue packet, he glanced at her and then away. "Make sure you take this with you. And use it, you know, if the need arises."

Should she be proud of him for quoting her? Or should she be embarrassed because her son saw the potential for condom usage on her first date in sixteen years?

Maybe I should be glad he's smart enough to remember he has one.

"Keep it. I have some." They'd probably expired long ago, but she'd make a run to the store to stock a fresh supply.

"Okay, if you're sure." He returned the Trojan to his wallet. "I'll go check the front while you finish back here."

"That package looked kinda worn around the edges. You might want to replace it."

His quick exit made her smile. As self-conscious as he had to have been, he'd proven to her once again what a fantastic kid she'd raised. She doubted many eighteen-year-old young men concerned themselves with encouraging their mothers to practice safe sex.

Twenty minutes later, they climbed the interior stairway to the second-floor apartments. A knock sounded on the outer door as she topped the steps. She grunted, having hoped for a quick shower before supper.

Zack waved her off when she turned down the hallway. "I'll get it. You want to eat at your place or mine?"

"Would you mind yours? I still have to unpack, and half the kitchen and living room are buried under suitcases and groceries." She'd also have the option of going home if Mortie decided to give her the third degree about Drew. She needed to return Drew's call yet as well, but he deserved more than a rushed five-minute conversation.

"No problem. Come on over when you're ready." Zack headed to the door, leaving her to wash away the afternoon's worth of deli smells and spatters.

A steamy shower and clean clothes did nothing to improve her disposition where her cousin's meddling was concerned, but she wasn't about to hand over any ammunition for a told-you-so comeback. He was the kind of family who had no qualms about saying it. Fortunately, she'd put the finishing touches on her plan.

She rapped twice before entering Zack's apartment. As she expected, Mort sat on the couch with feet propped on the coffee table and his hands hooked behind his head, looking like he was chilling out after a hard day's work. The laid-back pose didn't fool her for a second. He was taking in his surroundings, studying her every movement as she crossed the living room to sit in the chair across from him. His keen eye and people-watching skills had made him a shrewd and successful businessman.

The clink of glasses from the kitchen likely meant Zack was setting the table.

Just enough time to instigate some trouble.

"Hey, Mortie. How's it going?" She buried her annoyance at him and smiled.

His brief scowl amused her, the jab hitting its mark. "If you weren't my favorite cousin, I'd ruin you for calling me that. Give me a report on your meeting with Fulton, and then I'll tell you how it's going."

"Ugh. Seriously, you don't want to know. The man was about as pleased to find me squatting in his accommodations as I was about finding him there, and I'm pretty sure he drafted his resignation while we were snowed in. He was already pissed about having to work when he was supposed to be on vacation."

Usually lightning fast with a reply, he seemed speechless—and not terribly happy. He sat up, his open posture not betraying what had to be going through his head. The only tell was the barely noticeable tic in his right eyelid. She would've missed it if she hadn't known where to watch. Drew's half-serious remark about quitting his job had sparked her ingenious scheme.

"Supper's on the table."

Her son's announcement seemed to scatter Mort's tension, probably from years of hiding his emotions behind the well-rehearsed mask. "Good. Let's eat."

She didn't believe for a second he'd let the subject drop. It was on hold until he deemed it important enough to readdress.

"Starving? Did you work through lunch again?" Almost too tired to move, she groaned as she levered out of the chair.

In two steps, he was beside her, slipping his arm around her waist. "You okay?"

"Yeah, nothing a twenty-four nap won't fix." She let him help her to the kitchen table. Now was as good a time as any to lay on the guilt trip. "Hard to sleep when you have no power, water, or heat and the temperatures drop into the teens at night. Then I came home to one of my part-timers getting carted off to the hospital with appendicitis. Instead of unpacking and resting, I worked all afternoon."

His hold tightened a fraction. "You should've called me."

"Kinda difficult to do with no cell signal during the blizzard. Not that you would've been able to do anything it. The roads were impassable." Taking a seat at her entrée, she frowned at him. "And what could you have done about Ona?"

He sat in the chair to her left, his serious expression exposing far more than he probably meant to. "Why didn't you call in somebody else?"

Ignoring his question for a moment, she removed the lid from her carryout container and savored a deep whiff of heaven. "All my other workers are gone for winter break. With Ona sick, it's me and Zack."

His silence didn't surprise her. The man was a thinker when presented with a problem. He loved the challenge of creating the perfect solution.

A full minute passed as he uncovered his combo dinner and dug into his tamales. He poked a bite, pausing with it halfway to his mouth. "I can take the three-to-seven shift until one of them gets back."

Zack barked a laugh. "No offense, Uncle M—Kyle, but you're a desk guy."

Cutting into her enchiladas, she avoided looking up at her brilliant boy. He'd given his "uncle" the rope to hang himself.

Mort's fork thunked against the container. "You think I put myself through undergrad by sitting in an office? I'll have you know I worked in the deli with your mom for two years."

"Yeah, but wasn't that like twenty years ago?"

"Nineteen. Believe it or not, I still remember how to take orders and run a cash register."

Pepper bit her lip to keep from giggling. Mr. Kyle Morton, astute businessman, had walked right into her son's trap.

"Okay, if you think you can keep up." Evidently, Zack wasn't above egging him on, either.

"Yeah, I do. I'll be here by two tomorrow for a quick refresher."

Giving a nod, her chip off the old block scooped a forkful of rice. "Oh, by the way, I have seniority. That means you get restroom and mop duty."

Mort froze mid-chew. His eyes narrowed and he shifted in his seat. Lifting his napkin to his lips, he swallowed. "Why do I get the feeling I've been conned?"

She finally surrendered to a grin. "Never underestimate a woman's right for payback. I think we'll be even after you serve your sentence."

"I'm glad we're not enemies." His compliment was obviously all the acknowledgment he'd give her that he intended to fulfill his end of the bargain.

"Me too. Eat your supper." Done discussing her problems, she concentrated on her food, hoping he'd catch the hint.

"I'm sorry about the trip."

His apology seemed sincere, so she gave him the benefit of the doubt. Her hint had been too subtle, though. "Fine. Now drop it before I decide to hold a grudge."

"Okay, okay." He frowned, clearly not happy about her lack of disclosure, but he turned his attention back to his meal.

Although silence was unnatural for their trio, she relished the quiet while they ate. Exhaustion crept closer with every bite, and she set down her fork halfway through the second enchilada.

"Hey, Mom, you should go home and go to bed before you fall asleep in your plate." Zack pushed his empty container away from the edge of the table. "You want me to put the lid on the rest?"

She yawned as she stood. If she had any hope of calling Drew, she needed to do it now. "Yeah, thanks."

Thankfully, Mort only gave her his paternal look, the one that warned her he was about to become overprotective. "I can work from open to close tomorrow if you want to take the day off."

His offer softened her heart a little, but not enough to let him off the hook for his trickery. She took her leftovers from Zack and smiled when he kissed her cheek. "Nah. See you at two. And thanks for picking up supper."

"You're welcome. Sleep well." He muttered something to Zack as she shuffled out of the kitchen, most likely a comment about her working too hard and needing a man to take care of her.

Ignoring their exchange, she increased her pace, ready to fall into bed and update Drew on the success of their conspiracy. The obstacle course to her bedroom didn't faze her. She'd deal with the mess in the morning.

After her nighttime routine in the bathroom, she donned her flannel pajamas and burrowed under the covers. What she wouldn't give to have Drew next her, his body heat seeping into her as he caressed and held her. Somehow, three nights of sleeping with him had turned her into an almost normal woman.

A short search of the contacts in her cell yielded his number, and she tapped the screen to connect. At the third ring, a bud of disappointment threatened to make her wish she hadn't promised to return his call.

"Pepper?" He sounded breathless, as if he'd run to answer his phone—or come inside her only moments ago.

"You were expecting somebody else?"

His laugh spread over her, warming her chilled skin and chasing away the distress. "Just hoping for you. I've missed you today. You and your sarcastic bite. Speaking of which, my sister-in-law informed me I have a hickey on my neck. Any idea who could've put it there?"

A self-satisfied giggle erupted from her throat. "A hickey, huh? Good thing you didn't leave one on me. My nosy cousin never would've let me hear the end of it. He's convinced you're resigning, by the way."

"Good. No more talk about Kyle. Your emergency handled? Everything okay?"

His interest in her life reminded her why she liked him so much. "One of my employees was being loaded into an ambulance when I got home. Appendicitis. I had to work her shift."

"Wow, I hope she's okay."

"Her mom's supposed to let us know how surgery goes."

"You sound tired. Whenever you're ready to hang up, just say so."

He was easily the most considerate man she'd ever met. "Tired but not too sleepy to talk for a few minutes. I bet Kristin and Hannah are glad to have you home."

"Yeah." He paused. "I told them about you. I'd planned to wait a few days since they've been dropping hints about wanting me to get married again, but they kind of ambushed me."

"Oh?" She was anxious to hear how he'd escaped alive.

"They had a surprise for me. A ring from a vending machine like you see at the grocery store and a piece of paper with a woman's name on it. I was supposed to give her the ring. I'm not sure they understood why I can't."

If he didn't seem distraught that he'd had to deny his daughters, she might've been a twinge jealous. "That's very sweet. I bet they were disappointed."

"Yeah." His lack of elaboration suggested they'd been more than a little upset.

"Like run to their rooms and slam the doors unhappy? Or I'm running away and you can't stop me mad?"

He sighed. "Somebody who understands parenting. It was the run and slam version for Kristin. Hannah wanted to know if you were going to treat her like Cinderella."

"The evil stepmother curse." As soon as the words were out of her mouth, she regretted them. They hadn't known each other long enough to discuss marriage and stepparent problems. "They don't sound very receptive to meeting me right now. Maybe we should wait a while for an introduction. See how things go. Besides, you never know. We could date for a month and decide to call it quits."

"Or a month from now we could be engaged."

Her belly quavered at the thought. Whether from nerves or anticipation, she wasn't sure. "Let's not rush into anything."

"I'm just saying we'll handle whatever happens. If we're happy together, we'll convince the girls to be happy too. You're hardly evil stepmother material." His voice softened. "I don't think I'd like it if we called it quits. Gut feeling."

How could he have so much confidence in a day-old relationship? Was it even a relationship yet?

She rubbed her tummy. "My gut's a little queasy. The longest I dated anybody was about a week. That was in tenth grade."

"We're not sixteen, and our hormones aren't out of control. Well, maybe a little. But life isn't all drama and immediate gratification. I'm not interested in test driving every car on the lot if I really like the first one."

His corny analogy eased some of the tension in her muscles. "I'm a car, am I? What kind?"

"Let's see. With those amazing curves and that sassy personality, I'd say you're a red Ferrari on the outside. Inside, you're classy yet practical, like a Lincoln Continental with black leather interior. Oh, and there's a lacy red garter hanging from your rearview mirror."

"A garter, huh? What's that represent, other than the typical man-fantasy?"

"The hot and sexy side you have a hard time admitting you have. The womanly part. She likes to hide, but I know she's there."

His husky tone made her wish again that he was lying beside her.

Should she roll over to retrieve a vibrator from her nightstand drawer and beg him to talk to her while she pleasured herself? She wasn't anywhere near that brave, though. Besides, he'd probably think she was a pervert.

"Still awake, Pepper?"

"Yeah. Just thinking about what you said. It was nice."

"So you don't mind being compared to a car?"

"Nope. I like listening to you talk."

His low chuckle was mixed with a strangled cough. "Does it make you horny? Because I'm dying from hearing your voice. I can't wait until Saturday to touch you."

She grinned, glad to know she wasn't the only one suffering from withdrawal. Perhaps he wouldn't think she was a pervert after all. "Maybe I could earn some extra money by starting my own pay-per-minute phone line."

"You'd make a bundle, but I'd rather you only talk dirty to me. I don't like the idea of sharing you. Not even your sexy voice."

Taking his response as a green light, she switched her phone to speaker and pulled out her favorite toy. "How dirty do you want it, ad man?"

CHAPTER TWELVE

PEPPER'S QUESTION CATCHING HIM COMPLETELY OFF GUARD, DREW nearly choked on his tongue. His cock already ached from imagining her lying with him in bed, whispering in his ear. Phone sex would be a new experience for him, but he was willing to try it if she was. Saturday was too many days away.

Moving the phone from his leg to the bedspread, he worked the top button of his jeans free. "How about naughty instead of dirty? I'm not sure I can use the really raunchy words, for either of us."

"Works for me." Rustling noises came from her end of the line. "Are you in bed?"

"Yeah, and I'm taking off my pants. I wish you were undressing me." He lifted his butt to slide the denim and the layer underneath past his hips. "What are you wearing?"

"I *was* wearing pajamas, but I'm not anymore." A low buzzing hummed in the background. "And my favorite vibrator came out to play."

He kicked off his pant legs, sending his underwear sailing off the bed. "You have a lot of those?"

"A few. A celibate woman has to have some relief now and then. Do you have any toys? Or do you prefer to use your hands?"

Her words weren't even close to naughty yet, and he couldn't resist a slow stroke down and up his erection. "Hands, although I might be game for your toys some time. I'm so hard, Pepper. Do you like me that way?"

"Mm-hm. My nipples are hard too. If I lean my chin way down and lift my breasts, I can lick them."

He groaned on another downward stroke, the visual she inspired pushing him toward the point of no return. "Do it. And put the vibrator against your clit. I want to hear how good it feels. I want to hear you moan."

"Then you have to moan for me. Massage your balls while you pump up and down. Pretend you're inside me."

Her uneven panting ramped up his heart rate and his pulse echoed in his head. With her first soft whimper, he increased his pace. "Yeah. Just like that. God, I love listening to you."

"Mm." The achy sound could've been one of her sexy groans from when he'd fingered her to orgasm while he sucked her tasty nipples.

"I'm so close. More." He squeezed his sac and tightened the grip on his erection.

Each of her moans heightened the intensity building in his testicles. Increasing in pitch and volume, her sounds finally became a single drawn-out keening, and he let it draw him into his own release.

He closed his eyes, picturing her beneath him as he reveled in the rush of fluid from his cock. Too breathless to speak, he growled as he came, hoping she'd gotten as much pleasure from him as he'd gotten from her—even if it was a quickie.

"Holy cannoli. Masturbating was never this much fun before."

Utter satisfaction was no match for her comment, and he surrendered to a belly laugh. If she'd been lying next to him, he would've kissed her for bringing a bright spot to his evening. "God, I wish you were here with me."

She snickered. "Then we wouldn't have had unbelievable phone sex. I might last until Saturday now."

"Okay, you have a point, but I'll still miss sleeping with you." She'd quickly become a comfortable habit.

"Me too. I'm working ten to seven tomorrow." Her yawn reminded him of the long day she'd had. "Will you call me after the kids go to bed?"

"Yeah." He might text her a good morning before she went to work as well. "I've kept you awake late enough. Go to sleep, Pepper."

"Goodnight, Drew."

"Goodnight." He ended the call, hoping the day went fast tomorrow.

For the first time in over a year and a half, happiness truly seemed like it could be a part of his future.

"DADDY, WAKE UP. I'M HUNGRY."

"Me too. Can we go out for breakfast?"

Drew pried his bleary eyes open. He hadn't slept worth a damn, waking up several times when he'd reached for Pepper and she wasn't there. At least his older daughter was speaking to him this morning.

Rolling to his back, he yawned and stretched. "French toast?"

Hannah clapped her hands. "Is Uncle Flynn coming over to cook for us? Or Aunt Lily? She makes yummy muffins."

"Nope. I learned to cook a few things while I was gone." He levered up on his elbows to gauge Kristin's reaction. Her serious expression warned him she hadn't fully forgiven him and she didn't believe for a second he could make edible French toast. "Hannah, will you go down to the kitchen and wash two apples please? Careful on the stepstool."

"Okay! I will!" She made a beeline for the door.

When she thundered down the steps, he patted the bed. "Sit with me for a minute?"

Giving a shrug, Kristin perched on the edge of the mattress. Her attitude clearly hadn't improved much since yesterday afternoon.

"Are you still mad at me?"

She shrugged again.

"I want you to understand that I would never date a woman I

thought wouldn't be a good mother to you and your sister." He shifted, sitting up to lean against the pillows. "But—and this is a big one—I have to be in love with her to marry her. You two aren't going to be my little girls forever. You're going to grow up, and I need someone I want to be with for a long time. The lady I told you about is someone I think I could fall in love with. Will you give her a chance when the time comes to meet her?"

Tucking her hands between her knees, she glanced at him. "If I have to. You would've liked the lady we picked for you just as much."

Frustration forced him to count to ten. "But who's to say she'd like me? Life's more complicated than a fairy tale. I like this woman a lot, and it's important to me that you like her too. You can still be friends with the other lady even if she and I don't get married. Besides, Hannah looks up to you, and your opinion influences hers."

He didn't care for using older sibling pressure, but he needed her to see how much her behavior affected her sister's acceptance and how important Pepper was to him.

"You want me to be nice so Hannah will be nice." Leave it to his oldest child to cut to the chase. Her paraphrasing was an accurate, if not flattering, assessment of his request.

"Yes, and I want you to give her a fair chance. You said you don't want me to be lonely, but what about being happy?"

She frowned at him over her shoulder. "Of course I want you to be happy. I just didn't think you'd find somebody else before we could tell you we picked out the perfect lady. She has long black hair and she's a really good cook."

Leaning forward, he pulled her into a hug. "She's probably perfect for someone, and I appreciate that you were trying to help, but I'm pretty sure I've found the perfect woman for me already."

"More perfect than Mommy?"

Her words didn't spark the twinge of guilt he expected. Instead, he grasped Hannah by shoulders and held her away from him as he looked her in the eye. "I don't compare you to your sister or the other way around. You're two different people. Nobody's more perfect than anybody else. Got it?"

She nodded, her gaze dipping toward her lap.

He hadn't meant to sound harsh, but Kate hadn't been without flaws. She'd been human, like every person in the world. Idolizing wouldn't bring her back, and it would taint their memories until she no longer resembled the person who'd touched their lives. He wanted no part of that. They were all imperfect.

"You know I have enough love for all of you, right?" He kissed her forehead. "I'll never run out."

When she looked up at him, her eyes were filled with tears. "I'm sorry. I guess I was being selfish, huh?"

"Maybe a little, but your heart was in the right place." With a lump in his throat, he brushed a drop of moisture from her cheek. "Ready to help with breakfast?"

"Okay." She wiped her tears with her sleeve as she stood. "I love you, Daddy."

"Love you too, angel." He tossed back the covers, thankful he'd had the energy to put on a T-shirt and pajama bottoms after last night's adventure. "I'll meet you in the kitchen in a couple minutes."

Heading to the master bath, he scratched his stubbly jaw. Somehow, he'd managed to avert a disaster. Parenting as a couple was hard, but he had no idea how single parents survived with their sanity intact until their kids grew to adulthood. He'd have to ask Pepper what the secret was.

Pepper. Is she up yet?

After washing his hands and pulling on a sweatshirt, he grabbed his cell phone from the nightstand. The glowing numbers read eight fifteen, meaning she was probably wide awake. He tapped the message icon.

"Good morning. I hope you have great day. Looking forward to talking to you tonight."

He hit the Send button and waited for the beep that announced its delivery. With any luck, she'd see the text before she started her workday. She might even miss him half as much as he missed her.

Pocketing his phone, he aimed for the kitchen. The faint hiss of whispering carried to his ears as he neared the arched entrance. The whispers became murmurs.

"But—"

"No buts. Daddy likes her, so we have to try to like her too." His responsible daughter's willingness to defend his choice triggered a smile. She made him proud.

"What if she's mean like Cinderella's stepmother?" Hannah had never been a blind follower, and she was obviously staying with tradition.

"She wouldn't be able fool Daddy. He's too smart for that. Come on. If we're making French toast, we'll need bread and eggs."

Backtracking a few steps, he faked a noisy yawn this time as he entered the kitchen. "Apples ready, squirt?"

"Yep! And here's the bread." Plopping half a loaf of white bread on the counter, Hannah pursed her lips. "What's her name?"

He caught himself a moment before he gave away the fact that he'd been listening in on their conversation. "Whose name?"

"The lady you like." She perched her fists on her hips. "If we have to try to like her, shouldn't we know her name?"

Kristin set the eggs next to the bread, her eye-roll signaling her obvious disapproval of her sister's less than subtle method of getting information.

Glad for the interest in any case, he squatted in front of Hannah. "Her name is Pepper McCann. She owns a deli not far from where Uncle Flynn and Aunt Lily work."

"What does she look like?"

He straightened and raised his hand to his Adam's apple. "She's about this tall—maybe two or three inches taller than Kristin. Her hair is short, and she looks sort of like the fairies from your book. No wings, though."

Hannah giggled. "Of course not. Does she like kids?"

He picked her up, too aware she wouldn't let him do it much longer. "Yep, and she's pretty and nice and a really good cook. Enough questions for now. We have breakfast to make."

"What do we do first?"

Setting her feet on the floor, he tapped a finger to her nose. "Your job is to cut the bread into big chunks. I'll get out the casserole dish and slice the apples while Kristin breaks the eggs into a bowl and stirs them."

"Eww. Eggs are slimy. I think you should do that part, Daddy." His older girl stuck out her tongue and made gagging sounds.

"But you're lots better at it than I am. Do you want crunchy French toast?" He still wasn't sure he'd gotten all the eggshell pieces out of his and Pepper's omelets.

"Okay, I'll do it, but you have to mix them. That's the really gross part."

"You'll have to measure the brown sugar and put the apples in the dish then. Sounds fair, doesn't it?"

Twenty minutes later, he hoped for the best as he put the dish in the oven and set the timer. His training hadn't included a large repertoire of menu items.

Sending the girls to get dressed, he headed for the shower. He'd promised them two full days in a row together to make up for his trip. Work was off-limits, and his e-mail could wait until Monday. Christmas vacation would be over, leaving him to get down to business on Pepper's account. With any luck, he'd get to spend more time with her.

As he shoved his arms into his shirtsleeves, his phone vibrated against the top of the dresser. It buzzed again a second later. His insides did a dance at the thought that Pepper might've texted him a greeting.

He yanked the shirt over his head and then grabbed the phone. His heart leapt at the first message.

"Good morning. I hope you have a wonderful day with your kids. Can't wait to talk to you too."

His stomach twisted with the next.

"Something big has come up. I need to see you in the office before noon."

Kyle was a nice enough guy, but his penchant for spending every waking moment at his job had gotten old.

Tapping on the message box, Drew debated typing "I quit" in all caps. Then his and Pepper's payback scheme filtered into his brain.

"Will be there about ten thirty."

He reread her text, letting it chase away his frustration with her cousin. The workaholic would never know what hit him, and Drew hoped like hell he wouldn't have to follow through on the threat. As underhanded as Kyle had been setting up the "conference," he'd also been generous with the amount of time off Drew had needed for Kate's illness and flexible when he'd asked about working from home. Without Morton's manipulation, the chances of him giving Pepper more than a passing thought would've been slim at best.

Accepting the bad with the good was part of life.

The phone bleeped at him and vibrated against his palm.

"Excellent. See you then."

The girls stood at the oven door when he arrived in the kitchen. The timer ticked down to the last five seconds.

"We need to make a quick stop at the office on the way to the movie." At Kristin's sigh and Hannah's pout, he held up his index finger. "One minute is all. I promise. I just need to drop off a paper to my boss."

"We're going in with you." Straightening her spine, Kristin assumed her Hastings stance—chin up and feet planted. "If he tries to make you work, Hannah and I will start crying so he'll feel bad."

Hannah gave a vigorous nod.

"He isn't that bad, girls. But I suppose it won't hurt to have you go in and say hi." Drew winked at them and donned a pair of oven mitts. "Stand back. Let's see if breakfast is edible."

Forks clinked together as Hannah pulled them from the silverware drawer. "It *smells* yummy."

He agreed with her assessment, even if she sounded like she doubted its taste would live up to the smell. A waft of aromatic heat hit him in the face when he opened the oven door, and his mouth watered at the spicy-sweet scent. "Sure does."

Kristin set a stack of plates on the counter next to the stove as he placed the casserole on the stovetop. "Vanilla smells good too, but I'm not drinking it. You have to take us to get pancakes if it tastes bad."

Dishing up the first helping, he grinned at her. "Are you gonna be the guinea pig?"

"Nope. It was your idea. You have to try it."

With a shrug, he wiggled his fingers at Hannah. "Fork please."

She complied, and he cut off a steaming piece, allowing it to cool enough to save his taste buds. As the tender apple touched his tongue, a satisfied smile tried to spread across his face, but he chewed instead. After glancing back and forth from one daughter to the other, he finally swallowed.

"Is it good?" Hannah's eyes widened with every word.

"Sorry, girls." He shook his head. "It's way better than good."

"Daddy!" The chastisement came in stereo.

"Okay, okay. No teasing. Uncle Flynn would be impressed." Serving up two more platefuls, he handed them off. "Let's eat. I still have to print out the paper I'm dropping off, and we need to leave soon."

Their French toast disappeared in record time, giving him yet another reason to be glad he'd met Pepper. He wasn't anywhere near ready to admit it to his boss, though. The well-intentioned manipulator deserved to squirm a little while.

With the draft of his resignation letter in hand, Drew herded his daughters out the door and into the car a few minutes after ten. He took advantage of the fifteen-minute drive by practicing the lines he and Pepper had scripted for him.

He willed his muscles to relax as he parked outside the building he'd worked in for twelve and a half years. "Come on, girls. We don't want to be late for the movie."

Hannah met him at the sidewalk, her hand tucked in her older sister's. "We're ready to cry if we have to."

"I don't think you'll need to, but that's good to know." Grasping her free hand, he led them inside.

Kyle's secretary greeted them with a smile and continued clicking away at his keyboard. "Good morning, Mr. Fulton. Young ladies. You can go on in. Mr. Morton's expecting you."

Barely slowing, Drew nodded. "Thanks."

After a rap on the door, he entered.

"Morning, Drew." Kyle rose from the chair behind the desk and extended his hand. "You didn't tell me you were bringing the kids. Hi, girls. Did you have a good Christmas?"

Kristin ignored the offer of a handshake, as close as she'd ever come to showing her displeasure to anyone outside the family. "Yes, Mr. Morton. Thank you."

"It would've been better if Daddy wouldn't have had to go on that trip." Hannah tucked her hands behind her back and frowned.

Holding out the paper, Drew hoped to get down to business. "Would you mind proofreading this for me before you tell me why you needed to see me?"

Kyle grasped the letter and held it at arm's length. "I guess not."

The only sign that he might be bothered by its contents was his silence. Half a minute passed before he set it down in front of him and lowered himself into his chair.

Another thirty seconds ticked by.

"She said you weren't happy about the accommodations, but this? Are you sure?" Kyle's voice didn't waver as he spoke, but the man hid his emotions better than most.

Drew didn't have to ask who "she" was. Luckily, the girls didn't know.

Foregoing an outright answer, he raised his eyebrows.

He can interpret that any way he wants.

His boss slid a file to the edge of the desk. "You should take a look at what I had my lawyer draw up before you make this official."

Eyeing the folder, Drew hesitated picking it up. Curiosity almost got the better of him. Fortunately, Hannah tugged on his coat, reminding him he had more important things to do. "Okay, but I'll have to read it later. I have another appointment to get to."

With a wave, he led his daughters out through the reception area to the parking lot. The file drew his attention to the passenger seat several times, but he focused on the road and driving to the theater.

During the movie and a late lunch, he tried unsuccessfully to ban the contents from his thoughts. A trip to the grocery store didn't help, either. Anything to do with lawyers could only bring bad news.

CHAPTER THIRTEEN

THE DOORBELL CHIMED, BUT PEPPER IGNORED IT. SHE HAD SIX ORDERS to prepare, all of which were due for pickup in less than five minutes. Zack would handle the line of customers.

Tightening her grip on the scoop, she filled four single-serving containers with tabouli and then moved down the counter to the tofu antipasto.

"Need some help?" The familiar voice brought half a second of relief to go with her underlying annoyance.

At her cousin's question, she nodded. "You're early. Go wash your hands and put on an apron. We have tables that need cleaned out front. And make it snappy."

Not waiting for his response, she returned to her work.

Four black bean soups, three roasted veggie wraps, two spinach quiches. And a dozen whole-wheat cloverleaf rolls.

She bagged the orders, double-checking every item as she placed it in the sacks. "Kyle, put these over on the counter next to the register then grab the spray bottle on the bottom shelf and a clean towel. Those tables need cleaned five minutes ago."

Instead of spouting off to her, he followed her instructions to the letter. By the time she started on the last order, he stood behind the counter helping Zack with drinks and was far too subdued for her liking. His early arrival didn't surprise her, but he hadn't teased or provoked her once since he'd walked through the door.

She'd have to corner him later for an explanation.

By one thirty, the lunch rush ended, leaving a few stragglers to wander in the rest of the afternoon. They'd have time to refill the salads and make another batch of soup before supper.

As she strained the pot of vegetable stock, Kyle marched into the kitchen, stopping at the dishwasher. "Dining area is clean. Floors are swept and mopped. After I unload the dishes, I'll restock the salad case and check the restrooms."

His curt tone didn't fit his in-control personality, and his usual easy smile was nowhere to be found.

She set aside the pan. "Hey, everything okay? You seem a little out of sorts."

"No, everything isn't okay, but I can't say you didn't warn me." He added a bowl to the stack and huffed out a half sigh, half growl. "Drew came into the office this morning. Actually, I asked him to. Anyway, he handed me his resignation letter."

Her stomach dipped to her knees. "He *quit*?"

That hadn't been part of their plan.

"He might as well have. He wanted me to proof the letter for him." Turning to face her, Kyle leaned against the counter. "You know I was only trying to help two people I care about find each other, don't you? He gets along with everybody. I never thought for a second you guys wouldn't hit it off."

"Did you think of asking us if we were interested before you instigated your matchmaking scheme? Forcing a pair of strangers to share a cabin is bad enough, but you knew when we left there was a damn good possibility we'd get snowed in. How'd you like it if I did that to you? I'm sure I could find a woman interested in getting cozy with you."

He cringed. "Don't you dare."

"Then what made you think doing the same thing to me was okay?

And what business is it of yours whether or not Drew Fulton has a girlfriend?"

Dropping his chin to his chest, he rubbed his temples. "So maybe I should've just introduced you. I still think you'd make a great couple."

"An introduction—with mutual agreement to meet each other. You know damn well I'd never go out on a blind date, and I highly doubt Mr. Fulton would, either." She had no intention of commenting on his thoughts about hers and Drew's coupledom. What Kyle didn't know wouldn't allow him to stick his nose deeper into her private business.

His nod seemed to indicate his acquiescence. "You're right. I'm sorry. I fucked up."

"Wow! I better write this down. Mort the Great and Powerful admitted he was wrong." She scowled at him as she carried the pot to the sink.

"Only my methods. If you gave him half a chance, you'd like Drew. The guy deserves a special woman like you, and he'd treat you the way a guy should treat a woman."

The bait didn't appeal to her at all. One nibble, and she'd end up with Kyle trying to rule her love life. "Did you apologize to *him*? Or are you going to have to hire a new ad man for me?"

"I gave him the file from my lawyer."

Her heart skipped a beat, and she whipped around to face him. "Legal papers? You crotchety old miser, if you try to sue him for quitting, so help me I'll—"

"I'm not suing him." He held up both hands, as if he could fend her off her verbal attack. "I want to make him a partner. And, in case you've forgotten, you're only three years younger than me."

"A *partner*?" She almost strangled on the unexpected word. Her cousin was the poster child for control freaks. She'd only managed to keep him in line by being as stubborn as he was bossy.

"Yeah, a partner."

"But you don't let other people make decisions for you."

"I have a possible new business venture I want to keep a close eye on. To do that, I'll have to split my time between the business and the investment." His tight-lipped smile told her he wasn't yet used to the idea of forking over even partial control to Drew. "I've known him a long time. He's the only person I trust to keep me fully informed and not take advantage of me being gone more than half the time. Well, besides you, but you've got enough on your plate with the deli."

"What did he say? Is he taking you up on the offer? Because I bet that'll mean my stuff gets put on the back burner." Feigning vague disinterest wasn't easy. She and Drew hadn't figured on Kyle giving him a promotion in exchange for a fake resignation letter.

"I don't know." He crossed his arms in front of his chest, the first true sign of frustration he'd given. "I practically had to force him to take the paperwork. His kids were with him and he said he had another appointment, so we didn't talk about it."

The weasel left himself wide open for more badgering.

"*Kids*? And when were you planning to tell me he has children? Huh?" She dumped the vegetable waste into the compost bucket. "Or was that supposed to be a surprise too?"

At least Mort had the decency to blush. "Ah, hell."

"I guess that means you didn't think your plan all the way through this time. Must be one highly questionable investment for you to make that mistake." Plunking the pot in the sink, she gave what she hoped sounded like an angry snort. "Go clean the bathrooms before I decide to tell Fulton to quit so I can pay him under the table for the marketing package."

He opened his mouth like he might argue, but he evidently thought better of it. Lips pressed thin, he stalked out of the kitchen.

She had to give him credit for stepping into the role of low man on the totem pole without whining or trying for a hostile takeover. As helpful as he'd been to her over the years, he wasn't a follower.

Footsteps made her look over her shoulder at the doorway.

Zack chuckled as he stopped next to her. "I can't believe Uncle Kyle didn't realize you were feeding him a line of bull. You might want to have your boyfriend sign the partnership agreement before the truth comes out. I have a feeling somebody isn't going to be too pleased with either one of you beating him at his own game."

"Yeah, well, I wasn't terribly pleased with him setting us up the way he did. He can hardly complain about payback when he instigated the whole thing." Draining the leeks she'd set aside to soak, she lowered her voice. "Besides, he's getting his way in the end, so he should be his usual smug self."

"You really like this guy a lot, don't you?"

"Yeah, I do." She hoped her son couldn't tell that her stomach had filled with a horde of butterflies from thinking about Drew.

"I want to meet him when he picks you up on Saturday. To let him know I'm looking out for you."

"Don't you think it's kind of soon to meet him? I mean, it's just our first date." It also put a more serious tone on their relationship, not that it wasn't significant already.

He grunted. "You spent four days alone in a cabin with him. I kind of doubt the term 'first date' applies. If you're going out with him, you guys are way past handholding and a goodnight kiss. Not much to do during a power outage. That's why there's usually a lot of babies born nine months after weather emergencies."

Heat crept up the back of her neck to her ears. "Don't you have customers?"

"Nope. Last one left a minute ago." His smirk reminded her of Kyle's gleeful expression when he knew he'd won.

"Then go do a quick inventory for the bakery order. I have soup to make. Oh, and change the sign to leek and potato." Hefting the strainer filled with rinsed leeks, she mentally crossed her fingers he didn't push the subject any further.

"I still want to meet him." Zack marched out of the kitchen with a cocky grin before she had a chance to deny him outright.

She'd have to convince Drew to meet her at the restaurant if she wanted to escape the awkward meet and greet. Things were moving a little fast for comfort.

Annoyed that she'd let herself fall victim to the typical obsessive dating behavior, she hauled out a cutting board and knife to quarter potatoes. Running fifteen pounds of reds through the slicer would take the edge off her short temper and force her to focus on keeping all her fingers instead keeping her cousin and son out of her love life.

With the soup simmering, she finished the rest of the supper prep, avoiding the counter area and another discussion about the new man in her life. About the time she encouraged Drew and Zack to get to know each other, something would probably happen to end it all. She didn't want to jinx the budding relationship.

After another busy meal shift and cleanup, she checked the locks and waved to Kyle as he set off toward the parking lot. Luckily, her earlier reprimand seemed to have shut him up about Drew. She switched off the lights and then headed upstairs to her apartment.

Zack was close on her heels. "Sorry about earlier. I'm trying to protect you. That's all."

She turned to face him when she reached the top step, putting them almost eye to eye. "I know. And I appreciate it."

"So you'll make sure I get to meet him?"

"Nope. Not this time anyway." He opened his mouth, but she shook her head before he could speak. "Soon. Give us a chance to decide how serious we are about each other. No pressure. No rushing into anything."

His shoulders slumped. "Okay. But he better be good to you. I can find out where he lives."

"He's very good to me. I would've kicked him out into the blizzard if he wasn't."

He grinned. "Yeah, that's true."

Giving him a quick hug, she changed the subject while she had the chance. "Are you still going out for New Year's Eve?"

"Clay and I are gonna hang out with Trent at his house and watch movies. Maybe play video games. Eat pizza. I'm thinking we should stay all night. Safer not to drive. Too many crazies."

"Good plan." Relief at his forethought and responsible behavior eased the tension in her spine. She'd never stop worrying about him, no matter how grown up he was. "You'll let me know if you change your mind?"

He nodded. "I'll be at Uncle Kyle's by nine to help with dinner."

"Sounds good. Have fun tonight." Leaning in, she kissed him on the cheek. Then she took a backward step toward her apartment, anxious for a hot shower before Drew's call. "Happy New Year, Zack. Love you."

"I love you too, Mom. Happy New Year." He walked toward his door as she unlocked hers.

After sending him a smile and a wave, she ducked inside. A glance at the clock on her nightstand told her she had plenty of time to kill. More than likely, Kristin and Hannah would want to stay up until midnight, meaning she had at least four hours to wait.

She stripped off her clothes on the way to the bathroom, determined not to become one of those pathetic women who sat by the phone, wasting her free time. She'd lived without a man for almost two decades. Entertaining herself wasn't a problem. He'd call when he called, and she'd shower, finish unpacking, and throw together a late supper.

As she set her cell phone on the vanity, it buzzed against her fingertips, shifting her pulse into overdrive. The screen lit up to reveal a text message.

"I forgot tonight's New Year's Eve. Girls want to stay up until midnight. Maybe I can convince them to celebrate midnight in Greenland? Miss you."

She couldn't hold in a laugh at his ingenious idea, even though she had no delusions it would work. The last two words warmed her heart, but she got straight to the point. *"Lots to talk about when you can call. Read the papers in the file if you have time."* After tapping Send, she surrendered to the urge to type in another message. *"I miss you too."*

A few seconds later, the phone vibrated again. *"Okay. XO :)"*

She shivered at the strange tickle in her belly. What she wouldn't give to have his arms wrapped around her as he kissed her. After a smiley-face reply, she added condoms to the grocery list on her phone.

Saturday night couldn't arrive soon enough.

ADJUSTING THE COVERS OVER HIS YOUNGER DAUGHTER, DREW LEANED down to kiss her forehead. "Happy New Year, Hannah."

She'd lasted longer than her sister, but neither had been able to keep her eyes open to see twelve o'clock. Poor Kristin had given up the fight at eleven thirty, burrowing into her makeshift bed on the floor and falling asleep a good ten minutes before Hannah.

He switched off the lamp as he stood. Fortunately, his girls enjoyed camping out together in the family room, still sharing a strong bond he hoped never faded.

With a check of the locks, he headed for the stairs and thumbed in Pepper's number. He was more than ready to hear her voice.

"Hi. I guess they didn't make it to midnight, huh?" An obvious smile colored her soft greeting, triggering a rush of pleasure in his chest.

"No, but they gave it decent shot. Maybe next year." He entered his bedroom, letting the door click closed behind him. "I didn't wake you, did I?"

"Nope. I was reading."

"A new cookbook? Or a book, like fiction or a biography?" As little as he knew about her, he wouldn't allow this opportunity to slip through his hands.

She was silent for a few seconds. "Promise you won't laugh?"

"Of course not. I'd never laugh at you."

What could she read that would make her think he'd find it amusing? *Lady Chatterley's Lover*? *Pride and Prejudice*?

He had nothing against her having a hidden romantic side.

"Okay, if you promise. It's called *A Little Appetizer*." Clearing her throat, she seemed to hesitate. "A barbecue chef calls the owner of a construction company when he dials the wrong number, and they...*talk* on the phone a few times before they meet. Sort of like what we did last night."

Only one thing came to mind about last night's call, and it involved more than talking. "You mean they talk dirty to each other? And, well...you know."

Too many wicked thoughts filled his brain. No wonder his outspoken Pepper was uninhibited. She liked to read erotic stories.

Her giggle made him smile through the heat flaming his neck.

"Lots dirtier than we did, but, yeah. That's where I got the idea. You're blushing, aren't you?"

He didn't need to look in the dresser mirror to answer her question. "Aren't you? Or do you read about strangers having phone sex all the time?"

"A girl going solo has to have something to inspire her." Her blunt response shouldn't have surprised him. She'd been alone half her life, and she had a habit of saying exactly what she meant. "They're not all like this one, although it *is* my favorite. Maybe we can read it together sometime. I have some with light bondage too."

Every muscle below his belt reacted to her revelation. No experience didn't necessarily equal no interest.

"Damn, I can't wait to see you on Saturday." He was tempted to bring along a couple silk scarves to tie her to him forever. *So much for going slow.*

"I'm thinking we might have to have dessert before dinner. You know, to take the edge off."

He stretched out on the bed, wishing once again that she was there with him. "Yeah. Sleeping alone was hell last night, not that sex was all I missed."

Her voice softened. "I know. Me too. Waiting's a lot harder than I thought it would be."

"Waiting isn't the only thing that's hard."

"We need to change the subject or anticipation is going to lose the battle to satisfaction. I'd rather get it in person."

"You're right." Spying the file on his dresser, he took advantage of the chance to change the subject. "What's in the file? The girls wanted to play board games, so I haven't had a chance to look at it."

She was quiet for several seconds. "Are you sitting down? 'Cause it's a doozy."

Her warning made him narrow his eyes at the folder of papers his boss had given him. "Yeah, I'm sitting."

"First, I should probably tell Mort's really worried you're going to quit, so our little payback plan went off without a hitch. The kicker? He was planning to ask you to become a partner."

Sure he'd misheard, Drew sat up. "A partner? A *partner*?"

Of all the scenarios he'd imagined, being offered a stake in the company wasn't one of them. He rolled off the bed to retrieve the file, taking his phone with him.

"Yeah, a partner." Only Pepper's voice kept him from believing he was having some kind of weird dream. "He has a new investment he must think is going to need a lot of hands-on attention."

Drew dropped to the end of the bed, scanning the legal contract but not comprehending it. Kyle Morton wasn't a man who joked about business, and his proposition made an already complicated situation even more convoluted. With every day, the chances of them becoming related by marriage grew exponentially.

Marriage? I can't say that word out loud or I'll scare the daylights out of her.

Life wasn't simple, and neither were the decisions he had to make.

A flicker of light from his phone made one point clear. "Happy New Year, Pepper. You are, without a doubt, the best thing that happened to me last year, and I owe you a hell of a kiss Saturday night."

CHAPTER FOURTEEN

DREW CHECKED THE DASHBOARD CLOCK AS HE WAITED FOR THE stoplight to turn green. He wasn't exactly nervous about his date with Pepper, but they hadn't spent any time together surrounded by other people. The world had consisted only of her and him at the cabin. Would he even be able to keep his hands off her long enough to eat dinner?

They also had to discuss Kyle's offer. No matter what she thought about how fast things were moving, Drew could easily imagine falling in love with her and getting married. Hell, he was already at least halfway there. She deserved some say in whether or not he took the promotion if he was considering asking her to be his wife.

Flipping on his turn signal, he took a calming breath. Her apartment above the Red Hot Pepper deli was a block ahead. The drive had taken less than fifteen minutes, meaning he was early. He didn't care. Seeing her was his only wish at the moment.

He turned into the parking lot and followed it around to the back of the building to the outside stairway she'd mentioned. As he pulled his keys from the ignition, the door at the top of the stairs opened and a young guy scuttled down the steps.

Pepper's son?

The determined set of his jaw became more obvious with every step toward the parking lot.

Grabbing the bouquet from the passenger seat, Drew climbed out and braced himself for what would likely be an inquisition.

"Mr. Fulton?"

Drew nodded, offering what he hoped was a casual smile. "Yeah."

"I'm Zack McCann. Good to meet you, sir." He stopped an arm's length away and stuck out his hand.

Drew accepted the kid's polite welcome, glad not to have been greeted with a fist or a gun. "Nice to meet you, Zack. I guess you want to know what my intentions are."

"Nah. Uncle Kyle wouldn't try to fix my mom up with a jerk. All I ask is that you don't accidentally get her pregnant, because I won't let you off the hook, even if she does."

Taken aback by the boy's directness, Drew took a full five seconds to gather his thoughts for a response. "I'd never do that to her, but she's lucky to have you looking out for her. Is she ready? I'm a few minutes early."

"Yeah, I think so. Go on up. You'll need to ring the bell to let her know you're here." Zack gave him a quick smile before turning toward the only other car in the lot. "Have her home by midnight."

"Not a problem. I turn back into a dad at nine thirty."

A quick stop and pivot brought Zack back around to face him. His expression was unreadable. "You have kids?"

Pepper clearly hadn't shared many details with her son.

"Yeah. Two girls. Ten and six."

"How long have you been divorced?" Zack's stance widened and he crossed his arms in front of his chest, undoubtedly daring Drew to say the wrong thing. He made a fairly intimidating protector.

"Widowed a little over a year ago."

"Does my mom know?"

"Yeah, about both." Pressing the lock button, Drew pocketed his car keys. "Look, I—"

"Zackary McCann, don't you have someplace to be?"

At the sound of Pepper's voice, Zack winced. "I'm going, Mom."

She stood at the top of the stairway, her fiery hair glowing under the security light. The color suited her personality—passionate and short-tempered—and she'd apparently warned her son not to interfere with her date.

The car door clunked closed and the engine turned over before she finally looked in Drew's direction. As Zack backed out of the parking spot, she crooked her finger at him. "Want to come inside?"

"Yeah." The car finally rounded the corner of the building, and Drew took the stairs two at a time. Gathering her in his arms, he touched his lips to hers, fighting the need to truly kiss her until they had a bit more privacy. "Damn, I've missed you."

"My apartment. Now." Clasping his hand, she dragged him into a hallway with a single door on each side. A few seconds later, she led him through a living room and into what had to be her bedroom. "How fast can you get naked?"

A jolt of anticipation zipped from his brain to his balls, stealing his voice. He handed her the bunch of daisies and then toed off his shoes as he shed his coat. Working buttons and zippers, he stripped off the rest of his clothes.

With her nose buried in the bouquet, she laughed, the sound warming his heart. "That was pretty fast. I love daisies. Thank you."

"I'm glad you like them. I wasn't sure what to get." He hooked his hand around her waist and pulled her closer for the kiss he'd been dying to give her outside. Her wool coat was rough against his erection. "You're wearing too many clothes. Want me to help you get undressed?"

"Sure." She gave him a sly smile. Setting her flowers on the dresser, she released the overlapped edges of the front of her coat. Bare skin peeked out from the opening.

"Not so many clothes after all." He eased the covering off her shoulders, determined not to behave like a man with only one thing on his mind. "Weren't you cold outside?"

"I've been thinking about you all day. Being cold wasn't a problem." She wiggled, sending the sleeves sliding down her arms and baring her beautiful breasts to him. "I might even have a fever."

Unable to resist touching her, he slipped his thumbs into the waist-band of her loose-fitting sweatpants and pushed them past her hips. They puddled around her ankles. "No panties, either. I guess that means you want me to take your temperature."

Her giggle made him even harder. "You should probably use your meat thermometer."

"Damn right." He fished the condom out of his wallet. By the time he put it on, she'd stretched out on the bed. Eyeing her perky nipples, he climbed over her. "I think I'll start up here."

She gasped when he sucked a puckered tip into his mouth.

After a couple circuits around the taut flesh, he switched to the left one, lavishing it with the attention he'd wanted to give it the last four days. Her body called to him to move on, to enjoy every inch of her while he had the chance.

He crawled lower, kissing her ribs as he drifted toward her belly button. "Breasts are perfectly done. Tender and sweet. Better check those thighs."

Tangling her fingers in his hair, she gave a gentle tug. "Come up here and kiss me. And take my temperature already."

"Just a little taste? I've been going crazy without you." The earthy scent of her arousal urged him lower. He nuzzled her inner thigh and then dipped in for a sample. "Mm, delicious. You taste as good as you smell."

She squirmed against him. "Damn it, Drew. Stop teasing!"

Finally giving in to her request, he nibbled his way up her body again. He pushed inside her as he settled his lips on hers. His control almost slipped at the intense pleasure of connecting with her. "I missed you so much."

She groaned into his mouth and her body pulsed around him. "I missed you too."

Their moans blended, a welcome song to his ears.

The slow glide in and out did nothing to temper his need to claim her. He could try to live one moment at a time, but he'd still have to go home alone later. No matter how reckless it seemed, he was half a step from falling madly in love with her. The only thing holding him back was the fear and panic he'd likely cause by admitting his feelings to her.

Focusing on his rhythm, he vowed to enjoy the few hours they'd have together and not worry about tomorrow, next week, or next month. He'd found the woman he wanted to cherish for the rest of his life. Nothing would change that.

She hooked her ankles at his lower back, making him sink deeper.

He shifted to bury his nose against her neck. "You feel amazing."

"Mm. Yeah. Ditto." Her fingers dug into his shoulders. "I wouldn't complain if we stayed here and ordered pizza instead of going out."

As tempting as her suggestion was, he had no intention of letting their budding relationship turn into a series of sexual liaisons. "Sounds great, but that's not much of a date. I want to take my girlfriend some-place nice. Treat her right."

"You're taking me someplace fantastic right now." She rocked her hips upward, and he tensed his abdominals to ward off an accidental explosion. "But if you insist, we can go out to eat."

Her lack of response to his girlfriend reference assured him he hadn't misspoken. She certainly would've corrected him if he'd crossed a line. "Ready for a visit to the moon?"

"With you, always."

Thrilled with her response, he trailed a line of kisses along her jaw to her soft lips. He'd gladly accompany her wherever she wanted to go.

He licked the seam of her mouth, and she opened for him as they moved together. Her hips rose to meet his increasingly erratic thrusts, not quite keeping time with the mingling of their tongues. Every sound she made vibrated through him, magnifying the pressure building inside him.

Her pleasure was his pleasure. They were connected on a truly inti-mate level, his desire to bond with her going far beyond sex. He wanted to give her his heart. It already belonged to her.

She arched and cried out as her body gripped and pulsed around him, and he followed without hesitation. The release sent him soaring, but he refused to break their kiss to voice his physical satisfaction. That small freedom would allow him to say the three words he doubted she was ready to hear. Showing her the depth of his emotions wouldn't scare her off. Any hint of pressure to reciprocate probably would.

Time waited for no man, but he wouldn't rush her. New love was fragile, and he wouldn't risk hurting her—or endangering his second chance at happiness.

NOT READY TO LET DREW WITHDRAW FROM HER, PEPPER TIGHTENED her shaky legs around his waist to hold him in place. Even an inch of space between them would be too much.

She'd expected the urgent need to have sex with him, but the wish to go home with him and stay forever, not so much. In all her thirty-seven years, she'd never fallen in love.

Until now.

The prospect was more shocking than frightening.

Ending the soul-sharing kiss, she finally pulled in an unsteady breath and blinked up at him. His lips bowed into a sweet and sexy half smile that shone in his eyes. Her stomach did a little flip at the tangible affection in his gaze.

He skimmed a finger along her cheek, setting off a delicious shiver. His stare was soothing rather than uncomfortable. When he didn't speak, she tried and failed to suppress her own smile. She didn't have to hear the words he didn't say. They were written in his expression, and he was thoughtful enough to give her the opportunity to lead their relationship.

She told her son she loved him every single day, but could she hand over her heart and soul to this man?

A bit of contemplation and consideration seemed like a wise course of action.

Rubbing her palms along Drew's back and shoulders, she lifted her head from the pillow to gently kiss him. "Much better than phone sex."

"Mm-hm." He leaned his forehead against hers as he cupped her jaw. "I missed seeing your face and touching you."

His tenderness made her love bloom brighter. "Me too."

"I want to stay inside you, but I should get rid of the condom."
Easing back, he shifted his comforting weight off her. His slow discon-
nection tempted her to pull him back for more.

Her stomach rumbled, saving her from blurting out the thought
circling her brain. "Bathroom's through that door. We should probably
get dressed and go eat."

He nodded as he moved to the edge of the bed. "Do you want to go
first?"

"Not sure I can stand up yet. Go ahead." She rolled to her side, too
sated to do anything other than watch him retrieve his pants from the
floor and walk to the bathroom.

The shifting of his muscles drew her gaze to his strong shoulders
and then to his magnificent butt. He was as physically attractive as he
was kind and intelligent. She hadn't stood a snowball's chance in hell
of resisting him.

With the sound of running water, she forced herself up from the
bed. By the time he returned for his shirt and shoes, she'd donned dress
pants and a sweater. Their actions seemed almost marital, feeding the
emotions running laps in her mind. Thankfully, it wasn't an uncomfortable feeling.

She slipped on her shoes and reached for the bouquet he'd given
her. "As soon as I put these in water, I'll be ready to go."

He picked up their coats from the floor and then followed her
toward the kitchen. His arm closed around her waist from behind as
she stopped at the sink. "The daisies reminded me of you. Not flashy or
fancy, but beautiful and full of life all the same. And they smell nice."

Her chest tightened at the utter happiness his words brought, and
she focused on arranging the flowers in the vase so she wouldn't have
to try to speak. He'd probably worry that he'd said something wrong if
she choked back the tears blurring her vision. Her heart was every bit
as full as it'd been when she'd given birth to her son.

The arrangement done, she turned in his hold to kiss him. "Thank
you."

A whisper was all she could manage, but he didn't seem to notice.
"You're welcome. Ready to go?"

She nodded, accepting his help with her coat.

He clasped her hand in his, only letting go long enough for her to lock the apartment and exterior doors. After playing the perfect gentleman at his car, he didn't release her hand again until they arrived at the restaurant.

She'd found someone truly worthy of her love and trust, but could she take the leap of faith?

"You're awfully quiet." He gave her fingers a gentle squeeze as they trailed after the hostess to their table. "Everything okay?"

Her nerves calmed a little at his concerned tone. "Everything's great. Just trying to remember how to act on a date."

His low laugh stirred up her belly again. "Not sure I can help with that. How about we pretend it's our anniversary instead of a first date? Less pressure."

"Maybe for you. The closest I've had to an anniversary is my birthday and Zack's." She let out a shaky breath as they stopped at the table.

"We should fix that." Leaning closer, he pressed a soft kiss to her lips. "Happy anniversary, Pepper."

Warmth spread all the way to her toes.

"It's your anniversary?" The hostess set down the menus and clapped. "Congratulations! How long have you been together?"

Drew draped his arm around Pepper's shoulders. "Six days."

"Newlyweds! That's so romantic!" Opening a menu, the girl tapped at a section near the bottom of the page. "Dessert's on the house. Just let your server know which one you want to share."

Pepper suppressed a giggle as the hostess left them to settle into their seats. Bending to scratch her un-itchy ankle, she lowered her voice to a whisper. "She thinks we're married. Are you crazy?"

"Yeah, about you." He scooted his chair closer to hers. "You really shouldn't blame me for her assumption. Besides, we're not on our first date anymore. I'm much more relaxed now. How about you?"

The giggle finally escaped. "And I thought you were uptight. Yeah, I'm okay now."

"Good."

The silence didn't bother her as they studied their menus. It wasn't the awkward don't-know-what-to-talk-about quiet of a first date. Being with him and the occasional brush of his fingers against the back of her hand brought a sense of peace and contentment. Considering he was the first guy she'd developed a romantic interest in for almost two decades, did she dare think about a future with him?

"I read through the offer from Kyle." Closing his menu, Drew placed it on the end of the table. "He wants me to spend fifteen to twenty hours a week in the office."

She tried to read his expression, but he seemed to have mixed feelings about becoming Mort's partner. "Have you talked to your girls about it? I mean, they're used to you being home most of the time, aren't they?"

"I wanted your opinion before I bring it up with Kristin and Hannah." He unrolled the napkin around his silverware partway and then rolled it back. "Not to rush into anything, but I think there's a pretty good chance that we could be together for a while. You deserve some say in the decision too."

Her insides somersaulted, and she could only stare at him. Sharing important decisions was a whole new experience.

His lips thinned as he frowned. "I'm sorry. I'm going too fast."

"No, it's not that." She swallowed to wet her suddenly dry throat. He'd given her the perfect opportunity to reassure him he wasn't alone on the rollercoaster. "In fact, I can see myself with you for a long time. I'm not sure I can say the words yet, but what I'm feeling is pretty serious stuff."

A shadow fell over them, most likely the waiter. She'd probably heard enough of their conversation to know they weren't married.

"Drew. Pepper."

She jerked her head around at the familiar voice, and her heart dove to her feet.

The cocky smirk on her cousin's face told her he'd overheard their exchange. He waved as he continued past their table. "Good to see you both. I hope you enjoy your evening."

CHAPTER FIFTEEN

"DADDY, I CAN'T FIND MY NEW BOOTS!" HANNAH TUGGED ON DREW'S sleeve as he zipped his computer bag closed.

"Did you check downstairs by the garage door?" Scanning the top of the desk to be sure he hadn't forgotten anything, he grasped the case by its handles.

She raced out of the bedroom, her footsteps rumbling like distant thunder as she hurried down the steps in front of him. Taking the turn toward the kitchen, she slipped on the hardwood floor, making him wince at the possibility of a wipeout. He didn't have time for a trip to the pediatrician's office or the emergency room for stitches.

Somehow, she managed to skate out of the turn and speed down the hall to the kitchen. With a last-second grab for the wall, she skidded to a stop. "I found them!"

"Lunches are packed, Daddy." Kristin pursed her lips and shook her head. "Slow down, Hannah. You're going to give Daddy an ulcer. Your backpack is ready."

Boots on and fastened, Hannah pulled her hat and scarf from the hook. Wisps of brown hair stuck out every which way as she tugged the knitted band down to her eyebrows. "What's an ulcer?"

Curious to hear how his older daughter would explain, he closed his mouth and bit the inside of his cheek to keep a straight face.

"It's a bad stomachache from worrying too much." Kristin glanced toward him as she put on her coat. "Are you ready, Daddy? You shouldn't be late for your meeting with Mr. Morton, no matter how much he makes you work when you're supposed to be on vacation."

"Just need to put on my coat. Thanks for handling lunches today." Grabbing at Hannah's jacket, he helped her locate the sleeve she couldn't seem to find. The distraction made pretending he hadn't heard the complaint easier. "I'll be home in time for the school bus this afternoon."

Kristin handed off his lunchbox and gave him a quick hug before she opened the door into the garage. "I love you, Daddy. Drive safely."

"Love you, Daddy!" Her coat still unzipped, Hannah rushed out behind her sister. "Bye!"

He tapped the button to open the garage door. "I love you too. Have a good day."

The bus slowed to a stop by the mailbox as they jogged through the new dusting of snow on the driveway. He set his bag on the passenger seat and started the car while they boarded, waiting until the school bus began to move before shifting into reverse.

A year ago, he'd driven his girls to school every day, too afraid of losing them to let them be carefree kids. The fear had diminished, even if it hadn't disappeared.

Shaking off the reminder, he drove toward town. Kyle probably wouldn't let him off the hook without an "I told you so," but at least a brainstorming session with Pepper was on his agenda for nine o'clock. Seeing her would make up for his boss being smug as hell.

The light snow barely affected the flow of traffic, getting him to work ahead of schedule. He waved at the receptionist as he walked past her. Thankfully, she was on the phone and couldn't immediately announce his arrival. A little downtime in his office would prepare him for the upcoming meeting.

"'Morning, Drew. Did you enjoy your weekend?"

Tension grabbed him by the neck at Kyle's greeting from behind. Had his boss been watching out the window for him?

Drew continued into his office instead of turning around. "Yeah, I did. I don't suppose you brought me a cup of coffee?"

Kyle pushed the door shut behind them and then placed a steaming mug on the desk. "Black. No sugar. I owe you an apology for last week."

Drew raised his eyebrows at the admission. Not bothering with the effort to guess at his boss's motive, he set down his computer and shed his coat.

Sitting in the visitor's chair, Kyle gave nothing away in his expression. "I'm sorry for putting you and Pepper at risk."

"And?"

Amusement played in the other man's hint of a smile. "My methods might've left a little to be desired, but I'm not sorry for my actions or my reasons. I *was* right about the two of you after all."

The "I told you so."

Drew picked up the mug as he sat behind his desk. "Did you apologize to Pepper?"

"Yes. Did you have a good discussion with her about whether or not to accept my offer?"

"You know, I still have a copy of that resignation letter. Gloating isn't exactly aiding your cause." Drew counted down the seconds to the inevitable comeback while he sipped the coffee.

"I'm not gloating." Kyle leaned back and propped his ankle on his opposite knee. "Well, maybe a little. Mostly, I'm really glad to see both of you doing more than surviving from one day to the next. You were so wrapped up in each other last night, the damn building could've burned down around you without you ever realizing it. That's the kind of relationship you both deserve."

The relaxed position didn't fool Drew. His boss was always on. "Since when are you a romantic?"

"I'm not. Are you ready to sign the contract?"

The abrupt change of subject probably would've given most people whiplash, but Drew was used to Kyle's management style—control freak on mega steroids and massive amounts of caffeine. The guy steered conversations with the precision of a well-oiled machine.

The cup warmed Drew's chilled fingers. "Kristin and Hannah think I'll end up putting in way more than twenty hours a week here if I take the promotion. Actually, that's a concern of mine too."

"You're welcome to divide up the hours whatever way works best for you. Four hours, five days a week. Three hours on Monday, six on Wednesday, five and a half on Thursday and Friday. I don't care. My only stipulation is a minimum of three days a week unless we make prior arrangements. I need to know you're willing to oversee half the client load for at least two months."

"And if one of the girls gets sick? Kate's family has been great about babysitting in a crunch, but I'd rather not make them feel like I'm taking advantage."

Sitting up, Kyle steepled his fingers. "I'm a businessman, not an ogre. Have I ever refused you time off when you asked?"

His boss had him there. "No."

"I trust you to do your job. You're a professional. What are Pepper's objections?"

Since the jig was up, Drew saw no reason to beat around the bush. "She doesn't like the secrecy of this new investment, but she thinks becoming a partner is a good opportunity for me."

"She'll support whatever decision you make then?"

"Yeah. We're in agreement that I should finish her project before the partnership would take effect. A few of my accounts are due for review in the next few weeks too. I'd like to have those out of the way."

"I can arrange that. How does February first sound? You'll have four weeks to complete the Red Hot Pepper campaign and make the necessary tweaks on the other accounts." For all his hard-ass attitude and shrewdness, Kyle Morton was always fair. He withdrew his phone from inside his suit coat and tapped on the screen several times. "It's on my calendar."

Drew pulled the contract file out of his computer bag. "Okay. Let's get this done."

"You sound like you have doubts about this being the right decision."

He picked up the closest pen and flipped to the signature page. "If it was just me, I'd jump at the opportunity. But it isn't."

Kyle popped out of the chair and slid the sheaf of papers toward him. After he scribbled a few lines in the empty space at the bottom of the page, he shoved it back. "Fifteen hours."

"You're joking." Considering Morton's reputation for ruthless negotiating, Drew never would've expected that quick a concession. In fact, he'd fully intended to sign the contract without any changes.

"You know damn well I don't joke about business." Kyle's tone seemed to signal he'd misplaced his usual unflappable mood. He stuffed his hands in his suit pants pockets and flexed his jaw. "Look, you're the one person in the company I trust to handle the job. I need to be able to focus on this project. No distractions, no interruptions."

He'd practically handed Drew the weapon and the ammunition to make whatever demands he wanted. His trust evidently extended beyond the business aspect of their association.

Pen in hand, Drew initialed the handwritten addendum and signed on the line below his boss's scrawled signature. "Okay."

Kyle offered his hand. "I promise you won't regret it. I'll have my assistant make copies and give you one before you leave."

The firm grip assured Drew that the minor lapse in complete control was gone. "Thanks."

As he walked toward the door, Morton tossed a grin over his shoulder. "Tell Pepper I expect enough notice to buy a new tux for the wedding since I'll be giving her away."

Shaking his head, Drew relegated the request to his list of things to forget. Kyle was welcome to piss off his cousin with his arrogance all by himself.

Fifty minutes later, he parked behind the deli, anticipation almost convincing him to text Pepper to meet him upstairs. Unfortunately, as much as he longed to spend every second of the next hour making love to her, they needed to stick to business today.

She poked her head out the door as he rounded the front corner of the building. "We have company."

Shoving off the disappointment, he wrapped his arms around her and pulled her close enough for a slow kiss. "Mm, I missed holding you last night. Zack playing chaperone?"

"He says he's interested in our business discussion. You know, real-world experience for his marketing major. Mm, you feel nice."

"Excuse to spy on us or not, he could benefit from participating in the process. Besides, it'll keep us focused on getting your campaign done." He stepped back and slid his fingers through hers. Her strength soothed the little part of him that still doubted his earlier decision. "The partnership takes effect the first of February."

"Mort didn't pressure you to sign, did he?" Her frown suggested retribution if her cousin had forced the decision.

"Nope. Let's go inside before you freeze." He squeezed her hand a little tighter as she led him into the dining area. "I think he's afraid of messing things up between us. He cut the office time to fifteen hours without me even asking."

She spun to face him, her eyes wide. "You're kidding! He never does anything without a financial benefit in mind. Well, almost never."

"Hey, Mr. Fulton. How's it going?" Zack popped up from behind the counter, where he'd probably watched them making out at the doorway.

Aiming for the largest table in the dining area, Drew waved with his free hand. "Hi, Zack. It's been an excellent day so far. Want to sit in on the meeting? I have some ideas to run past your mom and wouldn't mind a second opinion."

"Sure. Can I get you something to drink?"

"I'm fine. Thanks." Drew held Pepper's chair for her before sitting down next to her. "I'm still a little wired from meeting with Kyle this morning."

Zack snorted a laugh as he set a cup of tea in front of Pepper. "Yeah, he does that to most people. The nature of the beast."

"Apt description. What areas of marketing are you interested in?"

"Consumer behavior. The psychology aspect. What factors make people choose one product over another? Is it the actual product? The way the product is marketed? Advertising strategies? Branding?" The glint in Zack's eyes suggested his choice of a college major was a good one. "What kind of ideas do you have for the Red Hot Pepper?"

Drew pulled the file from his bag and slid his standard questionnaire across the table. "This is what I start with when I have a new client. And you can call me Drew if you want to."

"Okay." Zack studied the form for a full minute before he pulled a pen from his apron pocket. "Mind if I make some notes on here?"

"Not at all."

Pleased to have something in common with Pepper's son, Drew dug into the nuts and bolts of how he created a marketing plan based on the needs on the business owner. Between nods and questions, Zack covered every empty space on the paper with blockish writing and arrows.

An hour later, Pepper pushed her chair back and stretched. "Okay, guys, I know you're having fun talking shop, but I have a restaurant to open in half an hour. Drew, you want to take some lunch with you?"

Trying not to stare at her delicious curves, he gathered his sketches and notes. "That'd be great. What do you have that'll go with the peanut butter sandwich and apple Kristin packed for me?"

Her eyes lit up with her smile, sending his heart hammering. "How about some soup? We have vegetarian chili, butternut squash, and leek and potato today. Oh, not the chili. It has peppers."

"You remembered. Let's go with the leek and potato." He stowed the files and his laptop in his bag while he gathered his courage. "Are you and Zack free for supper tomorrow night? Maybe six o'clock? The girls have been asking about meeting you and, well, I think it's time."

Zack adjusted his apron as he stood. "I think so too. Pizza?"

"Sure."

"Tomorrow night works for me. Are you brave enough to risk a public meltdown or do you want us to come to your house?"

"Zachary!" Pepper swatted at her son. "Go to the kitchen."

His laughter echoed through the dining room as he followed her order.

Drew waited until Zack disappeared to add his own chuckle. "He's right, you know. Hannah has no issues making a public scene when she thinks it's called for, and I have no idea how Kristin will react. She's been really moody the last couple days. Nice one minute and grouchy the next."

"Your house, it is." She glanced toward the counter and then bounced from her chair to his lap. Her wild hair tickled his ear. "We can pretend to clean up and have a tryst in your kitchen. By the way, you look very sexy in a suit."

"You look very sexy in everything. And nothing." He wrapped his arms around her waist to stop her from grinding her ass against his cock. "The kitchen is right next to the family room. I'll have to give you a personal tour of the house instead. Even a fairy princess movie wouldn't be enough of a distraction for two nosy girls. And Zack might have an issue with what I want to do with you."

"Maybe we can have a quick business meeting in your office after supper." Her lips grazed his neck, sparking a tremor from his balls to his abs. "Call me tonight."

As much as he enjoyed their phone sex adventures, they weren't enough. He craved long nights of making love to her and lazy mornings of waking up beside her. "Why did I keep my hands to myself those first two nights?"

"Because you're a good guy and we wouldn't be where we are now if you'd broken your promise."

She was right, of course. He'd also needed to realize that he was ready to move on with his life—with her. They hadn't wasted the time they had together, but patience was a virtue he could do without.

He buried his face in her hair for a fix to last him until tomorrow. "I'll call you after Kristin and Hannah go to bed."

"Geez, you guys!" Zack's voice carried from somewhere behind the counter. "People eat in there!"

Considering how much worse the admonition could've been, Drew could only laugh. "At least he didn't tell us to get a room. I might've taken him up on that suggestion."

She giggled against his shoulder. "He probably thought about it, but figured it wouldn't be in his best interest."

"I should go. You have a restaurant to open and I need to get busy reviewing accounts."

"Mm-hm." After a petal-soft kiss to his earlobe, she eased out of his arms and stood. "I'll get your soup."

As much as he would've preferred watching the sexy sway of her hips, he finished packing his portfolio and computer bag. Their relationship was about more than sexual attraction, and a little anticipation would make them appreciate their alone time even more.

Anticipation? She was smart, sassy, and the opposite of almost everything he'd ever expected to want in a woman, and making love to her was an experience like no other. Anticipation equaled frustration, with no outlet for the urgency and passion. Sharing his bed with her every night for the rest of his life might take the sharpest edge off, but the desire would never fade. She brought out a hunger in him that he hadn't known existed before they'd gotten snowed in.

"Here you go." Pepper set a brown paper bag and a paper cup on the table. "Your soup and some crackers. I thought you might want something warm to drink too. Decaf."

"Thanks." Raising the strap of his bag to his shoulder, he leaned in for one last kiss.

She rose on her tiptoes to meet him. "You're welcome. Talk to you later."

"Lo—, um, later."

The corners of her mouth curved upward, a good indication she'd noticed the casual declaration he'd barely caught as it tried to slip out. How had he fallen for her so fast and so far, and why did the words seem so easy?

He shrugged on his coat. "I should go."

She was silent as she walked with him to the entrance, but the knowing smile never left her face.

Cool air swirled around him when he opened the door and stepped onto the sidewalk. "I'll call you later."

"Can't wa—" Her gaze seemed to shift to something behind him and her smile lost its exuberance. "We're not open yet."

He turned, coming face to face with a dark-haired man about his height. Wire-framed glasses highlighted bright blue eyes. A click sounded, and Drew didn't have to ask why Pepper had locked the door behind him. She had a damn good reason.

Zack's father.

CHAPTER SIXTEEN

PEPPER HAD TO MAKE HER LEGS CARRY HER TO THE KITCHEN, BUT THE burning sensation in the pit of her stomach urged her to find a broom and channel her inner bitch. How dare that low-life, no-class pile of shit show up in her life again after nineteen years?

She grabbed a cucumber from the stack next to the cutting board and lopped off the stem end.

Zack caught it a second before it would've hit him in the chest. "Trouble in paradise already?"

"No." With controlled precision, she chopped her victim into dozens of uniform wedges.

He took a step back. "Then what happened? You're obviously pissed about something."

The thwack of the knife through a second cuke brought little satisfaction and no relief from her anger. "Kevin Pierce was at the door when Drew left."

Zack froze with his arm poised to toss the projectile in the compost bucket. "What did *he* want?"

"I don't know. I told him we weren't open and locked the door." She set the knife on the cutting board and plucked a seed from the smallest chunk of cuke.

"Good." Working his jaw, he crossed his arms in front of his chest. "I have nothing to say to him. He treated you like dirt and didn't take responsibility for his actions. I might have half of his DNA, but he isn't and never will be anything other than a sperm donor. He sure as hell isn't my father."

"It's okay if you're curious, you know."

"Stop trying to be understanding, especially when you're subconsciously hacking his penis to bits."

"Believe me, this isn't subconscious." At his laugh, she winked at him. "Every time I deseed one of these suckers, I imagine neutering him."

"Remind me not to get on your bad side." He kissed her cheek and leaned against the counter beside her. "Seriously, though, what are you going to do if he comes in?"

Thank the powers that be for making him wait until now. "Bite my tongue, fill his order, and send him on his way. Sure, he was a jerk, but he gave me you. More importantly, what are *you* going to do? I doubt he's here to see me."

The color drained from his face. "I...I don't know. I didn't think about that."

She returned to prepping the ingredients for the four-quart order of Thai cucumber salad due for pickup at four o'clock. "You might want to."

His frown deepened and he stalked toward the delivery entrance. "The only thing I want to know is what motivated him to show up now. Does he really think I'm interested in any of his excuses?"

The pile on the cutting board grew as he paced several laps of the kitchen. She added her victims to the soy sauce dressing and red pepper mixture then wiped her hands on her apron.

He stopped in the doorway to the dining room, likely giving him a clear view of the sidewalk. "Will you get mad if I talk to him?"

"No. You're an adult. It's your decision." The words were harder to say than when she'd practiced them, no matter how much she trusted his judgment. "Your relationship with him, or lack of one, has nothing to do with us."

He tapped the watch on his wrist. "It's almost time to open."

"Okay." After a final stir, she snapped the lid on the tub. "Would you mind putting this in the cooler? Oh, and I love you. I always have and always will."

"Love you too, Mom." He placed his hands on his hips as he turned toward her. "No sneaking to the door first. I don't want him anywhere near you without me, Mort, or Drew there."

There goes that plan. "So you like Drew?"

"Yeah. He seems like a nice guy, even if you two are doing things I don't want to think about." He hefted the plastic container and carried it to the far end of the room. His raised voice echoed out of the walk-in cooler. "Uncle Kyle trusts him, and that says a lot."

"I trust him too." *We wouldn't be doing those things if I didn't.*

"Good thing since you're probably going to marry him." His head popped out from behind the steel door, amusement gleaming in his eyes.

Maybe. She pulled a clean towel from the shelf closest to the door-way, stretching for an unobstructed view at the entrance.

Pierce still faced the glass, but another man stood on the sidewalk, his back to the deli. He tucked a folded newspaper beneath his arm and then turned up the collar of his black overcoat. When Pierce took a step toward the door, the other man moved to block him, revealing a familiar silhouette.

What are you doing here, Mort?

"What are you looking at?"

She jumped at Zack's voice behind her. "Somebody else is waiting outside."

"Who?"

"Kyle."

"Well, this should be interesting." He slung his arm around her shoulders. "Let's see if we can get one of them out of here before the lunch rush and a brawl."

How about both of them? Kyle hadn't harassed her about her date with Drew yet, but he probably wouldn't let this opportunity pass him by. With any luck, he'd leave without figuring out who his blue-eyed companion was as well.

She gave Zack a one-armed hug. "Say the word, and Kevin Pierce is gone. He has no control over us."

His nod was nowhere near decisive. "Let's go."

The walk to the front entrance seemed shorter than usual, and Kyle's scowl as she unlocked the door spoke loud and clear about his opinion of the man behind him.

Zack stepped in front of her as Kyle entered. "What are you doing here so early? You're scheduled to work one to five today."

His eyebrows dipped into a sharp vee above his nose. "I got a call from Drew about forty minutes ago. He said he wanted my opinion on something here at the deli."

"But he left forty minutes ago."

Kyle cast a glance over his shoulder as he sauntered toward the order station. "Actually, he left about ten minutes ago. Right after I got here."

He knows. They both know. Relief and anxiety doused the tiny spark of annoyance.

Zack poured a cup of coffee and set it on the counter. "I can't believe I'm saying this, but thanks for butting in, Uncle Kyle."

The resulting grin was full of self-satisfied arrogance. "Your mom could learn a little something from you. What are you going to do about the worthless bastard who came in behind me?"

Pierce's lips flattened into a grim line. The lines around his mouth and eyes deepened. "I'm here to talk to my son."

Kyle took a leisurely sip of coffee. "Really? I don't recall anyone admitting to being Zack's father."

"Knock it off, you two." Pepper stepped between them, keeping one eye on the door for customers. "This is a testosterone-free zone and I have a restaurant to run. What do you want, Kevin?"

The bulging vein on his forehead barely stood out among the wrinkles. He looked past her, presumably at the young man with his hair and eyes. "Can we have a private conversation outside?"

"No." Zack's voice was firm and clear, revealing none of the indecision he'd shown in the kitchen. "In the dining room or not at all."

That's my boy.

Kevin shoved his fists in his coat pockets and gave a curt nod. "Fine."

"You have five minutes. I'm working."

With his cheeks almost as red as the cashmere scarf around his neck, Kevin followed Zack to the farthest corner from the entrance. Their differences—height, build, posture, gait—stood out far more than their similarities as they walked to the table. Her son might have resembled his father nineteen years ago, but time hadn't been kind to the male half of Zack's chromosomal pool.

Ain't karma a bitch.

Coffee mug in hand, Kyle turned toward dining room.

She unlocked the register, without looking up. "Stop right there, Mortie. This is something Zack needs to do on his own."

A low growl rumbled in his throat, but he didn't move.

"By the way, thanks." Leaving him to guess the reason for her gratitude, she walked to the breaker box to turn on the open sign. As she switched the breaker, her phone vibrated in her apron pocket. A quick look at the screen sent her pulse racing.

"Please don't be mad at me for calling Kyle. I know he can be a pain in the ass, but he also won't let anything happen to you and Zack. Everything okay? That guy is Zack's father, isn't he?"

"Not mad. Yes. Grateful that you're perceptive. Zack can handle himself and Mort's playing watchdog." She tapped the Send button and then thumbed the keypad again. *"Thank you."*

"You're welcome. I can arrange for Colleen to pick up the girls at school and be there by 3:00 if you need me." A red heart popped up after his message.

"I don't think he's dangerous, but if he starts acting weird, I'll call the police. And Kyle's here until 5. I promise to let you know how things go."

"Okay. I'll try not to worry too much."

At the kitchen doorway, she bit her bottom lip to hide a giddy smile. Falling in love with Drew would be so easy if she let herself.

Who am I kidding? She may not have said the words, but the feelings were there every time she saw or thought of him.

Familiar laughter echoed through the dining area, except it was devoid of its usual humor. "You should've admitted the truth when you had the chance, Mr. Pierce."

The fury in her son's statement warned her that their visitor had made a tactical error of epic proportions.

She stepped through the kitchen doorway as a chair screeched across the tile floor.

Kevin stood and raised both palms toward Zack, like he expected an attack. "This isn't just about proving you're my son. I can make it worth your while."

"Yeah? How?" With his arms crossed in front of his chest, Zack straightened, making him at least two inches taller than the man who'd fathered him.

"If I can prove you're my son, you'll be entitled to a third of the Pierce estate. About four million dollars. Enough for you and your mom to live comfortably for a long time. All you have to do is let the executor take a swab sample for the DNA test."

"And what do you get out of it? The other two-thirds?"

The back of Kevin's coat stretched tighter across his shoulders as he raised his chin. "When my mother dies, yes. I'm the only Pierce heir. Besides you, of course."

"And how much do you get if I don't agree to the paternity test?"

"It doesn't matter. I'll get a court order if you refuse."

"Consider your request refused then. I have no problem going to jail for contempt if a judge is crooked enough to issue an order like that." Zack gestured toward the exit, his resolute tone making Pepper proud. "I'm not interested in your money. And since you just showed me all I need to know about you, there's no point in you coming back for father-son time, either."

Kevin tugged on his gloves and then glared in her direction as he slithered to the door. "This isn't over, not by a long shot."

As the door swung closed, Kyle tossed a notepad and a pen on the table closest to him and pointed to a chair. "Zack, sit. Write down everything he said and your responses. Pepper, I want to see you in the kitchen for a minute."

"I haven't been twelve for a long time, Uncle Mort. If you have something to say, just say it." Zack dropped into the seat and drummed the pen against the paper.

"Okay. I'm calling my lawyer about restraining order. I don't trust that greedy bastard."

"What else?"

"What makes you think there's something else?" Kyle slipped off his coat and hung it over his arm, a motion much too casual for the conversation.

"Because you never do anything halfway. You're probably planning to hire bodyguards or a security team. I wouldn't be surprised if you already have a private detective tailing Pierce so you can dig up every piece of dirt on him and find out all his secrets."

"Bodyguards *and* a security team. They have different responsibilities. The security team has been outside for the last five minutes and I've had a PI compiling a file on Pierce since Drew called me. He thought he recognized the guy from high school, so I already had a name."

Pepper buried her face in her hands and groaned. How had her simple life gotten so damned complicated?

"You okay, Mom?"

Before she could answer, a group of her regulars tramped in from the sidewalk, stomping snow from their boots. "Yep. Let's get to work."

The steady stream of customers that followed left few idle moments to think about anything but soups, sandwiches, and salads. Zack seemed quieter than usual, hardly unexpected after meeting his father for the first time and finding out he could be the recipient of more money than most people earned in their entire lives.

Kyle, however, clearly relished the challenge of pitting his intellectual and strategic skills against Pierce and his influential name. The occasional glint in Mortie's eyes and hint of a sly sneer could only mean a major confrontation was in the making—or so he probably hoped.

At ten minutes after five, he walked past her at the counter with a spray bottle and a clean towel, looking like he had no plans to leave at his scheduled time. Halfway through cleaning the first table, he pulled his phone from his pants pocket. "Morton."

She continued refilling the cranberry tabouli, not sure if she should be annoyed or grateful that he'd decided to stay late.

"Interesting. What's the net worth?" He nodded. "Offer seventy-five cents on the dollar from the Prizm account. If he makes a counteroffer, drop to seventy."

The barely suppressed glee in his voice almost made her feel sorry for his latest rival. His business sense may have rubbed off on her son to a degree, but thankfully his ruthlessness hadn't.

"Why the frown?" He slid his phone back in his pocket as he strode toward the window. "Is that bastard outside again?"

"Language, Mort." Snapping the lid on the nearly empty tub, she shook her head. "Not that I know of. Just wondering who you're bankrupting this week."

"Negotiating with. He needs money. I'm willing to buy interest in the company to protect it from a hostile takeover. We both benefit."

"A hostile takeover, huh? Yours, no doubt."

"I try to conduct business in a civilized manner. When that doesn't work, I might be willing to force the issue, depending on the situation."

The situation. She lowered her voice. "This *negotiation* has to do with Kevin Pierce, doesn't it?"

Moving on to the next table, he gave her a patronizing smile. "I'm not at liberty to say until the deal is finalized."

"You can be so damn pretentious sometimes. Just admit it. Instead of letting Zack deal with this greedy idiot, you decided to take matters into your own hands, by way of retaliation for his visit today." A snicker behind her warned she hadn't been quiet enough.

Zack draped his arm around her shoulder and kissed her cheek.

"Actually, he asked me if it was okay. It's partly my money, so he thought I should have a say."

"*Your* money? Where'd you get the kind of money you need to buy a company?" Her instincts were probably right, but confirmation would give her a legitimate reason to chew out her cousin for interfering—again.

Zack walked to the coffee maker. With his back to her, he removed the used filter. "Uncle Kyle started an account for me when I was three, in case I needed the money for college. He's been investing the money and made a killing right before the bottom dropped out of the market. Then we switched to a more conservative approach."

"We? How long have you known about this account?"

"Pep—"

"I didn't ask you, Mortie." She tucked the bucket of salad under her arm to stop herself from heaving it at her cousin, although he deserved a good smack in the head for the enormity of this secret.

"Don't be mad, Mom." With fresh grounds in the new filter, Zack slid the basket into place.

"How long?"

"Since I was ten." He faced her, but he didn't meet her gaze. "He let me help with the investment portfolio. We wanted to surprise you."

"Oh, I'm surprised all right. In fact, if you tell me it's worth as much as your share of the Pierce estate, I may just ground you for the rest of your life."

A snicker came from Kyle. "Looks like you're in big trouble, kid."

Her stomach dropped to her knees.

"As of the first of the year, the balance is about a hundred dollars shy of four million." Zack poured a cup of decaf and added his usual hefty serving of skim milk.

She steadied herself against the counter. "*Four million?* Just how much did you start with?"

Kyle moved to the next table. "A hundred thousand. He's got a real knack for picking investments."

"A hun—"

"College is expensive."

"Yes, but… Where in the world did you get that much money? You were barely out of grad school when Zack was three."

He scrubbed at a spot harder than seemed necessary. "Nothing illegal, if that's what you're implying."

His lack of a direct answer made the hairs on her neck stand on end. "Where did the money come from?"

"It's not important."

Zack gave a sharp hiss. "She's using her mom voice, Uncle Kyle. You better tell her the truth."

"Am I the only one who doesn't know?" She crossed her arms in front of her chest.

As her cousin pulled out the nearest chair, he gestured to the one next to it. "Come sit down."

She shuffled to the seat, her heart in her throat. "I'm not gonna like this, am I?"

"No, but I did what I thought was best for you and Zack at the time. Besides, your mom and dad deserved the payback for the way they treated you."

The lump in her throat dropped to her stomach. "I don't want their money. And I don't want my son to have it, either."

"They gave it to me as a graduation present. It was my money to do with as I pleased. I used half to start my business and put the other half in an account for you and Zack. If you don't want to touch the original principle, fine, but the rest is yours to keep."

She sat back in the chair, too stunned to argue. "Well, now I know why you offered to have your accountant do my taxes all these years. You sneaky twerp."

Instead of his usual smug pride at the insult, he kissed the top of her head as he stood. "You two are the most important people in my life. It's my way of saying thanks."

CHAPTER SEVENTEEN

"THEY'RE HERE, DADDY!" HANNAH'S THUNDERING FOOTSTEPS carried down the hall to the kitchen. She skidded to a stop a few inches from the breakfast bar and snitched a carrot from the plate in front of her. "She's so beautiful! Do you think she'll like us? How come the boy is so tall? Is his daddy tall like Uncle Flynn?"

With his stomach doing backflips, Drew set the handful of paper plates on the bar and hoped the evening went off without a hitch. "Be the polite and nice girls I know you are, and she'll like you fine. Zack doesn't have a good relationship with his father, so it's probably best not to talk about that. Did you put away your crayons and coloring books?"

"Yep. Let's go answer the door." She glanced toward the family room as she grabbed his hand. "Come on, Kristin."

His older daughter looked up from her math book and scrunched up her nose. "I'm doing my homework. Do I *have* to?"

Not willing to create another scene over Pepper, he ignored her disagreeable tone and her obvious attempt to draw him into an argument. "You don't have to come to the door, but finish up the problem you're working on and take your books upstairs. They'll only be here for a couple hours. You can do the rest before bedtime."

She rolled her eyes. "Fine."

And so it begins. Pretending he hadn't seen her disrespectful action seemed like the sensible thing to do, at least for now. More than likely, she hoped to be sent to her room, which wouldn't exactly be a punishment under the circumstances. *Sometimes you have to lose the battle to win the war.*

The doorbell rang as Hannah dragged him toward the front door. "Hurry, Daddy!"

Glad for some enthusiasm from one of his daughters, he jogged beside her down the hallway. He reached for the doorknob with his free hand. "Ready?"

A wide smile lit up her face, easing the disappointment of Kristin's rotten attitude. "Ready!"

As he opened the door, she squeezed around his leg, making his intent to greet Pepper with a kiss impossible.

"You must be Hannah." Pepper handed his younger daughter a plain white bakery box. "I brought dessert. Will you carry it for me?"

Hannah nodded. "What kind of dessert? I like cake and pie and cookies. Oh, and candy and chocolate, but Daddy says I don't need any more sugar 'cause I'm already sweet enough."

With her finger to her lips, Pepper giggled. "It's a secret until after supper. Your daddy's right. You are sweet."

"Can I call you Pepper? Daddy said that's your name, but I usually have to call grownups miss or missus. I like Pepper better than Miss McCann. It's a good fairy name."

"Well, Pepper it is then. I'm more of a sprite, though. I sometimes get into trouble because I have a quick temper."

"I get in trouble because I talk too much. Right, Daddy? Hi, Zackary. You're tall." Cradling the box in her arms, Hannah whirled around and scurried toward the kitchen.

Drew waved his guests inside. "Hannah the hurricane. She has two speeds—supersonic and recharging."

The sparkle in Pepper's eyes suggested she'd been much the same as a child. She rose to her tiptoes and pressed her cool lips against his. "She's adorable. Hello."

"Hi there."

Zack chuckled and slipped off his jacket. "Good luck sneaking away for some privacy."

Without releasing his light hold on Pepper, Drew grinned at her son. "We're counting on you to help, Zack. Pizza'll be here in about five minutes."

"Bribery, huh? You drive a hard bargain." After a quick handshake, Zack took his mom's coat and hung it over his jacket on the hook on the wall. "You're not going to make me dress up like a fairy princess, are you? Because I draw the line at wearing wings. I'm more of a cape man."

Kristin shuffled into the hall, a scowl on her face and her arms loaded down with books. Without a glance toward the front door, she stomped up the stairs. "Everybody knows capes are for losers."

When she disappeared into her room at the top of the steps, Zack let out a low whistle. "Wow. I guess she isn't thrilled about having visitors."

"Sorry about that." Drew guided his guests to the kitchen, angry enough to ground his daughter for a month but too aware of how little impact the punishment would really have. Should he make excuses about how difficult the holidays had been on her and how disappointed she'd been that his job had cut into their family time? Thinking that he planned to replace her mom was probably the last straw.

This is as much my fault as hers.

Pepper slipped her fingers through his and gave them a light squeeze. "Don't beat yourself up over it."

"She's never rude to people. If anything, she's always been the easy kid."

Her belly laugh didn't bode well. "First of all, she doesn't want to be a kid anymore. Second, speaking as a female, girls are never easy. They just lull you into thinking they are for a while. Third, I'm cutting into her time with you. She probably also thinks of herself as the woman of the household, and I'm threatening to take over her job. Give her some time."

"How'd you get to know so much about raising girls?" He rubbed his thumb along her chin, loving the softness of her skin against his fingertips.

"Well, I *am* a girl." Her mischievous smirk made his balls tighten.

"Yeah, I know." He wasn't likely to ever forget, either.

A tug on his sweater reminded him they weren't alone. "Are you going to kiss her, Daddy? 'Cause then you have to get married."

The hopeful look that accompanied her question hit a little too close to the part of his heart wanting to do exactly what she'd suggested. He fished his wallet out of his back pocket instead. "I think it's a bit more complicated than that, squirt. Why don't you go see if the pizza's here yet?"

Zack chuckled as Hannah charged down the hallway. "Nice save. I give you guys no more than a month before she demands an engagement."

"It's here!" She raced back to the kitchen. "Do you have a girl-friend, Zack? I really like weddings. And babies. There's always cake at weddings and baby showers."

A patch of color rose along his neck as fast as his hands popped up. "Don't look at me. No girlfriend, and definitely no babies yet. If I want cake, I'll make one or go to the store and buy one."

"Will you share it with me if I promise not to bother you about getting married or having babies again?"

Zack's hoot of laughter echoed through the kitchen. "Wheeling and dealing. She's a miniature Uncle Kyle. I have new respect for you, Drew."

"Somebody finally understands." Drew handed him enough cash to cover the pizza, delivery, and a respectable tip. "The first piece of pizza is yours. Hannah, will you run upstairs to see what's holding up your sister?"

His daughter sprinted past Zack before he took his first step toward the hallway. Then the rumble of her footsteps on the stairs was accompanied by a yell. "Kristin!"

Pepper hooked her arms around Drew's neck, pressing her breasts to his chest and putting her mouth even with his. "Alone at last."

Grateful for the few seconds of privacy, he greeted her with the kind of kiss he'd wanted to give her at the front door—slow glides of his tongue against hers as he held her close. The simple scents of her soap and shampoo surrounded him, reminding him of their last night in the cabin together, lying skin to skin with her while they made love. He ached to wake beside her almost as much as he wanted to bury himself inside her.

An angry shout shattered the mood. "I told you to leave me alone! Now get out of my room and stay out!"

A door slammed and a screech bellowed down the stairway. "I hate you! You're mean!"

"Good! Go away!"

The unmistakable prelude to a major bout of crying started with the usual, if infrequent, wail. It was followed by a shriek and then noisy sobbing. Hannah didn't cry often, but she did it the same way she did everything—with every ounce of energy in her compact body.

Drew rested his forehead against Pepper's. "Damn. Why did they have to pick tonight to do this? I just wanted a nice quiet supper where the girls could get to know you."

Her breath tickled his cheek as she spoke. "It's okay. Kristin's obviously not ready for you to be seeing someone. Things have been moving kind of fast. Maybe we need to slow down."

Her words sent a jolt of panic through him, and he jerked upright, grasping her shoulders to prevent her from leaving him. "Like hell we do. Life's too short and unpredictable. I'd do damn near anything for my kids, but I'm not giving you up because one of them decided to throw a fit."

She hid her face in his shirt. "Life *is* short and things don't always as planned, but that doesn't mean we have to get where we're going as fast as we can. You should be upstairs right now. Are you sure *you're* ready to be seeing someone?"

Her insinuation made his stomach cramp. After the time they'd spent together and the discussions they'd had about their pasts, how could she ask that question?

He released her and paced to the refrigerator, her sudden lack of confidence in him slicing him to the quick. A single remedy came to mind.

Mustering his courage and making a conscious effort to keep his voice low, he faced her. "Sisters argue, and I learned the hard way to stay out of it unless it gets nasty. I love you, Pepper. I don't know how or why it happened so fast, but it did. If you don't feel the same, you need to tell me now, because I thought we were on the same page."

She blinked at him several times with an unreadable expression. A noisy exhale followed as Zack entered the kitchen carrying a stack of pizza boxes.

"Looks like I was right about the meltdown." He set down their supper and glanced first at Drew and then presumably at his mom. "Uh-oh. How about if I take the top two and some napkins upstairs? Maybe they just need to eat."

After taking the smaller boxes from the stack, he grabbed a handful of napkins from the table and returned the way he came.

Say something, Pepper. Anything.

No, not anything. Say what I want to hear.

Another minute passed.

Unable to stand the silence anymore, he turned his back to her and rested his hands on the counter. "I guess this is it. Take what you want of the pizza. I don't think I can eat."

"Drew—"

"All your graphics are ready. I'll finish the marketing plan over the weekend and send it to Kyle on Mon—"

"Drew, I—"

"—day. Your contract outlines how—"

"Damn it, Drew." Her voice broke over his name, sharpening the pain in his gut. "Listen to me. Please."

What excuse would she give for shredding his heart and soul?

He lowered his head, too tired to argue. A pair of sock-clad feet entered his peripheral vision and he squeezed his eyes shut to block them—and her—from his mind. Those pretty little feet had tangled with his legs while he and Pepper had kept each other warm at night.

They'd shared blankets and body heat and secrets. Why didn't she leave so he could try to forget her?

A whisper came from beside him. "I love you too. I haven't said those words to anyone but Zack and Kyle for a long, long time. The problem is I know your girls have to come first in your life right now and one of them doesn't want me to be part of it. I won't make you choose."

Frustration welled up inside him, driving out some of the elation from her admission that she loved him. He reached around her, trapping her between him and the counter. The unreadable look on her face was gone, replaced by concern. He'd seen enough of that during Kate's illness to recognize it a mile away.

Sympathy wasn't what he needed. "I'm still not giving you up because Kristin's decided to be a pain in the butt. She doesn't even know you."

"She could make things very difficult for you. I know from experience that kids can get really creative when their parents aren't paying enough attention to them or they think they aren't getting the attention they deserve. This is more about her than it is me."

"Yeah, well, if she expects me to ever allow her to date, she's going to have to accept me dating you." As childish as it sounded, he wouldn't take the statement back. "I'm almost forty years old, widowed, and lucky enough to have found love a second time in my life. She should be happy for me. What happened to the kid who handed me a gumball-machine ring and a piece of paper with a woman's phone number a week ago?"

"Tween hormones? Second thoughts?" The softness in Pepper's tone suggested she might be weakening on her sacrificial stance. "I know what it's like to have your parents side with someone else."

"This isn't even close to the same thing, so stop trying to be noble. Your parents willingly ended their relationship with you." *Believe me, I know how that feels.*

Her fist connected with his bicep, but her effort lacked the vigor of her quick temper. "Quit being logical. I just want to make sure you and Kristin don't lose the special bond you have."

"No. Logic works well for me, especially when I'm dealing with my daughters." He gently raised her chin until she met his gaze. "I love you. We have a special bond too."

The tip of her tongue snuck out to wet her lips, tempting him to distract her with another kiss. "What if she doesn't—"

"No what-ifs. She'll get used to the idea."

"I guess I have to take your word for it."

"Yep."

She slid her arms around him and laid her head over his heart. "Fighting is exhausting. Can we eat now?"

Thrilled for the physical contact, he treasured the effortless peace of holding Pepper. "We weren't fighting. We were discussing how our relationship should progress in light of my child's hissy fit. Considering the amount of yelling and crying upstairs, I think we handled it pretty well. No one needs to apologize for saying something stupid and we found out our feelings are mutual. It's definitely time for pizza."

"Discussion, huh? Do you want to go up and get the girls while I pour drinks? Or would you rather let angry children lie?"

That she could joke about his older daughter's obnoxious behavior made him love her even more.

He savored a few more seconds of contact, grateful to have survived his family's disastrous first impression on the new woman in his life. "Drinks would be great. There's milk, juice, water, and tea. Kettle's on the stove. Tea bags to the left of the sink. I'll send Hannah down with Zack so I can have a talk with Kristin. Milk for Hannah and Kristin. Water for me."

"You run a tight ship for somebody who talks like he's barely staying afloat."

Lifting her onto the counter, he stepped between her thighs and gave her a quick but possessive kiss. "Must be the pirate in me."

Her sexy grin hit him straight in the groin. "You can shiver my timbers anytime."

"Hey, guys, keep it rated G." Zack's scolding made Drew's pulse jump. "Hannah's waiting on the steps. She stopped crying, but she says she only eats in her room when she's sick and, even though she loves pepperoni, she needs a cup of milk because it's spicy. Oh, and her sister is a poopy head."

Helping Pepper down from the counter, Drew thanked his lucky stars he didn't have to juggle two disgruntled daughters tonight. "I owe you, Zack."

"You bought the pizza, so we'll call it even." Zack opened the largest box and transferred three slices to a plate.

With two-thirds of his crises under control, Drew headed upstairs to troubleshoot the last third. He paused at the top of the steps, where Hannah sat with the pizza box on her lap. "All better?"

Although her eyes were red-rimmed and her cheeks were pinker than normal, she gave a decisive nod. "I like Zackary. He's nice. He doesn't have any brothers or sisters to argue with."

"I like him too." He ruffled the top of her head and ignored the growl from his stomach. "Do you want help carrying your supper down to the table?"

"Nope, I can do it. Besides, you need to go find out why Kristin is so grumpy." The box in her right hand and her left on the banister, she trotted downstairs.

A fortifying breath did little to prepare him for the confrontation he faced. Almost everything about his older daughter had come from her mother—her height, her build, her hair, her stubbornness. The Hastings women wore their obstinate streak with pride, and Kristin had inherited it in spades.

He rapped on the bedroom door three times, waited a beat, and rapped twice more. When she didn't answer, he turned the knob.

She didn't even glance up from the book in front of her as he entered. A single crust of pizza remained in the box on the desk. She'd managed to circumvent the possibility of him insisting she join everyone else for supper.

The battle or the war?

He swiveled the chair toward him and crouched in front of her so she had no choice but to look at him. "Pepper and Zack are guests in our home, and I expected you to be polite, the way you were taught. You need to apologize to them for being rude and disrespectful. Now."

Her eyes narrowed and her frown deepened. "And if I don't?"

Unaccustomed to this level of defiance, he counted backward from ten. At zero, he started again. What the hell had gotten into his calm child?

He stood, hating the ultimatum he had to give her. "Then you stay home and help me with laundry on Saturday instead of going ice skating with Aunt Merie."

She grabbed the edge of the desk and whirled away from him. "That's not fair! It was a Christmas present!"

I'm doing the right thing. "Apologize or no skating."

CHAPTER EIGHTEEN

SCRAPING ANOTHER BUNCH OF CHOPPED CELERY OFF THE CUTTING board and into the soup pot, Pepper stole a glance at the front counter. The guy with the matching hard hat and reflective vest was back for his two-fifteen coffee-and-sandwich break—for the third day in a row. She could've informed Mortie the disguise didn't fool her for a second, but as long as his watchdog and Kevin Pierce's minion—Mr. fake-Bronx-accent—ordered and didn't bother her other customers, she'd feed them without complaint. Road-crew Bob's adversary sat at his usual table with a bowl of soup and the business section, no doubt.

Wiping her hands on a clean towel, she walked to the doorway behind the counter for a peek into the dining area. *These guys are so obvious.*

She tried for her best nonchalant smile as she approached her newly returned part-timer. "Are you doing okay, Ona? Do you need a break?"

"I'm fine, thanks. It feels great to be back to work." Ona adjusted the tie of her apron and turned toward the next customer. "Good after-noon, sir. Can I help you?"

Pepper's phone buzzed against her hip, sending her stomach to her knees. If Drew had to cancel their plans, she might cry. They'd done nothing but play phone tag and send intermittent text messages since their failed family pizza night. Kristin's under-duress apology hadn't been the least bit sincere and she'd refused to participate in any attempt at conversation.

If looks could kill…

She retreated to the kitchen to answer the call. "Give me the bad news first."

"All good news. Date night is a go." The relief in Drew's voice signaled a man near the end of his rope who'd gotten an unexpected reprieve. "Merie invited Kristin to spend the night so they can head to the skating rink early. Maybe she can figure out what's going on. This attitude has to be about more than just us getting serious. God, if it's boys, I'm moving her to an all-girls school. Oh, and Colleen asked Hannah to sleep over so she wouldn't feel left out. They'll both be gone by four thirty."

"You mean—"

"Yep. We have the whole night, and I don't plan on sleeping."

A shiver raced over her skin. "My place or yours?"

"Mine. Then we can make all the noise we want, and I've been dying to hear you scream."

Two can play at that game. With a last look toward the counter, she sashayed to the walk-in cooler. "What kind of noises will you make when I suck your—"

"Hey, I'm already hard. No need to make it worse." His chuckle sounded more pained than amused. "I've missed you so damn much."

"I've missed you too." She hefted a bag of carrots with one hand and carried them to the sink. "Zack and Ona are closing today. I can be there by four forty-five."

"Good. We can have a little appetizer to take the edge off before we make supper. We're having spaghetti, by the way. I thought we could make the sauce together."

A giggle escaped before she could stop it. "Is that supposed to be some sort of euphemism? Or are we really making spaghetti sauce from scratch?"

His contagious laughter triggered a flutter in her lower belly. "You have a dirty mind, woman. A beautiful, sexy, dirty mind."

"Yours is right there in the gutter with mine, mister."

"We're going to cook together. In the kitchen. Um, with food." He groaned into her ear. "See what you started?"

Pleased with how easily she could arouse him, she lowered her voice. "I like cooking with you. In the kitchen. With food."

"Damn, I better get back to work. The girls'll be home from school in about an hour."

"See you soon."

"I can't wait. I love you."

A sensation that could only be joy spread through her entire body. "I love you too."

She pocketed her phone and returned to prepping vegetables for tomorrow's lentil soup, her mood lighter than it had been in days. Drew didn't seem too stressed about Kristin, and they could both probably stand a break from each other—not that Pepper fully understood the dynamics of a normal parent-child relationship. Her childhood had been the total opposite of what she tried to give Zack.

When she finished chopping carrots and onions, Pepper grabbed the cleaning supplies and headed to the dining area. The spy and his shadow had surely moved on by now, continuing their game of cat and mouse.

The newspaper lay scattered across Bronx guy's table, unlike the previous two days. On top of the mess, neat red letters stood out on a partially completed crossword puzzle. Going across, the word "document" was outlined, as was "sign" going down along the left side. The hair on the back of her neck stood on end and several more words caught her attention.

Wise. Decision.

Accident. Flood. Retaliation.

She slammed her fist on the table. "You slimy weasel."

"Who's a slimy weasel?" The sharp edge on Zack's question made her wish she'd kept her mouth shut.

Pasting on a smile, she turned to greet her son. "When did you get here?"

"Just now. Quit trying to change the subject. Who's the slimy weasel?" His gaze shifted from her toward the awkwardly folded section of newspaper. "What's this?"

"Definitive proof that Kevin Pierce is a moron. Go get ready for your shift. I'll call Mort so he can send in his security dude to check it out."

He leaned closer, clearly seeing the same not-so-subtle message. "You need to have Drew pick you up if he isn't already planning on it. I don't want you going anywhere alone."

"You're enjoying this cloak-and-dagger crap almost as much as Mort, aren't you? I suppose you're also going to cancel gaming night with the guys. Well, forget it. Pierce isn't so stupid that he'd hurt me." She tapped in her cousin's number.

"Probably not, but he wouldn't think twice about doing something to the deli. We're moving gaming night here, where I can keep an eye on things, just in case. We can hang out down here so we won't bother you while you're sleeping."

"Morton here." Kyle's curt greeting saved her from having to explain why they were welcome to make as much noise as they wanted in Zack's apartment.

She made a just-a-minute gesture to her son. "Daddy dearest's henchman left behind some incriminating evidence this afternoon. Tell one of your associates to come take a look."

"Enough for a restraining order?"

"Maybe."

"I'm on my way over. A woman wearing black boots and a purple ski jacket should be walking in the door right now. She'll know what to do."

The glass door swung open, admitting a gust of cool air. An innocuous-looking blonde matching his description entered the deli behind it. If ever the kind of no-strings female her cousin would go for existed, she was probably it—not that Pepper had ever seen him with a woman.

"You're scary, Mort."

"Keeps my adversaries in line. I'll be there in five minutes." The line went dead without a good-bye.

The purple ski bunny sashayed to the table, her leggy gait sending her hips swaying back and forth. She pushed her sunglasses to the top of head. "Ms. McCann, I believe you have something to show me."

Pepper pointed at the newspaper. "This was left by a customer who came in a few minutes after two. He's been coming in every day about the same time since Kevin Pierce was here to talk to Zack."

"The suit with the bad haircut." Her short inspection ended with a disgusted snort. "Stinking amateur. I bet he even paid with a credit card."

"I can check the receipts." Not waiting for a yay or nay, Pepper hurried behind the counter to check the last few sales. A scan of the credit slips yielded a corresponding amount and a name. "Found him."

"Good."

Another brief chill made her look toward the entrance again. Kyle stood framed in the doorway, his scruff-covered jaw stiff and his spine ramrod straight. The cold could've come from him as easily as the temperature outside.

He crossed to the blonde. "Thoughts?"

Her whole head moved when she rolled her eyes. "Laughably unprofessional. Kindergarten-level intimidation skills. Paid for his lunch with a card. Getting him to identify his boss ought to be a piece of cake. Can I rough him up if he doesn't spill right away?"

His answer came slower than it should have. "No. I'm after Pierce, not his peons."

If she was disappointed, she didn't let it show. "Okay. Ms. McCann, I need about three minutes of your time and anybody else who was present."

After what seemed a lot like a police interview in the kitchen, Pepper joined Zack and Kyle out front while Ona took a turn answering questions. Her cousin's demeanor hadn't improved during her absence. If anything, his scowl had deepened.

He shared a silent exchange with her son in a single glance before pinning Pepper in place with a stare. "Under no circumstances are you to be alone until I find out how dangerous this asshole is. Zack says you have a date with Drew. I'll drop you off at his house and he can bring you home. I want you to call me as soon as you get to your apartment and have all the doors locked."

With little choice but to admit her plans, she shoved her fists in her apron pockets and scowled back at him. "Not that it's any of your business, I'm not coming home tonight."

"Good."

Zack straightened his shoulders and looked down his nose at her. "You're staying overnight at Drew's? Don't you think you should've told me?"

"I just did. You weren't supposed to be here anyway, so don't try to play the protective adult-child card."

Kyle's eyebrows rose slightly and a hint of a smile appeared. "Drew told you what I said about giving me time to buy a new tux, didn't he?"

"A tux? You mean..." She dropped into the chair beside him and slumped forward. "God, Mort, can't you mind your own damn business for once?"

"You *are* my business, and I can't see Drew having a sexual relationship with a woman he isn't serious about. Marriage serious."

She massaged her forehead and fought the frustrated scream clawing at her throat. "Can we please not discuss my personal life?"

"You better back off, Uncle Kyle. She's going to take a swing at you in about two seconds." Zack sat down next to her, his long denim-clad legs stretching into the narrow strips of vision between her fingers. "I feel a lot better knowing you're staying with Drew tonight. Are you going to tell him about this?"

Considering he and his daughters could end up in the crossfire of this mess, she could hardly keep the latest development to herself. "Yeah."

"Okay. I'll open tomorrow so you don't have to worry about getting back early. Clay's hours got cut way back this week, so I can ask him to stick around."

She peeked out from behind her hands to give him a grateful smile. "Thanks, Zack. You know, Mort could learn a thing or two from you about respecting people's privacy."

"He could, couldn't he? Maybe if we find him a girlfriend, he'll learn the meaning of the word."

Kyle grunted. "Work is my wife and money is my mistress. What do I need with a girlfriend?"

His words sounded harsher than usual, making Pepper wonder if he'd been hiding a relationship and it had recently ended—against his wishes. Or maybe he was lonelier than he wanted to admit.

The ski-bunny sleuth approached their table, her expression revealing nothing. "Interviews are done, Mr. Morton. I'll have a report for you by five. Extra security is in place."

He gave a curt nod. "Good work. I'll be in touch."

None of the tension left the room with her exit, meaning the majority had to be coming from Kyle since Pepper was less worried than annoyed. He was normally more uptight than the average person, but this stress seemed like something outside the situation with Pierce, especially when he enjoyed a challenge.

Zack pushed up from his seat and shrugged out of his coat. "I guess I better go get ready for work."

Pepper waited until he disappeared into the kitchen before turning her attention to her cousin. "You know as well as I do that Pierce isn't about to hurt me or Zack. It sure wouldn't make either one of us cooperate with his stupid scheme. So what's got your jockeys in a twist?"

True to form, Kyle gave her a bland look. "My underwear are just fine."

"Liar. And what's with the scruffy face?"

He looked down at the phone in his hand and tapped the screen several times. "I'm working on business plan for the new investment and I hit a snag. Nothing I can't figure a way around. Trimming takes less time than shaving. When do you want to leave for Drew's?"

"I'll be ready at four thirty." His quick change of subject hinted at more trouble than a snag in a business plan. "Can I ask you a question?"

"Sure. I might not answer, but you can ask." He didn't so much as glance up from his phone.

She could almost guarantee he would when he heard her question. "Not that I have a problem with it, but are you...that is, are you having a...um, gender identification issue?"

His phone clunked on the floor a few inches from the toes of his right wingtip. Then he stared at her for a full ten seconds. "Are you trying to ask if I'm gay?"

His tone gave absolutely no indication of the answer.

"I suppose I am."

"No, I'm not gay. I'm not interested in acquiring a boyfriend, trying on women's clothing, or undergoing surgery to become a woman, although I was tempted to tell you that I am to prevent your interference in my love life."

"What love life? Yours has been as nonexistent as mine since..." *Since he took me in nineteen years ago. He sacrificed everything for me and Zack.* What had taken her so long to figure out the cause for his all-work-and-no-play existence?

His jaw tightened and he pivoted toward the far corner of the dining area, hiding whatever emotion he might have given away. "I have some calls to make. Let me know when you're ready to go."

Rather than pushing him to continue their conversation, she finished cleaning the last table and then headed upstairs to shower and change clothes. The warm spray allowed her mind to wander, giving her more reasons to feel guilty about Kyle's lonely life. What if he'd had a girlfriend and she'd been less than understanding about him inviting his pregnant cousin to live with him? Or had he chosen to focus on Pepper instead of a woman he loved?

Whatever the explanation, she was at least partly responsible for his decision to remain single and alone. She had no doubts about that.

She grabbed the tote on the floor beside her nightstand to serve as an overnight bag, but it didn't lift as easily as it should have. A quick peek inside reminded her how she'd intended to spend her free time during her trip to Hocking Hills. She grasped her iPad, intent on removing it, but reconsidered with it halfway out of the canvas bag.

Perhaps Drew would enjoy a few pages of the bedtime story that had inspired their mutually satisfying phone calls. Having a little extra foreplay on hand certainly wouldn't hurt.

Toothbrush. Change of clothes. No one could ever accuse her of being high maintenance, not even her enigmatic cousin.

Three minutes later, she scuttled down the interior stairway, counting the seconds until she could finally get naked with the man of her dreams again. Parenthood interfered with dating every bit as much as her parents had put a wrench in her life all those years ago.

Kyle still sat at the table in the farthest corner, with his back to the wall and his phone to his ear. His voice was too low for her to hear, but his tightly balled fist spoke volumes about his mood.

He glanced up and then rose as she weaved through several other occupied tables toward him. After what looked like a single-word response, he lowered his phone and slid it into his pants pocket. "Ready to go?"

A nod was all she could manage. The hints of gray at his temples and the lines at the corners of his eyes seemed more prominent, like he'd aged ten years since she'd gone up to her apartment. Had Pierce pulled a new stunt? Or had he gotten more bad news about the business investment he'd been so wrapped up in lately?

Without another word, he waved in Zack's direction and ushered her out the front entrance. Huge snowflakes drifted down from the overcast sky, creating a white curtain around them as they trudged to the rear parking lot.

They were both buckled into his car before she worked up the nerve to broach the topic he always seemed to avoid. "In case you don't already know, I really appreciate everything you've done for me. Not just now, but when I left home. When Zack was born. All of it. Sure, I tease you a lot about how protective you are, but I'm grateful for having someone who cares that much about me. And I'm sorry my problems interfered with your life."

He shifted the car into gear and switched on the wipers to clear the windshield. "I chose to involve myself. I wouldn't go back and change anything I did for you even if I could. If you think I'm alone because of you, you're wrong." Turning onto the road, he glanced in her direction. "Yes, I was in a serious relationship at the time, but you had nothing to do with the breakup. It was my choice and I don't regret the decision I made."

A sympathetic pang echoed in her heart. "You never found anyone else. Do you still love her?"

His brief hesitation suggested he didn't like the answer. "Sometimes love isn't enough. She moved on a lot faster than a woman with a broken heart should, so I'd say I chose wisely. I'd appreciate if you didn't bring it up again."

She blinked away the stinging in her eyes. *He's more human than any of us. He just hides it well.* "Okay."

CHAPTER NINETEEN

COLLEEN EYED DREW UP AND DOWN WITH A GRIN, MAKING HIM EVEN more anxious to send her and Hannah on their way. "Hot date?"

"That obvious, huh?" He shoved his hands in the back pockets of his jeans to keep from scraping them through his hair.

"Freshly shaved, recent haircut, and you've looked around me at least six times in two minutes. You're obviously waiting for somebody to get here." Placing a hand on her slowly expanding belly, she cast a glance upstairs. "Oh, and Hannah told me a really nice lady named Pepper came for pizza a few nights ago. The hickey lady? Must be serious."

"Maybe. Probably."

"That sounds like a yes to me." Her smile widened. "I'm so happy for you. I hope it works out."

Grateful for the support, he gave her a gentle hug. "Me too."

The hurried drum of footsteps on the stairs announced Hannah's approach. "I'm ready, Aunt Colleen!"

"Did you get your ski pants and extra gloves for sled riding? I don't think your dad wants to pick up a Popsicle tomorrow."

"Yep!" Hannah hefted the overstuffed duffle bag she'd dragged down the steps and tilted her face toward him. "I need a kiss, Daddy."

Since he'd barely gotten a good-bye out of Kristin, he treasured the moment by bending down to kiss her baby-soft cheek. "Love you, squirt. Have fun."

"I love you too." One arm circled his neck for a tight squeeze. A moment later, she squirmed free and opened the front door. "Come on, Aunt Colleen. Let's go. Bye, Daddy!"

His sister-in-law laughed and followed Hannah outside. "See you tomorrow."

Torn between hating how fast his daughters were growing up and thrilled to have some alone time with Pepper, he gave a halfhearted wave. Why did every good thing have to be accompanied by something bad?

Focus on the positive.

Pepper would arrive in roughly fifteen minutes. He'd washed sheets and remade his bed, restocked his condom supply, and bought the ingredients for what promised to be a simple yet tasty supper. Life wasn't perfect, but it was good.

He jogged up the stairs to double-check that he'd remembered matches to go with the candles on the dresser. As he entered his bedroom, something more important jumped out at him.

That could've been a real mood killer.

He picked up the frame that had stood on his nightstand for the last year and almost three months. Kate's carefree expression had changed only days after the picture had been taken, replaced by hard-fought bravery and determination. She'd wanted him to forget what cancer had done to her body when she was gone and fill their daughters' minds with good memories to drown out the sorrow and pain.

Sitting on the edge of the bed, he traced her smile, surprised by how little emptiness her absence brought now. When had that happened? Sadness and regret at not having more time still remained, but they didn't cripple him anymore, not the way they had in the weeks and months following her death-sentence diagnosis. He hadn't believed her when she said he'd find someone new to love and that he'd know when he was ready to move on with his life. "Ah, Kate. You'd like

Pepper. I bet you would've been friends if you'd known each other. She's easy to love."

He carried the framed photo to the closet and carefully placed it in the box of belongings he'd saved for the girls. Somehow, the world hadn't ended for him.

His pulse hiccupped with the ring of the doorbell, and he let out a slow exhale to calm his thumping heart. With a last scan of the room, he headed back downstairs, his hormones more out of control than they'd ever been.

He caught the distorted outline of Pepper through the sidelight as he reached the bottom of the steps, and a rush of heat flooded his groin. Only a week had passed since he'd made love to her, but it seemed like forever.

Too damn long.

Foregoing a civilized greeting, he yanked the door open and pulled her into his arms for a soul-melting welcome. Her tongue glided along his in a wicked dance, inviting him to delve deeper into the decadence of her irresistible mouth. Soft humming vibrated through his jaw, tempting him to undress her then and there.

Clinging to the tiny bit of sanity he had left, he reluctantly broke off the kiss. His ragged breaths turned the snowflakes decorating the tufts of hair sticking out from beneath her hat to water droplets. Her claim to be a sprite was right on the money. Everything about her was magic.

He caught a glistening bead on his fingertip. "Hi there."

"Hi." Her husky greeting fed his hunger to be inside her.

Taking the tote bag that had slid from her shoulder to her elbow, he led her into the foyer and shut out the world. "We're alone."

"Then why are you still dressed?" She tossed her hat toward the empty hook on the wall and unzipped her coat. It landed on top of the hat, along with her scarf and gloves.

"Take off your boots. The rest can come off in the family room." He took a step back from her, determined to make use of the romantic settings he'd prepared.

Her boots clunked on the floor next to his shoes. Then she led him by a belt loop toward the kitchen. "Let's go, stud muffin."

He slipped free of her hold and scooped her into his arms, unable to keep from laughing at her silly endearment. "This is faster, sex kitten."

A mix of purrs and giggles tickled his neck as she nuzzled against him. "Mmm. Pussycat needs lots of attention."

White-hot desire flooded his veins. While the words could've been innocent enough, her seductive murmur assured him she meant them in a very different way.

He stopped at the couch and lowered her feet to the floor, glad he'd had the foresight to hide a strip of condoms under the fleece throw tossed across the corner cushion. "You should probably undress yourself. If I do it, I'll tear your clothes."

As she peeled the sweater over her head, he cursed his choice of a button-down shirt and started with his pants instead. Her jeans, bra, and panties lay in a pile before he unfastened the third button of his shirt. The sight of her unclothed body stalled his progress.

"Need some help?" She guided his hands aside and made quick work of the remaining buttons. Then she brushed the shirt past his shoulders and down his arms, lingering at his biceps and again at his wrists.

With his hands finally free, he cupped her breasts in his palms and teased her nipples into tight buds with his thumbs. She arched against him, nearly driving him insane when her skin grazed his.

Her soft moan sent another surge of craving from his brain to his cock. "I want you."

He tried to speak, but the words wouldn't form. Showing her was better anyway, at least for now.

Pressing his erection to her belly, he touched his lips to hers in feather-light caress. Then he eased her down onto the couch as her tongue came out to meet his. A blind reach for the throw yielded the one thing stopping him from immediately sliding inside her.

He tore a package from the strip and donned the protection, reluctant to break the connection with her mouth. A quick glide through her slippery folds with his finger told him she was as ready as he was.

She grasped his cock, sending a tremor through him, and guided him to her entrance. He pushed as she rocked her hips upward, and a wave of lightheadedness swept over him at the snug fit of her body around him. This was where he belonged, where she belonged, joined together as one.

Her inner muscles flexed, pulsing around him and urging to him move faster, as she wrapped her thighs around his waist and gripped the hair at the back of his head. The slight sting threatened to steal what little control he had.

He sank into her again and again, each thrust driving him deeper. She gasped against his cheek with the movement and her fingernails dug into his ass. Her silky tunnel tightened, making his balls contract. Then she cried out, a sound so rapturous he could only follow.

The world splintered apart a moment later. Even as he floated out of his body, she kept him grounded, safe in her embrace and immersed in her love. His soul had melded with hers.

She stroked his shoulder blades, bringing him back to the real world—a world that was suddenly without problems. "I love you."

He braced himself on his elbows to stare into her unguarded eyes. She hadn't said the words first before, but the emotion shone from every inch of her blissful expression, and he didn't doubt for a second that she loved him as much as he loved her.

"I'm crazy, madly, irrevocably in love with you." He skimmed his lips along her hairline to her cheekbone. "I can't imagine my life without you."

His stomach rumbled as he shifted to lie beside her.

"If I didn't know better, I'd think you only love me for my cooking skills." She laughed and poked him in the gut. "Maybe we should start supper."

"In a few minutes. I've missed holding you." He closed his eyes, appreciating the chance to share private time with her. "I got spoiled at the cabin, being able to cuddle with you all night."

"I've heard most men aren't into cuddling." Her soft exhale cooled the perspiration on his chest. "I'm glad you're not like the average guy."

"They don't know what they're missing. The sound of your breathing. The feel of your skin. The smell of sex." Too comfortable to even consider getting up, he snagged the throw with his foot and pulled it over their naked bodies with his free hand. "I'd stay like this forever if I could."

"Me too." She snuggled closer, threading her leg between his.

Exhaustion tried to drag him into unconsciousness, but he fought the fatigue brought on from restless nights of sleeping without her. Enjoying every second of their limited time together was more important than sleep.

"Drew, are you awake?"

"Yeah."

"I don't want you to worry, but a guy who might work for Kevin Pierce left a cryptic threat today."

Panic raced up Drew's spine. He sat up so fast Pepper almost rolled off the couch. A quick clamp around her waist saved her from landing on the floor, and he pulled her onto his lap. "He threatened you and Zack?"

"No, but he hinted that something might happen to the deli if Zack doesn't agree to the DNA test. Kyle called in one of his security people and they've already got a name on the guy. They just need to link him to Pierce, which shouldn't be too hard since the guy left a trail a two-year-old could follow. Round-the-clock watch on the deli has doubled and I have the feeling my cousin hired a personal bodyguard for me." Her pursed lips said she wasn't happy about it, either.

Some of Drew's concern faded. "Did he call the police?"

"Not that I know of, but the woman from the security team acted like she is or was a cop, so I'm guessing she has connections with the local police. Maybe we can get a restraining order out of this, not that I expect Pierce would obey it. Greed does weird things to people." She scrambled off his lap and met his gaze. "I don't want to put you or the girls at risk. If he finds out—"

"You're making trouble where there isn't any, and I trust Kyle to keep things under control." Drew reached for his jeans as he stood.

"Let's go make supper. I hear chopping vegetables is your favorite stress reducer."

Her frown deepened. "What's Zack been telling you?"

He handed her his shirt, determined to make her smile. "I recall something about cucumbers and neutering. As long as you aren't imagining it's me, you're welcome to use my knives."

She dropped her gaze to somewhere below his chest and grinned. "I wouldn't dream of damaging your fruit. It gives me so much pleasure."

"Good to know." Donning his pants, he left the zipper down. "Do you need the bathroom before I go clean up?"

"Yeah, thanks." She slipped on his shirt as she walked away. The sleeves hung well past her hands and the hem hit her mid-thigh.

It was sexy as hell on her.

Drew shuffled to the refrigerator and then backtracked to the breakfast bar for the recipe Flynn had emailed. Making the marinara earlier in the day had crossed his mind, but cooking together had marked the beginning of their cooperation with and reliance on each other. Friendship and love had grown from it. How could he pass up the opportunity to recreate that magic?

He transferred each ingredient from the fridge to the counter. As he washed tomatoes, fingertips brushed along his ribs from behind, setting off enough tingles to make his satisfied cock stir.

"What kind of sauce are we making?" She peeked around him toward the sink.

"My brother-in-law sent me a recipe for vegetarian marinara. Tomatoes, onions, zucchini, summer squash, and mushrooms. I'm not sure how to peel tomatoes, but it sounds good." He gestured at the recipe with his elbow. "The girls might even eat it."

"If they don't, you can freeze single servings to reheat later." Handing him the dishtowel, she nudged him away from the sink. "I'll wash the rest of the produce and start the water heating to peel the tomatoes while you're in bathroom."

"Hot water to peel tomatoes? I figured I'd have to use a potato peeler." He laid the towel over her shoulder and rubbed his nose against her cheek. "Good thing you're here."

A chuckle accompanied the shake of her head. "You don't fool me. You'd have Googled it like a real man."

"Maybe so, but I'm still glad you're here." He traced the graceful curve of her neck. "Back in a minute."

By time he returned from disposing of the used condom and making sure he was clean for next time, she had a pot of water on the stove and a knife poised above the squash. "If you'll get out the rest of the ingredients, I'll do the chopping. Oh, and we'll need a bowl of ice water."

More than happy to let her boss him around in the kitchen, he checked the recipe. "I bought fresh garlic, basil, and oregano because it seemed like something you and Flynn would do. I have no idea how much of the dried stuff to use in place of them, not that anything we'd find the cupboard is less than two years old."

"Fresh is better." She lopped off the stem end of the zucchini. "I noticed the recipe calls for green bell peppers. Does your brother-in-law know they give you heartburn?"

"Yeah. He said leaving them out wouldn't hurt the sauce."

"Probably a good idea. I have plans for you after supper, and they don't include Milk of Magnesia or Tums."

He set his handful near the cutting board. "Plans, huh? I sure hope they don't conflict with mine."

Her sideways glance held a wicked gleam. "Somehow, I doubt that. Are we using marsala or a red?"

"Marsala. Flynn gave me some other recipes that call for it. The alcohol cooks out of it, right?"

"Yep. No worries. I cook with wine all the time." She ran her palm up his chest and around to the back of his neck. Then she pulled him downward for a lingering kiss. "Thank you for thinking of me. It was very sweet of you."

The lift of the hem on her thighs tempted him to carry her back to the couch for another round of lovemaking, but he settled for an almost accidental brush of his hand along her bare hip. "I have an ulterior motive. I want you in my bed all night, and not because you're sick."

Her soft hum came close to breaking his will, but then she turned toward the cutting board and picked up the knife. "No more distractions, mister. I'm going to be hungry soon and your stomach already growled at us once."

"Maybe I need to put my shirt back on."

The warning look she gave him over her shoulder would've been much more believable if she'd kept her eyes on his face. "Nice try. Is the water boiling yet?"

Steam rose from the pot on the stove in a rolling cloud.

"Looks like it."

"Okay. We won't mess with scoring the tomatoes since we're using Romas. They usually split enough on their own that they're easy to peel." The steady chop, chop, chop against the cutting board paused for a moment and then began again. "Use a slotted spoon to gently drop them into the water. In a minute or two, the skins will start to split. That's when you scoop them out and put them straight into the ice water. While you're waiting, get out a medium frying pan and the olive oil." Her all-business tone was no less sexy than her teasing.

Glad he wasn't on his own in the kitchen, he followed her instructions. Without warning, slits formed on tomato after tomato as they tumbled through the boiling water.

Slotted spoon. Ice water. "They all split at once. What if I don't get them out as soon as they pop open? Did I ruin them?"

"Just turn off the heat and transfer them to the bowl. It doesn't hurt them to blanch a little longer. Oh, and leave the water in the pot. We can use it for the pasta."

"Okay." He carefully scooped one after another into the ice water. The skins wrinkled after a few seconds and pulled away from the flesh along the split edges. "They look kind of like giant red raisins."

"Good. That means you did it right, not that I don't have the utmost confidence in your cooking skills." She spread a layer of paper towels beside the bowl. "Now take them out and put them on these. We don't want waterlogged tomatoes. The skins should peel right off. I'll remove the cores as I get them ready for the sauce."

Lifting the first of his victims from its icy grave, he waited for the drips to slow. "I'm a terrible cook. That's why you have to supervise."

"Not terrible. Inexperienced." She reached around him and turned on the burner beneath the skillet. "I can teach you all the important stuff."

"You already have. The heart is usually smarter than the brain." A tomato slipped through its skin and then his fingers as he tried to pick it up. It landed on the paper towels. "Slimy little bugger. You're not going to slip away like that, are you?"

CHAPTER TWENTY

P<small>EPPER SNICKERED AS SHE POURED OLIVE OIL IN THE HOT SKILLET.</small> "Depends on how slippery you make me."

Drew's laughter echoed through the kitchen, making her knees almost melt. "Slippery is good, but I'll be sure to hold on tight."

She hated to dampen the mood, but a major obstacle stood in the way. "What about Kristen?"

Another flop on the counter punctuated the sudden change in conversation, and his sigh probably had nothing to do with escaping tomatoes. "I don't know what's going on with her. She's never been rude to anyone before. If I didn't think it would backfire, I'd tell her how disappointed her mom would be in the way she's been acting. And don't you dare suggest that we put the brakes on, or I'm not letting you go home tomorrow."

"I thought we settled that last time. No kidnapping necessary." Touched and amused by his fierce preemptory declaration, Pepper dumped the garlic and onions into the pan. They sizzled and their pungent aroma rose in an invisible cloud. "When Kate got sick, Kristen became the keeper of the household. Oldest child syndrome—sometimes it's a good thing and sometimes it's a curse. She thinks I'm usurping her status. And she's getting to that age, whether you like it or not. Puberty can turn angels into devil's spawn."

He squeezed the last Roma free of its skin. "Ugh. I'm not ready for that at all."

"Nobody ever is. You have an amazing support system, though. Help is only a phone call away. Can you add the squash? Both kinds."

"Sure." His forearm grazed her breast as he added the zucchini and summer squash, sending a zip of pleasure southward. "So it doesn't bother you that Kate's family is still a big part of our life?"

"Why would it?" She handed him the wooden spoon. "Stir while I crush the tomatoes. They're your girls' grandparents and aunts and uncles. They need that connection. If anything, I envy your relationship with them."

"For what it's worth, I think your parents made a big mistake. Kyle has his faults, but at least he's loyal. Colleen's excited to know you're staying the night, and she and Merie want to meet you, which is kind of weird. I mean, I was married to their sister, for God's sake. And they've been pushing me to date. Definitely not what I expected."

Warm juice and flesh oozed through her fingers and landed in the bowl beneath her hands. She winced at the slight sting on her thumb that marked a recent cut. "What do you think Kate would say about you dating?"

He paused his stirring and frowned at her. "You really want to talk about this?"

"Yeah. Your marriage shaped who you are, and it's not like you're married now."

"She made me promise to find someone new to love. I didn't want to think about going on without her, even if it meant spending the rest of my life alone. We argued about it a lot when she first brought it up. I saw no possible way to love someone else after being married to her for over a decade and us having two kids together. I gave in because it seemed stupid to waste the time we—she—had left. I'm guessing she told her sisters to make me follow through on that promise. In a way, it's like starting over again, except I'm a single dad this time around."

Not sure she could speak without tearing up, she nodded and squished another pair of tomatoes in her fists.

"I've never talked much about it to anybody but you. Well, and Flynn a little since he moved back from Cincinnati. For some reason, it's easy to spill my guts to you." His footsteps behind her were the only warning before his mouth warmed a spot below her ear. "I'm glad I was wrong about falling in love again."

"Me too." She leaned into him, careful to keep her gooey hands over the bowl. Instead of making her feel vulnerable, he gave her the strength to trust her whole heart to him. "To be honest, I didn't expect to meet someone who would make being part of a couple better than being alone. And all it took was a blizzard. Timing is everything."

He chuckled and kissed her neck. "Yeah, and I think it might be time to add the rest of the ingredients. The squash is turning brown."

"You must be the real deal. Nothing distracts me from cooking." Handing him the bowl of tomatoes, she gestured with her head toward the stove. "Add these and stir."

"I can't wait until we can distract each other some more. Anything else need to go in?"

"Basil, oregano, salt, pepper, and marsala." She dropped the cores onto the pile of vegetable waste and rinsed her hands. "Then it needs to simmer while we get the pasta ready. Do you think you can behave yourself for twenty more minutes?"

"Maybe." His adorable smirk said otherwise. "When should we put the bread in the oven? It's one those take-and-bake baguette things. Oh, and I bought a bag of salad."

"I'll take care of the salad. You can cook the pasta while the bread bakes. Preheat the oven first and then put the pot of water on high." She double-checked the recipe on the way to the fridge. "There's a note at the bottom that says to add about a teaspoon of sugar. It's probably to tone down the acidity. I do that with my tomato-based soups."

"Oven's preheating and burner's on for the fettuccini. One teaspoon of sugar coming up. That's the smaller one, right?"

Spying the bag of mixed greens through the clear crisper drawer, she bent to retrieve it. "Yep. What do you want in your salad?"

"There are some grape tomatoes and croutons. Look behind the mayonnaise for the tomatoes and behind the oatmeal in the pantry for the croutons. I hid them so little girls wouldn't make them disappear. Why can't they like the lettuce instead?"

"Because life with children would be too easy if they ate everything we wanted them to." She moved the jar of mayo and added her find to the supplies on the counter. "Will I need a stepladder to reach the croutons? Kristin's almost as tall as I am."

"Nope." As the refrigerator door swung closed beside her, he lifted her off the floor.

She flung her arms around his neck and clasped her ankles at his lower back. The action was far more intimate than she was prepared for, her inner thighs coming in direct contact with firm abdominals. "You bad, bad boy. I thought you were going to behave."

Grinning, he carried her toward the pantry. "Just helping you reach."

"Uh-huh." Her line of sight was several inches higher than usual, with the oatmeal directly in front of her when he stopped. The corner of the package of croutons peeked past the edge of the box. "Got what I need."

He cupped her left butt cheek. As his fingertips edged closer to the apex of her thighs, a tremor rippled through her middle. "Me too."

Closing her eyes, she groaned. "No wonder you never learned to cook. You always want to skip ahead to dessert."

"Just making sure we're both ready for it."

"Somehow, I don't think that'll be an issue." A single beep came from the stove. "Done preheating?"

"Yeah. I've been preheating all week." He lowered her to her feet, making his shirt slide upward to her breasts and her skin brush against his. "We have some very long, lonely nights to make up for."

His need to make the most of their time together made her heart ache. "I'm not going anywhere tonight."

"I know. It's just that things can happen and we don't have any control over them. I don't want to have to live with any more regrets."

She hugged him as tight as she could, wishing she could see their future and reassure him that they had years and years ahead of them to share. "We don't have to worry that every second could be our last. I love you and you love me. I know it, whether we're cooking or laughing or making love. Even when I'm missing you. I spent too many years of Zack's childhood worrying about his father taking him away before I realized I can't stop life from happening. But I can enjoy the simple things without needing everything to be perfect."

The rigidness in his jaw loosened when she splayed her palms over his shoulder blades. "I can't help but wonder if I'm going to lose you too. What if—"

"What if we live happily ever after together?"

"I'd settle for happy most of the time ever after." He touched his forehead to hers. "Let's finish making supper so we can work on that."

"Do you want to me to cook the pasta and you make the salads?"

"Nah. I need the practice. The girls and I have been living on mostly canned goods and sandwiches long enough." He picked up the package of fettuccini and walked toward the stove. The wink he gave her confirmed she'd managed to lighten his mood a little. "Besides, I should have more than marketing and bedroom skills if I want to keep you interested."

With a laugh, she swatted at his delectable jeans-clad butt. "I don't know about that. Your bedroom skills are pretty remarkable."

"Good to know. Yours aren't too shabby, either. Do you like your pasta *al dente*?"

The bag of romaine popped open with a two-handed tug. "Yeah, but I usually subtract thirty to forty-five seconds from the recommended time so it'll absorb the flavors of the sauce when I toss them together. And I prefer firm to overcooked and starchy."

"You sound like Flynn. He's the one who told me what *al dente* means." Drew slid a handful of fettuccini into the water. "I never thought he'd end up cooking for a bunch of retirees. It worked out pretty well, though, since that's where he met his wife."

"How old *is* he? Not that I have a problem with the May-December romance thing, but don't older guys usually go for younger women?" She arranged the tomatoes on top of the lettuce.

His belly laugh made her tummy tickle. "He married his boss. Sort of, but not really. She was the acting director of the retirement village when he started working there last fall. She's a dietician. Her uncle owns the complex."

"Okay, that makes more sense."

"I can't imagine falling in love with someone twice my age. That'd be like dating your mom."

"Men do that all the time. You know, dating women young enough to be their daughters or granddaughters. I'm all for love and happiness, but it seems a little creepy to me. Wouldn't you rather have your girls find someone close to their own age?"

He held out the wooden spoon as he turned toward her. "Nope. My girls are *never* dating. Guys tend to think with their dicks and then do really stupid things, especially to women."

"I can't disagree with you there, but I'm betting they'll have something to say about it. I just hope all the talking I've done with Zack makes a difference." She scattered a handful of croutons on top of their salads.

"He's a good kid. Well, not so much a kid, is he? He's very protective of you. I doubt he'd ever treat a woman disrespectfully, knowing what you went through."

"Probably not. I guess I should be more worried about girls taking advantage of how nice he is. God, and the money. I don't think I'll ever get used to that, even after growing up with it. I still can't believe Mortie kept their investment plans from me. If I didn't know he meant well, I'd be tempted to strangle him." She carried the salads to the breakfast bar.

"About the money thing. There's something you should know."

Her stomach tensed at the apprehension in his voice. "Yeah?"

He gave the pot another stir and then turned to face her. "Add another zero to the end of Kyle's net worth, and that's what I grew up with. My dad got into politics when I was in prep school, and he expected me to follow in his footsteps after college. Kate didn't come from a family in his social circles, so he was pretty pissed off about how serious I was about her. I asked her to marry me and he hasn't spoken to me since."

A sympathetic twinge pinched her heart. "What about your mom?"

"We were supposed to meet for lunch once not long after Kate and I got engaged, but she never showed. I'm guessing he found out about it and used the him-or-me blackmail to stop her. It wouldn't have been the first time."

She balled her fists so tight her fingernails dug into her palms. "Nice. I wouldn't be surprised if he was one of my father's friends, especially since you went to school with Pierce."

"You're not going to hold that against me, are you?"

"No. You don't get to pick your family. Unfortunately."

As she crossed the kitchen, he opened his arms, his smile making her feel more welcome and wanted than her parents ever had. "I suppose not. I'm damn glad I finally get to spend some time with you, but I never expected to waste it talking about all this stuff."

Resting her cheek against his bare skin, she let his familiar scent help her escape from the not-so-pleasant memories of their pasts. "I wouldn't call it a waste. I like talking to you, and being disowned is something else we have in common. Not many couples can say that."

"It isn't exactly something to brag about, but you're right. Talking isn't a waste." The timer beeped behind them as his stomach rumbled again. "Finally. I'm starving."

"Me too." She enjoyed a last thump-thump of his heart in her ear and then stepped out of his reach before he got too distracted to drain the pasta.

Five minutes later, he sat beside her at the breakfast bar, a fork in his right hand and a hunk of warm baguette in his left. Other than an occasional appreciative groan, he seemed completely captivated by the meal. Rather than interrupt the companionable silence, she enjoyed their delicious creation and recharged her body for a long overdue night with the man she loved.

Was real marriage like this? Or did desire drive them to satisfy the most basic of their needs? Her own life certainly hadn't taught her anything about healthy man-woman relationships.

She twirled the last noodles onto her fork and put the bite in her mouth. Their conversation had been introspective enough without dissecting her lack of experience with this kind of love.

Drew tucked his finger under her chin. "Why the frown? I'm hardly a chef, but I thought supper turned out pretty good."

"It was very good." Stacking her salad bowl on her plate, she grimaced. "Just overthinking."

"I have a cure for that." His fingertips grazed her thigh as he stood. "As soon as I put away the leftovers and load the dishwasher, neither one of us will have thinking on our minds."

"Want some help?"

"Nope, it'll only take a minute." He picked up a pile of dirty dishes with each hand and carried them to the sink. The silverware clinked and dishes rattled as he rinsed and added them to the nearly full racks.

The efficiency of his movements spoke of a man who had become relatively self-reliant over the past two years, even if he lacked the knowledge to produce many meals from scratch. He was a quick learner, and he obviously didn't expect her to take care of him.

Pushing the start button on the dishwasher, he waggled his eyebrows at her. "Done. Let's head upstairs."

Pepper hooked her hand in the back pocket of his jeans as she followed him along the hall to the stairway. Then she grabbed her bag on the stairs without slowing.

When they reached the top, Drew halted. "Wait here a second."

He walked to the master bedroom and disappeared inside. The faint scent of burning matches and then vanilla carried to her nose a few moments later.

Candles? How had she found this amazingly sensitive man?

Reappearing in the doorway, he crooked his finger at her. "Ready."

"Me too." She unfastened the button between her breasts and sauntered toward him. With each slow step, she freed another button. When she finally stood in front of him, his shirt hung open.

His eyes darkened, and he slipped the fabric from her shoulders and down her arms. One kiss after another followed the unhurried path of bare skin, sending delicious shivers along every inch of her body.

She clung to him to keep her legs from giving out beneath her. As he lifted her into his arms, his lips finally met hers. The stroke of his tongue against hers and the coarseness of his chest hair against her nipples pushed her need for him to new heights. He lowered her to the plush covers, only releasing her long enough to shed his jeans and roll on a condom.

Then he was beside her again, skin to skin, their bodies aligned. She welcomed him inside and savored the total connection with every part of him. He moved in time with her, the motion unhurried this time, as if they had all eternity to nurture and treasure these irreplaceable moments together.

The gentle touch of his palm on her jaw told her everything in his heart, how much he loved and cherished her. She didn't need to hear the words, and she offered the same to him, holding him close enough to feel the steady vibrations of his heartbeat drumming in time with hers.

Without a doubt, he was the love of her life.

CHAPTER TWENTY-ONE

DREW IGNORED THE LIGHT TRYING TO PENETRATE HIS EYELIDS, RELISHING the feel of Pepper's body and the utter contentment of waking up next to her instead. The scent of sex and candles still lingered in the air and her slow, even breaths lulled him back toward sleep, but his stomach protested.

She wiggled against his already half-hard cock. "Good morning."

"G'morning." Happy to encourage her play, he settled his erection into the cradle of her bare bottom. "Hungry?"

"Depends on what's for breakfast." She skimmed her fingertips up his thigh to his right butt cheek.

"Mm. French toast? Omelets? I bought some bacon."

"I'd rather have a salami." Her uninhibited laughter made him slip free. "Any condoms left?"

"One, plus a new box in the nightstand drawer." He reached behind him, hoping to snag the last packet without having to move away from her. "Got it."

Before he could tear open the package, she grabbed it and pushed him onto his back. "My turn to suit you up."

He bit the inside of his lip and groaned when her hand closed around him. Rather than getting down to business, she stroked his length down and up, teasing him until he wanted to flip her over and dive inside. Then she finally positioned the latex on the almost painfully swollen head and unrolled the condom.

Every base instinct called to him to forget the damn protection and screw her until she screamed. "Torturous wench. God, I need to be inside you."

"I'm getting there." Her lips parted as she lowered herself onto him.

Every nerve ending sprang to life, the connection to her more essential than air. He traced her spine upward as he sank into her. Her body tightened around him with each smooth in-and-out stroke, pulling him into the sensual world he'd found with her. Their synchronized movements reinforced what his gut had been telling him since the night they'd made love at the cabin. They belonged to each other. Together, they were stronger.

Breaking the steady rhythm, she sat up and locked gazes with him. Her muscles trembled beneath his palms on her upper thighs, hinting at her readiness to once again drown in the pleasure they'd already shared several times since her arrival yesterday.

Unable to resist, he cupped her pale breasts and circled the darker flesh surrounding her nipples. Each successive circuit brought him closer to the taut buds. She closed her eyes and her head fell back as she arched into his touch.

He rocked his hips upward, and a gentle brush of his thumbs over her nipples yielded the response he longed for—the rapid contraction of her muscles around him and a high-pitched cry. Another rocking motion earned him more of the same and urged him toward his own release.

Her fingertips dug into his biceps, triggering an unexpected plea-sure-pain reaction as he tried to prolong her orgasm with a faster pace. He fought to breathe through the overwhelming need to let go of control and join her.

Release hit him when she gasped and trembled again, obliterating any thought that their time together would soon come to an end.

Surrender was easy. Sharing the incredible bliss of being one with her satisfied the simplest of his desires.

She wilted onto his chest, her mouth finding his for a kiss more loving than any before that moment. Between erratic breaths, he welcomed the unspoken words she offered, treasuring every part of their connection. He wouldn't take anything for granted ever again.

The buzzing of his phone against the nightstand broke through his serenity. "Damn. So much for post-coital cuddling. I better see which of the girls has to come home right this minute."

She levered off of him and rolled to the edge of the bed. "I need a trip to the bathroom anyway. I hope it isn't anything serious."

Enjoying the sway of her hips as she walked to the master bath, he picked up his phone. A quick check of the message brought relief as well as annoyance at the interruption.

"Free for lunch today?"

He tapped in a response to his brother-in-law since the mood had already been intruded upon. *"Hey, Flynn. Lunch sounds great. Around noon at Montgomery Crossing?"*

"Works for me. See you then."

"Everything okay?" Pepper slipped on his shirt and fastened several buttons on her way to the bed. The worry in her eyes said she was as concerned about a problem with his daughters as he'd been.

Drew nodded. "Just my brother-in-law wanting to get together for lunch. He has terrible timing. I wonder how he'd feel about me texting him tonight after he goes to bed with his wife. They're still newlyweds."

"Newlyweds, huh? That's kind of mean, especially if he didn't know you were having a sleepover." A wayward lock of fiery hair fell across her forehead, adding to her already impish look. "It could've been worse, you know. Your phone could've gone off before we did."

"I'm not sure I would've noticed. You're very distracting." He pulled her onto his lap and nuzzled the soft spot behind her ear, careful not to scrape her skin with his razor stubble. "Ready for breakfast?"

"I need food first." The arch of her foot glided up his calf, triggering a tingling sensation all the way up his leg.

"Wicked little nymph, I meant food. The other can wait until after we eat. I could use a little recovery time."

Her laughter vibrated through his lap, tempting him to roll her over onto the bed again. "I brought something to show you."

"Oh?" He'd seen, touched, or tasted every inch of her. What else was left?

"Remember the book I told you about? You know, the one with phone sex? I brought my iPad with me. It has a shower scene."

Her reminder sent another jolt of sexual current southward. "Are you going to read to me while I cook?"

She gave him a doubtful look as she leaned away. "I think we should save the reading part until we're done cooking. Crisp bacon is fine, but burnt to a crisp isn't. Besides, I believe you still need to learn how to make scrambled eggs that aren't slimy and yucky."

"There is that. Your shower scene better be worth the wait." He lowered her to her feet as he stood.

Her mouth skimmed along his shoulder to his chest. The tip of her tongue darted out to connect with his nipple, sending an unexpected jolt to his groin. "Oh, it is."

"Then let's get to it. I'll meet you downstairs in about two minutes." He hurried to the bathroom before his body convinced him to forego feeding her for another round of lovemaking.

Pepper McCann had turned him into a sex fiend. That was the only logical explanation for the urge to spend every waking moment naked with her. He hadn't been this crazed as a teenager high on puberty hormones.

The pungent scent of brewing coffee met him as he entered the kitchen. Pepper added eggs to the supplies she'd already gathered on the counter, his shirt hanging mid-thigh on her once again. It was a delicious cross between domestic and racy. That look was something he wouldn't mind waking up to every day for the rest of his life.

With ring shopping in the back of his mind, he joined her at the refrigerator. "Find everything okay?"

She opened the cabinet door near his head. "So far. Do you have a broiler pan?"

"Yeah." He retrieved it from the stove drawer, the stacked pans clanking together as he rearranged the contents. "What are we broiling?"

"Not broiling, baking. Bacon shouldn't be swimming in grease as it cooks, so the broiler pan lets the fat drip into the bottom pan. Middle rack in the oven. Preheat to four-fifty. Then crack four eggs in a bowl while I get the bacon ready."

"Yes, ma'am."

Her efficient motions yielded a single layer of meat that covered the entire surface in less time than it took for him to follow her instructions and fish two pieces of shell out the mix of egg whites and broken yolks.

As she washed her hands, he snuck in beside her. "What's next?"

"Salt, pepper, and milk, and parsley, if you liked it in the omelet. Dried is fine." She handed him the towel. "Do you have an iron skillet?"

"Yeah, in the pantry, but I thought you had to cook eggs in nonstick."

"Only in the omelets-for-beginners lesson. You can use well-seasoned cast iron for almost anything." The preheat alert beeped once, and she slid the broiler pan into the hot oven. More beeping sounded as she set the timer. "We'll need to check the bacon in about eight or ten minutes and flip it over."

"How much salt, pepper, milk, and parsley? Do they go in before or after I beat the eggs?"

Her muffled voice came from the pantry. "All but the milk go in before. About an eighth of a teaspoon of salt. Two or three good shakes of pepper. Teaspoon or so of parsley. Whisk until you can't tell the yolks from the whites."

He added the seasonings and then picked up the whisk. "Bubbles or no bubbles?"

"A few big ones are fine. Mixed well but not frothy." She reappeared with the skillet. "This should be out where you can use it. Did you know you have a cast iron Dutch oven in there too? It doesn't look like it's ever been out of the box."

The excitement in her voice reminded him of Hannah on Christmas morning.

He grinned without looking up from his task. "It hasn't. I don't know how to use it."

"You can bake with it in the oven, but the flavor's best with a wood or charcoal fire. We should build a fire pit in the back yard when the weather gets nice. Then I'll show you how to roast a whole chicken. It's divine." She set the pan on the counter and clucked her tongue. "This thing needs seasoned a bit before we use it. Where's the vegetable oil?"

"Sounds great. You being here and the chicken. Oil's in the lazy Susan. Milk now?"

"About a tablespoon should do it. Then stir again." Her bottom wiggled back and forth as she rubbed oil into the pan. "While this heats, I'll flip the bacon and you can get out the toaster and the bread."

As she opened the oven door, the salty, smoky aroma of bacon filled the kitchen, distracting him halfway through his new task. "God, that smells good. I'm really glad you aren't a vegetarian."

Her boisterous laughter brightened his mood even more. "Me too."

With the broiler pan back in the oven, she waved him over to the stove. The time for his most challenging test in the kitchen had evidently arrived.

He joined her, beaten eggs in hand. "I have more eggs if these don't turn out right."

"They'll be fine." She guided his hand into an oven mitt. "The number one rule of cooking with cast iron. Never touch the handle of a hot skillet with your bare hand. It *will* burn you. And it hurts like hell."

"Experience speaking?"

"Yep." She plopped a dab of butter in the pan. It sizzled and spread across the hot surface as it melted. "When the butter starts to brown, slowly pour in the eggs. Then stir until they're completely opaque. Shiny and see-through means not done."

"Okay." Following her instructions, he carefully emptied the contents of the bowl into the skillet. The mixture oozed to the curved edges, bubbling and turning light yellow beneath the liquid on top. A few swipes through the goo yielded what looked like the beginnings of scrambled eggs.

"Good. Keep stirring, all the way around. Just like that. Scrape and stir. See how they peel away from the pan? That means we used the right amount of fat and the skillet's the right temperature. Not too high. Not too low. They're almost done. Anywhere you still see brighter yellow spots, stir and flip that part over. I'll start the toast."

Pale yellow fluffs rolled from one side of the skillet to the other with each stir. Although they were uniformly colored, he continued moving them around for another count of thirty. "I think they're cooked all the way through. They aren't slimy looking anymore."

"Move the skillet off the burner and come man the toaster while I check on the bacon."

He paused to give her quick kiss on the lips in passing as they switched locations. "You're sexy when you're bossy."

"Ha! You didn't think so at the cabin." The teasing grin she gave him over her shoulder sent his heart into a tailspin.

"That's because I didn't know what I was missing." He buttered the first batch of toast and started a second while she transferred the bacon to a couple layers of paper towels. "Here are the plates."

As the toaster popped a second time, she set two plates on the breakfast bar. "The eggs look great. Maybe we should try oatmeal next time."

Next time. I don't want you leave this time. He added the toast to their plates and sat beside her. "To be honest, I think I can live without knowing how to cook oatmeal."

"You've never had mine."

His prejudice against oatmeal vanished with the first bite of his breakfast. "Hey, these are good."

"Of course, they are. You're not a bad cook. You just need a few more lessons." She paused with her fork halfway to her mouth. "Now eat up so we can read a scene or two."

Caught between wanting to enjoy the best breakfast he'd had in a week and wanting to share a little naughty reading, he made a sandwich from the eggs, bacon, and toast. "You need to eat faster."

The wobbly feeling in his stomach her laughter triggered made him wish this moment could last forever. He had to find some way to convince Kristin to accept her—and soon. Going days without seeing and touching Pepper had already gotten old. Phone calls and clandestine meetings didn't come close to satisfying his desire to be with her.

He washed down the last tasty bite with a slow sip of perfectly brewed black coffee, something else that made him appreciate their time together. She tucked her last piece of bacon in her mouth as he took another sip.

Picking up both their empty plates, he stood. "I'll clean up while you read."

"Sounds like I'm getting the better end of that deal."

"Not really. I get to listen to you talk naughty. That's definitely a win for me."

"We'll start with the shower scene and see if you can stand the heat." A flash of wickedness sparkled in her eyes as she tapped the tablet's screen. After another tap, she leaned back in the barstool. "Here we go. *A Little Appetizer*. That's the name of the book. Very appropriate since Nash and Lucie's first few encounters are on the phone."

Not sure he was ready for the listening equivalent of voyeurism, he rinsed the silverware and added it to the dishwasher. The sooner he finished with cleanup, the sooner he could experience another encounter with Pepper.

"Lucie speaks first." She cleared her throat and lowered her voice to a husky pitch.

"I think I've created a phone-sex monster." She pulled her most life-like dildo from the vanity drawer. *"Not that I'm complaining, mind you. Sexual creativity is an important quality in a man."*

"I kinda like that quality in a woman too, not that I knew how much until last night. Ready for some fun in the shower, Lucie?" Shivering at Nash's husky tone, she reached past the shower curtain to turn on the water. *"Any time you are."*

Heat crept up Drew's neck at the picture in his head. "I think a 'life-like dildo' might be a little much. What else do you have?"

Pepper snickered, but she didn't complain about his low tolerance level for kink. "Okay. Let's try this one instead. It's called *The Main Dish*. Mason is a caterer and Ginger works as a food critic for an online newspaper, sort of, and she hired him to cater her wedding reception."

The wet plates almost slipped from his grasp. "You mean she's cheating on her fiancé?"

"No, no cheating, at least not by her. She caught her fiancé with… someone else, and she decides to act on her attraction to Mason. Just listen."

"I didn't drink to get over what they did. It all makes sense now. I should've seen it before." Ginger pulled her other foot from the boot in his grasp and then leaned forward until their faces were inches apart. Her long, dark lashes brushed her cheekbones with a slow blink. "I drank to be brave."

With his heart thumping a mile a minute, Mason dropped the second shoe next to the first. "Brave for what? Not something foolish, I hope."

"When you kissed me, I felt alive. I want to feel that way again." Not a single word came out slurred. "I need to be brave enough to tell you I want to have sex with you."

Alive. Kissing Pepper had made Drew feel alive again too. Making love to her made him want to live forever.

He ignored the broiler pan, using the excuse that the bacon grease was probably still too hot to dispose of to call his work done. "Come on. I want to have sex with you, and I don't need a drink to say it."

CHAPTER TWENTY-TWO

PEPPER STOMPED THE SNOW FROM HER BOOTS AND STRIPPED OFF HER gloves as she entered the double doors. The sudden wall of heat that met her was pure heaven after the biting-cold walk across the parking lot. A sign inside the second door indicated all visitors were required to check in at the office and a large arrow pointed to the left.

Tucking her gloves in her pocket, she turned in the direction of the office, thankful for another sign above an open doorway. A security camera stared down at her as well.

The layout was similar to Zack's elementary school, but not enough years had passed to prevent a tiny swell of apprehension. Every phone call had sent a wave of panic through her, not so much because she worried about her son being ill or in trouble as the possibility that his father had decided to claim him.

Of course, this school visit was almost as stressful. After a week of phone tag and no face-to-face time with Drew, her patience had reached its tattered end and tonight's second attempt at a family supper didn't look terribly promising, either.

She stepped into the office and smiled at the woman behind the counter. "Hi, I'm Pepper McCann. Drew Fulton made arrangements for me to pick up his daughter Kristin. She isn't feeling well."

"Good morning. She's in the nurse's office resting. May I see your ID? And you'll need to sign her out." The receptionist set a clipboard in front of Pepper and handed her a pen.

"Sure." Pepper slid her driver's license from the slot in her wallet. "Mr. Fulton will be in meetings part of the afternoon. Hannah hasn't complained of a stomachache or headache too, has she?"

The woman's pursed lips emphasized the deep wrinkles around her mouth. "No, I can assure you that Hannah is quite her normal self today."

Pepper completed the required information and signed her name, not about to let the receptionist's obvious disapproval stir her temper. "Thank goodness. One sick little girl is more than enough. Is Kristin ready to go?"

"As soon as we get her belongings from her locker." The pinch-faced woman picked up the telephone and punched in a short set of numbers. "Hi, Margie. Can you send Kristin Fulton's coat and back-pack to the office? Thank you."

A familiar voice came from behind Pepper, prompting her to look over her shoulder.

"I told Mr. Scholtz, and he didn't do *anything*." Framed in the doorway, Hannah stamped her foot and crossed her arms in front of her. "Carson is a meanie and I refuse to sit by him anymore."

With a mighty effort, Pepper barely held in a laugh. Strong-willed was an apt description for Drew's younger daughter. *No wonder we get along so well.*

"Pepper!" Hannah zipped through the office door, stopping inches from Pepper. Then she perched her fists on her hips and glared at the two adults who followed her into the room. "Pepper's going to be my new mom and she told me that telling on someone to a grownup isn't tattling when they do bad things to you. How did they know to call you, Pepper? They always call Daddy, but I'm glad you're here instead. Tell them I'm allowed to pull Carson's hair if he pulls mine first and the teacher doesn't do anything to stop him."

The woman on the left glanced at the man beside her and frowned, but it was downright friendly compared to the malicious look the middle-aged man aimed in Hannah's direction.

Hold on to your shorts, buddy. I'm big enough to stand up for myself and you can't sentence me to detention. Pepper nodded to his superior in greeting. "Pepper McCann. Is that true? Hannah told Mr. Scholtz a boy pulled her hair and he did nothing? So Hannah tries to protect herself and she gets in trouble? Something is very wrong with this picture."

The woman cleared her throat. "I'm Mrs. Sowers, the principal. I can only discuss the situation with Hannah's legal guardian. I don't believe Mr. Fulton has notified the school that there's been a change."

"Well, then by all means, call him. I'm sure he'll be interested to know that his daughter should expect to be punished for trying to stop a boy from hurting her while in the school's care." The principal made no move toward the phone on the other side of the counter, so Pepper reached into her pocket for her cell. "Or I can call him."

Hannah tugged on Pepper's coat. "Can you? I want to talk to Daddy."

With a patronizing smile, Mrs. Sowers patted the girl's arm. "There's no need to overreact."

The little girl rolled her eyes. "I'm not overreacting. You're *under*reacting."

Maternal instinct urged Pepper to call out the principal for her lack of concern, but letting her temper get the best of her wouldn't help. *Being the mature one sucks.* "You know what, Hannah? I'll call your dad and tell him what happened, but I think you should go back to your classroom. You're here to learn, not spend time in the office. I'm sure Mr. Scholtz will be happy to move Carson's desk away from yours so he can't bother you anymore. Isn't that right, Mr. Scholtz? And Mrs. Sowers can let all the kids know that hurting others is not acceptable. Does that sound fair?"

"Yep." Hannah wrapped her arms around Pepper's waist and squeezed. "You're the best, Pepper. I love you, and I can't wait until you and Daddy get married."

Married, huh? The girl's earlier comment about a new mom registered half a second later. "We'll talk about that another time. You head back to class."

"Okay. Can you come over tonight? I miss having a mommy."

Pepper hugged Hannah to hide the emotions roiling beneath her fake composure. "You bet. I'll be there right after I close the restaurant. Oh, and Kristin isn't feeling well, so I'm taking her to the deli to rest until your dad gets done with his meetings."

"I want to come too. Can I please?"

"Sorry, kiddo. No can do. You have to show Carson that you solve problems, not run away from them."

After a bit of grimacing, Hannah sighed. "Okay, but you have to read me a bedtime story."

"You're a master negotiator, Miss Fulton. One bedtime story it is." A firm handshake sealed the deal. When her possible future stepdaughter and Mr. Scholtz disappeared down the hall, Pepper turned her attention to the principal. "Hannah's father and I will be following up with her after school to make sure she's no longer seated next to Carson."

Mrs. Sowers expression turned as sour as her name. "You've made my job and that of Mr. Scholtz more difficult by undermining our authority."

"'Undermining your authority?' I thought I behaved quite diplomatically, actually, considering the circumstances. If you'd disciplined the child who created the problem instead of the one trying to solve it —without any help, I might add—I wouldn't have had to bargain with her to go back to class. You undermined your own authority by letting that boy think he's gotten away with something and treating Hannah like the troublemaker." Pepper swallowed the urge to continue her rant. If the woman didn't get the point by now, she never would. "Is Kristin ready to go?"

"I'm right here." A rather pale Kristin stood at the end of the counter, her hint of a smile suggesting she'd overheard at least part of the altercation. "Can we go now?"

Oops.

A boy entered the office with a coat and backpack hanging from his arm. He handed them to Kristin and then returned the way he came.

"I think so."

Mrs. Sowers glanced toward the receptionist, who gave a curt nod. "I'll be contacting Mr. Fulton to set an appointment to discuss this further."

Taking Kristin by the hand, Pepper reigned in her boiling temper and walked to the doorway. "I'll be discussing *this* with him too."

The trek to her car was silent, but as Pepper slid behind the steering wheel, she let out a long exhale. "I don't remember Zack's teachers and principals being so—so..."

"Condescending? Rigid?" Drew's daughter closed her eyes and leaned against the headrest.

"Exactly."

"Mom hated going to school for Hannah's conferences. She said they always acted like she was a bad parent. At the open house after Hannah started kindergarten, Mrs. Sourface said she needed to be on medication. Boy, Mom got really mad that time."

"Mrs. Sowers. No matter how much you dislike her, you should always be respectful." *Even if she doesn't deserve it. Maybe next time I need to ask to see her medical degree.* Pepper stopped at a red light and placed her palm on the girl's forehead. "Your mom sounds like she was a great parent. Hey, I thought you were sick. You seem fine to me."

Kristin's cheeks flushed bright pink. "I do have a stomachache and I feel kind of achy all over."

Looks like I got thrown in the deep end today, but at least she's talking to me. "Tell me the truth. Are you faking?"

"No." Her defensive tone was mixed with a helping of firm indignation.

"Okay. Then can I ask you a personal question?"

"Um, sure. I guess."

Fairly certain her instincts were right, Pepper managed a glance at her passenger as they followed the road north toward town. "Did you start your period at school? First time?"

A groan came from the passenger seat. "Is it that obvious?"

"We'll just say I'm perceptive. That sounds better, doesn't it? Your dad is *so* lucky I could pick you up today. Well, you're lucky too, because I know the best way to get rid of those nasty cramps." Making the right turn into the deli's parking lot, she winked at Kristin. "Let's get you settled on the couch with a movie, a heating pad, and a bowl of soup. I just finished baking a batch of cookies when your dad called. You like snickerdoodles, don't you?"

"They're my favorite." The girl sounded like she had mixed feelings about it, though.

Finally, I did something right. Pepper parked in her usual spot behind the deli and shut off the engine. "Mine too."

Kristin lunged across the center console and flung her arms around Pepper's neck. "Thanks for taking care of me."

Thrilled to finally develop a positive bond with Drew's older daughter, Pepper returned the hug. "You're very welcome, but I bet every one of your aunts would've done the same. Your grandma too."

Kristin pulled away and wrinkled her nose. "They'd tell Grandpa I wasn't feeling well and then he'd want to know what was wrong. I don't care if he *is* a doctor. I can't talk to him about girl stuff. That's too weird. It's almost worse than telling Daddy."

"Good point. Grab your backpack and we'll head upstairs."

As they walked to the outside stairway, Pepper's phone vibrated against her gloved hand inside her coat pocket. More than likely, Drew wanted an update on her errand. Unfortunately, the unexpected issue with Hannah wasn't something they could handle via text messages.

"Will you tell him? Daddy, I mean. He'll worry if he thinks I'm sick in a bad way."

At the top of the steps, Pepper unlocked the exterior door and waved her guest inside. "If you want me to. It's his job to worry about you, you know. That's what parents do. Or what they're supposed to do anyway."

"He worries too much, though, because of Mom having cancer."

"You're probably right. I'll make sure he knows there's nothing to worry about." Pepper ushered her visitor along the short hallway to the apartment. "I have plenty of feminine hygiene products in the bathroom. You're welcome to take some home with you if you need them. When you need more, we'll make a run to the grocery store. No need to make your dad uncomfortable."

"Thanks. I'm sorry I haven't been very nice to you. It's hard thinking about somebody taking Mom's place." Following Pepper into the living room, Kristin pointed behind her. "Who lives across the hall?"

"I'm not close to my mom, but I understand. Apology accepted. Zack lives in the other apartment. When he started college, he wanted to be more independent. This was a better option than living on campus since he works part-time in the deli. Cheaper too." After a quick tour of the kitchen and bathroom, Pepper led Kristin back to the living room. "While you get comfortable on the couch, I'll run downstairs for some soup. Minestrone or creamy potato soup? Crackers or a sandwich?"

"Minestrone has tomatoes and peppers in it, doesn't it? What's in the potato soup?" Kristin dropped her backpack on the couch and took off her coat.

Like father, like daughter. "Yeah, the minestrone has fresh tomatoes and bell peppers. The potato is basically mashed potatoes with enough milk to make it the consistency of soup and has sautéed onions and carrots."

"Can you make a grilled cheese sandwich to go with the potato soup?"

"Yep, but there's a catch. You have to choose your flavors. Italian, wheat, or rye bread? Swiss, cheddar, colby, or Muenster cheese? Oh, and plain butter or garlic butter?"

The girl's eyes widened. "Wow. I never had fancy grilled cheese before. Garlic butter, Italian bread, and... Boy, that's a hard choice. Um, Muenster?"

"My favorite combination, although I enjoy colby or cheddar on rye now and then too. So, um, did your mom or one of your aunts talk to you about your period?" *I can do this.* Having no prior experience with "the talk" from a parental or pubescent perspective didn't have to mean hiding her head in the sand.

A bit of pink colored Kristin's cheeks, but the cause could as easily have been the cold as embarrassment. "Yeah. Mom talked to me about lots of things when she was sick. She said she wanted to make up for not being here when I needed to ask questions. Do you think she felt bad for leaving us?"

With her heart in her throat, Pepper sank onto the couch beside Kristin. "Maybe, but I bet she mostly wanted to make sure you'd be okay without her. I can't even imagine how difficult it must have been for her to come to terms with not getting to watch you and Hannah grow up. She made the most of the time she had with the people she loved. Remember that about her."

"It feels kind of weird talking to you about her."

"A little, but I'm okay with it if you are." Afraid to lose the precious ground she'd gained, Pepper patted the girl's knee and stood. "I'll be back in about ten or fifteen minutes with lunch. Movies are on the shelf and you're welcome to help yourself to something to drink."

"Okay." Kristin unzipped her backpack, evidently content to let the subject drop.

As she hurried downstairs, Pepper pulled her phone from her pocket. She shook her head and fought a laugh at the messages waiting for her.

"Thanks for picking up Kristin."

"Do you think she needs to go to the doctor?"

"I hope she doesn't make you sick. What if she's contagious? Neither one of us can afford to miss work."

"Tell me if she's rude to you. Maybe I need to have another talk with her tonight."

"Are you back from the school yet?"

Rather than hoping he'd understand a series of short answers, she tapped on his contact.

A single ring was all that sounded. "Hello? Pepper? Is everything okay?"

"I have good news and bad news. Well, not exactly *bad* news."

"Okay. Let me have the bad news first." His pained exhale in her ear made her wish she hadn't put it that way.

"Kristin is growing up. She's becoming a young woman."

"Well, yeah. Oh. Ohhh. You mean… Man, that explains a lot. The mood swings lately. God, I'm not ready for this. Give me the good news."

On her way to the bread rack, she grabbed the cheese and the garlic butter from the fridge. "She's just having some cramps and a headache, and we had a whole conversation without any snide remarks or sassy facial expressions."

"Yeah, that's good news. So you don't mind taking care of her?"

"Nope. It's fine. I'm making her lunch and she's going to watch a movie upstairs." Bread knife in hand, she opted for disclosure, at least in one respect. He probably didn't want to know the details. "We talked some about Kate."

His long moment of silence gave her no clue what he thought about that revelation. "Hmm. That sounds awkward. Does that fall under good or bad?"

"It was a little weird for both of us, but I think it helped. She might actually like me without feeling like she's betraying her mom now. Progress."

"That's a relief. Did the school let you sign her out with any problems?"

She carried the buttered bread and sliced Muenster to the grill. "Yeah, but I have the feeling I've made an enemy of the principal. Most definitely Hannah's teacher."

His groan summed up exactly the reaction she expected. "Hannah got in trouble again?"

"More like the teacher needs a lesson in teaching boys to treat girls with respect. A boy pulled her hair, so she told Mr. Scholtz. When he didn't do anything, she pulled the boy's hair. Guess who got blamed for being the bully." With the sandwich cooking, she ladled potato soup into a carryout container. "I convinced Hannah to go back to class and then Mrs. Sourface accused me of undermining her authority. You'd think a woman principal would encourage her teachers to prevent bullying and victim-blaming, especially with girls."

"Mrs. Sourface, huh?" His bark of laughter seemed to indicate he wasn't bothered by the way she'd handled the situation. "You must've gotten that name from Hannah."

"Kristin, actually. I told her she shouldn't call her that, but it fits so damn well."

"It does, doesn't it? Kate and I talked about trying to find a different school, but then she got sick and I didn't want to disrupt the girls' lives even more. Maybe it's time to start looking. I'd like you to help if you have time." Something beeped in the background and he growled. "I need to go. My next appointment is here. Can you still come over to the house later?"

"Already planned to. Hannah finagled the promise of a bedtime story out of me. If Kristin doesn't mind, she can stay and ride with me. Then you'll have a chance to talk to Hannah about what happened." Partly excited and partly terrified about the prospect of sharing parenting responsibilities with him, she flipped the sandwich. "Want me to bring supper?"

"Sounds like a good plan, but I'll take care of supper since you handled the school stuff. I love you."

"Love you too. See you about six thirty." Tucking her phone in her pocket with one hand, she transferred the garlic-scented sandwich to a box with the other. "Perfect."

A snicker came from behind her, Zack obviously having overheard her conversation with Drew. "I would've liked to seen you butting heads with the principal. I bet you put her in her place. You're probably Hannah's hero now. Poor kid."

"Hero? I doubt it. She held her own just fine. That girl is way smarter than her teacher and the principal." The bell above the entrance chimed as she bagged the soup and sandwich. "Looks like the lunch rush is starting. I'll be back as fast as I can."

"No hurry." Retying his apron, he headed to the counter.

Pepper headed in the opposite direction, taking the inside stairwell back upstairs. A touch of maternal reflex hit when she entered her apartment.

The opening credits of a Harry Potter movie flicked across the TV screen and Kristin lay curled up on the couch, the fleece throw draped around her. Peppermint-scented steam wafted from the mug on the end table.

She sat up when Pepper approached. "I made tea. Is that okay?"

"Yep." Pepper handed her the bag. "Here's your lunch. I need to get to work, but I'll be up to check on you in about an hour or so."

"Thanks." Kristin nibbled on her lower lip and unfolded the top of the plain white sack. "I'm sorry I acted mean. You didn't deserve it."

Touched by the sincerity of the gesture, Pepper risked kissing the girl on the top of the head. "Apology accepted. Do you want to hang out here instead of having your dad pick you up after work? Then I can drive you home and read Hannah her bedtime story after supper."

"Can I?"

"Sure." *That was easy.* "I'll see you in a little while."

The happy dance on the return trip downstairs had to suffice for a celebration. Noises carried a bit too well in the stairway to let out a whoop of relief.

Pepper joined Zack at the counter. "Did I miss much?"

His tight-lipped scowl sent her stomach rolling in a somersault. "Pierce is here. He wants to talk to you."

CHAPTER TWENTY-THREE

SLIDING BEHIND THE STEERING WHEEL, DREW TOSSED HIS PORTFOLIO onto the passenger seat. With ten workdays left before the partnership took effect, he'd managed to review his current accounts and come up with updated marketing plans for all but three clients. Kristin had finally accepted Pepper, and tonight he would pop the question.

So what if he'd met her less than three weeks ago?

His life finally seemed to be moving forward again after almost two years of barely treading water, and he loved her, something he'd never expected to happen so quickly or easily.

He flipped on his turn signal as he neared the exit of the parking lot. Then he turned toward home, wishing that was his next stop. Although he wasn't looking forward to his last meeting of the day, it was a necessary evil.

Twelve minutes later, the bright yellow school zone sign sparked a twinge in his gut, and he followed the paved entrance to the south side of the building. Pepper had handled the Hannah situation pretty damn well, and now he would finish the discussion with the people he'd entrusted with his daughter.

The receptionist greeted him as he entered the office and immediately ushered him toward the principal's closed door. She knocked. "Mrs. Sowers is expecting you."

I hope so since I made an appointment with her. When the door opened from the inside, he stepped into Sourface's lair. "Did someone tell Hannah she isn't riding the bus home today?"

The principal walked to the far side of her desk and gestured for him to sit as she took the seat across from him. "Yes. I understand you'd like to discuss what happened with her earlier in the classroom. The teacher saw her pull a boy's hair and had to call for assistance when she refused to come to the office."

Instead of sitting, he paced to the window and back to the desk, allowing his temper to simmer. "What about the boy who pulled her hair first? And the teacher who ignored her when she told him about it? Since when does asking for help get punishment and instigating the trouble doesn't?"

"I see Ms. McCann talked to you." Her disapproving tone sounded more condescending than usual.

"Yes, she did. She said Hannah was brought to the office, but the boy who pulled her hair wasn't. Is this what's been going on for the last—"

"Mr. Fulton, the teacher saw her pull the boy's hair. He didn't see the boy pull her hair."

"So it didn't happen if the teacher was too busy to see it? If a tree falls in the forest and nobody hears it, it still makes a noise. And don't give me some nonsense about tattling. You should be teaching these kids that telling an adult when something bad happens is the right thing to do. Or maybe you'd like the police to ignore you if someone breaks into your house and they didn't see it. I want to know how long you've been making my daughter the bad guy because she's had to protect herself."

"That's quite enough." Mrs. Sowers pushed her chair back and rose. "This isn't the first time Hannah's gotten in trouble for tattling. The school—"

"No, it isn't enough. Hannah's being blamed for something you and the teacher should be handling. You admitted that she told the teacher about the problem and he did nothing. How many other little girls has this boy bothered and they didn't say anything because they knew the teacher, or you, wouldn't do anything about it?"

Sowers clenched her fists in her lap. "I don't like what you're implying."

"I don't like the way you're treating my daughter." Tired of beating his head against this brick wall of a women's thick skull, he headed to the closed door. "I'm withdrawing my girls from this school. Today. I expect your full cooperation in forwarding their records as soon as we find a more suitable learning environment."

The principal's hateful expression reminded him of the nasty headmaster who'd replaced Dumbledore in one of Kristin's favorite movies. Her lips thinned to almost nothing and her flushed cheeks clashed with her purple sweater.

He forced himself to walk at a relaxed pace to the outer office, relief already easing the stress that had been building for months.

The receptionist looked his direction with wide eyes and then away, hinting that she'd likely eavesdropped on the whole private conversation. "I'll have Mr. Scholtz send Hannah to the office while you sign her out."

Sent to the office twice in one day? I don't think so. "Actually, I'd rather go down to her classroom to get her after school is dismissed. I need to help her clean out her desk and her locker. Please tell Kristin's teacher I'll stop in there when I'm done in Hannah's room." Turning his back to her, he slipped his phone from his pocket and opened his text messages.

"Are you busy, Pepper?"

Several long seconds passed before the prompt that she was in the process of responding appeared. *"Just got done checking on Kristin. Everything okay?"*

"These people have no idea how to deal with boys picking on girls. I can see why you told off the principal. I pulled Hannah and Kristin out of school. Any chance you have time to help me find a new one by the end of next week?"

"I'm sorry they weren't more cooperative. We can talk about it

tonight with the girls and make plans on Monday. I have a couple ideas. Maybe some school visits Monday, no, Tuesday morning? Monday's a holiday."

His pulse slowed at her calm offer of a solution. *"Sounds good. I appreciate this more than you know."*

"You're welcome. I'll see you in a few hours."

He pocketed his cell and stood facing the wall of glass between the office and the hallway. A few hours seemed like forever to wait, but it would likely go fast with all that he needed to do before she arrived at the house. Tonight's supper had to be special, a way to set the tone for a romantic proposal after they put the kids to bed. Maybe Hannah would have a suggestion or two when they stopped at the grocery store. Her imagination was still unhindered by the fear of failure.

The sharp ring of the dismissal bell made his pulse jump and his heart race. The sick feeling in his gut that had faded returned. The noise signaled another change in his life, one he hoped marked another positive step forward.

Voices carried through the glass and children filed into the hall, loaded down with winter coats and backpacks. Bittersweet memories crowded in, memories of the first day of school for both his girls and enough musical programs that they all ran together. He and Kate had attended every one together, even after she'd gotten sick and the trouble had started with Hannah.

The time to move on had arrived, staring him in the face and challenging him make the changes he and his girls needed. Familiarity didn't necessarily breed contempt, but it wasn't always the best option, either.

The hallway cleared almost as quickly as it had filled, the long holiday weekend probably great motivation to hurry. Without looking back, he exited the office and followed the hall to the first-grade classrooms. The man standing outside the second doorway cast a glance in his direction and crossed his arms in front of his chest. If Drew hadn't already recognized the teacher, the defensive stance would've given him away.

I hope for your kids' sakes you don't have any daughters. Drew entered the room without slowing, too pissed off to do more than offer a terse greeting to the jerk. "Mr. Scholtz."

"I'd like to have a few words with you if you don't mind, Mr. Fulton." The teacher shadowed him to the wall of lockers where Hannah stood.

"I do mind." Greeting his daughter with a smile, he leaned down to whisper in her ear. "I heard what happened. Pack up everything but the stuff that has to stay here. Pepper's going to help us find a different school."

She threw her arms around his neck, almost knocking him off balance. "Really, Daddy?"

"Yep."

"Kristin too?" The concern in her question was uncharacteristic.

I want my confident Hannah back. "Yeah, both my girls. Get the rest of your things."

"Okay." Without a moment's hesitation, she marched past her teacher to her desk. One item after another went into her backpack. Then she did the same with her locker. "Ready."

He grasped her outstretched hand, still ignoring Scholtz and his bully-faced stare. "Let's go clean out your sister's locker."

The trip to Kristin's classroom brought a small dose of remorse, but her ability to conform instead of rebel had made her the perfect student. A sympathetic shrug from the woman sorting papers at her desk was evidence enough that word of this afternoon's disagreement had traveled quickly. Her lack of attempt to talk him out of withdrawing his kids spoke louder than any words she might've said. Keeping quiet probably offered better job security than making waves.

Within ten minutes, he unlocked his car doors and loaded the armful of his older daughter's belongings into the passenger seat. "Climb in, squirt. We need to stop at the grocery store and pick out something super special since Pepper's coming for supper tonight."

Hannah swung her backpack onto the seat beside her and then buckled her seatbelt. "What about Kristin? Are we going to pick her up after that?"

"She's coming home with Pepper so we can have some time together."

"Why?" Her pouty lip caught his attention in the rearview mirror as he backed out of the parking space. "Are you mad about me getting in trouble today?"

Before he turned onto the road, he took a second to glance back at her over his shoulder and shake his head. "Nope. You probably shouldn't have pulled the boy's hair, but you did the right thing by telling your teacher what happened. Is this the first time he did something like that?"

"Carson never pulled my hair before, but he tried to take my pencils once. And Mr. Scholtz called me a fibber when he snuck the pencils back on my desk. He broke my ruler on purpose too and he tripped me on the playground. He's mean. I wish all boys were nice like you, Daddy."

Damn, I should've done this sooner. He slowed as they approached the first four-way stop. "You know, you don't have to say that. I promise I'm not mad about the hair pulling. Or any of the other times the principal said you were in trouble."

"I know, but you're the nicest boy I've ever met, even when I give you an ulcer."

An involuntary laugh escaped. "My stomach's fine, squirt. Your sister was exaggerating."

"Oh, okay. When are you going to marry Pepper?"

Soon, I hope. "I haven't asked her yet."

"Why not? You love her, don't you?"

Finally, an easy question. He made the turn into the grocery store parking lot. "I love her a lot, but I wanted to make sure you and your sister were comfortable with the idea of her being your stepmom first."

"I don't want to call her that. She isn't mean, even if Kristin doesn't like her." A gasp came from the backseat. "Oops. I shouldn't've told you that. Now she's gonna be mad at *me* too."

"Nah, it'll be okay. Pepper's good at fixing things. What do you want to call her?"

As soon as he shut off the engine, she unlatched her seatbelt and leaned through front seats. "How about Mom? She can't be Mommy because Mommy was Mommy. And Zack calls her Mom. Can we have a little brother when you get married since we'll already have a big brother?"

Nerves about proposing could've caused the sudden attack of butterflies in his stomach, but most likely the thought of becoming a father again was the culprit. "A baby? I'm not sure about that, but I *will* tell you a secret. After supper tonight, I'm going to ask Pepper to marry me."

She flung her arms around his neck and squealed. "You are? I can't wait to tell Aunt Colleen and Merie and Grandma and Uncle Flynn!"

"You have to keep it a secret for now. No telling, or even hinting, until I say it's okay."

"I promise, Daddy! Are you going to give her *the ring*? You can't ask her to marry you without a ring."

How could he be diplomatic about the fact that he'd already bought a real diamond engagement ring? Pepper deserved better than a gumball-machine prize. "You know what? I was kind of thinking that maybe you and Kristin should give her the one you picked out. Um, to show her that you want her to be part of our family too."

"Oh! We could ask her to be our mom." Hannah bounded out of the car and opened his door. "Come on, Daddy! We need to pick out a special cake and we have to get some flowers. It'll be just like Valentine's Day!"

Her enthusiasm chased away the case of nerves, and he tucked her hand in his as they hurried past the row of parked cars. "Let's hope it's even better than Valentine's Day since we're cooking. What do you think? Steak on the grill and baked potatoes?"

She hopped over an icy spot on the pavement. "Yep! Cooking outside in the snow is fun!"

Even though she'd had a tough day at school, her disposition seemed none the worse for wear as they walked into the store. She rushed between the cakes, pies, and cookies, insisting on inspecting the whole bakery department before finally making a decision and then leading him to the floral section.

He stopped near the refrigerated case of long-stemmed roses and some other exotic-looking flowers. Traditional was probably a good choice for a marriage proposal.

"Roses are pretty, Daddy, but Mom's more like these." She pointed to a modest bouquet of hot pink and white carnations with yellow, pink, and orange daisies poking up in between. It was vibrant, colorful, and natural—a perfect match for Pepper.

Mom. Maybe this won't be as hard as I thought. "You're right. Good thing you're here to help me." A glance at his watch warned him they'd have to hurry through the grocery shopping part of their outing if he wanted to have supper ready on time. "Let's get a move on, squirt. We don't want to be late."

They made quick work of picking up the few remaining items on his mental list and then headed to the express checkout. When he caught sight of his brother-in-law's wife in the next lane over, he ducked behind the magazine display. Explaining the flowers and cake would be easy compared to justifying how fast his new relationship had gotten serious enough for a proposal. At least Flynn and his almost-boss, Lilith Montgomery, had known each other and worked together for almost three months before they walked down the aisle.

"Hi, Aunt Lily!" Hannah darted to Lilith and hugged her around the waist. "Whatcha buying? We're buying stuff so we can ask Pepper to marry us tonight. Daddy's cooking, and we got cake and flowers."

So much for keeping secrets. Stifling a groan, he gave his newest sister-in-law a weak wave as she jerked whatever was in her hand behind her back. The simple lettering on the small purple box registered a second later. To his advertising brain, the packaging was unmistakable. EPT had branding down pat.

Her smile brightened. "I won't tell if you won't."

He grinned, as happy for her and Flynn as he was for himself. Not that long ago, he would've thought the worst of her. "Sounds fair."

She set the box on the conveyer belt and kissed the top of Hannah's head. "You and your sister should come for a sleepover sometime soon."

At the ingenious distraction, his daughter clapped her hands. "Can we make pineapple upside-down cake with Uncle Flynn? It's my favorite."

"You bet, kiddo." The line moved forward, putting Lily across from the cashier. "My turn. I'll call you next week."

"Okay!" Hannah weaved her way back to him as he unloaded the cart. "Aunt Lily is lots happier since she married Uncle Flynn."

He nodded. "Uncle Flynn is too."

Her blue eyes lost some of their gleam. "Daddy, will all your sadness go away when you marry Pepper?"

The question picked at the wound that hadn't yet healed all the way —might never heal completely. "I'll always be kind of sad about your mom. That's okay, though. I loved her a lot."

As answers went, it didn't begin to cover the full range of his emotions, but trying to explain his feelings to his child held no appeal. Starting over with Pepper was almost like living another life, one far removed from his time with Kate. She'd wanted him to move on, to find happiness again. Somehow, he had, and guilt over not feeling guilty still snuck up on him unexpectedly.

Setting the last of his purchases on the conveyer belt, he abandoned the maudlin trek toward memory lane. The past was done and he was ready to plan for his future.

CHAPTER TWENTY-FOUR

STILL SEETHING FROM KEVIN'S EARLIER VISIT, PEPPER PASTED ON what she hoped was an easygoing expression and entered her apartment. Slamming the door behind her might've released some of her pent-up anger, but she buried the urge. Showing her red-hot temper was probably a bad move since Kristin had finally warmed up to her.

The girl glanced up from the same spot she'd been parked on the couch all afternoon. The lamplight brought out a tinge of red in her brown hair Pepper hadn't noticed before. "Is something wrong? You look like Daddy when he's trying to not be mad."

"Good observation." Plopping into the adjacent chair, Pepper growled. "You know what? It isn't important and I'm not going to let it stress me out. Did you save some cookies for me?"

Kristin giggled. "I don't think I could eat three dozen snickerdoodles even if I wanted to. It's awfully close to suppertime, but I suppose a cookie won't ruin your appetite too much."

"Thanks, Mom." With a wink, Pepper rose to find the cookies on her way to the bathroom. "I'm going to take a quick shower. Then we'll head to your house. I won't be long, maybe ten or fifteen minutes."

As Pepper snapped the lid back on the container, Kristin's tentative voice followed her to the kitchen. "I wouldn't mind having you for a mom."

Thankfulness and relief chased away the remains of Pepper's anger. "I wouldn't mind having you for a daughter."

She took a bite of her treat and hurried into the bathroom before anything could ruin the perfect moment. In the grand scheme of things, Kristin's change in attitude was a hell of lot more important than Kevin's antics. His threats and cajoling had backfired, and he'd trashed any chance of convincing Zack to cooperate with his money-grubbing conspiracy. Between Kyle's security cameras and her brilliant thought to record the conversation on her phone, a restraining order finally seemed doable.

The warm water soothed her stiff neck muscles and washed away the lingering scents of raw onions, green olives, and bleu cheese. Even if Drew liked eating those things, he probably wouldn't enjoy smelling them on her all evening.

Ten minutes later, she slipped a sweater on over her tank top and went in search of her shoes. "Hey, Kristin, ready to go? I just need to find my boots and grab my coat."

"Yep. Your boots were sticking partway out from under the couch, so I put them on the rug by the door. That's okay, isn't it?" Kristin wrapped her scarf around her neck as she stood. The fleece throw lay folded in a neat rectangle on the back of the couch and not a single empty mug or lunch wrapper remained on the end table.

"You bet." Pepper bent to tug on her boots. "I can be a bit of a slob when I get busy."

"This is nothing compared to Hannah's room sometimes." With her coat zipped and snapped, the girl slipped on her gloves. "She's way more of a slob than you are."

"Will I be able to get to her bed to read her a bedtime story tonight? Or do I need to take a shovel with me?"

Slinging her backpack on her shoulder, Kristin laughed, a genuinely happy sound that brightened Pepper's mood even more. "It's not that bad. She just needs to be reminded to put her stuff away."

"I could use a reminder like that from time to time myself." Keys in hand, Pepper led the way down the outside stairway to her car.

Her passenger was quiet during the drive, but not in the awkward way she would've expected this morning. The occasional flash of light from oncoming traffic across the Kristin's face revealed the most content expression Pepper had seen on the girl.

As they turned off the main road, darkness hid all but the half-circle of light from the headlights and the brighter patches of snow along the road. The peacefulness of the surrounding woods matched the serenity that had finally developed between them.

"Are you going to live at our house when you and Daddy get married? Or are we going to move?"

The question caught Pepper by surprise, and she tightened her hold on the steering wheel to make the turn onto Drew's street. "You sound awfully sure there's going to be a wedding. He hasn't asked me, in case you're wondering. And I haven't asked him, either."

"But he bought a ring. I saw—" Kristin clapped her hand over her mouth.

Pepper stopped a few feet from the garage door, thankful she hadn't been driving in heavy traffic during Kristin's obvious slip of the tongue. Marriage had come up, but only in a casual at-some-undefined-time-in-the-future way.

"Oops. I shouldn't have said that. You have to act surprised when he gives it to you." The girl slumped in her seat and groaned. "He's going to be *so* mad at me for telling."

Patting Kristin's shoulder through her coat, Pepper tried to calm her racing heart. "We'll talk about living arrangements when the time comes. As far as your dad being mad, I think you're way off the mark. He's been worried about you getting along with me, so I doubt he'll do anything until he's sure you're okay with me becoming part of your family."

Lanky arms wrapped around her waist. "I'm going to tell him I like you and that I don't mind if he wants to marry you. I'm glad he's happy again."

A tear leaked from Pepper's eye, and she rubbed a glove along the side of her nose to wipe it away. "I like you too. We should go inside before your dad comes looking for us."

After another squeeze, Kristin released her. "Thanks for taking care of me today. I feel lots better."

"You're very welcome." Pepper opened her door and hoped the wetness on her cheeks didn't freeze.

The other door clunked closed. "Mm. Do you smell that? I think Daddy's grilling. He isn't very good in the kitchen, but he's the best at cooking out."

Savoring the mouthwatering aroma hovering in the chilly air, Pepper followed Kristin along the sidewalk toward the front porch. "I'm pretty sure that's steak. I might propose before he does."

"That'd be awesome. Then he wouldn't know I told you about what I wasn't supposed to see."

"I wouldn't be too sure about that. Parents tend to know those things." Scuttling up the porch steps, Pepper gave her co-conspirator a sideways grin. "Come on. I'm hungry."

Five minutes later, they stood in their stocking feet at the French doors leading to the deck. Drew and Hannah were huddled in front of the grill, the red glow of hot coals making their faces look pinker than they probably were. Pepper tapped on the glass, waving when her chefs turned at the noise.

Drew's mouth turned upward in an inviting grin. He raised two gloved fingers and his muffled voice carried through the double-paned glass. "Two minutes."

She nodded and didn't fight the giddiness that came as involuntarily as breathing. How had she fallen so completely in love with this man in such a short time?

Kristin snickered beside her. "You guys are worse than Uncle Flynn and Aunt Lily, and that's saying a lot. You're going to ask him tonight, aren't you?"

"Maybe." The idea wasn't as ludicrous as her irrational nerves seemed to think it was. It put her in control, and the time she and Drew spent alone together had included discussions of their future together. Proposing wouldn't exactly be out of character for her, either. *Forget traditional. I can damn well ask him to marry me if I want to.* "You'll need to make sure your dad and I have a little privacy at some point this evening."

"Leave it to me." The impish sparkle in Kristin's eyes warned Pepper that Hannah wasn't the only one of Drew's daughters with a taste for subversion.

"You sound too much like me at your age, which is a little scary. And here I thought you were the live-by-the-rules sister." Pepper crooked her finger at her new buddy and headed for the kitchen cupboards. "Let's set the table while they finish cooking."

As Kristin finished adding silverware to the place settings and Pepper filled the glasses, Drew and Hannah clomped in the back door.

"You're finally here!" Hannah glanced up at her dad and pressed her lips together, making a zipping motion across them with her gloved fingers.

Holding out the covered platter in his grasp, Drew raised his eyebrows at his younger daughter. "Boots off. Then go hang up your coat. Kristin, will you set this on the table? And, Pepper, can you come here please?"

The desperation in his voice sounded so similar to the time he'd been trapped in wet jeans at the cabin that she had to suppress a shiver. Although he didn't seem to need help with his coat or shoes, she shuffled over to him anyway. "Everything okay?"

He hooked his arm around her and pulled her in for a slow but mostly chaste kiss. "Almost. This isn't exactly how I planned it, but Hannah's too excited to keep the secret and the timing just feels right."

When he dropped to one knee in front of her, her stomach dropped with him—especially after hearing about his recent purchase.

"Pepper, I love you and I want to spend the rest of my life with you." He removed a blue jeweler's box from his coat pocket and flipped open the lid, looking every bit as adorable as he had in rubber-duck-covered boxers. "Will you marry me?"

With her heart hammering in her chest, she had to swallow twice to clear the tightness in her throat.

Hannah and Kristen clapped behind her. "Say yes! Please say yes!"

Drew grinned in their direction, probably thrilled that his older daughter was part of the coaxing. Then he met Pepper's gaze. The openness and warmth is his relaxed smile propelled her even deeper in love.

Touching her fingertips to the laugh lines at the corner of his lips, she surrendered to the overwhelming urge to seize her chance at true happiness. "Yes, I'll marry you."

He turned his head and kissed her palm. The gentle caress sent tingles along her skin. "Soon? I've never seen the point of long engagements."

While his girls would likely prefer a full-blown wedding, an intimate ceremony with a few friends and family members was more her style. "How long? A few weeks? A few months?"

"I was thinking two weeks from Sunday. The thirty-first." He rose as he slipped the ring on her finger. "I can ask Lily about having the wedding in the party room at Montgomery Crossing and Flynn can put together some food for the reception. Simple but classy, and not a lot of stress for us."

The chill of the thin circle of metal contrasted with the warmth coursing through her. "That sounds wonderful."

"Can you take the girls shopping for dresses and whatever else they need? I can help Zack at the deli if you need to take time off."

"Just how long have you been planning this?"

Hannah squeezed in between them. "I told Daddy all the things we have to do to get ready for the wedding while we were making supper. Me and Kristen, oops, Kristen and I helped Aunt Lily with hers and Uncle Flynn's. They had wreaths and trees with lights and bows 'cause it was Christmas Eve. We need lots of flowers, and who says the ring bearer has to be a boy? I want that job."

"Are you sure?" Pepper brushed a few stray strands of hair toward Hannah's loosened ponytail. "I was going to ask you and your sister to be my bridesmaids."

The little girl's jaw dropped. "A bridesmaid?"

"Yep, but I suppose Kristen could be my maid of honor and you could carry the ring, if that's what you want."

Drew's older daughter squealed, all her usual composure evidently lost in the excitement. "Really? You want me to be your maid of honor?"

Hannah stepped back and put her fists on her hips. "But… Can I be the best man then?"

Waving his girls toward the table, Drew kicked off his shoes. "Supper's getting cold. Eat first. We'll talk about wedding details later."

Pepper leaned in close enough to hide a whisper behind a kiss. "Good save."

"Ha! I'm tempted to elope, but I don't think the girls would like that much." He removed his hat and hung his coat on the doorknob. Then his chilly hand closed around hers. "I can't wait until I get to wake up beside you every morning."

"Me too." She kissed him again, too in love not to show him.

Unlike a week and a half ago, supper was a relaxed, enjoyable meal with no outbursts, hateful looks, or unpleasant comments. Married life wouldn't be perfect, but she could live with normal, average, or some variation thereof. Their combination of stepparents and stepsiblings wouldn't matter. They'd be a family in the truest sense of the word—there for each other, through good times and bad.

While the girls cleared the table and Drew stowed the leftovers, Pepper tapped a message to Zack into her phone. *"Any plans for two weeks from Sunday?"*

Less than five seconds passed before her cell vibrated in her hand. *"Nope. What's up? Getting married?"*

She laughed aloud and shook her head. *"Maybe. No saying I told you so."*

"Awesome! I seem to recall predicting an engagement within a month. Tell Drew I said it's about time. LOL"

"How do you know I didn't ask him???"

"Did you? I can see you doing that."

"No, but only because he beat me to it. I was going to tonight."

"Haha! I'm happy for you. He's a good guy. What about Kristin?"

"He is. That's not a problem anymore. We bonded over snickerdoodles and girl talk. See you when I get home tonight."

"Told you you're a great mom. :) Love you."

"What's so funny?" Drew placed a pickle jar full of flowers in front of her. "These are for you."

She handed him her cell and then brushed her fingertips across the colorful blooms to release their sweet perfume. "They're gorgeous. Thank you."

Amusement lit up his eyes as he scrolled through the series of text messages. "I'm a little sorry for messing up your plan. I guess great minds really do think alike."

She lowered her voice, even though the girls were busy loading the dishwasher. "It was partly Kristin's idea, if you can believe that. I'm not sure I would've considered doing it otherwise."

"I didn't want to have to tell her I was marrying you whether she liked it or not, but I would've at some point. Patience isn't my best virtue." He glanced toward his daughters as he draped his arm across her shoulders. "Looks like cleanup is done. Are you ready for dessert?"

The girls were headed to the table with a bakery box, but her mind had already veered off in another direction. She covered a giggle with a cough and waggled her eyebrows at him. "Definitely. It's been a long week."

The corner of his mouth curved upward before he kissed her. "Very long."

Hannah squeezed under his arm with paper plates and plastic forks while her sister set the box beside the flowers. "We bought a cake with hearts on it since this is kind of like Valentine's Day. Oh, I almost forgot!"

She ducked backward and dragged Kristin toward the breakfast bar. After almost a full minute of whispering and nodding, both girls returned to the table.

With Hannah bouncing at her side, Kristin held out her hand, a gaudy gumball-machine ring in her open palm. "Pepper, will you marry us too?"

Pepper pulled in a shaky breath, caught off guard by the flood of emotion brought on by the invitation. Unable to speak past the urge to cry like a baby, she nodded and reached for the token. The girls crowded in next to her as she slid the ring past the knuckles of her right pinkie. It flopped to one side.

Lifting her hand, Drew wiggled the bauble back and forth. "Want me to make it smaller so it stays put?"

"In a sec." She hugged his daughters in turn, deeply touched by their gift. "Your dad told me you gave him the ring for a lady you thought would be a good wife to him and mom to you. That you'd give it to me… It means so much to me."

Hannah looked toward her sister. "Now?"

Kristin's grin was wide and genuine, a welcome change from the smiles she'd faked to avoid getting in trouble. "Yep."

The younger girl clutched her hands behind her and stood with her feet glued to the floor. "We love you as much as Daddy does and we're really glad you're going to be our mom. Now it's time to eat cake."

"I love you too. Both of you." Pepper swiped at her teary eyes and then held out her pinkie to their father. "Okay. Ready. I don't want to lose this."

With a gentle squeeze, he adjusted the band to fit her finger. "Perfect."

"Yeah." She'd found the perfect man—and his kids—to spend her life with, even if they all were a little imperfect.

Hannah set the first piece of cake in front of Pepper. "Now can we talk about wedding stuff? And babies. I want a baby brother."

CHAPTER TWENTY-FIVE

Ushering Kristin and Hannah into the deli, Drew greeted the gorgeous redhead behind the counter with a grin. Even in a food-spattered apron, Pepper took his breath away. The feeling hit the spot even better than his morning coffee.

She set an empty white tub on the cart beside her and stepped toward the order station. Leaning forward, she met him with a quick kiss. "Hi, guys. What a nice surprise! You're never going to believe who's here. The principal from one of the schools on my list. It's only a few blocks from here—maybe half a mile? She'd like to meet you."

"Hold still." He pulled a paper napkin from the dispenser and wiped what looked like a tomato seed from her chin. Then he kissed her again. "Can you take a little break and make the introductions?"

Hannah scrunched up her face. "She better be nicer than Mrs. Sourface."

Kristin pressed her lips together, clearly trying not to show her approval of the name her sister used. "If Pepper likes her, she must be okay. Right?"

"Of course I'm right. You'll see. Mrs. Beecham was Zack's favorite teacher before she became a principal." Tugging the dirty apron over her head, Pepper whirled toward the kitchen. "Ona, I need to go out to the dining room. Can you cover the register for a few minutes?"

A dark-haired young woman appeared in the doorway. "Sure. The second pot of black bean soup is cooking."

"Great. Thanks." Pepper pointed to the end of the counter. "Meet you down there in a minute. I need to wash my hands."

He waved the girls forward to the opening past the salad case, but a quick scan of the dining room didn't give him the slightest clue about who Mrs. Beecham might be. Four women sat at separate tables, each one as different from the others as they could possibly be, except for age. Only the blonde closest to him looked too young to run a school, but good genes and a decent hairdresser could probably help a forty-something-year-old pass for thirty. Her fur-lined purple ski jacket and tall black boots hardly fit the image of a principal, though. The others were all probably at least fifty.

His younger daughter yanked off her gloves. One dropped to the floor as she shoved them in her pocket. "Which one do you think she is?"

Kristin picked up her sister's glove and handed it to her without so much as a sigh or an impatient reminder to keep track of her belongings. "That's easy. The lady reading the book."

"Nope." Pepper's fingers slipped through his, linking their hands together, and she led them to a table next to the window. "Good guess."

A fiftyish woman dressed in some sort of white karate outfit sat with her booted feet crossed at the ankles in front of her. She tossed her silver-streaked braid over her shoulder as she looked up from the kitting in her lap. Her gaze went straight toward his girls. "You must be Kristin and Hannah. Zack's mom told me all about you. I'm Mrs. Beecham. Would you like to join me? And, of course, you too, Mr. Fulton. Pepper said you might be interested in attending my school."

Impressed that the woman chose to focus on his children instead of him, Drew gestured for the girls to sit. "It's nice to meet you, Mrs. Beecham."

"My pleasure."

Hannah plopped into the chair beside her and smoothed her fingers over the butter-colored yarn. "Hi. Whatcha making?"

"A scarf. It matches a hat and a pair of mittens I made." Mrs. Beecham held up her unfinished project. "They're going to girl about your size. Should we see if it's almost long enough?"

"Okay." Hannah shrugged out of her coat and stood stock still while the woman measured the length of the scarf against her neck. "Are you her grandma? Grandma Hastings says she can't do crafty things to save her life, but put her in the kitchen and she can feed an army."

Dimples deepened in the women's cheeks. "No, I don't have any grandchildren. Not the regular kind anyway. This is for one of the kids I met at the homeless shelter. Her favorite color is yellow."

"I like yellow, but red is my favorite."

Edging closer, Kristin held out her hand. "Hi, Mrs. Beecham."

The principal shook her hand. "Hm. Hastings. You two have to be Emily Hastings' granddaughters. I worked with her years ago and I remember the picture she always kept on her desk. You, young lady, are the spitting image of her oldest daughter. Kate, isn't it?"

Drew bit the inside of his lower lip, praying the conversation didn't turn into a flood of tears.

"Yes, Kate. She was our mom. She died." Kristin's voice revealed only a hint of sorrow.

Mrs. Beecham frowned for a moment and patted her arm. "I'm so sorry. That must've been very hard for you and your family. My son died when he was a baby. I was sad for long time, but I decided to do something positive with all the love I had to give, so I started taking special care of the children at school and the shelter. He'd be happy about that, I think. I know I'm happier giving away the love I have for him than keeping it all to myself."

"I think Mommy would be happy that we love Pepper. She's going to be our mom in two weeks from tomorrow."

"She told me. You're a lucky bunch. Pepper has a big heart." She picked up the cell phone next to her crumpled sandwich wrapper and *tsked*. "I have leave for an appointment, but I enjoyed meeting you and your sister. Mr. Fulton, if you and your young ladies can come by the school on Tuesday, I'll be glad to give you a tour and answer any questions you may have."

He shook her hand and relaxed at the sudden weight off his shoulders. "That sounds terrific. I'll call in the morning to confirm the time. I really appreciate you letting us interrupt your lunch."

As she stuffed her knitting into the bag, she stood. "Psh. I was already done eating. Besides, food for the soul is just as important as food for the body. I met three new wonderful people today I didn't know before. That's some good food."

Hannah giggled and Kristin joined in, feeding his own soul in a way he'd never tire of.

After giving Pepper a brief hug, Mrs. Beecham strolled toward the exit as if she didn't have a care in the world. "And the soul doesn't have to worry about too much dessert."

Dropping into the chair she'd vacated, Drew pulled Pepper down onto his lap. "I don't know about you guys, but I think we just found the right school. What do you say we go out for supper tonight to celebrate? Pepper's choice since she arranged the whole thing."

She snuggled closer, making him wish their wedding day was today instead of fifteen days from now. "Luck and timing. I told Mrs. B we were looking for a new school and you just happened to stop in. Mexican?"

Hannah's eyes widened. "I *love* tacos. And fried ice cream."

"How about you, Kristin?"

"Mexican sounds great." Kristin's gaze seemed to skip back and forth between him and Pepper. "Would it be okay if I stay here with you while Daddy goes to talk to Uncle Flynn and Aunt Lily about wedding stuff?"

"Sure, as long as he doesn't mind."

Bouncing in her seat, Hannah raised her arm. "Me too! Me too!"

Pepper tensed in his arms and glanced first at him and then toward Kristin. "Hm. That depends on whether your dad says it's okay and whether you're willing to listen to your sister. I'm going to be working, so she'll be in charge of you if you stay."

Drew shrugged, content to let the women in his life settle the negotiations on their own. "I don't have a problem with it if Hannah and Kristin are willing to follow your rules."

Kristin's slight smirk said she'd definitely consider exchanging a little time away from her sister for a taste of authority. "Works for me."

With pursed lips, Hannah tapped her fingers on the table, obviously weighing her options. "I guess that's okay."

Amazed at how easily they'd come to an agreement, he nuzzled Pepper's ear, hoping neither of his daughters noticed his whisper. "They must like you better than me. I don't blame them."

She snickered, the sound barely audible. "So, girls, do you want to hang out down here or go upstairs?"

Hannah grabbed her coat and slung it over arm. "What's upstairs?"

"Two apartments where Zack and I live. Kristin watched movies up there yesterday, but I also have some puzzles and board games. Oh, and cookies."

"Cookies?"

"Mm-hm. Kristin, can you head upstairs with your sister? I'll be up in a minute."

His older daughter nodded. "Through the kitchen?"

"Yep. Just be careful." Pepper was silent until Kristin and Hannah stepped through the doorway. "One of Mort's security people is sitting a few tables over. I'm not sure how she knew you were coming, but I feel a lot better with her keeping an eye on things while the girls are here."

Although the thought of being followed unsettled him, he preferred his boss's minions to Pierce's peons. "Any more visits or warnings?"

"No, and it worries me."

"I know you won't let anything happen. Or Kyle. In this case, being a control freak is a damn good thing. I wouldn't be surprised if he had surveillance cameras installed."

She sighed as she slipped out of his hold and stood. "He did. I should go let the girls into my apartment and get back to work."

With a last kiss, he walked with her as far as the counter. "I'll be gone for about an hour, hour and a half at most. Any special requests for the menu?"

Mischief and more lit up her eyes. "You."

"Soon." He turned toward the exit before he gave in to the temptation to haul her to the walk-in fridge for some privacy.

She was gone by the time he reached the door.

Curiosity stalled him for a moment since the other three women still sat at their respective places, each one a few tables from where he, Hannah, and Kristin had met Mrs. Beecham. None of them looked like a bodyguard or someone capable of taking down a bad guy, but that was probably the point.

He pulled on his gloves and headed outside. At least with someone following him, he wouldn't have to wait for the auto club if he had car trouble or got stuck in the snow.

The short drive through town didn't give him time to ponder what Pierce might have planned. He had undoubtedly gotten the message that Zack wasn't interested in a sizable inheritance or cooperating, with or without the threat of legal action. Morton probably had enough connections to the local judges to derail any attempt at a court order, but Pierce had evidently been too slippery for a restraining order so far.

Drew parked in the same visitor spot of the Montgomery Crossing Retirement Village parking lot he'd used a week ago. His brother-in-law probably wouldn't be surprised by the news of an engagement. A wedding in two weeks could be a different story.

A tap on the passenger car window made him jump. One of the more eccentric seniors greeted him a wave and a wide grin. Purple tufts of curly hair peeked out from under her stocking cap. "Where are those delightful young ladies of yours?"

He met the petite firecracker at the sidewalk with a quick hug. "Hi, Alice. A better offer came along. Walk me to the kitchen? I need to talk to Lily and Flynn."

"You bet! Well, to the building anyway." She set off at a brisk pace. "Those two lovebirds are happier than a pair of clams. I suspect they've been busy making a baby, but don't tell 'em I said so."

"I promise not to say a word." The automatic doors whooshed open as they approached the entrance to the main building and he laughed under his breath.

"I still have another lap to go. See you later, hot stuff!" She pivoted and charged along the snow-dusted sidewalk away from him.

Two steps into the hallway, his brother-in-law's wife popped around the corner leading to the administrative offices. "Hey, Drew. How'd your dinner plans go last night?"

"Perfect." Her glow seemed to indicate a positive result on her part as well, but he wasn't about to ask about something that personal. "Are you free for a few minutes? I was hoping to talk to you and Flynn."

"Sure. I think he's working on next month's menu." She slipped her arm through his and steered him toward the dining area. "When do we get to meet your bride to be?"

"Soon, I hope. Did Flynn tell you about her?" Although their lunch last Saturday had involved some discussion of Drew's new personal life, he hadn't shared more than the basics for fear of jinxing the relationship.

"Just that she owns or manages the vegetarian deli here in town. I forget which. I do know it has an excellent selection of soups and salads. She doesn't happen to have short red hair, does she?"

As they neared the open space with about a dozen scattered round tables, he caught sight of his brother-in-law hunched over a laptop near the entrance to the kitchen. "Yeah, and it suits her."

Lily burst out laughing, and Flynn looked up from his work. He greeted her with a kiss and Drew with a goofy smirk. "What brings you here?"

"Any chance I can book the party room for a small wedding and a reception on the thirty-first? Catering too."

"January thirty-first. That's a Sunday." His matter-of-fact tone assuring Drew he'd seen the whole thing coming, Flynn sat and clicked the keys on his laptop. "Not a problem. We can be done with brunch and cleanup by twelve-thirty. It's all yours after that. What kind of reception? Appetizers, buffet, formal dinner?"

"You could've acted at least a little surprised."

"Why would I do that?" He shared a conspiratorial grin with his wife. "I know what love does to men like us, and one look at you last weekend was all it took to see your fate. Then you opened your mouth and never stopped talking about her. Goner in seconds, same as me."

"Yeah, well, I probably would've asked her to marry me sooner if it wasn't for Kristin. Her stubborn streak is every bit as wide as the rest of the Hastings women. I don't know how you survived those three sisters." After holding a chair for Lily, Drew sat across from the couple. "We want something simple, not too fancy. Maybe twenty, twenty-five people. You, your sisters and mom and dad, Pepper's son and cousin. Just family. Enough food and cake to feed everybody."

"Are you going to invite any of your family?"

"No plans to, no." After fifteen years with no communication, they'd made their feelings perfectly clear and he didn't want or need more disapproval.

"What about her parents? Any brothers and sisters?"

"None." Drew leaned back in the chair, hoping the tension in his shoulders didn't show.

Lily clasped her hands on the table in front of her and pursed her lips. "Are you sure she's okay with your former in-laws being there? It might be a little uncomfortable for her."

"She knows the situation and doesn't have a problem with it. She thinks it's great how close we've stayed. One of things I love about her is how uncomplicated she makes things. When she gets pissed off at me, it blows over pretty fast. Of course, we were also total strangers trapped together in a blizzard, so I don't expect—"

"Oh, I want to hear about this!" Lily's concerned expression gave way to laughter again. "How did you get trapped together? Weren't you on a business trip?"

A flash of heat crept up Drew's neck. "My boss is her cousin and she was my new client, under duress. He set us up in one cabin. Forced cohabitation."

"That sounds interesting. Good thing your boss has crazy-good matchmaking skills." She slid Flynn's notepad closer and picked up the pen. "Let's hear the rest of those wedding plans."

CHAPTER TWENTY-SIX

WITH THE GIRLS' NEW DRESSES HANGING FROM HER FINGERTIPS AND her own dress draped over her arm, Pepper dug for the ringing phone in her coat pocket. Her keys fell to the driveway, vanishing into the fresh snow as she tapped the screen to answer the call. "Pepper McCann is suffering from temporary insanity and will return your call shortly."

Hannah and Kristin rounded the hood of the car, each with a shopping bag containing new shoes and accessories to match their wedding clothes and happily-ever-after expressions written all over their adorable faces. The outing had been successful, but a nap sounded almost as inviting as a cup of tea and a comfortable chair.

Drew's low chuckle sent warm shivers to her belly. "I was going to ask how the shopping expedition went, but I'm not sure I want to know the details. That bad, huh?"

"Not bad. Good, actually. I'm just exhausted. I wasn't prepared for expert-level mall hopping." A nudge through the depression in the snow yielded metal scraping against the pavement but no visible keys.

He laughed again. "I blame that on their aunts. Did you find everything you need?"

Kristin handed her bag to her sister and then reached into the hollow. "Found 'em."

"I think so." Mouthing a thank-you to Kristin, Pepper led the way toward the front door. "We just got home. Do you want me to start supper?"

"Nope. The girls and I are cooking tonight. Oh, and can you remind Hannah to make sure all her dirty clothes are in the hamper? I should be there in about half an hour, maybe forty-five minutes. Now go put your feet up and relax."

"Okay." Certain life couldn't get much better than this, she stepped aside so Kristin could unlock the door. "I love you."

"Love you too. See you soon."

Hannah skipped inside, her wet soles squeaking on the floor. "Can we try on our dresses and shoes together?"

Her sister grabbed her by the sleeve. "Boots and coat."

"Oops! I forgot. Can we, Mom?"

Pushing the door closed with her hip, Pepper didn't even try to fight the warm, fuzzy feeling in her heart. "Your dad told me about a chore you need to do, but you can try on the whole outfit after you're finished."

"Ugh. Not laundry again." Boots thudded onto the rug.

Kristin shook her head as she hung up her coat. "I told you before. If you don't throw your dirty clothes on the floor when you get undressed, you won't have to pick them up later."

Hoping to avoid an unpleasant ending to a good day, Pepper shooed the younger girl up the steps. "I'll help this time. Go get started and I'll be up in a minute."

"Okay." The shopping bag swinging all the way, Hannah scampered upstairs and into her bedroom.

"How did you get her to do that without arguing?" Kristin pointed in the direction her sister had gone. "Daddy always has to tell her *over and over.*"

"Can you hold these while I take off my coat?" Handing the trio of plastic-covered dresses to the older girl, Pepper slipped off her boots. "Thanks. You know she's only doing it to impress me, don't you? I figure it'll work a few times and then the novelty will wear off. For now, she likes having a mother again. Do you think she remembers much about your mom?"

"I don't know. We talk about her and we have lots of pictures of things we did together, especially when she started getting too sick to get out of bed. I think Hannah keeps a flashlight under her pillow so she can look at the photo albums we made every night before she goes to sleep."

Pepper bit her lower lip to keep from sitting on the steps and bawling. Losing a mother who gave her children the love they needed and deserved was far worse than having parents who didn't give enough of a damn to care if their child was okay. *Better to have loved and lost? I don't think so.*

Her eyes still stung, but she took the armload. "Do you want to try on your whole outfit too?"

Kristen's expression brightened. "I probably should. Can we try making the fancy braids the saleslady talked about too?"

"You bet." Pepper trudged up the steps behind Kristen, determined to take advantage of every positive moment. "Give me a few minutes to help your sister with her laundry then we'll play with hairstyles. I'm going to need a lot of practice. I haven't had long hair for at least twenty-five years."

"I can't picture you with long hair. Short fits you." Kristen paused at her bedroom doorway long enough to take her dress. "After I get dressed, I'll set out everything we need for braids in the bathroom."

"Great. Hannah and I will be there shortly." Pepper continued on to the bedroom next door. A pile of clothes blocked the entrance. "Hey, how am I supposed to help if I can't get in?"

"I'm done!" The muffled call came from somewhere across the room.

A peek past the doorjamb revealed the girl pulling her hand out from under her pillow. Had today's focus on the wedding made her miss Kate more than usual?

"Good job." Pretending not to notice Hannah's guilty hands-behind-her-back pose, Pepper bent to sort the darks from the lights.

"Come help me sort and put these in the laundry basket, and then we'll do a practice run of the big day."

"Can I wear the locket Daddy gave me with my new dress?"

"That's a great idea. Does Kristin have one too?"

"No, she got a bracelet. They both have hearts, though, 'cause Daddy loves us."

"You bet he does." Pepper hefted the full basket. "Why don't you get undressed while I take these to the laundry room? Then I'll help you with your dress when I get back."

"Okay." Hannah yanked her sweater over her head and flung it to the floor. As she grabbed the hem of her undershirt, she froze for a full second. Her undershirt followed the sweater. "I have to put it on again, so it doesn't matter if I throw it on the floor."

Shaking her head, Pepper carried the basket downstairs. The girl was as messy as she was. By the time she returned, a new scattered pile of clothes covered the end of the bed.

Hannah's fists peeked out of the pleated sleeves of her dress. A static-filled mane of hair pushed through the head hole, snapping and standing on end. Her face popped free next. "Can you zip me and tie the bow? Oops! Please?"

Pepper combed through the mass of strands in attempt to find the zipper. Several zaps buzzed through her fingertips. "You could power half of Ohio with all this electricity."

Giggles erupted from the little girl. "You're silly! I forgot to tell Daddy I need more cream rinse."

"We'll tell him when he gets home from work. Hold still so I can zip you up." The zipper slid upward, pulling the loose fabric around Hannah for a perfect fit. "Do you need help with your tights?"

"No, I can do it." The package flew across the bed when the girl tore through the plastic.

Stifling the urge to supervise, Pepper picked up her own wedding clothes and headed for the master bedroom. A hole in a pair of nylons wasn't the end of the world.

As Pepper slid on the ivory pumps that matched her dress a few minutes later, Kristin knocked on the partially open door. "Mom, can you finish zipping for me? I can't reach."

"Sure. Come on in."

"Look what I can do!" Hannah scooted past her sister and then twirled toward the bed. The dress flared out, making the lace trim dance up and down around her knees. "It's a fairy gown!"

With far more dignity, Kristin approached the mirror in the corner of the room. She smoothed her palms over the fitted waistline and down the full skirt. The delicate floral pattern complemented her reserved personality as well as the style fit Hannah's playful side. "I thought I liked the blue dress better, but this one is just right."

Pepper moved the older girl's ponytail aside and eased the zipper upward. "I'm glad we found something you both like. Hannah said you have a bracelet that matches her locket. I bet your dad would love for you to wear them."

Kristin's face lit up. "That's a great idea."

"I can't take credit for that. It was actually Hannah's idea."

Hannah scrunched up her mouth as she plopped on the end of the bed. Considering the amount of recent friction between them that Drew had mentioned, she likely expected her sister to change her mind.

"Well, I love it." Kristin clasped Hannah's hand and pulled her toward the hallway. "Come on. It's time to figure out how we're going to wear our hair. Then we need to take pictures."

A great deal of giggling accompanied Pepper's braiding efforts, but she finally managed to arrange both girls' hair into non-Medusa designs after several attempts. She snapped a few photos with her phone and emailed them Drew.

A glance at the time as she tapped the Send button warned her they needed to change back into their everyday clothes. "The dress-up party's over for today. Your dad will be home soon. Shoes in their boxes, tights in their packages, and dresses on their hangers. Inspection in fifteen minutes."

Kristin gave Pepper a quick hug. "Thanks for taking us shopping today. And everything."

She followed her sister out of the master bedroom with a brighter than usual smile.

Raising girls would undoubtedly be different from parenting a boy or an only child, but the day had gone surprisingly well. Neither of her soon-to-be stepdaughters had pushed any boundaries or tried to manipulate her into getting their way. Drew deserved a pat on the back for at least part of that. He was a good father.

Pepper stood in front of the mirror for a last look at the first dress she'd bought in years. It wasn't anything like the wedding gown she'd imagined as a little girl. The sleeves weren't lace and the bodice wasn't covered in beads and pearls. The hem skimmed her knees instead of touching the floor. She didn't need a veil, either. If not for the girls, she would've been equally happy in jeans and sweater. Marrying the man she loved mattered more than fancy clothes.

She twirled once, sending the skirt rippling up and down like Hannah had done. As she turned to face the mirror again, a flash of something metallic reflected in the glass behind her.

My earring?

Reaching for the side zipper to undress, she walked toward the nightstand, glad she hadn't had to explain to Kristin or Hannah how her jewelry had gotten in their dad's bedroom. The object caught the light again, but it wasn't the small gold hoop she'd lost.

The twinge in her belly came and went in a fraction of a second. Drew could've had his old wedding ring out for any number of reasons, the most obvious being their upcoming wedding reminded him of the wife he'd lost. Kate would always have a place in his heart. Pepper had accepted that fact the first time they'd made love.

Without touching the gold band, she changed into her street clothes and hung the dress on its hanger. They both had pasts and neither of them had to look back anymore except to remember.

"Mom! I'm done!" Hannah burst into the room at full speed, her socks flapping in her left hand. "Come see."

"Me too." Kristin appeared in the doorway, prim and proper as always. "I put everything in my closet. If you don't need me for anything else, I'll go start chopping the vegetables for supper. Daddy should be home in a few minutes."

"Great job, girls." Taking her purchases with her, Pepper followed her companions into the hall. "Do you need some help with dinner prep?"

With her lips pursed, Kristin paused on the top step. "Daddy said you're not supposed to cook on your day off."

"Did he now? I guess that means your sister can practice her reading with me until it's time to eat." Pepper cast a sideways glance at Hannah. "Upstairs or downstairs, kiddo?"

"Upstairs!" The younger girl tugged Pepper toward her room. "I want to read one of my fairy stories."

"That sounds wonderful." With a wink at Kristin, Pepper followed her guide. "We'll be down in a little bit. Come get me sooner if you need help."

The book already lay on the bed, along with Hannah's dress on its hanger. They hid most of another book, its cover and pages like that of a scrapbook.

Tightness spread through her chest, but Pepper sat. *If she wants to share memories of her mother, who am I to deny her?* "Isn't that the same book we read a few nights ago?"

"Yes, but you read it then. I'm going to read it this time." Hannah climbed onto the bed. As she flipped through each page, she never hesitated at the more difficult words.

Even though memorization probably had a lot to do with it, Pepper kept her observation to herself. "You're getting to be a really good reader. Next time I'll bring some books from my apartment. I have one about pirates that was Zack's favorite when he was about your age."

"I like pirates. I dressed up like one for Halloween when I was five. Mommy had to stay home and help Grandma give out candy. She was too sick to go trick or treating with us." Biting her lower lip, Hannah slid the other book from under her wedding clothes. "She dressed up like my favorite fairy just for me. I have a picture. We didn't get to play dress-up anymore after that 'cause she had to go to the hospital."

Pepper draped her arm around Hannah's shoulders and gave her a gentle squeeze. "Aw, sweetie. I'm so sorry. It must've been really hard to..." *Lose your mommy? Watch her die? Let her go?* No words seemed right to finish the thought. Her mom wasn't lost, and watching her die sounded too harsh. Drew and his children had only let her go because they had no choice.

"It's okay. Mommy told me not to be sad. Just 'cause I can't see her doesn't mean she isn't here with me." Hannah flipped the book open to a page near the back with a single photo—obviously, the last one her mother had added to the collection. "Lookie. This is how I knew you were going to be my new mom."

The woman in the picture stared back at Pepper. Although Kate's face was gaunt and grayish, her smile was genuine. She was clearly enjoying every minute she had left with the girls on either side of her. Wisps of short hair brushed her forehead and cheeks to frame dull but intelligent blue eyes. A ring of pastel flowers rested on the cap of orange-red hair, a near match for Pepper's. If not for the sickly tone of her skin, Kate Fulton could've been more than one of the fairies from Hannah's book. She could've easily passed for Pepper's sister.

"Mommy had to wear a wig with her costume since all her hair fell out. She used to have it long like Kristin's. It was the same color and everything. Grandpa says Kristin looks just like his Katherine when she was a little girl." Hannah removed a pink envelope from the next page and held it to her heart. "When I got my first haircut, Mommy put some in my baby book, so we decided I should have some of hers in my Mommy book."

With her insides cramping and her throat too achy to talk, Pepper nodded. Nothing could've prepared her for the gut-wrenching emotions swirling in her stomach. How could she ever live up to Kate's selfless-ness? The woman deserved sainthood for putting her children's memories before her own pain and suffering. She'd made sure they celebrated her life instead of mourning the loss of it. Kate was more angel than fairy.

"Mommy told me Daddy would need someone magical like a fairy to make him happy again. And I just knew it was you when I saw you." Hannah rose to her knees and wrapped her arms around Pepper's neck.

"I'm glad I was right. Daddy loves you and I love you. And I think Kristin does too."

"I love you too." The words were easy, even if emotion made speaking in anything other than a whisper impossible. Pepper hugged the girl closer. "Thanks for sharing this with me."

The heavy clunk of a door closing and Hannah wiggling free saved her from what would've surely been an ugly fit of sobbing. "Daddy's home!"

"Why don't you go down and set the table, and I'll hang your dress in the closet?"

"Okay." Hannah scrambled off the bed and darted out of the room.

Glad for a few minutes alone, Pepper put away their shopping haul and made a quick stop in the bathroom to splash cool water on her blotchy cheeks and red-rimmed eyes. Holding in tears took more out of her than crying. After a slow, calming breath, she draped her plastic-covered wedding dress over her arm and stepped into the hallway.

Drew stood at the bottom of the stairway, his carefree smile soothing her agitation in an instant. "Do you have any idea how much I love having you here when I come home?"

She scuttled down the steps to greet him with a quick kiss, careful not to drop her armload. "I love being here. And no peeking."

"I wouldn't have thought you'd be afraid of the groom-seeing-the-bride's-gown-before-the-wedding curse." Pulling her against him, he touched his lips to hers again. "Oh, and your phone was ringing a second ago."

"Not afraid, just cautious." Three cash register *ka-chings* sounded from near her feet as she placed her armful over the banister. Another followed two seconds later. "That's Kyle. I better see what he wants."

Drew handed her the purse she'd left on the stairs. "Yeah. He won't leave you alone until you answer."

Her cell made several more noises in quick succession. "It must be urgent, at least to him."

"You placate him while I go help Kristin with supper."

She dug for her phone as he skated toward the kitchen in his stocking feet. With a silent chuckle, she tapped in the passcode. Nearly a dozen messages, three missed calls, and an equal number of voice-mails waited for her. *What's so damn important, Mort?*

Not in the mood to hear his overbearing voice, she opened her texts first. Her neck muscles tangled tighter with every word.

"Answer your phone."

"Where are you?"

"Pepper, you need to call me."

"It's the deli."

"The police are here."

"Zack had to close early."

"Call me."

"Call."

"Me."

"NOW."

The cell buzzed and sang in her hand with an incoming call from her cousin. She tapped the answer button. "What's going on, Mort?"

"The toilet in the men's restroom had a major leak." The tightly controlled words warned her the situation wasn't that simple.

"The police are there for a broken toilet?" She sat on the bottom step and slipped on her boots.

"It might have been deliberate. I called in a plumbing expert because, from the looks of it, one of Kevin's thugs put liquid nitrogen or something in the tank."

"*Flood.* That low-life piece of scum. I'll be there as quick as I can." Not waiting for an acknowledgment, she ended the call and shoved her arms in her coat sleeves.

"Everything okay?" Drew's voice from behind made her jump.

She set down her cell to pull on her gloves. "No. I'm sorry to skip out on dinner, but I need to get to the shop. Mort says there's a problem with the plumbing."

His lips flattened into a grim line. "Pierce?"

Unable to sugarcoat the situation, she nodded. "Maybe."

"I don't want you to go. The guy is desperate, and he's liable to do something really stupid. It's not safe." He grasped her gloved fingers.

"I think you should stay here until the police—or Kyle—takes care of this."

"Aw, Drew. You have no idea how grateful I am that you want to protect me, but I have to handle it." She eased away from him to grab her dress and the bag hooked over its hanger. "The police are going to need a statement. I need to contact my insurance company. If I close the deli until Kevin's caught red-handed, he wins, and I'm not giving him that power."

His hand closed around her upper arm as she moved toward the door. "Damn it, Kate, I'm scared of losing you."

The air evaporated from her lungs, and his full realization of the misspoken name came a full second later, the shock evident in his horrified open-mouthed stare.

She pulled away from his hold and hurried out the door before he could recover from his gaffe or try to explain. The most obvious explanation was usually the correct one.

Drew wasn't anywhere near being over the loss of his wife.

CHAPTER TWENTY-SEVEN

Too dazed to sleep, Drew sat up and switched on the bedside lamp. He blinked at the sudden brightness, a flash of gold on the nightstand catching his attention as his vision adjusted.

Damn it. He'd meant to drop off his old wedding band at the jewelry shop while he was in town today. The ring held a special place in his life, but changing it into a pair of matching heart charms for his girls had seemed like a good way to preserve it and make room for his future with Pepper. Then again, forgetting it might have been a subconscious trick his mind had played on him.

No matter how many times he replayed the scene, he couldn't find fault with Pepper's reaction to his inexcusable blunder. She'd had every right to walk out. Considering her temperament, he was lucky she hadn't decked him before she left. At least she hadn't heaved her engagement ring at him, not that she would've thought to do that after what he'd said. The shock and dismay in her eyes would haunt him forever.

What if calling her Kate means I'm not ready to get married again? He picked up the symbol of commitment from his first marriage. *Is this a sign?*

As much as his heart ached right now, he hoped that wasn't the case. Falling in love with Pepper had been so easy, and she fit in his life like she'd belonged there all along.

But it's only been three weeks since we met.

Funny how one slip of the tongue could cause so many doubts.

She was a victim of his past as well as her own. He'd proven to her that men couldn't be taken at their word. Whether unintentional or deliberate, hurt was hurt, and his pain probably didn't begin to compare to hers.

He reached for his phone and then stopped before he picked it up. A text message was no way to apologize. Neither was a phone call. In fact, an apology couldn't make up for what he'd done. Even flowers and a romantic dinner for two would fall far short. Groveling might be enough to convince her to forgive him, but she deserved better.

A glance at the clock informed him not even an hour had passed since he'd climbed into bed. He shoved back the covers and swung his legs over the side of the mattress, determined to distract himself from the downward spiral of depressing thoughts. How many times after Kate's death had he worked through the night to avoid sleeping alone? To keep from seeing her take her last breath in his dreams? To convince himself to accept reality?

Reality. Pepper was alive, but gaining her trust again would probably be almost as impossible as resurrecting Kate.

Phone in hand, he shuffled to the desk and dropped into the chair. Her marketing package was finished and he had only a couple accounts that needed minor updates. In two weeks, his partnership would take effect, but the growing anticipation was gone. None of it mattered.

Sooner or later, he'd have to explain Pepper's disappearance to his daughters. They might have accepted his excuse about an emergency at the deli, but it wouldn't fly for long. How could he tell them truth? What was the truth?

The vibration of his cell jolted his arm like an electric shock. *Pepper?*

Another vibration followed, and another. The number on the screen wasn't hers.

He tapped the icon to answer the call and hoped his voice didn't give away anything. "Hey, Kyle."

"Drew. I just wanted to let you know Pepper's okay and my contractor's already on site to clean up the water and fix the damage to the shop. He said no more than a week. She should be able to reopen by Monday."

"Great. Thanks."

"I'd rather she didn't know, but I had cameras installed inside as well as out after the newspaper incident. My security team is reviewing the video now and should have a face and a name soon. Then it's just a matter of following the money trail. She and Zack are staying at my house until Pierce is caught."

"Good." *At least she's safe.*

"You should take advantage of her free time this week. Do Kristin and Hannah like to swim? They're welcome to use the indoor pool. I won't be in the office tomorrow and I'm headed out of town Wednesday morning. My housekeeper will be there to let you in or if you need anything. I should be back Friday evening by eight."

Pepper clearly hadn't shared any details of Drew's screw-up with her cousin. Unfortunately, it didn't give him any indication of her intentions where their relationship was concerned—if they still had one.

Not prepared or in the mood for an inquisition, Drew offered the most noncommittal response he could think of. "Okay."

After an uncharacteristic pause, Kyle sighed. "I didn't like interrupting your evening with her, but she needed to know."

"You're right. It's fine." *Why the hell is he so chatty?*

"Okay. I'll see you in a few days." The line went silent without a good-bye.

If Morton suspected something was wrong, he sure hadn't hinted at it. Once word got out, though, their partnership agreement could go up in flames too. The job could be gone, even though Kyle had been the instigator of the whole damn mess.

Preparing for the worst, Drew clicked on his most recent financial spreadsheet. The numbers blurred, maybe because he needed to put on his glasses, but probably from the tears he'd fought since Pepper had walked out without a word.

He rubbed the moisture from his eyes. What right did he have to fight for her?

His phone buzzed again, sending his stomach into a tailspin again. Hi brother-in-law's name and number glowed on the dark background. "Hey, Flynn. What's up?"

"Hi, Drew. I didn't wake you, did I?"

"No, I'm working." He swiped his fingertip across the touchpad as the computer screen dimmed. *It isn't a lie.*

"You're sitting down?"

"Yeah." *Get to the damn point already.*

"Lily said she saw you at the store the day you proposed to Pepper and that you, um, saw what she was buying. Well, we figured you should be the first to know. Lily's pregnant. We're having a baby."

The awe in Flynn's voice brought a lump to Drew's throat. "That's great. Congratulations."

"Thanks. Is everything okay? You sound like something's on your mind. Did Morton try to talk you into more hours in the office?"

"No." Drew shoved the chair backward and stood. "I fucked up."

"It must be pretty serious for you to use the F-word."

"Remember when you thought you were going to have to quit your job at Montgomery Crossing and you asked if you could stay here?"

"Yeah. That was a rough time for Lily and me. Oh no, not you and Pepper." Flynn muttered something and then a door clunked shut. "I'll be there in two minutes."

The line went silent.

Doesn't anybody say good-bye anymore?

As he padded downstairs, Drew discarded the idea of pulling out the bottle of Jameson like he had during Flynn's and his last commiseration talk. A hangover would only make getting up in the morning more difficult. Alcohol wouldn't dull the pain or change a damn thing. Besides, he had to take Kristin and Hannah to visit their new school.

Fuck.

At the bottom of the stairs, he flipped on the porch light and unlocked the front door. The glow reflected off the snow, lighting up the yard. A pickup truck turned into the driveway and Flynn appeared on the sidewalk a few seconds later.

Drew greeted his brother-in-law with a sincere attempt at a smile. "I'm thrilled for you guys. Really. How's she feeling?"

"We didn't expect it to happen so soon, but..." Flynn shrugged, the excitement evident in his grin. "Lily's happy, and that's all that matters."

"Want a cup of decaf?"

"Decaf, huh?" Flynn followed him down the hall. "At least let me make it. So, what's going on with you and Pepper?"

"It's all yours." Taking a seat at the breakfast bar, Drew couldn't help but picture cooking with her in the kitchen, making love to her on the couch, proposing to her next to the patio doors. "You know how you're just kind of rolling along, enjoying what seems like a perfect life after pure hell, and then, bam, you do something so stupid that you screw it all up? I never even saw it coming."

"Come on. It can't be that bad. Stuff like this always seems a lot worse than it is." Flynn scooped pre-ground beans into the filter and shuddered. "Next time, I'm bringing my own coffee. What happened?"

"I called her Kate." His transgression sounded even more unforgiveable out loud.

"Yikes. That is pretty bad. Not fatal, but definitely not good."

"*Pretty bad?* You should've seen the look on her face. And I didn't even realize I was saying it." Drew grabbed a napkin from the holder and tore it in half from corner to corner. "I love her. The girls love her. She's perfect for us, but all I can think about is maybe I—"

"Stop right there." Flynn crossed his arms in front of his chest. "You've met other women in the last year. Not one of them made you want to get married again—or even date. And don't give me some bull-shit about thinking it was time to move on. You stopped wearing your ring right after I met Lilly. That was long before Morton set you up."

"Then why did it happen? It just came out by itself."

"Unless you were having sex with her at the time, it's fixable. You weren't, were you?"

"*No.* She took the girls shopping for wedding clothes today. When I got home from work, she got a call from Kyle. Evidently, there was a problem with the plumbing. Her son's father has been a real pain in the ass lately, making threats and stuff, and he might've done something to the water pipes at the shop. I asked her not to go, but, of course, she said she had to." Drew balled up the shredded napkin and heaved it toward the bag of coffee.

Without missing a beat, Flynn nabbed the projectile a few inches in front of its target and put it in the wastebasket under the sink. "So, I'm guessing you were upset that she wouldn't listen to you."

"I panicked. This guy's a grade-A prick and I'm scared to death he's going to hurt her."

"I'm no psychologist, but you need to cut yourself some slack. Your wife—my sister—died from something neither of us could prevent or protect her from. It makes sense you'd do your damnedest to keep Pepper safe. The name thing? That's just your subconscious trying to make up for being helpless with Kate." The coffeemaker gurgled as the last of the decaf dripped into the carafe. Flynn pulled two mugs from the cupboard. "See? Simple. It has nothing to do with you not being ready to get married again or wanting to bring back Kate."

"You want to tell that to the hot-tempered redhead I'm in love with? She has the Hastings' stubborn streak beat by miles."

Hooking his foot around the stool next to Drew's, Flynn somehow balanced the two mugs as he pulled out the chair. "The only option besides talking to her about it is letting her go, because it doesn't sound like she'll come looking for an apology or an explanation. Are you willing to do that?"

"Talking isn't the problem. I have no idea what to say or if she'll listen." Steam rose from the cup, twisting and twirling in a dissipating cloud above the coffee the way she'd disappeared earlier. "I'm not sure *I'd* listen to me if I was her."

"You're throwing away your best chance of getting her back? Are you *crazy*?"

"I doubt she'll even agree to see me."

"Lily sat next to my truck in the freezing cold for who knows how long, waiting to apologize to me, and look where we are. I didn't think I ever wanted to see her again after the way she dumped me, but that wasn't my heart talking. Not that I'd want do it all again, I would, knowing what we have now. Love is hard sometimes." Flynn blew across the top of his coffee and set it back on the counter. "But, hey, it's up to you."

"What if—"

"What if she understands? You won't know unless you try."

"You're—"

A faint thud came from somewhere between the hall to the front door and the stairs. "Shhh!"

The patter of footsteps on the stairs followed a second later.

Drew winced. "How much do you suppose they overheard?"

"Probably enough to know there's trouble in paradise." Flynn's grimace most likely matched his own. "Why don't I get out of your hair so you can do some damage control?"

"Chicken. Just wait. Your time is coming." After a gulp of coffee, Drew pushed out of his chair to walk his closest friend to the door.

Flynn laughed. "I can only imagine. I think I'll enjoy taking care of Lily and our little bean sprout for now."

"God, I miss those days."

Shoving his arms into his coat sleeves, Flynn smirked at him. Then he jangled his keys in his palm as he went out the front door. "You and Pepper could do something about that too, you know. Talk to her."

Annoyed at the lack of sympathy, Drew shut and locked the door. If he somehow managed to convince her to still marry him, a discussion about babies would come after the wedding, the abbreviated honeymoon, and a real honeymoon—if at all. It wasn't anywhere near the top of his priority list, especially since he was closing in on forty. He already had his hands full with a pair of spying daughters.

Coffee mug in hand, he switched off the kitchen light and trudged up the stairs. A narrow strip of pale yellow light beneath Hannah's bedroom door became darkness as he reached the top step. Whether she'd acted on her own remained to be seen, but another hissed whisper suggested she wasn't alone in her snooping.

As he reached for the doorknob, hurried footsteps carried to his ears and then came the shuffling of what had to be bedcovers. Not bothering with stealth, he twisted the knob. "I know you're awake."

"I told you not to make so much noise." Kristin's admonishment wasn't anywhere near as harsh as it would've been a week ago.

"It's too hard to be quiet." Hannah crawled to the end of the bed, her shadowy outline barely visible by the light from the master bedroom. "Daddy, did you and Pepper have a fight? You're still getting married, aren't you?"

Kristin switched on the lamp, momentarily blinding him. "It wasn't a fight. If you'd been listening instead of talking, you would've heard what he said."

Raising his eyebrows at the pair, he sat on the side of the bed and patted the spot next to him. "Listening in on a private conversation isn't nice."

Hannah wiggled onto his lap as his older daughter plopped down beside him. Her pouty lip quivered. "I didn't mean to, and Kristin tried to stop me. I just wanted to know why you got so sad after she left. It reminded me of when Mommy was sick. Pepper isn't dying, is she?"

Tightening his hold on her, he thanked his lucky stars for the answer to that question. "No, she's fine. We're both fine."

Kristin frowned at him and crossed her arms in front of her chest. "Whatever you did, you *have* to fix it."

Her staunch assumption that Pepper wasn't at fault shouldn't have surprised him given her recent change of heart, but it did. "I know."

Scrambling out of his arms, Hannah glared at him. "She isn't coming back, is she? But she's our new mom and I have a new dress for the wedding and…everything! I'm very mad at you, Daddy."

He nodded as he rose. At least he always knew where he stood with his younger daughter. "I'm mad at me too. Go back to bed so I can figure out what to do."

Without a backward glance, he walked to his bedroom and closed himself inside. Procrastination would only prolong his misery and alienate his daughters more than he had already. What Pepper decided to do with his apology and explanation was beyond his control, but letting her temper cool off wouldn't help his cause.

Before his nerves could get the better of him, he tapped in her number and held his phone to his ear. Each ring sent his stomach into another disconcerting somersault. Then the generic greeting from her voicemail recited her number and a beep followed.

Not the least bit surprised that she didn't answer, he took a fortifying breath as he paced from the desk to the bathroom. "Pepper, it's Drew. I'm so sorry. I know how it looks. It's just that the thought of something happening to you… I wanted to protect you. It has nothing to do with Kate, except that I feel helpless. I don't like not having control of things. God, this business with Pierce makes me worry every second you're not with me. Please call me. I love you."

He dropped into the chair as he ended the call. What the hell would he do if she didn't give him a chance to make up for his horrible blunder? Even his own children might never speak to him again. *Maybe not ever, but definitely more than a few hours.*

The deafening silence was interrupted by a faint chime.

Ignoring the sick feeling in his stomach, he took a swig of coffee and then shuffled to the hall. At Kristin's bedroom, he waited for another telltale ding from her cell phone. It sounded again, but the chime came from downstairs.

As he descended the stairs, a glint caught his eye halfway down. Pepper's phone lay on the third step from the bottom—the place she'd likely set it to put on her coat and boots.

He picked it up as he continued to the kitchen for the box of cookies she'd brought the day before. *So much for that apology.*

Was the entire world against him today?

CHAPTER TWENTY-EIGHT

"WHERE *IS* IT?" PEPPER EMPTIED THE CONTENTS OF HER PURSE ON THE bed and sifted through the pile of receipts, notes, and assorted necessities. *Damn it.*

She growled as she dug through her coat pockets for the third time. Admitting defeat meant the one location she had no intention of looking was the only possible place it could be. She'd prefer replacing her phone to facing Drew, except Mort probably wouldn't let her leave his fortress without an escort in either case.

Four swift raps on the door added to her irritation.

"Mom, you awake?"

At least her cousin hadn't come to insist she join him for breakfast. His all-knowing, all-seeing skills might turn her into a criminal on this terrible Tuesday morning. Hopefully, her son would think her mood was a product of the damage to the deli.

"Come on in." She tossed her coat on the chair, adding to the chaos from her search. At least she'd found her missing earring.

Zack peeked his head inside, his expression more grim than last night. "I have some news. Holy cow. What happened in here?"

"I lost my phone and I'm pissed off at the world right now." She moved her suitcase from the settee to the floor and gestured for him to sit. "What kind of news? If it's bad, I don't want to hear it."

He weaved through the trail of clothes and sat with his hands braced on knees. His fingers flexed several times as he looked at her and then away. "I suppose it depends on who you are. Sort of good news for us. Really bad news for Kevin Pierce."

Relief tried to edge in, but she shoved it aside in favor of cautious optimism. "His hired saboteur ratted him out?"

"Not exactly." He cupped the back of his neck with his left hand, still avoiding eye contact. "He's dead."

"*Dead*?" Unable to maintain her balance on suddenly rubbery legs, she grabbed the footboard and slumped onto the bedcovers. "What happened? You're sure?"

"Yeah. No details yet."

She flopped onto her back to stare at the ceiling. As much as she disliked the man, she'd never wished him dead. *Castrated maybe, but not—* "Oh my God. Kyle didn't do it, did he?"

Her son's laugh seemed grimmer than his usual not-amused chuckle. "I doubt it since he said the loser saved him the trouble."

"Then he knows about it? Oh, what am I saying? Kyle always finds out about everything before anybody else." The mix of relief and unexpected grief pushed her from the bed. She sat beside Zack and rubbed his back. "Are you okay? I know Kevin wasn't your dad by any stretch of the imagination, but he was your father."

He shrugged. "It's kinda weird. He was just this imaginary guy until he showed up. I never expected to meet him and find out he's a bigger jerk than I thought. Was. I guess I'm glad I had the chance to see for myself what he was really like."

"Still, I'm sorry."

His crooked smile assured her that he'd be fine. "No big loss. Besides, Drew's going to be a much better stepdad than Pierce could ever be a father. He wasn't too worried about you coming to the deli last night, was he? He's almost as protective as Uncle Mort."

"Yeah." She tensed against the sharp ache the mention of Drew sparked. Grabbing a handful of the clothes scattered near her feet, she rose. "But it's fine."

"You're cleaning your personal space. Nothing is fine. Did you guys have a fight?"

She picked up another handful and then dropped her armful into the open suitcase. "No."

"Then what's wrong?"

"I lost my phone, my shop is flooded, and your father conveniently kicked the bucket." Footsteps followed her toward the bathroom, but the tears threatening to turn her into a weeping fool kept her from confronting him. "Isn't that enough?"

His palms closed over her shoulders. "Something else is bugging you. Are you pregnant?"

"No, I am not pregnant!" She wiggled free of his hold and pointed to the door. "Out. I don't want to talk about it."

He stepped in front of her, forcing her to look at him or the floor. "It has to do with Drew, though, doesn't it?"

A tear leaked from the corner of her eye, despite her best effort not to cry. "Did you not hear what I said?"

"Of course I did, but I know you. The harder you push people away, the more you need somebody on your side. So you can either tell me what happened now or I can follow you around all day until you do."

She leaned her forehead against his chest to hide an unwanted smile. "God, you're stubborn. I love you."

"I learned from the best." His arms closed around her, easing some of the pain in her heart. "I love you too. Now tell me what's going on."

One quick rip seemed like a better option than drawing out her misery for hours. "I can't marry him. He's not over the death of his wife."

"Okay, that could definitely be a problem, but how do you know that?"

"He got upset about me going to the shop last night and he called me Kate. He didn't even realize he said her name at first." The specter of that moment revived the same horrible sensation of falling into a deep, dark pit with no chance of escape.

"People sometimes say things they don't mean when they're under stress. I learned about it my psychology class. The thinking part of the brain shuts off during fight or flight."

"Yeah, well, I just wanted to get the hell out before he said what I was thinking. And I really want to go to the shop and forget about everything but the deli for the rest of the day. No more thinking or talking about it. I have too many other things to do." After a quick hug, she ducked away and went in search of shoes. "The sooner we reopen, the better."

He was silent while she dug through the last pile on the floor and led the way downstairs with her boots in hand. Unfortunately, Kyle stood in the hallway with an overnight bag at his feet as she headed toward the kitchen for some breakfast.

"Good. You're up." Her cousin pulled a pair of black leather gloves from his coat pocket. "I'm leaving early for my trip to Columbus and I'll be back by Friday evening. I don't expect any more issues with Pierce since his appropriate and timely demise, but I still have a few people standing by just in case."

She straightened his perfectly draped scarf, playing with the temptation to tighten it around his neck. "Good morning to you too. Zack, would you mind making me a cup of tea while I have a few words with Mort."

Kyle's lips thinned into his usual annoyed grimace. "Harriet is more than happy to prepare your tea. I, however, would appreciate not being addressed by that name."

"Tough cookies, *Mortie*. Zackary?"

Her son edged past their host. "I'll go ask Mrs. Weisser about that tea."

As soon as he was out of earshot, Pepper gave Kyle her frostiest glare. "How dare you be so thoughtless in front of him? Whether you liked Kevin Pierce or not, he was Zack's biological father and making light of his death is insensitive."

"For God's sake, the idiot electrocuted himself. Or more likely, he didn't pay one of his amateur thugs and the guy made it look like an accident." He picked up the suitcase and then kissed her cheek. "I'll check on you this evening."

Unable to shake the unbidden image of Kevin lit up like a bolt of lightning, a nod was all she could manage as her cousin walked out the front door. Thank goodness Zack was normal compared to the other men in her life.

Footsteps sounded on the wood floor behind her. "Mrs. Weisser said she'll have your tea ready in three minutes and she wants to serve us breakfast in the dining room."

Pepper pasted on what she hoped was a neutral expression and faced her son. "Thanks. Kyle can be so damn annoying sometimes."

Zack's snort echoed through the foyer. "You know it's to prove somebody needs him, don't you? As long as he feels needed, he can pretend being alone doesn't bother him."

With a halfhearted smack at her son, she set off toward the dining room. "Enough of the psychoanalysis already. Besides, being alone is better than being with the wrong person."

He trailed after her, the steady squeak of his boot tread against the floor comforting. One day soon, he wouldn't be there every day.

Maudlin thoughts plagued her through breakfast and the drive into town. Thankfully, Zack seemed more intent on driving than talking.

As he pulled into the empty parking space next to her car, a burly guy with an armload of cracked porcelain rounded the corner of the building. He heaved it into the dumpster and headed back the way he came.

The sick feeling in Pepper's stomach almost made her wish she hadn't gotten out of bed this morning. "Looks like we need a new toilet."

"Yeah. Kind of a crappy way to start the day, isn't it?" Zack unhooked his seat belt and opened the door.

She groaned, but was glad one of them still had a sense of humor after recent events. "That was really bad. Let's go see if we can help with the cleanup."

A chorus of pounding, drilling, and voices greeted her at the front entrance. Drop cloths covered every inch of the counter and a tarp hid the kitchen doorway. Several construction workers gathered around a guy with a clipboard near the only visible table. The sharp scent of coffee made her stomach cramp, the smell too much like the early-morning breakfasts at the cabin.

Then a woman in a hard hat and coveralls ducked past the edge of the tarp and joined the group. "The basement plumbing is in good shape, but I found four places where water leaked through the floor."

Clipboard guy pointed to the bearded man on his right. "Go down and check out the subfloor and joists. Set up a fan on the steps when you're done. I want that basement dry."

"Right away." Beard man pivoted in the direction of the kitchen and then back again. "Miss McCann is here."

After a short burst of instructions to the remaining workers, the group dispersed and clipboard guy clomped toward Pepper. "G'morning, ma'am. Everything's moving right along. Less damage than I first thought, considering the type of leak. We should have you ready to reopen on Friday."

She removed her glove to shake his hand. "I really appreciate the time you and your crew are putting in."

"Mr. Morton said you needed the job done fast. Having him call us to do the work is as good as winning the lottery."

She smiled instead of warning him about the implications of falling short of her cousin's expectations. "Thanks for agreeing on such short notice."

"Glad to. I can't give you a tour of the work yet, but you're welcome to ask questions if you have any." He shuffled through the papers on his clipboard and pulled one free. "This is what we found during the initial inspection. Some other minor repairs have popped up as we've gone through the list. Those are included on the back."

"You mean I can't stay and help?"

"Sorry, ma'am. Can't risk an injury."

"Okay." *What am I going to do for the next three days? Damn you, Mort.*

Zack guided her to the exit. "Let's go upstairs. You can catch up on paperwork while I go to class."

"Fine." Protesting wouldn't change a damn thing, so she tramped through the thin dusting of new snow with him, following the path of their earlier footprints.

A black SUV crept along behind them into the parking lot and the uneasiness in her stomach struck again. The last thing she needed right now was more drama.

Zack stepped in front of her, blocking her view. "D'you suppose Pierce was mixed up in organized crime? Or wanted by the FBI?"

"I'm kind of hoping he was an alien, and these guys are MIB." As she peeked past his shoulder, the driver shut off the engine. "We hit the ground if they have guns, agreed?"

"Yeah." His voice squeaked and he clutched her hand. "Stay behind me, okay?"

She ducked under his arm before he could stop her. "I can't see anything!"

The driver set one foot on the ground, revealing a creased charcoal-gray pant leg over galoshes. The door swung wide as he stood and a flat gray cap on a mostly bald head appeared above the window. He shuffled to the passenger side, his gait hardly that of a mobster or a federal agent.

A taller man with more-salt-than-pepper hair climbed out, towering over his chauffeur as he straightened. His bright blue gaze landed to the right of Pepper. "Zackary McCann?"

Shifting slightly, her son nodded. "Yes, sir. Can I help you?"

"You're still the spitting image of your father." The man hobbled toward them, his cane clearly for balance and not a weapon. He stopped a few feet from the SUV and waved off his driver's outstretched arm. "I'm fine, Carl. Why don't you wait in the car?" After a few more steps, he stopped again. "You'd probably like to know who I am and what I'm doing here, wouldn't you, young man? And you, Miss McCann."

Zack lifted his chin. "You're my grandfather, the one with the will.

The way Kevin Pierce talked, I figured you'd already passed or were about to. My condolences."

"You've heard about my son then. Thank you." Mr. Pierce gestured toward the steps, resignation more than grief seeming to fill a soft sigh. His foggy breath drifted upward and vanished. "Would you mind if we sit and talk? Getting old is rough, but at least I have a new knee. I suspect you have no interest in any part of the family money, even with your father gone. I do, however, have a proposition for you."

"I suppose it won't hurt to hear you out, but I have to leave for class in about fifteen minutes." Her son's standoffishness didn't surprise Pepper.

"We'll be done in ten. Your studies are more important right now than an old man's legacy." Mr. Pierce reached toward her and then seemed to think better of it. "You've a raised a fine boy. Will you join us?"

Not about to leave her son alone with another possible conniving member of the Pierce family, she climbed three steps and sat. A few minutes of civility—and cold—wouldn't kill her. "Thanks. I'm sorry for your loss."

"Believe me when I say his loss was greater than mine. I wish he and I could've seen eye to eye on a few things before… I guess that'll be one of those regrets I can't do anything about." The old man maneuvered his way onto the second step with his cane and laid it across his lap. He waited until Zack settled next to him. "I'd hoped he might change by meeting you, but greed blinded him."

Lines deepened along Zack's forehead and his lips formed a grim line. "You knew about me and used your will to get him to acknowledge me?"

The man's eyes widened enough to suggest he hadn't expected such a direct question. "Yes."

"How long have you known?"

"I suspected your mother was telling truth all those years ago, but I wanted to believe my son had integrity. After seeing how he treated his business colleagues, especially women, it was obvious he'd lied. I did a little research and found you without too much trouble when you were about six years old. One look, and I knew you were a Pierce, but my wife convinced me not to disrupt your life. You seemed happy and well cared for without our interference. It was her idea to change our wills now that you're an adult."

Some of the tension in Zack's shoulders seemed to ease. "I appreciate you leaving us alone. My mom and Uncle Kyle would've given you a lot of trouble if you'd tried to get custody or something, and I wouldn't have gone with you willingly."

"Margaret said I should be satisfied with the knowledge that I had a grandson for the time being. She was right, of course." Mr. Pierce unfolded his coat collar up around his neck, not hiding a shiver. "We'd like the opportunity to get to know you now. Your mother too."

"Maybe, but I'm not changing my last name. Oh, and you still haven't told me about this proposition you want to make."

Pepper suppressed a burst of triumphant applause at Zack's ability to stand up for himself.

The man pulled an envelope from inside his coat, satisfaction written all over the older version of her son's face. "The papers contain the latest prospectus for my company as well as a detailed account of the business. When you finish your degree, I'd like you to start training to take the reins at Pierce Enterprises. My phone number is there if you have questions or want to talk about what the job entails. Miss McCann, have your contractor send me the bill for the repairs to your building. It's the least I can do for Kevin's stupidity." He rose, using the railing and his cane to get to his feet. His progress to the waiting SUV was slow but steady. "I enjoyed meeting you, Zackary. I hope the feeling will be mutual some day soon."

CHAPTER TWENTY-NINE

"Come on, Daddy!" Hannah skidded to a stop and held out a lunch sack as Drew shrugged on his coat. "It's time to go!"

"I'm coming, I'm coming." He slung the strap of his computer bag on his shoulder and then took what was probably a peanut butter sandwich, carrots, and an apple. "Did you remember your library books?"

"Yep, and I'm going to get some new ones today." The new hole in her smile peeked at him as she spoke, assuring him that she hadn't caught the irritation he hadn't been able to hide.

The week had been full of firsts—the first day at the new school Pepper had helped him find, Hannah's overdue loss of her first baby tooth, Kristin's successful attempt to cook supper by herself—even if she'd been less than thrilled to have been assigned that job. He'd wanted to share those good things with Pepper. She would've celebrated those milestones with them if his mouth hadn't decided to have a mind of its own.

Instead, she'd kept a low profile. Her car was probably still missing from its spot at the deli, as it had been Tuesday afternoon and both times he'd driven past Wednesday and yesterday. Her silence spoke a lot louder than any words her temper might've allowed.

He followed Hannah through the garage door and locked it behind him. As he slid behind the steering wheel, Kristin's dark cloud of a mood surrounded him, dragging him deeper into the mix of melancholy, frustration, and anger. The chilly blast from the heater didn't begin to compare with the frostiness coming from the back seat. At least one of his daughters had finally progressed beyond the not-speaking-to-him stage.

Their low whispers grated on his nerves during the drive into town, making him wish he'd accepted Lily's offer to give the girls a ride to school in the mornings. Kristin's annoyed shushing was as recognizable as the exasperated sighs she'd taken to giving him lately. Life sure had a way of sucking the life out of him.

His phone buzzed in his pocket as he made the last turn. *What now?*

He inched forward through the drop-off lane until they reached the unloading area. "Do you have everything, Hannah? Kristin?"

"Um, yes, Daddy." The slight hesitation in her response made him glance at the rearview mirror. She didn't meet his gaze before she flung open the door.

"Uh-huh." Kristin glowered at him and then slid across the seat, following her sister onto the sidewalk.

Ignore the attitude. The battle isn't worth it. "Have a good day. I'll see you after school. I love you."

Hannah turned back with her mouth open, but Kristin grabbed her hand and pulled her into the herd moving toward the main entrance. Less than a minute later, they disappeared inside.

I love you too, Daddy. The words didn't sound right in the voices he'd committed to memory.

Although the thought of working from home was far more inviting than going to the office, he waited his turn to exit the one-way loop and drive toward the other side of town. He may have failed his parents, Kate, Pepper, and his kids, but failing Kyle wasn't an option—unless he wanted to add a business partnership to his list of relationship fatalities.

Following the shortest route, he slowed as he passed the Red Hot Pepper deli. The same plumbing van and three pickup trucks with trailers from all week sat in the rear lot, and several workers stood at the open back end of the van. Zack's car entered from the side street, but only a single occupant was visible—not that seeing Pepper would change a thing. She probably wouldn't want to hear his excuses, even if he could convince her they were true.

Drew focused his attention on the road and hoped for an uneventful Friday. Not much could make the day worse than it already was, but more stress might push him past the edge of sanity.

The sight of Morton's car at the office made Drew's stomach sink even further. Whatever Kyle had lined up in Columbus had either been canceled or he'd pulled an all-nighter so he could get back to find a loophole in the partnership agreement. He'd likely sent the text message during Drew's morning commute.

Just when you think things can't get worse, somebody finds a way to prove you wrong.

He parked in his usual space and retrieved his cell from his pocket. Kyle's name and message stood out on the dark background of his phone.

"Returned earlier than expected. Come straight to my office."

The coffee and toast in Drew's stomach turned into a gurgling mess, coaxing him to go home and back to bed. Unfortunately, it would only delay the inevitable.

Faking a dignified gait, he stalked into the building and past Morton's secretary, who looked far less cheerful than usual, without slowing. After two raps on the door, he entered his boss's office. "You wanted to see me?"

With his back to the door, Kyle drummed his visible fingers on the arm of his chair. "Close the door and sit."

The order held more contempt than Drew had ever heard in the man's voice. *I'm so screwed.*

"Things haven't gone as planned." As Morton spun toward the desk, his steel-eyed glare hit Drew full force. "I had to cut my trip short to handle the situation myself, and I'm not pleased about it."

I guess that means I won't be getting a favorable recommendation letter. While Drew had heard rumors of Kyle's expert intimidation skills, he'd never been on the receiving end of them or seen them first-hand. Silence was probably the best option until the man finished his tirade.

"An offer like that doesn't come along every day. A few concessions here and there wouldn't be amiss. Don't you agree?"

Did he expect Drew to go back in time and change the words he's said to Pepper? *Don't you think I would if I could?*

Kyle's fist connected with the top of his desk, his always under-control temper revealing itself for the first time in nearly twelve years. "Ungrateful and petty, that's what she is. Damn spiteful woman."

"Woman?" Drew hoped his confusion and relief didn't show.

"Yes, woman." The chair rolled backward into the floor-to-ceiling bookcase as Morton stood. He paced to the window and crossed his arms in front of his chest. "Who in their right mind refuses a legitimate offer when they're looking for a reputable financial backer? She should know a good investor's going to want to keep a hand in the business until he's earned out the initial outlay of funds. How else will he protect his investment?"

Unaccustomed to discussing matters beyond the scope of clients and accounts, Drew trusted the question was rhetorical and kept his mouth shut.

"I have no idea how you can surround yourself with females and remain sane. They're completely illogical and unpredictable." Disdain was written all over Morton's face. "I want you to help me find a way to convince this woman to accept the investor's terms."

Only one possible solution came to mind. "Compromise. Adjust the terms enough that she'll agree to them."

Kyle prowled to the coffeepot and filled a mug. "I offered to meet with her lawyer to discuss possible changes to the contract. She said she doesn't have a lawyer, that she's capable of handling the negotiations herself."

"Okay. Meet with her yourself. Find out what it'll take for a deal."

The slow sip of coffee might have been an occasion to consider that alternative, but the way Morton's hand flexed around the mug suggested it was something else. "I can't meet with her until after the papers are signed and the deal goes into effect."

A light bulb flicked on in Drew's head. "So you…" *Didn't call her after a one-night stand? Dumped her when she started getting serious?* "You've had dealings with her before? And she won't sign if she knows you're facilitating the contract?"

Kyle gave a curt nod and then lifted the coffee cup to his mouth. It only partially concealed the twitch in his jaw. When he lowered the cup, the superior look of satisfaction was back. He returned to the desk and scribbled something on a sticky note. He handed it to Drew. "I want you to be the intermediary. You get half now and half once we work out an agreement."

Stunned by the number on the paper, Drew blinked, certain he'd read it wrong. The same five digits written in black ink still stood out on their stark-white background. "You're kidding."

"You know damn well I don't ever joke about money." His boss sat in his chair, the invisible aura of stress suddenly gone. "You've worked hard this month to prepare for the partnership and your accounts are all in great shape, so you have time to do a little side job for me. Any man who can keep two little girls and my cousin in line must be a master negotiator."

A sarcastic bark almost escaped. "I'm not so sure about that. Isn't that why you have Godecki on retainer?"

"You have a face people trust. She's more likely to talk to you than a lawyer." Morton's brusque tone meant he wouldn't take no for an answer.

Giving in was easier than arguing his lack of mediation training. Besides, the extra money could go into his daughters' college fund and the distraction might keep him from dwelling on things he couldn't change. "Okay. I'll do it."

"Check or direct deposit?"

A twinge in his gut warned Drew the whole conversation had probably been premeditated, not that he planned to back out of the agreement. "Direct. Do I need to make arrangements for a meeting or are you setting that up?"

"A meeting is set for one to two thirty today." Kyle pulled a folder from the top drawer and snapped it onto the smooth mahogany surface, his confidence triggering equal amounts of annoyance and appreciation. At least he'd arranged the meeting around the school's pickup schedule, even if it was short notice. "Here's a file with the original offer and a list of areas the investor is willing to negotiate on. If something comes up that I haven't covered, text me the details and I'll tell you how to respond."

If Morton had overlooked a single detail, the woman meant a hell of a lot more to him than he let on. Those exact limits could indicate how much control she had over him and how much he didn't like it.

Drew flipped open the file. "Where are we meeting?"

"Her restaurant, Hot Tamale, in Streetsboro. She wants to open a second location by August of this year, but she wants a silent investor instead of taking out a loan."

"And your investor wants some say in the business decisions since she'd be using his money to expand?"

"Of course. Successful or not, she has to expect some input on her business and marketing plans. Good businesspeople aren't in the habit of putting their money into blind speculation."

"Makes sense." A scan of the first page revealed the slightly deceptive use of a generic-sounding company name. "I'm guessing you want me to refer to the company as Sharp Capital and Investments?"

"SCI, the group, the company. Any of those are fine. As far as she's concerned, it's a group of anonymous investors who pick and choose which projects they want to support. The names are confidential." Kyle poured another cup of coffee and handed it to Drew. "I solicit investors in addition to taking advantage of some opportunities myself."

"Okay." Already intrigued by the handy diversion from his personal problems, Drew tucked the folder under his arm and rose to leave. "How big a hurry are you in? Do you want the new terms settled on today? Or do I have some flexibility?"

"Today would be great, but I don't expect it. Women are stubborn."

As much as he agreed with the sentiment, Drew simply nodded and headed to his office to study the pages of legal documents and notes. It might prepare him for Kyle's retaliation over Pepper after the deceptive wheeling-and-dealing scheme succeeded or failed.

Fail? If that happens, my ass'll be in a sling long before he finds out about how I screwed up with Pepper.

AT FIVE MINUTES TO ONE, DREW STEPPED INSIDE HOT TAMALE'S entrance to south-of-the-border décor and the mouthwatering scent of peppers, onions, and Mexican spices. *Bad omen or an invitation to heartburn?*

"*Hola.* Welcome to Hot Tamale." A dark-haired young woman greeted him at the sign asking him to please wait to be seated. "One for lunch? Or are you meeting someone?"

"I'm Drew Fulton. I have an appointment with Ms. Valero." He showed her the business card he'd found in the file. Why the SCI card already had his name on it wasn't worth pondering.

"Follow me please." His guide hurried past the main dining room and down a hall to a closed door. After a knock, she pushed open the entrance to a private banquet room. "Mamá, there's a Mr. Fulton here. He says he has an appointment with you."

A woman with a coal-black braid down her back turned toward her daughter. She rose and gestured for him to enter. An embroidered blouse hugged her curves and a flowing skirt danced around her calves as she walked toward him. The casual clothing did nothing to tone down her piercing dark gaze or the intimidating force that emanated from her. She exuded grace, intelligence, and timeless beauty. "*Gracias*, Marta. Come in, Mr. Fulton. Would you like something to drink? Iced tea? Coffee?"

If he'd had any doubts about Kyle Morton's previous dealings with her being personal, they were gone now. Their similar personalities guaranteed enough intensity, fire, and destruction to compete with a volcanic eruption. No wonder ashes had been left in their wake.

"I'm fine, thanks." Drew extended his hand as he met her halfway to the table. "Drew Fulton. My card."

Her unreadable eyes bore into him for several more seconds. "You don't look like a lawyer."

"I'm not. Sharp Capital and Investments has asked me to serve as its representative during the contract negotiations. I have the authority to present and accept terms within specific limits. Any changes beyond those limits require approval of the investors." He waited for her to sit before he took the seat adjacent to hers.

"The company comes highly recommended, but I don't like that the investors themselves won't meet with me. Secrecy almost always equals deception and lies." She closed the laptop in front of her and slid the stack of papers closer.

"Even if I was at liberty to say, I don't know who's involved in this project. Only the CEO of the company has that information and he's unavailable today. Let's see if we can work out a compromise that satisfies everyone." As he removed the file from his portfolio, the tension in the room faded to the new-acquaintances kind.

"Okay. The first point I'd like to discuss is item one." Pen in hand, she recited the entire paragraph, picking apart the details she didn't like and underlining the acceptable sections.

An hour and twenty-five minutes later, Drew added four pages of notes to the contents of the file and zipped his portfolio closed. "I think we covered everything. I'll have a copy of the updated contract sent over as soon as it's ready. Probably Monday afternoon."

Ms. Valero pushed her chair away from the table and stood. "I appreciate it. I'll walk you out."

At the exit, he shook her hand. "Feel free to e-mail me if you'd like to go over the final draft before you sign. We can set up another appointment for next week."

"Thank you." She gave him what seemed to be a genuine smile. "I didn't expect much cooperation, but you made an honest effort to make the terms fair. Bankers and lawyers could learn a lot about conducting business from you."

He returned her smile as he headed out the door. "You're welcome. Good to meet you, and I hope your expansion is successful."

The satisfaction of finding common ground for her and SCI stayed with him to his car and the drive to school. After this long week of hell, something positive had finally happened in his life. Even the sun had come out sometime during the meeting. Maybe it was a sign.

He stopped behind the last car in the line stretching from the main entrance to the street and traced the outline of Pepper's phone in his coat pocket. Kyle's casual mention of going to the deli had to mean it had reopened today. She was less likely to toss him out if his daughters were with him, wasn't she? Wouldn't returning her cell earn him the right to apologize?

A short text to his boss killed the minute or so before kids poured out onto the sidewalk, excitement for the weekend showing in the energetic race to their rides. A striped hat like Hannah's appeared in the rush of bodies, but it disappeared and then emerged at the sidewalk on the head of a girl with blonde hair.

The cars in front of him crept forward as the crowd thinned and the line moved toward the exit. One by one, they turned out of the pickup lane onto the street until only a few stragglers were left.

Not in any hurry and used to his younger daughter's tendency to forget things, he leaned against the headrest and closed his eyes. Lack of sleep had chased him all week and lured him with the chance for a few seconds of downtime. A knock made him jump and he opened his eyes expecting to see his girls waiting for him to unlock the car door.

Instead, Mrs. Beecham waved and motioned for him to roll down the window. "Long week? Didn't Kristen and Hannah find you?"

He shook his head, still a little dazed from his catnap. "No. I didn't see them."

"I said good-bye to them as they came out of the building. Hm. Maybe one of the girls forgot something and they went back in. Why don't you wait here while I check?"

"I told them I might be a little late since I had to go into the office today. They might've gone to the gym for the after-school program."

"Okay. You're probably right. I'll look there first." She hurried away, pausing only to talk to one of the office staff at the doorway.

Both women vanished inside.

After what seemed like an eternity but wasn't more than five minutes, she returned, with several adults following close behind. A concerned frown had replaced her earlier smile. As she approached his car, the group in her wake fanned out in three different directions.

Trepidation spread through his chest. If anything happened to his kids, he'd never survive.

When the principal stopped at the driver's side of his car, he lowered the window and swallowed to soothe his suddenly dry throat. "Where are they? Are they ready to go?"

She glanced toward the far end of the building. "Some of the teachers are checking the playground and the area around the school. A girl in Hannah's class said she heard her and Kristen mention running away from home during recess. They can't have gotten far."

Panic equal to what he'd experienced at Kate's diagnosis froze his heart. Bad could always get worse.

CHAPTER THIRTY

PEPPER SWIPED HER FOREARM ACROSS HER CHEEKBONE TO KEEP TEARS from dripping into the pot of lentils as she scraped the cutting board clean. *Damn onions.*

The burning in her eyes eased as she chopped celery, carrots, potatoes, and eggplant for the soup of the day, but the ache in her heart persisted. Preparing for the reopening of her shop was a much better distraction than catching up with paperwork and swimming laps in Mort's pool, although licking her wounds in private had had its advantages.

She gave the soup a final stir and turned on the flame beneath the pot. As she rinsed the cutting board, Zack pushed the cartload of salad containers through the kitchen doorway, his quick glance away from her betraying his unending concern. "I'm fine, so just concentrate on getting everything ready."

"I didn't say a word." His disapproving scowl matched the tone of his voice.

A stab of guilt wormed its way into her conscience, but she hacked a head of cabbage in half instead of dwelling on her nasty mood. The world wouldn't lend her fifteen minutes for a meltdown and it wouldn't solve a damn thing anyway.

Footsteps halted behind her. "I decided to go to Kevin's service instead of class today, so I'll be here about two thirty, quarter to three. Ona said she'd cover for me until I get back."

The knife clattered against the cutting board, her grip suddenly gone. "Your, um, grandfather didn't guilt you into it, did he?"

"Nah. I figured he might appreciate the company. I also heard a woman in the background when I called him yesterday. She sounded kind of upset that he met me without her. I'm guessing she's my grandmother. God, that sounds weird."

Pepper couldn't disagree. "I think most people have some dysfunction in their family. I sure can't throw stones."

"I just never really thought about having grandparents. Your parents don't deserve the title and Kevin Pierce wasn't real enough to waste time thinking about." Zack kissed the top of her head. "You and Uncle Kyle have always been all the family I needed."

Another tear leaked down her cheek. What had happened to her practical take-whatever-life-dishes-out backbone? Her explosive temper had been the only display of her moodiness. She wasn't a whiner or a complainer—and she sure as hell wasn't a crier.

Ignoring the trail of moisture, she picked up the knife and cut each piece of cabbage in half again. "Did you check the fountain machine? The last thing we need during the lunch rush is to have to change out a syrup or CO_2 tank."

"Already done. Iced tea is made and the cash drawer's ready. I'll go shovel and salt the sidewalk." He gave her shoulder a gentle squeeze and then lumbered toward the dining room. His pause halfway to the front counter set off her internal alarm. "You need to talk to Drew. Give him a chance to tell you what's going on in his head instead of making assumptions, because I'm pretty sure he's as miserable as you are."

Zack ducked through the doorway before she could heave a wedge of cabbage at him.

"I am *not* miserable." She sliced off the triangle of core and tossed into the waste bucket. No amount of talking would fix what was wrong with their relationship. *We don't have a relationship anymore.*

The admission hurt, but she was a realist. Eventually, she'd get over it.

The sooner, the better.

Eight shredded cabbages later, she stowed tomorrow's Chicken House Coleslaw in the cooler and stirred the lentil soup on her way to the front of the shop. A last check of the food cases and the dining room relieved some of the stress nagging at her neck muscles. The deli was set to open ten minutes ahead of schedule, a major accomplishment considering she and Zack hadn't been able to get into the building until almost eight o'clock in the morning. After three whole days of not working, opening early would be a treat.

She crossed the new tile floor to the window that faced the street. As she raised the blinds, at least a dozen of her regular customers waved at her from the sidewalk. Unable to control the urge to sob, she turned away and buried her face in her hands.

"Why are you crying, Mom?" Zack hugged her to his chest. "You're supposed to be happy. Everybody came out to surprise you and show their support."

"I know." She sniffled, hoping to stop the ridiculous outburst. "I'll be okay in a minute. Damn it, I need to go wash my face and blow my nose."

"Take your time. I can handle opening."

Glad he didn't push the Drew issue again, she hurried to the restroom. He might be right about clearing the air with her former fiancé, but the thought of seeing him and having to let him go would hurt a thousand times worse than having an eight-pound baby.

Former? Then why the hell am I still wearing this blasted ring? And the one from his girls?

A few splashes of cool water got rid of the blotchiness on her cheeks, if not the redness in her eyes. Lack of sleep was as much to blame as crying. Half a dozen deep breaths calmed her emotions enough to return to work.

Although the long line out the door threatened her composure, she tucked the necklace with the gumball-machine ring into her sweater and joined her son behind the counter. Each order drew her attention to soups, salads, rolls, and wraps instead of the complications that had upended her life.

When Ona arrived at eleven thirty, Zack excused himself and disappeared into the kitchen, his bleak expression a sign that he wasn't crazy about his choice to be a good grandson. Thankfully, Pepper had exercised a little self-control and kept herself from ordering a black flower arrangement with a "Good Riddance" card attached.

She dropped into a chair at the far corner table at two fifteen. The nearly endless stream of lunch patrons had dwindled to the point she could finally take a lunch break, but she was too exhausted to eat. Steam rose from her cup of tea and bowl of vegetarian chili, making her long for her fuzzy slippers and fleece robe.

"Pepper?"

She blinked at the sound of Ona's voice. "Hm?"

"Are you awake? There's somebody here to see you."

What now? Lifting her head from the table, Pepper refrained from groaning. While a visit from the Publisher's Clearing House people would make her day, the chances of catching the plague were far higher. "Who is it?"

As she sat up, Drew stepped around Ona. He was as handsome as ever in a dark suit, loosened tie, and wool pea coat. Dark circles rimmed his eyes, but the pure terror written on his face sent her stomach plummeting. "The girls are missing."

She grabbed for the table at the rushing sound in her ears. "Missing?"

"They ran away from home. Kristin won't answer her text messages and nobody's heard from them." His voice cracked on the last several words. "I thought they might have come here."

"No." With her heart in her throat, she shoved the adjacent chair backward with her foot. "Sit. Details. How long have they been missing? Didn't they have school today? You called Colleen and Merie and Flynn?"

He sank into the seat and rested his elbows on his knees. "I went to pick them up, but they didn't come to the car. The principal checked inside and found out from one of the other kids that they planned to run away from home after school. I called everybody I could think of and a bunch of the teachers searched the school property. There wasn't any sign of them on the way here. I don't know what to do."

Touching her hand to his, she wracked her brain for some way to help. "Did anyone call the police?"

He nodded. "I knew they were upset about us, but I never thought they'd do something like this. Anything could've happened to them. Shit, Pierce. What if he—"

"Didn't Kyle tell you? Pierce is dead."

"Dead?"

"Yes." Wrapping her arms around him, she rested her forehead on his shoulder. His familiar soap-and-shaving-cream scent surrounded her. *I miss you so much.* "We'll find them."

"This is my fault."

She combed her fingers through his windblown hair. "Stop. We need to focus on finding them. Do they have any new friends who live close by?"

"Not that I know of. They wanted you. I want…" He released a shaky breath and straightened. Without meeting her gaze, he stood. "I'm sorry for bothering you. Will you call me if they show up?"

Bereft from his withdrawal, she crossed her arms in front of her to keep from reaching for him. "Of course. And you'll call me as soon as you find them? Crap, I lost my phone. You'll have to call the deli."

He pulled a cell phone from the inner coat pocket and handed it to her. "You left it at the house. I should've returned it sooner, but I…I figured you wouldn't want to see me. I'm sorry about that too. For everything."

How could she tell him he was wrong about her not wanting to see him without looking like a pathetic fool?

"Hey, Drew." Zack sauntered toward them, his wide smile out of place for someone who'd come from his father's funeral service. "Did you and Mom finally talk things out? I hope so, because she's been really cranky all week."

"Zackary McCann, you need to mind your own business." She

didn't often want to strangle her son, but this time he'd crossed that imaginary line. "Kristen and Hannah are missing."

His eyebrows rose as his grin became thoughtful. "Missing or ran away? I can totally see them forcing your hand by running away. Good idea, actually. Well, maybe not good, per se, but inventive, for sure. Effective? I suppose that remains to be seen."

Something in his speculative tone set off her motherly radar. "Did you help them with this disappearing act? You were in on this from the beginning, weren't you?"

"I can honestly say I had no part in the planning."

She pushed out of her chair and gave him the look he called the "mom stare." "But?"

He cast a glance between her and Drew. "But nothing. You guys should take advantage of this opportunity to discuss a reconciliation."

A growl rumbled up from her chest. "Damn it, Zack. What do you know about the girls?"

His casual shrug fueled her temper—and suspicion. "I've been sworn to secrecy until such time as the wedding is back on."

Drew snagged her son by the arm as he turned toward the counter. "They're okay? You know where they are?"

"Yes. I picked them up from school. They're hanging out with Uncle Kyle's housekeeper. She'll drop them off here after you guys kiss and make up."

Relief replaced the anguish in Drew's voice and on his face.

Although Zack's assurance overjoyed her, his smug expression warned her he meant business. Unfortunately, he didn't understand how impossible the situation was. She couldn't change how Drew felt about Kate or the fact that he'd projected those feelings onto her. She wasn't the woman he wanted to spend the rest of his life with. That woman had died.

Pepper weighed the consequences of sacrificing her heart at the demands of two well-meaning little girls. "No."

Both men stared at her like she'd sprouted a second head.

"Zackary, you tell Drew where Kristen and Hannah are right now so he can take them home. We've been manipulated enough to last a lifetime and then some." She picked up her uneaten lunch and carried it into the kitchen without looking back.

"No can do, Mom." Her son's denial followed her to the sink and did nothing to ease the ache in her heart.

She considered taking a bite of soup, but her appetite was gone. As she dumped her tea, the click of men's dress shoes on the floor signaled Drew's arrival behind her. Her cousin always announced his presence with the same distinctive sound.

"Can we talk? About us and what happened, I mean." His quiet request flowed over her, making goose bumps rise on her skin and tempting her to listen to his weak reasons and flimsy excuses.

"You said you were sorry. I accept your apology. That's all I need." That was a lie, but she wasn't about to take it back. "I know you're willing to do whatever's necessary to find out where the girls are, even marrying me, but I'm not."

"I love you, Pepper. I made a mistake, one I'm going to regret for a long time, and I'd like a chance to prove it's you I want."

She rinsed her mug and set it on the shelf to dry. "You can't. It's your word against your word. You can't un-say what you said. Besides, I saw your wedding ring on the nightstand. You were obviously already having doubts. Better before the wedding than after."

"My ring? God, you're stubborn." Hadn't he used that irritated tone and the same words on her at the cabin? "You think an old ring and a panicked misspoken name mean I can't possibly be in love with you? Fine. I'll prove it."

Every desperate attempt to convince her of his loyalty ripped another hole in her heart. "Please don't make this any harder."

"What's hard is your head and those damn walls you put up around yourself. I'll be back in twenty minutes with proof. Then we're going to tell our kids we made up and that the wedding is on." He spun her around by the shoulders and didn't let go until she met his gaze. Then he touched his lips to hers in the lightest of kisses, sending shivers through every part of her traitorous body. "And don't you even think about leaving."

CHAPTER THIRTY-ONE

WITH SIX MINUTES TO SPARE, DREW SHUT OFF HIS CAR AND WAFFLED between grounding his daughters until they graduated from college and rewarding them for their ingenuity. If he somehow managed to persuade Pepper his intentions were genuine, some of both might be in order. At least they'd had the sense to involve Zack in their scheme. Unfortunately, they'd probably taken ten years off his life today alone.

Digging deep for as much stubbornness as his second chance at love had displayed, he jogged to the front of the deli. A flurry of snowflakes blew through the entrance with him.

Fight or flight flickered across Pepper's face as she folded the top of a carryout bag at the register. He clearly hadn't gone too far with his order that she stay put.

He rounded the counter and caught her by the waist as he continued into the kitchen. She stiffened slightly, but didn't try to free herself from his grasp. "I let the school and the police know Hannah and Kristen are safe. Now we can concentrate on us."

She laid her cheek against his chest, her determination to end their relationship once and for all apparently not as cut and dried as she'd tried to convince him it was. "I do love you, Drew, but I have to exercise some self-preservation here."

"I get it. I made you question my feelings for you. But I think I can prove how much I love you, if you'll give me an honest chance." He pulled the package from his pocket and handed it to her. "Look inside."

Indecision clouded her features as she unfolded the crumpled little shopping bag. She removed the first box. "You don't know me very well if you think you can buy me with expensive gifts."

"I know you well enough. Open it."

She set aside the bag and flipped up the lid of the blue velvet box. "A wedding band isn't proof. It just means you're trying to convince yourself—"

"Stop telling me what I feel and read the writing on the inside."

She scowled at him and then, lifting the ring toward the light, tilted it between her finger and thumb. With any luck, her mile-wide streak of tenacity had narrowed with her eyes. Her silence stretched to a full count of ten.

My red hotheaded Pepper is stubborn too. "Read it out loud."

"Fine." Her petulance seemed like an indication that her stubbornness didn't have a leg to stand on. "'My second chance, but second to none.'"

"There's another box. And look at the receipt, including the date."

After setting the first box aside, she pulled out the other one and a wrinkled paper. Lines etched her forehead when she popped open the second box. She ran her finger along the curved edges of matching heart-shaped charms. "I don't understand."

"They're for Hannah and Kristen." The charms had turned out more beautiful than he'd hoped. "Read what it says on the order receipt."

"'Two heart charms from men's 24K gold wedding band. Inscription – Daddy's Girl. ASAP'"

"And the date."

"January eighteenth."

"Monday afternoon. I stopped to have the inscription added to your wedding band *before* I screwed up."

Her lower lip trembled and tears pooled in her eyes.

"That's why I had the ring out too. I meant to drop it off at the jewelry store that morning to make sure the girls had them in time for the wedding, but I forgot it. I was too busy thinking about the next time I'd get to make love to you." He smoothed away a trail of dampness zigzagging between her scattered freckles. "Is that proof enough for you? Or do I need to grovel some too? I will if it'll help. Whatever it takes."

She dropped her chin to her chest. "I'm sorry. I shouldn't have jumped to conclusions."

"You had every right to." Thankful to have her in his arms, he buried his nose in her fire-kissed hair. "I should've known better than to play protector to a woman who's done a damn good job of taking care of herself most of her life. You're stronger than I gave you credit for."

"What if I'm the one who isn't ready?"

"I'll wait if I have to, as long as you understand I'm not giving up. I might be able to survive without you, but I don't want to." He lifted her chin, needing to connect with the emotions she might be holding back. "I can't promise everything will be perfect, but I'm willing to risk it."

Nothing in her expression hinted that she didn't believe him. His worry drained away with her whispered response. "Okay."

"Does that mean you still want to get married next weekend? Because I do. In fact, you should go ahead and move in today." As crazy as the request sounded to his own ears, he wasn't about to waste another day waking up without her.

She blinked at him. "What about Kristin and Hannah? How—"

"Do you really think they'll have a problem with us living together after what they did today? Not that they have any say."

"Well, no, but—"

"Then the only one holding things up is you." He returned the boxes to the bag and hooked the handles over her wrist. "I'd marry you today if I thought Flynn and Lilith could have everything ready by this evening. In the meantime, we're packing you an overnight bag and celebrating our re-engagement. Come on. Zack and Ona can take care of business and the girls are in good hands."

She scurried after him when he grabbed her hand and headed for the stairway to her apartment. "We need to have a talk about your bossiness and the length of your legs."

The urge to laugh almost stopped him halfway up the steps, but it wasn't worth the delay. Once he had her where he wanted her, she wouldn't be in the mood to argue with him anymore. "Unlock the door."

Her expression darkened.

He kissed the tip of her nose. "Please."

She withdrew a key ring from somewhere beneath her apron and dangled it from her finger.

The hallway wasn't his first choice of location for making love to her. He would, however, make do if he had to. "Or I can break it down."

"Since you put it like that." She slid the key in the knob and twisted.

As door swung inward, he lifted her into arms.

With a squeak, she flung her arms around his neck. "In a hurry?"

"Mm-hm." A well-placed nudge with his foot sent the door banging closed behind them. He carried her to the bedroom, weaving through a maze of suitcases and piles of clothes.

"Drew, would you have come here today if the girls hadn't run away?"

He lowered Pepper to her feet next to the bed. Did she have any idea how empty his life had been without her? "I drove by every day this week on my way to drop them off and pick them up from school. Every time, I checked to see if your car was in the parking lot, on the off chance I'd get to try to fix things between us. I came straight from a meeting in Streetsboro this afternoon, so I didn't drive past when I was picking them up, but I planned to stop on the way home."

"Why didn't you come to Kyle's house?" She pushed his coat and suit jacket off his shoulders and down his arms.

Her apron untied with a light tug on the strings, and he let it fall to the floor. "Because I wanted privacy when you forgave me. Having sex in my boss's house seemed kind of weird."

"True. You must've been pretty sure I'd accept your apology and explanation."

"Not at all, but I didn't plan on giving up. I can be just as stubborn as you when I need to be." The nimble way she loosened his tie and slipped the buttons free on his dress shirt made his breath catch. "We belong together."

"You make it sound so simple." Her fingertips brushed his chest as she sent his shirt down the same path as the outer layers.

"It is." He lifted the hem of her sweater and guided it over her head. The gaudy ring hanging between her breasts suggested she hadn't truly given up on him. "You're still wearing both rings. Condoms in the nightstand drawer?"

"Mm-hm. I never said I stopped loving you." She unfastened his pants and shoved them down his legs. "Hurry up with that condom while I get rid of my jeans."

Kicking off his shoes, he reached for the drawer. By the time he untangled the pants from his ankles and found a foil packet, she lay naked across the middle of the bed. He switched on the lamp to counter the growing dusk, illuminating the fiery halo around her face. The soft curves of her breasts and hips drew his gaze along her body. As beautiful as she would be with their child creating a swell over her abdomen, he was too selfish to share her with anyone else—at least for now.

He rolled on the protection and stretched out beside her. A slow caress from her shoulder to her knee and then up the inside of her thigh earned him a low moan.

She arched closer and hooked her leg over his, giving him the access he needed. Her breath warmed his cheek as her cool palm splayed over his heart. All the love he could wish for shone in the depths of her color-changing eyes. She didn't have to say the words for him to know everything he felt for her was mutual.

Touching his lips to hers, he savored the emotions and passion building in his body and soul. An unhurried glide of his fingers through the slick folds between her thighs heightened his desire to make their connection physical as well as emotional. He took the kiss deeper, meeting every smooth thrust of her tongue and mimicking the motion with his fingers.

She groaned into his mouth and moved his hand to her breast. A moment later, she guided his cock inside her. Tremors vibrated through her muscles, pulling him into the heat of her welcoming body. She closed around him, the fit more perfect than the last time they'd made love.

He rocked forward, letting the pure bliss of their union surround him. How could he have doubted his true feelings for this woman? For even a second? He needed her in his life, in his arms. She'd taken up residence in his heart that first night.

The lamp flickered as he stood at the edge with her, its light burning brightest when his orgasm overtook him and going out while he floated back to reality.

Her panting breaths tickled his neck. "Power went out. Generator'll kick on in a minute."

He reached out in the near darkness for the lamp and switched it off. "Nope. We're snowed in, and we're right where I want us to be."

THANKS FOR READING! IF YOU ENJOYED THIS STORY, PLEASE CONSIDER leaving a review on the retailer's website, BookBub, and/or Goodreads to help other readers find their next book! Join my Facebook reader group for fun discussions and subscribe to my newsletter to receive the latest news about releases, sales, book signings, and more.

ABOUT THE AUTHOR

Mellanie Szereto is the *USA Today* Bestselling Author of over forty romcoms and contemporary romances, most with characters who have plenty of life experience like herself. Whether you call them older, seasoned, mature, experienced, or later-in-life protagonists, they deserve love too! Her stories are often set in small towns with quirky main characters, fun secondary casts, and lots of humor. She enjoys gardening, cooking, and baking—as well as hiking to work off the fruits of her labor—and incorporates food into all of her stories. She lives in an old farmhouse in rural Indiana with her husband of thirty-seven years.

Visit her website for more information about her books!

www.ingramcontent.com/pod-product-compliance
Lightning Source LLC
Chambersburg PA
CBHW070834250626
47159CB00003B/777